ELUSION

ELUSION

CLAUDIA GABEL & CHERYL KLAM

KATHERINE TEGEN BOOKS
An Imprint of HarperCollins Publishers

3065400580

C

Katherine Tegen Books is an imprint of HarperCollins Publishers.

Elusion

Copyright © 2014 by Claudia A. Gabel and Cheryl Klam

Library of Congress Cataloging-in-Publication Data
Gabel, Claudia.
  Elusion / Claudia Gabel and Cheryl Klam.
      pages   cm
  Summary: "Teens uncover the dangerous secrets of a virtual reality program that's taking the country by storm"— Provided by publisher.
    ISBN 978-0-06-212241-4 (hardcover bdg.)
    [1. Virtual reality—Fiction.   2. Conspiracies—Fiction.   3. Science fiction.]
I. Klam, Cheryl.   II. Title.
PZ7.G113El   2014   2013015452
[Fic]—dc23   CIP
                                                                          AC

Typography by Erin Fitzsimmons
14 15 16 17 18 LP/RRDH 10 9 8 7 6 5 4 3 2 1
❖

First Edition

To Ben and Brian—we couldn't have done this without you.

ELUSION

PROLOGUE

"DON'T BE SCARED, REGAN," MY FATHER says. "I'll be next to you the whole time, I promise."

But I'm not scared at all. The reason my breath is coming out in quick, little gasps is because I'm excited. After all, I've waited for this moment for such a long time.

I shift in my seat, carefully listening to my dad as he gives me the instructions, to the point where I'm actually focusing on every syllable.

Place the microlaser visor over your eyes.

Insert the audio buds into your ears.

Slip your hand through the acrylic wristband.

Click on the app with your finger.

I follow each step, double-checking myself so I don't screw this up. This trial run is way too important to him. Computer scientists still don't believe in his work—an alternate reality program and device he's spent the last four years building—but all that is going to change.

We're going to prove them wrong.

My dad said that to me, just before we assembled our Equips and locked our hands together.

We.

I haven't heard that word in a long time. I think I forgot how amazing it is when he's around.

Within a few moments, trypnosis sets in and I begin to feel my body drifting away from me. Piece by piece, molecule by molecule, I break apart and dissolve until there is nothing left.

Nothing but absolute happiness.

When I open my eyes, I'm in this other dimension, which for now is only made of gauzy, incandescent light. A soft wave of electricity trickles along my skin. It almost feels as though I'm being lifted off the ground by an invisible current and suspended in midair. I've never felt anything like this in the real world, and since it's generated by a hypnosis program that's preloaded onto my Equip, I never will.

"The light is going to fade in a bit," I hear my father say. "And then the real magic will begin."

I smile. He is right by my side, just like he promised.

"When you see it all, you'll understand everything," he says.

He sounds almost apologetic, and I'm wondering if by "everything," he means this inaugural trip to Elusion will somehow explain the late hours my dad keeps at Orexis; how he constantly breaks plans with my mom and me so he can work in his computer lab; all the time he spends with Patrick, showing him how to code and design every inch of this place.

A warm breeze blows a piece of wavy strawberry-blond hair right into my eyes. Normally I get upset when I think about how my father has been for the last couple of years, but none of it bothers me now.

"Can you see me yet?" he asks. "It might take another second or two for the visuals and other sensory perceptions to kick in."

I blink a few times and my dad slowly comes into focus. Although his silhouette is outlined by a shimmering golden glow, he's wearing the same plaid flannel shirt and khaki pants he had on in the living room. His salt-and-pepper hair is still messed up and in need of a wash. His brown eyes twinkle as he reaches out to me and takes my hand in his.

"Great. Now just breathe in and out very slowly. It will increase the dopamine response and help your body adjust."

I inhale, noticing a deep, sweet scent that's carrying on the wind. "It smells like . . ."

"Pine trees. Just wait till you see them."

"Are you kidding me? There are actual pine trees here?"

A world with plant life and fresh air instead of Florapetro factories, grease clouds, and acid rain. I can't even begin to imagine it.

"The one thing I want you to remember while you're here is to trust your thoughts. Don't discount the power of your mind.

What you're experiencing is very real."

I loop my arm through his and gently lean my head on his shoulder. "Okay."

"I know it's confusing, but everything will make sense soon, I promise." My father grins. "All right, brace yourself. Here come the fireworks."

I raise my head in awe as I watch the veil of white light float up from the ground like a fog and evaporate to reveal a sapphire sky. Dad and I are perched on top of a rocky cliff. Miles and miles of dark green forest are stretched out in front of us. The view is so crisp and clear I can almost see every leaf and needle jutting out from each spindling branch. Beyond is a chain of mountains with snowcapped peaks, which borders a large lake with shimmering swirls of turquoise and jade. Everything is subtly traced with a translucent glittering substance, almost like fairy dust.

It's an incredible sight. And although I've never been a fan of heights, here I am, standing at the edge of a steep embankment, feeling that sweet electricity being absorbed by all my nerve endings.

"It's amazing, Dad. It's . . . it's like a dream," I say. "Is this Escape based on a real place?"

"Yes, a spot near Lake Michigan," he says, sounding oddly prideful, like he somehow created one of the Great Lakes himself. "It's long gone, though."

I take another step forward and spread my arms out to my sides as rolling clouds cast shadows all around us. My feet are firmly planted on the earth, but inside it feels like I'm flying.

"Remember what I used to say to you when you were little?" he asks.

"Stop wearing your oxygen shield inside the house?"

He laughs. "What else?"

I turn around and squint at him. "Hmmmm, let me think."

"Come on, I know you remember," he says playfully.

"A meaningful life is filled with contributions," I say, reciting his favorite mantra perfectly.

"Well, this is it. My biggest contribution yet, Regan." He walks up right beside me and tucks that unruly strand of hair behind my ear. "This is how I'm going to give us our planet back."

"People are going to love this, Dad."

My father tips his head toward two red weight-shift gliders that are parked less than ten feet away. "So, want to get a closer look?"

Normally, the thought of hang gliding over a ravine would completely freak me out. But standing on this cliff, here in Elusion, looking at the beautiful world below, I feel as though I can do anything. Before I know it, Dad is helping me into the hang glider's harness. I feel a tiny jolt to my brain, and my arms twitch.

"That was Elusion streamlining the apparatus's instructions into your subconscious," my dad says. "It only takes a second."

"This is amazing," I say. "I wish I could have stuff streamlined into my head at school."

My dad laughs and then gives me a playful wink. "Now remember, you can't get hurt in the Escapes, okay? Just allow the program to guide you."

"Got it," I reply as he finishes snapping me in.

"You know how to work this?"

For once in my life, I feel no self-doubt. "Yes, I do."

"Great, just wait for me to get set up with my—"

But I can't wait. That electric feeling inside of me is rising with every passing second, so I have no choice but to run forward as fast as I can and . . . JUMP!

"Hell, yeaaaaaah!" I squeal with delight as the wind picks up the wings of the glider, causing me to soar high into the iris-colored sky. I lift my gaze toward the golden sun, relishing the warmth on my face as I expertly zigzag in and out of the clouds.

Soon I catch sight of Dad flying right next to me. He doesn't look the slightest bit angry that I left him behind. In fact, he's smiling. Together we burst through pockets of mist and zoom over a long plain of grass filled with a rainbow of tall wildflowers twisting and bending in the direction of the wind.

"Race you to that mountain?" Dad's brown eyes flash with excitement.

My heart beats faster as my thoughts start to lose their shape. I'm not concerned about the ticking clock on my wristband and how much time we have remaining in Elusion. I'm not sad about how my father will have to spend days—maybe even weeks—at the office, leaving right after we wake up from the trypnosis. There's only one realization that's firmly set in my mind.

Soon, Elusion will change the world and everyone's lives as they know it.

Especially mine.

"Game on!" I laugh in reply, swinging my hang glider to the left as I charge ahead of my father and into the miraculous, digitally painted sunset.

ONE

FIVE MONTHS LATER

I'm packed in tightly among motionless bodies with barely any room to breathe. I tell myself to relax; I'm only going to be on the Traxx for a little while longer—fifteen minutes tops, if the Inner Sector express line doesn't have any delays. I try to ignore the harsh chill coming through the vents of the air purification unit just above my seat. The cold bites at the skin on my bare legs.

An eerie silence hovers in the train as the hundred or so people crammed into the seats sit perfectly still—their heads bobbing to the side and their eyes covered by sleek one-size-fits-all visors. Apparently I'm the only one aware of the cold or the large clusters of synthetic oil refineries whizzing by at two hundred miles per hour outside my sludge-streaked window, the only one worrying about things, like whether or not I passed my chem exam this morning.

The rest of my fellow travelers are all someplace else—a world with no pain, no concerns, and no stress; an enchanting, make-believe world that exists solely in their minds.

I could Escape along with them if I wanted, but I haven't been to Elusion since late December. Not even for a quick zip-trip, like these people are having.

Actually, I'm not sure I'll ever use my Equip again.

The connecting car door slides open and a concession salesperson—a thin, gray-haired woman in a blue-and-red uniform—begins to make her way up the aisle. She's carrying a medium-size square cooler, her eyes scanning for signs of life in this crowd of zonked-out Elusion users.

"Huh, you're awake," she says to me with surprise.

"Shocking, isn't it?"

"Very. I'm so used to seeing everyone with their Equips." The woman leans over, opening the top of the cooler to reveal an assortment of junk food and beverages. "It's nice talking to someone for a change. See anything you'd like?"

I spy a pack of triple-flavor-shifting gum and my mouth waters almost instantly. "I'll have one of those," I say, pointing to a small box marked *Citrus-Mint–Dark Chocolate*.

"That'll be fifteen credits," she says.

I grab my bag and rifle through the contents to find my passcard. In an effort to hurry things up, I dump my bag out on my lap. Lately I've been so disorganized and distracted. I just can't lose my passcard. If I don't find it, I'll probably get kicked off the train. I also won't be able to buy anything, get into school, or unlock the front door at home. It's the key to everything.

"I haven't bought an Equip yet." The salesperson carries on, oblivious to the fact that I'm becoming more flustered by the second. "But my grandkids can't get enough of it. They're always telling me about their adventures. My grandson said he went rafting last week in an adventure Escape," she says proudly. "My other grandkids live in DC and they're so jealous. Can't get Elusion there. At least not yet."

Thank God, I finally find my passcard. Stupid thing was hiding under my O2 shield. "Here you go. Sorry."

The woman takes the card and scans it, then hands it back to me, along with the pack of gum I just purchased. She also continues to ramble like someone who hasn't had a real conversation in months.

"That Patrick Simmons kid is going to be a zillionaire when the CIT approval comes through. I don't want to even think about how old he was when he invented Elusion."

"He didn't invent it," I correct her. "David Welch did."

The woman raises a curious eyebrow. "Wait a minute. I think I heard about him on the news a while back. HyperSoar accident, right?"

I nod my head and avert my eyes. I avoid discussing my dad with my mother or Patrick as much as possible, so I'm certainly not going to turn all chatty with some stranger on the Traxx.

"What a way to go. Burning up in the atmosphere like that." The saleswoman leans her upper arm against the headrest of a man sitting on the end of the opposite aisle and he doesn't even flinch. "No pain, though. I'm sure that's a comfort to his family."

Oh God.

I dig my fingernails into my hand, hoping the sting and pressure in my palms will distract me.

I will not cry. I will not cry. I will not cry.

All of a sudden, the Traxx loses speed, causing everyone to lurch forward in their seats. A robotic-sounding voice notifies passengers of a stalled turbotrain on the T line, the central connection for the entire transport system. The saleswoman mutters something about how awful all this construction is on the Traxx and curses some guy in charge of the expansion program before stalking away, leaving me alone as she moves down the aisle and into another car.

I let out a sigh of relief and stretch forward a little, so I can see past the man on my left and out of the Traxx's egg-shaped window into the Florapetro cloud–filled sky. No other trains are lurking in the distance. That's a good sign. Perhaps they'll be able to return to full throttle soon.

I twist my head to get a better view of the city beneath. We're on the outskirts of the heavily industrialized Inner Sector, the giant cinder-block factories and towering steel skyscrapers forming an impenetrable wall. Nearly nineteen million people live and work here, making the Inner Sector stations the most congested. There are always delays.

Luckily, the train isn't stopped for long, and within a few minutes it's rocketing past huge electronic billboards, many of them flashing advertisements for Elusion and the company that manufactures it—Orexis.

A better world is inside your mind.

Orexis will take you there!

It's never been so easy to get away.

Find the perfect destination with Elusion!

I place a piece of gum on my tongue and wince at the tart citrus taste. I glance at the redheaded identical-twin sisters perched in the seats across from me, totally spacing out behind their visors, their mouths agape in the same zombie-like fashion. Dressed in pencil skirts and fitted blazers, they look like they're traveling for work. Most office jobs operate on the Standard 7 cycle—seven a.m. to seven p.m., seven days a week. Whatever Escape they are in right now is probably the closest they'll ever get to a real vacation, given how hard it is for people to take time off.

My mom was like that—a successful nurse-practitioner with a hectic reverse-shift schedule. Somehow she always found a way to make time to be with her family, but now . . .

I rub the back of my neck, willing myself to think of something else, but it's really hard to do with all these Equips around me, triggering memory after memory of the way things used to be. I know my father would have been so happy, seeing how much people are enjoying Elusion. And if he were here, he'd probably ask me why I'm not one of those people.

Elusion could help me feel better—make me forget how difficult it is, living each day without him—even if only for a short while. But the last time I Escaped and came back to reality, the pain of losing him was a thousand times worse.

A few moments later, my gum has changed from citrus to mint and the robotic voice of the Traxx crackles through the speakers once again, announcing our arrival in the Inner Sector. All around me, Elusion wristband alarms begin to sound, lulling everyone out of their Escapes. The twins sitting across from me move in slow motion, taking off their visors before pulling the buds out of their ears. Their eyes flutter open and they stare into space, the muscles in their faces quivering. My stocky neighbor lets out a deep moan as he disconnects from his Equip and then sits there, almost like he's catatonic.

Some people think Aftershock symptoms are a small price to pay for time in Elusion, but I don't miss the side effects one bit.

The station we're pulling into isn't far from the Orexis building. Even though I'm running late, I think I can make it there on time if I use the pedestrian bridges and take a couple of illegal shortcuts. I grab my bag and rush to the cabin door, getting in line to exit before everyone else in the car. Once the door opens, I leap off the train and push my way through the mob descending down one of the fifty jumbo-size escalators that weave together in what looks like a gigantic aerial spiderweb.

I race out of the station, glancing toward the giant billboard that projects the latest air quality report. It's a negative ten, which means this area is a currently a red zone, so O2 shields are highly recommended. Although it's going to cost me time, I break from the surge of people who are streaming out into the streets and duck behind a towering copper pylon to pull out the pear-shaped plastic mask and place it over my mouth and nose. Once it's correctly positioned, I press the silver button on the right side, activating the suction that will keep the shield fastened to my face and emit the steady stream of oxygen that I'll breathe until I go indoors.

And then comes the acid rain. Just a couple of drops at first, but by the time I navigate my way through the hundreds of cars and buses crippled by traffic and reach the base of the first pedestrian bridge, it's coming down in sheets of gray. I dig inside my bag again and find my umbrella, but when I try to open it, the top spring jams, preventing the special oil-proof vinyl material from staying up.

For a split second, I consider turning back. Maybe this is a sign that I'm supposed to skip Patrick's press conference. Maybe the universe is trying to tell me that going to Orexis is a bad idea—I won't be able to escape the memory of my dad there.

But then I think about the train a few minutes ago and how Elusion was everywhere. After today, there'll be no place for me to hide.

At least not in the real world.

So I toss my umbrella into the trash and spit out my gum as I take the first step up the bridge.

"I don't see you on the admittance log," the stocky, surly-looking Orexis guard says, his eyes glued to the view screen in between us. He touches my passcard to the code reader on his glass desk once more, scanning it again.

Orexis headquarters is located in the refurbished Renaissance Center, or the RenCen, as it's been referred to ever since it was built. A titanium building complex on the shores of the Detroit River, overlooking Canada, it has a 200-story hotel, a mall, and a variety of office buildings. It's practically a city within a city—or a "brilliant micrometropolis," as the *Detroit Daily News* labeled it. The lobby is packed with people eager to witness Patrick's big announcement. It took me nearly a half hour just to reach the ID checkpoint at the elevator bank. If I don't hurry, I'm going to miss the start of the press conference. Even though my demerit count is dangerously high, I still skipped my last class at school in order to be here, so I definitely want to make the most of my AWOL time.

"I'm sorry, but you're not on the list of media that has been cleared to attend the event," he announces loudly, his eyes focused on the information from my passcard that has popped up on his glass desk.

"I'm not with the media," I say. The stocky guard has my passcard, and clearly my name isn't ringing any bells, so I lean over the desk and whisper, "My dad is . . . was David Welch."

God, I really don't want to make a scene—being here is uncomfortable enough, knowing my father is never going to walk through this lobby again. "Patrick Simmons invited me himself."

"Ms. Welch!" A tall guard with a shiny head devoid of any hair whatsoever comes hurrying over as soon as he recognizes me, his voice high-pitched and eager. "Do you want to use the private elevator, or—"

People are beginning to stare. So far no one else has placed me, but if I went up in the VIP elevator, I would kiss my anonymity good-bye. My father's HyperSoar accident was headline news, and I don't want reporters hounding me like they did a day or two after the funeral. Some of them even camped outside my house.

"If you could just swipe me in, that would be great," I say quickly.

The tall guard yanks my passcard away from his coworker and scans it, handing it back to me. I give him a grateful nod of thanks and then hurry through the gate, scooting inside a crowded elevator. I'm pressed up against one of the rectangular mirror-paneled walls. My eyes shift down toward my feet, but not fast enough. I catch my reflection, and to put it mildly, I look disgusting.

Due to the rain, my strawberry-blond hair has a strange dullness to it, and my bangs are in desperate need of a flatiron. My mascara is caked around my lashes, making my green eyes appear washed out and almost translucent. My uniform—an ugly navy cargo skirt with an ivory button-down shirt—is wet and clinging to me in all the wrong places, streaked with soot-like residue from the tainted precipitation. I run my fingers through my hair in a vain attempt to freshen up, but it doesn't help much.

Only a full-blast decontamination shower could help me now.

When the elevator doors open, I step off to the side, letting everyone move ahead of me. There's a crowd hovering near the theater entrance, probably because it's already full. My best bet is to sneak in through the back. I walk through an unmarked automatic door a few feet to my left and enter a gigantic hallway.

The soaring ceilings are glittering with lights and the glass walls are projecting glowing, larger-than-life testimonials regarding Elusion: a paraplegic who became an expert skier in a mountain Escape, a single mom of six who takes a relaxing "vacation" to a beach Escape every day on her way home from work, and a doctor who claims that using Elusion regularly can significantly relieve tension.

I stop at another unmarked door and wait for it to slide open.

I step inside the auditorium, my back now up against the wall. The two-thousand-seat auditorium is packed, including the enclosed observation deck at the top of the cavernous room. Even though the paneling is slightly tinted, hiding the faces of the people inside, I spot the silhouette of Patrick's mother, Cathryn. She has a distinctive figure that is hard to miss—poufy bobbed hair, wide-set shoulders, and a tall frame. Patrick's mom always makes him a bit nervous, so it's a good thing she isn't sitting in the first row.

The lights dim and Patrick takes the stage, appearing more confident and proud than I have ever seen him. He is also being projected on a gargantuan screen, so it's easy to see that his Italian suit is a little big on him. His mom is probably pursing her lips in disapproval, but I kind of like that he hasn't fully bought into the whole young-businessman thing. Patrick's also wearing a tie that my father gave him the day he began working at Orexis full-time. I can't help but smile at his sentimentality. Like me, he holds on to the things that matter the most.

The crowd bursts into feverish applause. The two brunettes standing beside me start snapping pictures of him and gasping as if he were some Hollywood heartthrob. Patrick grins and his chin dimples. I can tell from the twinkle in his eyes that he doesn't mind the attention one bit.

Suddenly, something inside me begins to hurt.

No matter how much I want to believe it, the demanding schedule Patrick has been keeping lately is clearly not just a busy phase. Then again, Patrick has been pretty much fully booked as long as I've known him. His standardized test scores were off the charts, starting from kindergarten, so even though he's just two years older than me, he graduated from high school when he was fifteen—as valedictorian. When he wasn't studying, he was doing some kind of extracurricular activity during his free time. I often wonder how he managed to make room for me, but he always did.

I take a deep breath once all the clapping dies down, moving away from the back wall of the auditorium and hoping that Patrick will somehow be able to see that I'm here to cheer him on. To hell with how I look. Patrick's my best friend. He's not going to care about what I'm wearing or that I'm having the worst hair day in the history of my life.

"First off, thank you all for coming today, and on such short notice." Patrick glances down at the teleprompter, hesitating for a moment before looking up and flashing the audience a gleaming smile.

"As you all know, for the last six months Elusion has been available on a trial basis in only three cities: Los Angeles, Miami, and Detroit."

At the mention of Detroit, the room bursts into a small round of applause.

I hold my fingers to my lips, whistling like my father taught me on a summer road trip to Montreal. I see a sliver of a clearing in the center aisle and make my way toward it. Patrick stops in the middle of his speech as if he heard my little birdcall. As he canvasses the dark auditorium with his blue eyes, I begin to push through the crowd a bit harder.

"Shane, can you bring up the house lights, please?" Patrick asks.

And just like that, the auditorium is bathed in brightness. When I look toward the stage, Patrick is staring right at me, the corners of his lips curving up.

"There," he says. "Now I can see you all much better."

I grin back at him and mouth the words "good luck."

Patrick nods and picks up where he left off in his speech. "For the past hour, Orexis has been flooded with calls, spawned by the rumors that Elusion is about to be released nationwide. Well, I don't know where your sources are getting their information, but they are one hundred percent . . . correct! Elusion finally received the coveted safety seal from the Center for Interface Technologies, and by the end of next week, both Equips and apps will be available for purchase in ten more cities. By the end of the month, the entire country will have access to the most exciting technological advancement of the century!"

The auditorium once again erupts in thunderous applause.

A woman holding a large box of sparkly acrylic wristbands walks in front of me. She presses one into my hand and then points to the left.

"Miss, you're going to need to sit down for the demonstration. There's an empty seat in row L."

"Wait, what kind of demonstration?" I whisper. "Are we all going to Elusion together?"

I'm not ready to go back there. Not even close.

The woman shakes her head. "No, of course not. It's just an immersive video accompanied by some music and acupressure hypnosis. Will you take a seat, please?"

I blow out a nervous breath as I walk up the aisle and spot the empty seat on the left. It's practically in the middle of the row, which means I have to crawl over dozens of people to get to it.

"The new Elusion app is an updated version of the program that has been on the test market," Patrick continues. "Our team has worked very hard to give you the most dynamic, original Escapes we could think of, and we'd like to give you a taste of the Elusion Universe today."

With my bag slung over my shoulder, I hunch down and try to get to my seat discreetly, apologizing for brushing against people's legs and temporarily blocking their view.

"Please put on your wristband," Patrick instructs us. "There is no need for earbuds or a visor. Sound will be provided through the speakers. Just bear with us for a minute while we set everything up."

A murmur floats through the crowd as the house lights slowly dim again.

I flop down in the seat, my bag firmly in my lap. I gather my hair and put it in a messy bun as Patrick's larger-than-life presence appears on the screen. The moment I slip on my wristband, earsplitting guitar chords come barreling through the speakers. As the music crescendos, a milky haze forms on the screen. When it fades into a sheet of pitch black, a million dots of white appear and glow with fierce intensity. I duck for cover when a streak of flames bursts from not only the screen but the walls around me. Balls of fire ricochet across the room, exploding in midair.

It's as if the auditorium itself is careening through the galaxy, narrowly avoiding collisions with gigantic asteroids, orbiting planets, and crescent moons at every turn.

I wince as a round ball of fire heads straight toward me, veering off to the right at the last second. This isn't real, I remind myself. But it sure feels like it. There is no pretty fairy dust here, and this is not the serene Elusion that my father introduced me to—this is something more terrifying and bewildering. Then I feel a shred of something I've felt many times before but have forgotten these past few months. A tiny surge of electricity rises in my chest, and within seconds it spreads all the way through my arms and down to my fingertips.

This ghost of a feeling is enough to take me back to when my father first brought me to Elusion, but then a shimmering, warm glow fans out in front of my eyes, distracting me from my thoughts completely. The hard-rock music disappears, and soon a soft murmur of a sound—almost like the white noise one might hear on an antique radio—radiates through the air. A large constellation comes into view, twinkling in a soothing, rhythmic pattern that loosens all the tension in my neck and shoulders. I feel every muscle in my body unwind.

One of the stars lights up brighter than the rest, hues of neon yellow and shades of orange and magenta flashing in the most radiant spectacle I have ever seen. I can feel the power pulsating at the core of the star. I inhale deeply as I stare at the unreal beauty of the universe around me.

For the first time in what seems like forever, I think . . .

Everything is going to be okay.

TWO

WHEN THE SCREEN GOES BLACK A FEW
minutes later and the only sound I can hear is my pulse pounding in my ears, I sit back in my seat, staring straight ahead but
seeing everything as a faint blur. I shake my hands out and roll
my shoulders forward, trying to snap myself back to normal.

"Don't be alarmed," Patrick says to the crowd. "It might
take a minute to regain your equilibrium. It's to be expected."

My gaze shifts around the room. Other people seem to be
rubbing their eyes, blinking as they fight to readjust to the real
world. I join in the pockets of applause that are coming from
different corners of the auditorium.

"What you just experienced was a sneak peek at another
new feature of Elusion," he continues. "It's called the Exhila-
ration Setting, or ExSet for short. Now users can control the

amount of brain stimulation they experience inside Elusion, and the intensity of their destination will change accordingly. CIT was truly amazed by this."

So am I. At least, I think I am. The thoughts in my mind and my eyesight are still a little bit fuzzy. I squint to see if that helps anything, and luckily it does.

"Whenever you're ready, I'd like to open up the floor to questions," Patrick says as a podium made of translucent material rises from a secret door in the floor of the stage.

"Mr. Simmons, will this universe-themed Escape be a standard dimension along with the World?" a bespectacled reporter says into the ladybug-size Orexis-issued microphone that's attached to his jacket.

"Yes, it will, and I really hope that users enjoy traveling into these uncharted destinations together," Patrick replies. Then he points over my shoulder. "You in the gray blazer."

"Is it true that Elusion will be released with higher trypnosis settings that will allow you to stay in your Escape longer and with less Aftershock?" a tall man with a neatly trimmed beard inquires.

Patrick shrugs. "Not exactly. Instead of the five minutes in the prototype, Aftershock will only last a minute—unless you're on a zip-trip that lasts less than twenty minutes. Then Aftershock is pretty mild. Also, the amount of time allowed in an Escape has not changed. It's still an hour."

Wow. The symptoms of Aftershock now only last a minute? My dad would be really impressed. He hated that users had to suffer through Aftershock and struggled to figure out a way make the symptoms less severe.

Patrick gestures to a woman in a red suit toward the rear of the room. "Ma'am?"

"Mr. Simmons, my followers are in Ohio, where Elusion hasn't been available. Could you please explain the technology used in the Equip and the app? It's still foreign territory for a lot of us."

"Absolutely. To put it simply, the Equip and the Elusion app work together. Kind of like an EEG machine, but operating in reverse."

A hint of a grin forms on my face. This is the exact analogy my dad used when trying to show me why the project he was slaving over was so groundbreaking.

"Instead of measuring all the rhythmic changes and patterns that occur in our brain waves, the computer hardware in the Equip components redirects them through the use of trypnosis, so that we experience a deep level of consciousness called trance. The software in the app acts like a remote control, giving us plenty of channels or settings we can visit while we are in a trance state."

My father would be so proud of Patrick right now.

"Fascinating," the reporter says, typing notes furiously on her tablet. "So how does trypnosis work, exactly?"

I can recite the answer to this question in my sleep. When my dad was alive, he and my mom used to talk about medicine and trypnosis over dinner. It used to bore me a little, but today

I'd give anything to have one of those nights back.

"Trypnosis is a combination of hypnosis techniques, created by three distinct computer-generated tools, which make up the Equip components," Patrick responds. "The visor has microlasers embedded in the lenses, which tap into the cerebral cortex and create an imbalance of brain-cell activity. The earbuds utilize aural symphonics, like humming sounds and voice triggers, to lull the brain into an even deeper level of consciousness. Lastly, there are two raised pieces of plastic on the inside of the wristband that apply pressure to nerve endings connected to the meridian centers of the body."

Patrick pauses to clear his throat and then steals a happy glance at me. In this moment, everything about him is so self-assured, and so . . . adult. Sometimes I wish I could leap forward with him and go straight to being in control of my own life.

"When all of these elements, including the app for Elusion, are engaged, trypnosis is achieved. At the risk of sounding immodest," he continues, "it is one of the greatest achievements in science and technology. The more often Elusion is used, the better it gets at delivering the type of experience the user prefers. The consumer can be transported to a toxin- and stress-free alternate reality in the safety of their own mind."

"*Safety?* How can you say that with a straight face?" says a loud, booming voice from the center of the auditorium. I spin around in my seat to see an auburn-haired teenage girl in a vintage army jacket and glasses, standing in a fighting stance and holding clenched fists at her sides.

Ugh. Avery Leavenworth.

"What do you have to say about Elusion addiction? It's a big problem here in Detroit, especially with kids my age," she barks. "I know my viewers would love to hear how you plan on addressing that. Although first you'd have to admit your product is more like heroin than a great achievement in science, right?"

Self-righteous student activist and star of the famously stupid vlog *AveryTruStory*, she is impossible to miss at school because she's always wrapped up in some kind of campus uprising. How did she even get in here? Did she really get legitimate press access? That never would have happened if Dad were around. He was very strict about which media outlets were allowed to cover his conferences. Apparently, Patrick is running the show a bit more loosely.

"Miss Leavenworth, Elusion is not a drug, and medical addiction isn't possible," Patrick says calmly. "If it was, then the CIT wouldn't have approved it, now would it?"

"You're screwing with people's brain chemistry! You said so yourself!" Avery shouts, refusing to back down. "My sources tell me that the Elusion system releases levels of serotonin and dopamine so high it's like the user is totally strung out."

"No!" I yell. "You're wrong!"

There's a faint murmur in the audience.

Oh. My. God. Did I just jump out of my seat and scream that out loud?

I peer toward the stage. Patrick grins and nods toward someone beside him. Before I know it, a man dressed in black approaches me and clips a mic to my shirt collar. I shoot Patrick a discouraging look, hoping that he'll step in and carry on this confrontation with Avery. But he just bows his head and smirks.

He's giving me the floor. In front of thousands of reporters. On a day where I look like something stuck on the bottom of someone's shoe.

"The serotonin and dopamine aren't *released*," I say, my words now reverberating throughout the entire auditorium. "That makes it sound like they're coming from another source, which they're not. All Elusion does is stimulate the body's production of certain chemicals that are already in the brain."

Avery crosses her arms over her chest and glowers at me like I just slapped her face, but that doesn't deter me at all.

"The sensors in the visor and the wristband both have safety controls that are monitored by a special server that keeps tabs on every single Equip. If the levels are too high, the signal is cut off. End of story."

Patrick is practically beaming with approval when the audience claps for me. "I'll take one more question. Yes, you in the green sweater."

I sigh in relief as I unclip my mike and give it back to an Orexis staff member. I catch sight of Avery out of the corner of my eye. She's being escorted toward the auditorium doors by two burly guards. Her mike has obviously been turned off, but her mouth is still moving and her face is red with rage. I think about following Avery outside and giving her an even bigger piece of my mind. How dare she throw accusations at Patrick like that, and give Dad's prized work a bad name?

But before I can grab my bag or come up with any insults to sling, my tablet buzzes. I pull my tab from my back pocket and unfold it. A note has popped up on the screen.

Meet Mom at M&W. 6:30.

Damn. If I don't leave now, I'll be late for yet another commitment, and Patrick is fielding a scandalous question about Elusion's rising "virtual hookup" rate, which I definitely want to hear about. I've never had one of my own, but at school the rumor is that making out with someone in an Escape is way more intense than the real thing. Still, as much as I want to listen to all the details, I don't have the heart to keep Mom waiting. I'm going to have to sneak away and text Patrick why I had to leave.

For a moment, I feel bad that I won't be able to tell him in person what a fantastic job he did today, but from the adoring looks he's receiving from everyone in the room, I figure he'll get to hear it.

Maybe even a few thousand times.

Where is she?

I'm pacing inside the lobby of Morton & Wexley, Detroit's largest and most prestigious depository. Every thirty seconds I look at the automatic doors, hoping to see Mom walk through them. I barely made it here on time—there were more Traxx delays, of course—but when I arrived, the clients' lounge was filled with people who were hooked up to their Equips, zip-tripping in Elusion, and my mother was nowhere in sight. I scoped out the clerk area to see if the meeting had already started, but all the employees were either on their tablets or conducting business with their customers in the confines of their glass-walled cubicles.

I check my watch. I've been waiting for nearly a half hour, and the building is about to close. I tap on my tablet to see if I can get a signal, but the reception is completely blocked, prob-ably because the depositories in this sector are steel-enforced and take strict security measures so that people can't coordi-nate a heist from inside the building with the help of their handheld devices.

After another minute ticks by, I throw up my hands in frus-tration and perch myself on the last empty chair. I drum my fingers impatiently against the curled armrest, praying that nothing bad has happened to my mom. Expecting the worst in a situation like this is pretty understandable, given what we've both been through, but I can't afford to latch on to those kind of negative thoughts. Not here anyway.

"Ms. Welch?" A bald-headed man with a mustache is now standing in front of me, wearing a badge that reads Mr. Xavier Burton. "Are you and your mother ready to recover your father's items?"

"I need a few more minutes, please. My mom still isn't here."

When he inspects his watch, his lips press together in a way that is all too familiar. My English teacher, Mrs. Thackeroy, has the same annoyed expression on her face when I'm late to her class, which is pretty often, considering that it's the first one of the day. With Mom at home to look after, I never seem to make it out of the house on time in the morning.

"We're only open for another ten minutes. You'll have to come back tomorrow if she doesn't arrive by then," Mr. Burton says, straightening his suit jacket with a harsh tug at the sleeves.

"Is there any way I could claim the contents of the security box myself?" I ask.

"No, I'm afraid not. The ledger states that pursuant to his will, Mr. Welch's wife becomes the principal owner of the contents. I'm sorry."

"That's okay. I'm sure she'll be here soon." I give him a somewhat insincere, halfhearted smile.

Mr. Burton issues me a curt nod and ducks behind a glass cubicle with a ribbon-like image scrolling around the middle with the words "Assistant Manager" in square-block digital lettering, and an update of the stock market.

I look at my watch again. In seven minutes, the staff of

Morton & Wexley is going to kick me to the curb. True, Mom and I could always come back another day, but then we'd have to spend more sleepless nights wondering what was so important to my father that he kept it locked up here, without anyone else knowing until his lawyer executed his will.

Did Dad have some kind of dark secret?

"Hey, Ree."

My head pops up when I hear the familiar voice. Patrick is walking toward me, a sympathetic smile on his face. I'm so happy and surprised to see him I hop off my seat and give him a big hug.

"What are you doing here?" I ask.

"Just wanted to see if you needed any help. I tried calling, but then I remembered my dad and all of the security rules at his trust company." He pulls back a little as he grabs hold of my hands. "I hope I'm not intruding."

"No, not at all," I say, grinning. "But don't you have stuff to do? What about the conference?"

"Once I left the stage, my job was over."

"Yeah, right," I say with a laugh. I know he's just saying that to make me feel better, and I appreciate it. "I don't know how you managed to sneak away, but you just scored major best-friend points for showing up here."

"Good." Patrick peers around the lobby as he lowers his voice. "How's your mom handling everything?"

"No idea. She hasn't even shown up yet. And of course, I can't call her in here . . ." I shrug, frustrated.

"Did you ask the manager to use their emergency phone line?"

"I don't want to go through all that. Maybe she got stuck on the Traxx or something. There's construction everywhere."

"Yeah, I'm sure it's something simple like that."

"Or maybe she just blew me off. It wouldn't be the first time," I say, my voice tinged with irritation.

It isn't fair of me to be angry. Mom is doing the best she can.

Patrick squeezes my hands gently. "It's going to be okay, I promise."

"How? This place is about to shut down for the day and I'm not authorized to receive my own father's . . ." I swallow hard and slip my hands away from Patrick's. "Forget it. We should just leave."

"Give me a second. I'm going to talk to the manager," he says.

I roll my eyes. "Don't even bother. He has a Mrs. Thackeroy attitude."

"I have no clue what that means, so I'm going to talk to him anyway. Be right back."

I keep my gaze trained on Patrick as he wanders into the clerks' area, waving at Mr. Burton through the glass door of his cubicle. The man's face lights up when he recognizes Detroit's most famous resident standing in front of him. Patrick shakes the assistant manager's hand and chats with him like he has known the guy for years. It takes less than a minute for Mr.

Burton to nod his head in affirmation and begin finger-pounding the screen of his tablet. Patrick looks out at me and gives me a thumbs-up.

It's official. Patrick has just advanced to hero status.

Once Mr. Burton and Patrick emerge from the glass cubicle, an announcement sounds over the loudspeaker.

"Ladies and gentlemen, Morton and Wexley will be closing in five minutes, so please complete your transactions. Thank you for your business."

I expect Mr. Burton to quicken his step, since he was so conscious of the time, but his stride is just as leisurely as Patrick's, who doesn't even try to hide his self-satisfied grin.

"Miss Welch, I'll take you to security block G now," the assistant manager says as he gestures toward a corridor off to the right, which leads to a large elevator bank.

"But aren't you closing up?" I ask.

"That shouldn't concern you, Ms. Welch." Mr. Burton pats me on the hand. "We are more than delighted to extend you and your family every courtesy."

I glance at Patrick, who just smiles at me innocently and shrugs.

What the hell did he do?

"Thank you, Mr. Burton. That is very nice of you."

As we follow Mr. Burton toward a foyer filled with industrial-sized elevators, Patrick and I nudge each other playfully. The assistant manager halts in front of the elevator marked *SBG* and pushes a button labeled *28*. Once the doors whoosh open, Patrick and I file in behind Mr. Burton.

"This block is subterranean, so it takes a little while to descend. Are either of you claustrophobic?" the man asks.

I shake my head. "No, I'm not."

"Neither am I," replies Patrick.

"Good. Then enjoy the ride," Mr. Burton says.

Patrick waits a minute before pulling his tab out of his interior suit-jacket pocket and typing on it. He's probably trying to get some work done; he's such an overachiever. He'll figure out soon enough that signals can't be sent outside of the building. But then I feel my rear pocket vibrating. I reach back and pull out my tab, noticing I have a text. It's from Patrick.

At first, I'm a little bewildered—how can I be receiving a message inside the depository? But then I remember just how advanced Patrick's hacking skills are. He probably found some kind of back door in their security system and glommed onto an admin network, making a signal available to both of us while we're in the elevator.

I drag my thumb and pointer finger across the screen so I can zoom in and read his note.

Patrick: How awesome am I? Go on tell me, I can take it. ;-)

When I laugh out loud, Mr. Burton cranes his neck and stares at me like I'm nuts. I mutter "sorry" under my breath, and thankfully he spins back around.

I quickly type a message back to Patrick.

Regan: Your awesomeness can't be measured. What did you say to him?!?!

Patrick: I said you were my illegitimate sister.

Regan: Ha-ha, very funny. Now tell me or I'll drop-kick you.

Patrick: I love it when you make empty threats.

Regan: TELL. ME!

Patrick: Fine! I promised I'd open a huge account here if he gave you access to your dad's box.

My cheeks flush. Since Dad's accident, Patrick has been making grand gestures like this for me, and each time he does, I feel a little more embarrassed. His intentions are good, no doubt about that, but as the months rack up, I just . . . I just can't help but feel like I owe him a million and one favors—and have no way of paying him back.

Regan: Thank you. For everything.

Patrick: Thank you—for coming to Orexis today. I know that couldn't have been easy.

Regan: Well, you were GREAT! Did you create that demo?

Patrick: Me and my nerd army. We are invincible.

Regan: Can't say the same for Avery. She had a lot of nerve, spreading lies like that. What an attention whore!!!

Patrick: You totally shot her down! I can't believe he missed it.

A breath catches in my throat, but luckily it only hurts for a second.

Regan: Yeah. My dad would have been really proud of you.

The elevator comes to such a soft stop that I barely even feel it. When the doors slide open, Mr. Burton exits and waves at Patrick and me.

"Follow me, please," he says.

We tuck our tabs away, and Patrick puts a reassuring hand on my shoulder. Obviously, he senses the sudden tension that has taken hold of me once we walk out of the elevator and into a long, narrow corridor that looks like it belongs in a morgue. The dimly lit hallway extends in both directions for what seems like a thousand yards, and there are multiple sets of steep metal staircases leading to other floors filled with windowless rooms.

"Don't worry, I'm right here," he whispers.

I take Patrick's hand, locking fingers with him. "I'm fine," I lie.

Mr. Burton guides us to the left and ahead a few feet before pausing in front of a set of stairs and offering me an orange passcard.

"Your father's security box is waiting for you in chamber twenty-eight. It's on the middle level and you'll have complete privacy there. Feel free to take your time. I'll wait to escort you back up to the main floor when you're done," he says.

"Thank you, Mr. Burton," I say.

Patrick and I walk up the steps to chamber 28, still hand in hand. I let go to swipe the passcard in front of the code reader, and the door whooshes upward, barely giving us enough time to enter before swooshing back down again behind us. Inside is a large, brightly lit, gray cement room with a tall aluminum table surrounded by several black high-backed stools. On the table is a square metallic box affixed with an electronic lock.

I shoot Patrick a nervous glance, but his calmness doesn't waver at all. I hate to admit this, but I'm actually kind of glad that my best friend is here right now instead of my mom.

"Go ahead," he says, prodding me a little.

I inhale and wave the passcard in front of the lock. I hear the click of a hinge, and the top of the box snaps open just enough so I can see a crack of darkness. I draw in another breath and lift it up the rest of the way. There's only one thing inside—an old, worn paperback copy of *Walden* by Henry David Thoreau.

A book? Dad left Mom a used book?

While I'm really relieved that there isn't anything scandalous in here—like a birth certificate revealing that I'm adopted, or an apologetic letter from Dad admitting he has a secret family stashed away in China—I don't know what to make of this.

I gently pick it up and flip through the pages, hoping that some kind of hidden meaning will jump out at me.

"Is there anything else?" Patrick asks. "Like notes in the margins?"

"No. Nothing."

Patrick leans over and inspects the book over my shoulder. "What about an inscription?"

I check both the title and the copyright pages to see if my father wrote my mom or me a message.

Still nothing.

"I don't understand," I say quietly. "Why would he put a book in a safety-deposit box?"

"What if it's a collector's item? It could be worth a lot of money," Patrick suggests.

"I doubt it. There's a bunch of dog-eared pages, and the

cover is just holding on by a thread."

"Well, maybe it doesn't make sense right now," Patrick adds. "But there has to be a reason why David kept this here, and why he wanted you and your mom to have it."

When my dad was alive and Patrick would give me insight into his behavior, it made me feel like such an outsider, like he understood my dad better than me. And the sad thing was, he did. But it always bothered me, and given the ripple of heat that's creeping across my brow line, it obviously still does.

"You're right." I tuck the book into my bag and close the metal box, crumpling my emotions up into a little ball. "Do you think you could give me a ride?"

"Sure, but what about your mom? Shouldn't we wait around a bit longer?"

I smile at Patrick but shake my head. "That's okay. I think I know where she is."

"Really? Where?" Patrick asks.

I swipe the passcard near the code reader, and the door rises to the ceiling again.

"Right where I left her."

THREE

MY MOTHER IS CURLED UP ON THE COUCH
with a pillow tucked underneath her head and a throw covering her legs. As I sit beside her, I see the sprigs of gray in the
roots of her chestnut-colored hair and the deep lines in her
forehead.

She's so worn down. Sometimes I fear she's going to give up.

I lean over and whisper, so I don't startle her too much.
"Mom? Mom, wake up."

She stirs a bit, turning from her left side so that she's flat on
her back. But that's all the response I get. I notice a tiny circle
imprint near her right temple, and my eyes flick over to the
end table next to the couch. Near the base of the silver halogen
lamp are the components of her Equip. I clutch Dad's book in
my hands so hard that it bends into an arch.

Mom has been back and forth between reality and Elusion so much lately that sometimes I'm not sure she knows which is which. She's trying to do the impossible—Escaping so that she can feel a release from the agony of losing her husband—but all I needed was one trip to understand what she can't accept just yet.

Coming back from Elusion is like finding out he's dead all over again.

High pollutant levels or no, I need some air.

I stand up, setting the copy of Walden in my place, and sneak out of the living room through the front door. There's a chill outside that wasn't there fifteen minutes ago when Patrick dropped me off, and it's enough to make me shiver. The cool temperature feels really good against my flushed skin, so I push up my sleeves and unbutton the collar of my shirt down to my breastbone. But when I breathe deeply, it feels like something is scraping against the back of my throat.

I know I should get my O2 shield. Dad was so militant about protecting ourselves from inhaling Florapetro residue. He would have a conniption if he caught me without it. Still, retreating into our house isn't an option right now.

To me, it seems more toxic inside than it is out here.

I park myself on the steps and look down Hollow Street, which hasn't changed since the day I was born. The rows of historic brick townhomes are all perfectly indistinguishable, with one exception, of course. The pathway in front of our house is the only one with the shape of a star pressed into the concrete, signaling that someone important—in this case, my father—once lived here. Usually I walk right over the seal and pretend it's not even there, but tonight it takes a Herculean effort to keep my eyes focused on the pops of light coming from behind my neighbors' windows.

Thankfully, the roar of a V12 synthetic-oil engine pulls my attention somewhere else and my head turns. A bulldozer-size delivery truck lurches down the road and comes to a stop a few feet away. I rise to my feet when a slender man in a light gray shirt and black pants exits the driver's side, carrying a large parcel. When his shoes walk across the star on our pathway, it feels like something is coiling around me and squeezing.

"Regan Welch?" The man's words come out quick behind his O2 shield, like he's in a big rush, so I just nod. He sets the package down on the steps with a thud and types on his tablet, his eyes never meeting mine. Then he shoves the tablet in front of me. "Scan here, please."

I reach into my pocket and pull out my card, tapping it against the screen. Once we hear a chirping sound, the deliveryman yanks the tablet away from me so he can dash toward his truck, practically knocking over the package in the process.

"Thanks for being so careful!" I shout sarcastically, but he slams the truck door in reply and slowly chugs away, a stream of exhaust hurtling behind him.

Sighing, I pick up the package, which is surprisingly heavy considering that it's packed in a durable foam box. The tag reads Alessandra Cole. The trendiest boutique in the Heights Sector.

It wasn't my birthday. Who would send me something from Alessandra Cole?

I'm about to rip it open on the steps, but when I see how secure it is—there are thick, orange strips of quick-seal on every side—I realize I'm going to need a laser pen to tear into it. The other thing I realize is that I'm starting to wheeze a little, so going back inside the House of Darkness is an absolute must now.

I hold the package in between my knees as I wave my passcard in front of the lockpad near the front door, unlocking it and pushing it open with my left hand. I gently set the box on the ground and nudge it forward until it passes through the entryway. The door shuts softly behind me and I lift the package up with both hands, almost dropping it when I see my mother standing in the middle of the living room, her back to me. She's holding the book my dad left in the lockbox.

She must sense me, because she slowly glances over her shoulder, her eyes meeting mine. She doesn't seem rested at all. In fact, from the dark half-moons that have formed right above her cheeks, it doesn't look like she's slept since December.

"Where did you get this?" she asks, her voice weak and hoarse.

For a moment, I worry that she's upset with me, but then I notice the small smile forming on her lips, like she's trying to remember how to be happy.

I set down the package, but I hesitate. I know that when

I respond, the small smile is going to disappear. I consider lying and telling her I found the book hiding somewhere, but she keeps this house like a shrine to my dad—everything he owned is still sprinkled around this place—so she wouldn't believe that for a second. I almost feel a little angry with her for putting me in this position.

"At the depository. It was in his lockbox."

"Oh my God, Regan. The appointment." Mom covers her mouth with her trembling hand, and just like that, the smile is gone. "I'm so, so sorry. I got a call from Orexis about Elusion's CIT approval a few hours ago, and I just got so worked up, thinking about your dad; I went to Elusion, and then I was just so tired. I sat down on the couch and . . ." She shrugs, choking back tears. "I must've fallen asleep."

"It's okay, Mom. Really."

I want to believe what I just said. I tell myself I just have to be more patient. But I know what she's going to say next.

"All I need is a little more time. I'm going to do better tomorrow, I promise."

Mom wipes her eyes with her shoulder so she doesn't have to let go of the book. My heart immediately replaces anger with guilt, and the shift makes me hunch forward. Suddenly, I have the posture and regret of a woman five times my age.

"You're right—tomorrow will be better," I say.

She sits back down on the couch to collect herself and looks up at me. There's a lot of red around her green irises, but that doesn't stop her from forcing a grin for my benefit. I know this sounds selfish, but I wish she'd do that more often. Just to let me know she's fighting to come back from wherever she is.

"This book," she says, tapping on the cover, "this is the first gift I ever gave your father. It was his birthday, and we hadn't been dating that long. But I knew he was a nature buff, so I just ordered it on a whim. I had no idea he still . . ."

When she pauses for a while, I sit down next to her. "Well, he liked it enough to keep it under lock and key. That's really sweet."

"I suppose. I just thought he, I don't know, was protecting something more important than this."

"What do you mean?"

"The monthly fee of a security box at Morton and Wexley is almost a thousand credits a week. I'm sure this book represented a lot of fond memories, but it's strange he'd spend so much just to prevent it from getting damaged or lost."

"Or stolen," I say, even though that thought seems a bit ridiculous.

Mom must think so too, because she chuckles a little. "Regan, who'd want to steal this? It's not worth anything; it's falling apart."

"I know. I'm just trying to make sense of it."

"Well, sometimes things don't make sense right away, so you might as well put them aside and wait until they do."

She finally lets go of the book and takes my hand. I was expecting her skin to feel cold, but it's just the opposite. Her palm is warm and soft.

"So what's inside the package?" she asks me, a hint of playfulness in her tone.

"I don't know, something from Alessandra Cole."

My mother's eyes brighten. "Oh good, it's your dress. I'm so glad I called over there this morning to confirm delivery. They totally messed up the dates."

It takes me a second to register what she's talking about, but when I do, my stomach performs a little flip of excitement. Before my dad died, she and I went to Alessandra to get fitted for formal ball gowns for Cathryn Simmons's huge spectacle of a fiftieth birthday bash, which Cathryn has been planning since the day she turned forty-seven. I had seen a dress I loved, but because it was so expensive, I had put it on hold, intending to get my friends' opinion before buying it. With everything that happened, it had slipped my mind entirely.

"Well, don't keep me in suspense. Open it up," she says, squeezing my hand.

The way I spring off the couch catches me by surprise. I'm not really a girly-girl who squeals at the thought of putting on a pretty dress. But my mom is, and since she is clearly looking forward to seeing me in something sparkly and decadent, I don't want to sour this moment.

Maybe she's trying to find her fight.

After running into the kitchen to snag a laser pen from the utility drawer, I come back into the living room and waste no time aiming the red dot at the quick-seal and slicing through the sides of the box. Inside, there are a lot of small foam peanuts, tissue paper, and plastic to wade through. I have to admit, it's fun throwing it all onto the floor. When I finally dig deep enough and get to the dress, I remember every single detail I loved about it.

The sweetheart neckline adorned with sequins. The mermaid fit that makes my waist look freakishly tiny. The bold emerald color that contrasts my light complexion perfectly.

As I pull it out of the box and hold it up to myself, my mom almost gasps.

"It's every bit as perfect as I remember it," she says proudly.

As much as I hate to admit these things, she's right—it is.

"Go upstairs and put it on; then make an obscenely dramatic staircase entrance," she adds, laughing.

This feels so good, being normal with her.

"Okay, but only if you try yours on with me," I say, holding out my hand. We had also picked out a dress for my mom to wear. "Is it upstairs in your room?"

She visibly stiffens, and I feel my arm dropping.

"Regan, I'm sorry. I . . . I can't go with you to the party."

And suddenly, I'm clinging to the dress like it's a security blanket. "Why not?"

"Honey, it's tomorrow night," she says, casting her eyes away from me. "I don't think I'm ready to be out in public just yet."

"But you just said that tomorrow you'd be better."

God, I sound like such a little brat. What I said is so manipulative and whiny, and I want to take it back, but it's too late.

"I will be better. Just not enough to be social in a group of people who are going to want to talk about your father," she explains. "Can you understand that?"

I want to say yes, but my bottom lip is quivering. I'm so ashamed for acting like a five-year-old who's not getting her way, but . . .

Doesn't she understand how hard it is to miss both Dad *and* her?

Mom gets up, leaving *Walden* behind on the couch, and comes over to hug me. My dress might get wrinkled, pressed between us like a pancake, but I couldn't care less.

"Listen to me, Regan. I want you to go and have a great time with Patrick," she says as she strokes my hair. Then all of a sudden I feel her start to shudder, like she's about to cry too. "And don't be afraid to keep living your life, either. Whatever it takes for you to heal from this, that's what you should do."

I want to say something, but if I let one word escape my lips, I won't be able to hold us up anymore. So we stand like that for a while, quietly, until we're both strong enough to let go.

I don't look or feel at all like myself.

Maybe it's because I'm not used to wearing haute couture, diamond chandelier earrings, waist-length hair extensions, or the pound of makeup that I let my mother layer on my face.

Or maybe it's because the last time I followed hordes of guests up the polished granite walkway of the Simmons estate, Mom and I had just finished watching an empty coffin being loaded into our family crypt.

I inhale deeply, trying not to remember Dad's memorial service or the reception that Patrick's mom hosted for us afterward. But images from that day start flooding my mind, and I freeze, right in the middle of Cathryn's stream of incoming party guests.

The boring black shift that I mindlessly slipped on that morning.

The minister bestowing blessings that I paid no attention to.

Mom doubled over when we said our final good-byes with the help of two single red roses.

I was in so much shock then; I didn't even shed one tear. Perhaps if I'd seen my father's body, I might have cried.

As I stand here, unable to move in my perfectly fitting, two-thousand-credit designer gown, I wish that shock had never gone away. Sometimes I desperately miss the beautiful numbness that gets you through that first stage of grief or, if you're lucky, makes you think that what's happening to you isn't even real.

Before my dad's accident, Patrick and I used to Escape together with our Equip prototypes so we could feel that wonderful nothingness, but now . . .

Running my hands up my bare arms, the same way I did at my dad's funeral, I feel like all the nerves on my skin are raw and exposed. It only gets worse post-Aftershock.

I know it. And so does my mom.

Suddenly, two women whiz by in identical hot-pink pantsuits, almost knocking me over. I'm actually thankful for their rudeness, because it propels me forward, although in baby steps. I steel myself and set my gaze on the enormous villa that Patrick grew up in. I don't recall this place looking so intimidating, which is strange, because it's the size of a city block and, with its large, domed ceiling, bears a strong resemblance to the old Detroit Observatory. It's also on top of a steep hill in the exclusive Heights Sector, far from the reaches of Florapetro pollution, so no one has to worry about putting on their O2 shields.

I glance at the sparkly little white lights that coat the postmodernist sculpture garden and the three-tiered outdoor fountain, which bookend the house. Strands of silver garland are skillfully hung over the front of the forty-foot-tall arched windows. I've never seen the estate so impeccably decorated before, but I suppose that's because a few years ago, Dad thought I was too young to attend galas like these.

If only he could see me now.

I wait for the crowd to thin out a bit before I approach the grand entrance, and when I do, a long-legged woman in a gold spandex leotard holds out a scanner and smiles at me.

"Passcard, please," she says.

I open my silver beaded clutch and pluck the card out. While Goldie scans it and politely gives it back, another woman walks over, decked out in a similar blue costume and batting her glittering eyelashes.

"Follow me, Ms. Welch," she says, motioning toward the right.

I know the way, of course, but I let her lead me because it makes it seem like I'm a stranger around here, and I have to admit, pretending feels kind of good right now. Along the way, I catch a flash of long spiral curls and shimmering green in one of the mirrored walls. I don't even register that the reflection is actually of me until Blue Lady and I are just about to step into the ballroom.

But when she opens the doors, I don't know where I am anymore, let alone who.

The ballroom has been transformed to imitate the space theme of the Universe Escape. A hologram show beams brightly colored images of stars and planets overhead. They flash in synchronized patterns above the guests, who seem totally delighted by the scene that's playing out on the cathedral-style ceiling.

I meander through the room, noticing the stage that's erected at the far end, where enormous speakers blare hybrid classical-techno music while shirtless male models wearing the new Equip and purple lamé boxer-briefs strike statuesque poses on towering platforms. Tuxedo-clad men and ornately dressed women crowd the dance floor as silver-painted cocktail waitresses sporting Elusion visors weave among the masses, holding large trays filled with crystal glasses of champagne.

Clearly, this party isn't just celebrating Cathryn's fiftieth birthday.

I take a deep breath as my eyes scan the crowd, hoping to find Patrick's friendly face. Instead they connect with someone else, someone totally unfamiliar. He's standing only a few feet away and wearing a uniform—small bronze medals and pewter buttons are sewn onto his gray jacket, and his black pants have thin red stripes up the sides. His sandy-colored hair is cut close to his scalp, making his cheekbones stand out as much as his amber-tinted eyes.

Military academy. No doubt about it.

And from the small grin he's giving me, there's also no doubt he just caught me staring at him.

I blow out a sharp, nervous breath and glance to my right, praying that a champagne girl will be in reach all of a sudden so I can grab a glass of bubbly and wash the embarrassment away in one big gulp.

No such luck, though. Soldier Boy is now standing a few inches from me, rocking back on the heels of his spit-shined shoes and looking like he's trying to think of something to say.

We're both silent, and I'm thinking too—about who he is and why he's here. I feel a stroke of heat spreading up the back of my neck, and then a loud voice slices through the music, catching me off guard.

"Regan!"

I spin around and see Patrick moving through the crowd. Even though he's slowed down by the throng of admirers who want to shake his hand, he keeps his gaze fixed on me. He looks absolutely fantastic, dressed in a retro Edwardian-style tux, but his blue eyes appear a little bit bloodshot, which happens whenever he spends too much time working.

I hate to say it, but I kind of wish he'd find someone else to talk to right now. I'm on the verge of a conversation with Soldier Boy, after all.

But lo and behold, there is someone tagging along with Patrick, though he's moving so erratically across the dance floor she can barely keep up—Zoe Morgan, the daughter of one of Orexis's biggest stockholders and one of the most popular seniors at my high school. Since she's a grade above me and way above my popularity status, my only personal contact with her has been at corporate, family events. But it's well acknowledged in school that every boy lusts after her great body, flawless mocha-colored skin, and long, raven-black hair. And tonight, her ivory spaghetti-strap dress and elaborate updo make her look even more perfect than usual.

"You're here!" Patrick says to me as he finishes saying hello to his mother's friends and business partners. He wraps me up in one of his signature bear hugs, and the part of me that just wished he'd leave me alone clamps its mouth shut. "You look amazing," he whispers in my ear.

"Thanks to Alessandra Cole." I pull away and pick up the skirt of my dress, then playfully dip into a curtsy.

Patrick laughs. "Did you learn that from a princess or something?"

"As a matter of fact, I did."

Patrick does the gentlemanly thing and nods at Zoe. "You two know each other, right?"

I extend my hand toward Zoe and she shakes it.

"Yeah, it's good to see you, Zoe," I say.

"You too," she replies with a smile that's nothing but genuine. "That dress is a knockout, by the way."

"Oh, this?" I say. "I just . . . threw it on."

Zoe laughs good-naturedly at my lame joke, but when Patrick puts his arm around me, her smile fades a little bit.

"I'm so glad you could come," he says to me. "Is your mom—"

"She had to work tonight," I blurt out.

I'm not proud of myself for lying just now, but the thought of Zoe Morgan knowing my personal business makes me queasy for some reason. Patrick gives me a quick squeeze, signaling that he understands, and graciously changes the subject.

"So did you scare Josh off or something?" he asks me.

"Who?"

"Mr. Buzz Cut," Zoe adds, grinning. "You were standing next to him a minute ago."

I peer over my shoulder and my stomach tightens. The boy I was staring at has completely disappeared.

"Oh, I didn't notice," I fib.

"How is that possible? That boy is one-hundred percent man candy," Zoe says.

"Man candy? I wouldn't go that far," Patrick says with a slight twinge of annoyance.

"Don't worry, you're still the most eligible bachelor in the country," Zoe teases him.

I can't help but smirk. I'm so used to girls fawning over

Patrick that it's nice to see him with someone who can hold her own.

"You saw the splash page on Celebrity.com, didn't you, Regan?" she asks me.

"Of course. Patrick sent me the link the second it went live," I joke.

"No, I didn't," he protests, as if embarrassed.

Zoe smiles, touching his elbow flirtatiously with her well-manicured fingers. "I'm going to freshen up; try not to miss me," she says.

When Zoe is out of range, I pull away from Patrick and gently nudge him in the ribs.

"She's really nice, Pat."

"She is nice. She's just been following me around all night."

"Maybe she just wants to get to know you."

"Yeah, well, there's only one person who'll ever really know me, and that's all I need."

I know he means me, and it's a sweet thing to say. But it leaves me feeling like a spotlight has just landed on me and everyone expects me to do something I can't, like . . . sing the national anthem without sounding like a frog.

"Well, what about this friend of yours? Josh. How well does he know you?"

"Remember that sleepaway tech camp I went to?" he answers.

"That camp in Canada? The one where they made you hike with a sprained ankle?"

"I only sprained my ankle at the end," he says, embarrassed. "Anyway, that's where I met him. In fact, we were pretty tight."

"Then why is this the first time I'm hearing about him?"

"Probably because that was a million years ago, and back in those days I didn't feel it necessary to share every single detail with you," he says with a grin. "We lost touch when he was shipped off to the academy. I haven't heard from him since—until I got his text today. Turns out he's in town visiting family, so I invited him." He takes my hand and grins, giving me a little bow. "Enough about Josh. Do you want to join me on the dance floor?"

I back up a couple of steps. "No way—I'm still limping from the country-club thing we did last year."

"Come on, we have so much to celebrate," he pleads.

I smile for a moment, because in his world, Patrick's right. Life is pretty much all wine and roses.

"Please. It'll be fun," he urges.

I'm about to give in, when the music dies down and a hush falls over the crowd. Patrick tips his head toward the stage, and when I look in that direction, I see that the shirtless male models have left so Cathryn Simmons can own it herself. She's wearing a black empire-waist chiffon dress and a small microphone headset, which she adjusts a bit before addressing the room.

"I hate to interrupt a good party, but I just wanted to thank everyone for coming here tonight." She pauses for a moment to allow her guests to applaud and puts her hand over her heart. "I have such amazing friends and colleagues, and I swear, you make fifty feel like thirty!"

God, she's so incredibly poised, no matter what the situation. After my dad's accident, she just stepped in for my mom and took over all the planning for the memorial service.

"But as you all know, there are more important things happening right now than my birthday," Cathryn says with a gigantic grin. "Yesterday, my little company had its most cutting-edge property, Elusion, approved by the Center for Interface Technologies. Soon, Equips will be in homes across America, and I just have to thank the person who made it all possible. My son, Patrick!"

The person who made it all possible?

I love Patrick, but he's not the person who conceived of Elusion and spent years creating the trypnosis technology within the Equip. My father was, and everyone in this room knows that.

"Patrick, could you come up here and say a few words?"

As another round of clapping stabs at my ears, Patrick kisses me on the cheek, his smile easy and light. He walks away from me without a word of regret or a hint of awkwardness, waving to all the people who are cheering for him, including Zoe, who returned from the bathroom just in time to pump a celebratory fist in the air.

But I can't stay here.

Not for another minute.

I've retreated to the main veranda—my favorite part of Patrick's house. When he and I were kids, sometimes we would come out here at night with his precious pocket telescope so we could lose ourselves in the glow of the moon and constellations. We could never do that at my house—the oil clouds always cling to the sky in the Historic Sector, making any kind of stargazing pretty impossible.

Now here I am, looking up at the billion little flecks of light scattered above me and wishing I were anywhere but here.

Last night, Mom said she didn't want to come to this party because there might be too many people who'd talk to her about Dad, but how wrong was she? From the crowd's reaction to Cathryn's thank-you speech, it's like everyone inside that ballroom has suddenly forgotten my father altogether. Seeing that self-satisfied smile on Patrick's face when his mom acknowledged him, watching him accept her invitation to come onstage to be recognized . . . it felt as though they were betraying not only my dad, but me as well.

I know I'm probably overreacting, but I can't stamp out the feeling of hurt that's gripping me so tightly it aches to breathe.

I clutch at my sides with my hands and bow my head, hoping to hide my flushed cheeks. There are a few guests and Lycra-clad waitstaff milling around on the veranda, and I don't want them to see me all worked up. Then again, does it really matter if anyone catches me like this? If my dad isn't alive and well in the Orexis family's collective memory, then I'm probably not either.

"Garlic bread?" a soft but commanding voice says from behind me.

I turn around, expecting to see a man holding a serving tray, but instead I'm met with a pair of devastatingly beautiful amber-colored eyes.

Patrick's long-lost friend Josh is standing next to me, straight as an arrow. His broad shoulders are pulled back so his chest sticks out a little.

Instead of being embarrassed that he might have seen me trying to collect myself, I have the exact same stunned yet overstimulated feeling I had after the demonstration at Orexis yesterday. My fingers are hot and tingling, like I just burned them on a stove. I'm standing here, staring at him again, wondering why I find it so hard to say something, or even move.

But then he holds up his plate and gives me a serious look.

"Before you say no, it has melted cheese on it," he says, pointing to the last remaining slice.

When I laugh, it's like someone has taken a pin out of me, and my entire body loosens.

"Oh really? Well, that changes everything."

I pluck the piece of bread off the square white dish and pop it in my mouth.

"Wow," I say, even though I'm not done chewing. "That's good."

Josh nods, his lips curving into a full smile. He doesn't have perfect teeth—there's a slight gap in between the front two—but I find that kind of endearing.

"Feel any better?" he asks.

The sincerity in his voice surprises me, and it makes me look away. I guess he did notice something was wrong with me.

"Sorry. I just saw you walk out here a minute ago. You seemed sort of upset," he says.

I shift my gaze back to Josh, shaking my head in denial. "No, I'm fine. I just needed to cool off."

"That's why I came out here too," he replies.

I smile, adjusting the top of my dress and hoping that I don't smell like garlic when I talk.

"So you're a friend of Patrick's. Tech camp, right?"

"Yeah. A long time ago." He puts down his plate of food on an end table and extends his hand toward me. "I'm Josh Heywood."

Taking his hand in mine, I smile yet again. "I'm Regan Welch. Nice to meet you."

Just as our fingers slip apart, I hear the sound of footsteps coming fast and hard along the veranda's black laminate flooring. I crane my head toward the automatic sliding doors and see Patrick walking straight at us, still radiant with pride.

"There you are," he says brightly. "I've been looking all over for you."

Josh takes a few steps back and gives me some room. Maybe he noticed how my stance changed from relaxed to rigid in no more than a heartbeat. Unfortunately, Patrick doesn't seem to pick up on it at all. I nod in Josh's direction and Patrick turns, facing him.

"You enjoying yourself?" he asks Josh, swatting him hard on the back.

Josh shrugs. "Yeah, sure."

"Good," Patrick says. "Let me know if you need anything."

But even though his words are kind, the light in his eyes has dimmed, and he's clenching his jaw like he always does when he's worried.

"What's wrong?" Patrick whispers to me. "Did I do something to piss you off?"

The minute I see his brow crease with concern, I start to doubt my emotions. This is Patrick. My best friend. He'd never do anything to hurt me. Not intentionally, anyway. Still, I feel the need to tell him how disturbing it was to see him stealing some of my dad's thunder. It may be unreasonable of me, and a bitchy thing to do, considering how sensitive he is. But I can't hold it in. I just can't.

"What was that in there?" I say, gesturing to the grand ballroom.

"What was what?" Patrick's light blue eyes flicker with confusion.

"Your mom, saying that you made Elusion possible." The words are coming out all accusatory, so I take a deep breath and try to steady myself by putting my hands on my hips. "It just didn't feel right."

Patrick shoves his hands in his pockets and glances at Josh, who has turned his back to us a little.

"Regan, there are a lot of investors at this party. My mom is only trying to remind them that we've got Elusion under control. You know, since the original creator isn't in the picture anymore," he explains, looking at me again, his voice almost pleading. "Your dad would understand."

What Patrick says is perfectly rational, and I know it should comfort me, but the tone he takes really gets under my skin. *Your dad would understand.* It sounds like he's insinuating he knew my dad better than I did.

"Maybe he would, but I don't," I say.

"Well, maybe if you hadn't walked out, you would have," Patrick snaps. He's clearly not happy with how this conversation is going. "I just made a little speech in there, and all I did was talk about David, how much he did for Orexis and for me. Give me some credit. Don't you think I miss him too?"

Patrick and I hardly ever fight, but if we keep going like this, one of us is bound to take us into a battle.

"I think I should go home, Pat."

"You don't have to leave," he says with a deep sigh, like he's trying to surrender. "Stay. After everyone goes home, we can go to Elusion together. It's been so long since we've done that."

It's true, but that's no accident. I haven't told him that I've only used my Equip once since my dad died.

"I'm sorry, I can't," I say. "We'll talk later. Just go back inside and enjoy the rest of the party."

"At least let me call you a car. It's getting late."

"I can take her home," Josh pipes up.

Patrick and I look at him, surprised. I think we both forgot he was standing a few feet away.

"Are you sure?" Patrick asks. "She lives in the Historic Sector, so it's a long drive."

"I don't mind," Josh replies, walking toward Patrick and giving him a nod of reassurance. Then he glances at me with a small smile. "It's a beautiful night."

FOUR

MY HEART RACES AS JOSH'S HIGH-SPEED electric motorcycle weaves between oversize sedans and double trailer trucks, the headlight carving a path through the dark night. The skyscrapers that surround Jefferson Highway—the six-lane main drag that leads to the Historic Sector and continues on into the city—are zooming by us so fast they form a long, gray haze along the side of the road. If my mom ever knew I was on one of these "donor cycles" (that's what people at her hospital call them), she would definitely have a stroke. But Josh and I are wearing helmets with built-in O2 filters, so we've taken that precaution, at least.

Most of my dress is bunched up around my thighs, but part of the hem is trailing above the back wheel like an emerald-colored plume. My hands are placed on either side of Josh's waist, and my chest is pressed up against his back. I can't help but feel what life at the academy has done to his body, and suddenly I'm able to forget the harsh chill of the wind and what feels like a coat of frost on my skin.

But then the motorcycle veers off an exit ramp, and after a mile or two it screeches to a halt. Josh cuts the engine and parallel parks in between two Florapetro-powered econocars. I rub my arms to bring some heat back to them and look up at the silver tower looming above us. With space in Detroit at a premium and air quality levels unpredictable, this type of building has been springing up all over recently. In fact, almost all the historic landmarks on Jefferson have been replaced by these identical, narrow pillars with panoramic windows hidden by decorative Florapetro covers that only open when air quality levels allow a view worth seeing. The tower we're sitting in front of has a flashing two-story MealFreeze sign on it.

Josh twists around and grins. "Hungry? I know we had appetizers but—"

"Sure," I say through the helmet mic, before he even has time to finish his sentence.

As nice as the ride was, it would feel good to get both feet on the ground.

He grins and steps off the chopper, holding it steady for me. I gather my skirt and awkwardly slide off. Before I know it, Josh is shooting me a look, and I'm not sure what to make of it. He seems annoyed or frustrated for some reason, and then he starts unbuttoning and pulling off his military jacket, revealing a plain white crew-neck tee underneath. Josh puts the jacket around my shoulders without saying a word.

I smile, thinking that he might be mad at himself for not having offered his jacket to me earlier, like before we took off on his motorcycle.

"What is this place?" I ask, pulling the lapels across my chest as we begin to poke our way across the crowded sidewalk.

Josh gestures at a passerby who is holding an extra-large red plastic cup with a yellow straw in it. "You've never had a MealFreeze?"

"Nope," I say.

"It's the food of the future," he replies, his amber eyes widening with excitement. "One six-ounce drink gives you all the protein, carbs, and vitamins of an entire meal. We have them a lot at the academy."

The doors of the MealFreeze open automatically, and we're treated to a blast of icy refined air as soon as we take off our helmets. I inhale deeply, trying to ignore the way my heart is banging against my rib cage, which I reassure myself is just a residual postmotorcycle reaction.

A few minutes later, I sit across from Josh in a tiny metallic booth surrounded by neon-blue antigraffiti-lacquered tiles, so close our knees are almost touching. The smell of lavender, piped in through the vents, wafts around us like a cloud of incense. I run my fingers over the velvety-soft textile seats and stare at the red thermal cup. On Josh's advice, I ordered the standard freeze, a vanilla-flavored substance that is supposed to contain forty grams of protein and a whopping six hundred calories. But it looks a little . . . gray. I hope that the color is due to the dim lighting in this place.

I glance at Josh, who gives me an encouraging nod, and take a sip. It's cold and creamy, and the taste is quite delicious, like it came from a real vanilla bean. But the consistency is a little too thick, like a big glob of Greek yogurt, so I have a hard time getting the first gulp down my throat.

Josh grins. "That bad, huh?"

I give him the okay sign with my right hand, and finally the MealFreeze makes it beyond my tonsils.

He picks up his drink and takes a long sip, then wipes his mouth with his napkin. "I guess this stuff is an acquired taste."

"No, it's really good," I insist. "After you finally swallow."

Josh laughs. It's deep and hearty and contagious, and soon I'm giggling right along with him. Once our laughter dies, I smile and look down at the half dozen colored badges neatly pinned on the breast of his academy jacket, which is still wrapped tightly around me.

"So what did you have to do for the black one?" I ask.

"That's for combat skills."

"Really?"

"Everyone at the academy has to apply for that badge. No exceptions, no excuses." His eyes suddenly cloud over, like he's remembering something he'd rather not. It's a look I'm sure I've perfected by now.

"Wow, it's hard to imagine being required to physically fight someone at school."

Josh doesn't say anything. He just mindlessly runs one of his hands over the top of his head, like he's expecting to find some hair there.

"What about the others?" I motion toward the orange and blue badges below the black one.

"Orange is for survival skills."

"What did they do for that? Drop you on a desert island or something?"

"No," he says with a chuckle. "It was a written exam. There aren't many remote spots in the world left for them to take us, I guess."

"I know," I say, my voice faltering a bit at the thought of how much my dad did to find a way back to the wilderness.

Josh leans over the table and points to the left side of his jacket. "The light green one. That's my favorite."

"Which skill is it for?"

"Computer science," he says proudly. "I officially reached master level."

"Sounds like Patrick has some competition, then," I say, raising my eyebrows.

Josh bows his head for a second, biting his lip, and I realize how suggestive that may have sounded. He glances back up at me and there's a beat of silence as we look at each other. I want to say something else, but I'm not sure what. Thankfully, he speaks up and saves me from gawking at him.

"So how did you meet Patrick?" he asks.

I twist a strand of hair around my finger until it turns a dark shade of pink. This question could lead us into touchy territory, but I don't want to seem evasive.

"Our parents worked together at Orexis for years, so we've known each other since we were kids."

"Right. He used to talk about your dad a lot when we were at camp. David, was it?"

"Yeah, they were pretty close."

"I had no idea he had anything to do with Elusion. I thought it was Patrick's invention."

I glance away and look across the aisle at the twentysomething couple sitting a few feet from us. They're nestled on the same side of the booth, their hands touching as their heads slump backward, eyes closed, Equips on. There's a moment where I wish we could trade places with them, so we wouldn't have to talk about uncomfortable things, so we could be free from all our feelings, good or bad, and just . . . be.

When I shift my eyes back to Josh, he's staring at his drink, a shadow of remorse passing over his face. "I was eavesdropping. When you and Patrick were talking at his house. I'm sorry."

"I suppose there is a badge for that?" I joke.

He tries not to laugh, but he can't contain himself. "No, I don't think so."

"What a shame." I smirk a little.

"I just want you to know"—he hesitates—"I think it was

nice of you to come tonight, considering your dad and every-thing."

"I couldn't miss Cathryn's birthday," I reply.

"It was her birthday?" Josh squints with confusion. "I thought we were celebrating Elusion's world domination."

"World domination?" I push aside my cup and lean forward a bit. "That sounds like one of Avery Leavenworth's lines."

"Avery," he says plainly.

At first I roll my eyes, wondering how he couldn't know Avery and her loud, obnoxious mouth, but then I realize that he might not have much access to the media inside the academy.

"She's this girl at my school who's famous for her ridiculous, indignant, so-called activist vlog." I shake my head and say, "She's obsessed with discrediting Orexis and saying Elusion is addictive. She even attacked Patrick personally at his press conference yesterday."

Josh straightens in his chair. "Why?"

"Maybe she's just trying to get more followers or view-ers; maybe she just wants more exposure and to promote her agenda. Honestly, I don't really care. I just want her to leave Patrick and Elusion alone."

The muscles in his jaw seem to tighten. Did I say something wrong?

"Look around," he says. "We're the only people who aren't zoned out in Elusion. Don't you think she might have a point?"

I do a quick scan of the room and notice he's right. It's not like the "restaurant" is packed, but out of the handful of Meal-

Freeze customers here, Josh and I are the only two who are awake. Still, that doesn't mean that Avery has a leg to stand on.

"Okay, if what she said was true, why am I not addicted? Why isn't Patrick? We've gone to Elusion more than anyone in the test market and we're just fine. How do you explain that?"

Josh flicks his straw across the room and directly into the open recycling chute built into the wall. "I don't know."

I could let this drop right here. Talk about something else, like I wanted to do a few minutes ago. But I feel so protective right now. My father isn't around to defend himself or the project that was his life's passion. Don't I owe it to him to face down anyone who doubts him and his work?

So I press on.

"Elusion was my dad's dream. He worked so hard on it . . . for years, he'd go in early and come home late. He worked through holidays and . . ." I lock eyes with Josh and notice how the tension in his jaw has now spread to his forehead and cheeks. "He wanted to make people happy, bring them some joy," I continue. "He wanted to preserve the beauty of the natural world and give people a chance to experience nature. All this excitement for Elusion just means he was successful. Most people can see that. This is a *good* thing."

"So you go to Elusion all the time, then?" he asks. "For the joy, obviously."

I try to ignore the sour tone of his voice. "I haven't been in a while. But like I said, I used to. A lot, in fact."

"How long has it been since you last Escaped?"

"I can't remember."

He searches my face for any trace of nervousness, like he doesn't believe me.

I let out a defeated sigh. "I've only been once since my dad died."

"Why? Are you afraid?"

"No!" I protest. "Nothing like that."

I blow out a frustrated breath as Josh crosses his arms in front of his chest.

"I don't mean to butt in," he says quietly. "But my uncle has this saying: 'Where there's smoke, there's fire.'"

Our eyes meet, and for a moment neither of us moves. We just sit there, staring each other down.

"I should get you home," he says finally, standing up as he glances away.

Even though I don't know him at all, I suddenly realize I can read the expression in his eyes. It's disappointment.

I have to admit, the feeling is mutual.

A half hour later, Josh and I are standing on the steps of my brick townhome. When I checked the air quality meter on his bike a moment ago, it read a negative eight, so I wore Josh's extra helmet to the door. I can actually feel particles of residue sprinkling down from the sky and settling on the back of my neck, which is unbearably gross.

It was an uncomfortable ride home, at least for me. I couldn't stop thinking about my confrontation with Josh. I suppose I ruined the light mood at our table by bringing Avery up in the first place, but what could I do after he seemed to be taking her side? Pretend like it didn't bother me?

But as he helps me slip out of his military jacket and I feel his fingers quickly graze my elbows, I wish that I'd just kept my mouth shut. We were getting along so well. I was having fun. He was easy to be around.

Now there's an awkwardness. And so we stand in front of my house, both shifting our feet as we avoid looking at the other, trying to figure out what to say and do.

"Thanks for the MealFreeze," I say, and push the Eject button on the helmet. As I yank it off my head and shake my hair extensions out, I realize that we'll only have a couple of seconds to say good-bye. It also occurs to me that I might not ever see him again, and something inside twinges a little at the thought, strange as that sounds.

Josh reaches out and takes the helmet from me. "Take care," he says simply.

All I can do is nod. If I open my mouth, I'll ingest all the garbage floating around in the air, and I'll be coughing up synthetic oil debris throughout the night. I yank my passcard out of my purse and swipe it in front of the lockpad. The door pops open, and I'm about to step inside when I feel a hand wrap around my wrist.

I turn around and see Josh grinning at me. He doesn't say anything, but he gives my hand a gentle squeeze and then bounds down the steps to his bike. Thankfully, I manage to hold my breath as I watch him drive away.

I close the front door behind me and exhale. The house is silent. I wheeze a little bit when I glance toward the stairs, and for a split second, like a habit I just can't break, I wonder if my dad is home from work yet. It must be the lemon-scented candle that is placed on the entranceway table. My mom used to love turning on the battery-operated candles in the evening, right before she left for the hospital, thinking the ambience would soothe my dad after a long day at Orexis. She still puts them on, every night at 6:20 p.m., and I wish that she wouldn't.

As I make my way toward the stairs, the track lights turn on automatically, thanks to the built-in motion detectors. I walk up to the second floor, pausing outside my mom's room. I press the manual control switch for the lights on the wall and dim them just in case she's sleeping.

But when I take a peek inside, I see that she's dressed in her ankle-length cotton nightgown, lying on top of the yellow velvet duvet with a slight, peaceful smile on her face. Her visor is still in her left hand, but her earbuds, wristband, and tablet are on the bed.

I can hear Josh's voice in my head.

Where there's smoke, there's fire.

My mind starts ripping through random memories of the past few days. While there are hundreds of blank faces that I can't really place, there are images of Equips everywhere. The Traxx, the depository, the restaurant, here at home . . . one of the only spots where people were not using Elusion was at school, where it's not allowed.

I think back to Patrick's press conference and Avery's outburst. She didn't offer up any proof to back up her claims, and what I told her about Elusion was true. But there are so many things I don't know, details I'm unaware of because my father and Patrick aren't talking about it over our dinner table any more.

As I look at my mother and think about how often she Escapes, I'm flooded with fear that something changed right before my very eyes and I didn't notice it because I wasn't looking for the signs. There are aspects of Elusion I haven't even tried, like the ExSet feature.

Maybe it's time for me to go back and see for myself.

I tiptoe out of there and down the hall to my room, the door sliding shut behind me. The autolights flicker on, and I see that Mom has folded down my linens and left my father's book on my bedside table. My eyes tear up at the thought of my mom parting with this, even for just moment. It's a sweet gesture—she obviously wants me to have a piece of him.

I kneel on the floor beside my bed and reach underneath, pulling out the titanium case with the new Equip that Patrick sent me a week or two before the conference. I sit on the edge of the faded quilt my grandmother made for me when I was born, and place the case beside me. I snap it open. All the components are neatly wrapped in quick-seal, tucked into their own foam slots.

Using my laser pen, I gently open the packages, placing each silver component on the bed beside me: tiny lightweight earbuds, a slim visor with mirrored lenses, and a soft acupuncture wristband with a chrome keypad that is no bigger than the face of a regular watch. Although my original equip contained all the same items, everything here is significantly smaller, sleeker, and lighter. I pick up the acrylic wristband and study the destination codes and time settings. There are some new destinations, but what really catches my eye is the red emergency ejection button on the bottom of the keypad, in case of a "rare equipment malfunction."

I kick off my platform heels and give my sore feet a quick rub, staring at the Equip components. I try to push away a rush of anxiety that's needling at my shoulders like bee stings.

I know the return from my Escape will hurt as much as it did a few months ago, but I have to take this risk. After all, how can I defend my father and Elusion if I'm not truly honoring what he created? And how can I say without a shadow of a doubt that it's not dangerous if I'm not facing this one fear of mine?

My tab vibrates on my steel-top window-ledge desk, signaling that I have an unread text. I snatch it up and swipe my finger across the touch screen to wake it out of sleep mode.

There are not one but two messages.

Patrick: Let me know when you get home, okay?

and

Patrick: Can we pretend tonight didn't happen?

I close my eyes and laugh. God, it is so hard to stay mad at him.

I glance down at my tab, my fingers dancing across the screen. I quickly type:

Regan: Stopped for something to eat. Back home now. TTYL

I'm about to hit Send when my hand hovers over my tab and freezes.

A minute passes and then another.

I finally send a text.

Regan: Going to Elusion to check out the Universe. Come with?

I guess, deep down, I don't want to go back there alone.

I touch the screen and the blue status bar zips along the bottom as my tab attempts to engage the Elusion program. A second later, a message pops up on the screen: *ELUSION® is only supported by Tecno 115 or higher. Press Enter if you would like to download now.*

I press Enter and wait for the app to be updated. A message pops up: *Download successful. Installing ELUSION®.* My heart banging in my chest, I sit down on my bed again and slide the wristband on, making sure the tips align with the pressure points and the digital dial is facing up. I press my start code on the small numeric keypad, connecting it and the tab by satellite to the main server.

An emergency warning flashes on the screen, a warning I'm guessing was CIT mandated:

If your wristband alarm sounds, please leave Elusion immediately. Staying in Elusion longer than recommended might result in brain injury.

I reach for the earbuds as my tablet buzzes with a message.

Patrick: Meet you there. 7-3-4-8

My pulse is picking up steam. I enter his companion code into the keypad and then wait.

A second later, I have another prompt from Elusion on my tablet:

User 7348 has accepted invitation request.

Another instruction flashes on-screen.

Please insert earbuds.

I take my earbuds and slip them in place.

Please engage video visor.

I slide the visor over my eyes, balancing it on the bridge of my nose, and push the switch on the temple forward. At first I'm surrounded by darkness, but then a glowing panoramic rainbow, created by the microlasers, stretches out in front of me.

A robotic female voice begins to speak in a droning tone, accompanied by a low hum, the kind of sound that electric transformers make.

"Escape immersion in five . . ."

I lie back on my bed, my hands folded comfortably over my stomach in what Patrick always refers to as the "casket" position.

Four . . .

I have a vision of Josh in his uniform, his amber eyes staring at me intensely as if he's trying to read my mind, but just as quickly it's gone, replaced by a fuzzy white airiness.

Three . . .

I'm beginning to feel a little light-headed, like I did after Mom and I painted my room three years ago. I see her standing on the ladder, her brown hair pulled back in a ponytail, the familiar laugh lines etched around her eyes as she smiles and says, "At least pretend like you're trying not to get it on the ceiling . . ."

Two . . .

A bright, all-encompassing white light dances around me.

One.

I'm floating in outer space among a cascade of stars, slowly spinning in circles, my arms stretched above my head and my open hands dangling loosely from my wrists. I'm amazed by how weightlessness feels—it's like swimming through a pool filled with the fuzzy petals on one of those flowers you make a wish and blow on. I can't remember what they're called. Actually, it seems like I can't remember much of anything—the name of my calc teacher, what sector I live in, or why I've been away from Elusion for so long. I keep searching the recesses of my memory for anything to hold on to but I'm coming up empty.

It's the most soothing feeling I've ever known.

Patrick's virtual universe—all the planets, moons, and stars—is completely astounding. Luminous yellows, greens, and reds come together like large blotches of oil paint mixing together on a blue-black canvas. Pinpricks of glowing white light are scattered everywhere, like someone has thrown confetti up into the air and it's never sprinkled back down. Strangely, the sound of nothingness is something I can taste on the tip on my tongue—it's sweet and soft, like melting caramel. I look down and see that I'm dressed in an aquamarine neoprene jumpsuit and heavy moon boots that have soles built for maximum traction.

My body feels warm, every cell channeling an indescribable energy that makes me believe in things I know aren't true, like my father is still alive, and I belong out here, hurtling through the galaxy. When I arch my back, I swing into an elegant, gravity-defying somersault. And then I see it—a comet blazing toward me. But unlike the one in the Orexis demonstration, it seems as though this comet has been designed just for me, in all my favorite colors. Vivid streaks of blue, purple, and magenta fill a sphere of charcoal gray, and orbiting around it is a wide stream of neon-pink stars.

It's getting closer, and moving faster. Although it looks like we're going to collide and I'll be incinerated on the spot, I don't feel anything but pure elation. I reach out with my hands in front of me, preparing to graze the comet with my fingers as soon as it's within my grasp.

All of a sudden something snags me by my arm and I'm yanked to the surface of the comet, where a familiar face is there to greet me. Patrick's blue eyes are electric, and his legs are straddled across the back of the flaming ball of violet and periwinkle. His neoprene suit is a gorgeous shade of cobalt, but it's a bit looser than mine.

"Ready for the ride of your life?" He grins, shifting me behind him. I wrap my arms around his waist as he types something on the keypad of his wristband.

"Yes! What are you waiting for?" I shout.

"Hold on," Patrick says as he presses one more button. Then he grabs what appear to be reins made of fire. "Okay, here we go!"

The comet blasts off and the planets whir past us, creating an endless blur of color. We're going so fast we barely get a chance to take any lingering looks at the wondrous scenery before us—there is a patch of hazy lavender fog that seems to go on into infinity; a gigantic tide of crimson rock formations spins out of control in every direction. And in the center of this marvelous splendor is a soulful, encompassing silence that totally blankets me.

It's exhilarating and serene all at once.

I lean around Patrick for a better view as we soar through a network of indigo-tinged nebulous clouds.

"Duck!" Patrick shouts as he maneuvers the comet under a sparkling silver asteroid. We're zooming downward at a ninety-degree angle, practically at the speed of light. Patrick's blond hair is blowing back in my face, and it feels like a thousand little feathers are tickling my nose. I smile and breathe in the smell of his shampoo—a delicious blend of rosemary and ginseng. Once we're out of harm's way, Patrick navigates our comet in a winding pattern, dodging a spectrum of tangerine-colored aerolites.

"Let's do that again!" Somehow, my words feel like delicate whispers, even though I am shouting them.

"Maybe later," Patrick says as he steers the comet away from the belt of fluorescent crater-covered rocks. "I want to show you something."

Once again the comet launches into flight, and we descend at an alarming rate. My head whips back and I squeal as my stomach dips.

Patrick releases one of the flaming reins and points into the distance. "Phobos," he says, as we careen past a sepia-tinged rock that looks like the shape of a skull. "It's one of Mars's two moons."

I hook my arms underneath his and grip him by the front of the shoulders. "I can't believe it. This feels like—"

"Heaven," Patrick says, turning around just enough to look me in the eyes. His cheeks are rosy, and I notice a small birthmark near the corner of his lips that I don't ever remember seeing before. When he smiles at me, I swear, I don't think I've ever seen him so clearly.

"Want to see Mars?" he asks.

"I want to see everything," I say.

It takes no longer than a split second for our comet to streak by the Red Planet, or at least that's how it seems to me. Time peels away here, and that's probably my favorite thing about

Elusion. Patrick pulls the comet so close to Mars's dazzling scarlet glow it's like we're skimming along the outer rims of its vaporous atmosphere.

Patrick yanks the reins and the comet stops, hovering above the giant mass in midair. I've seen plenty of pictures of Mars, but nothing could've prepared me for how it really looks—a swirling globe of reds, oranges, and pinks.

"I designed that myself," Patrick says, his voice filled with pride.

"It's so beautiful."

Patrick turns around again to face me, his intense gaze sending a ripple of heat up my spine.

"Like you," he says.

He touches my cheek, caressing my skin with the backs of his fingers, which slowly drop down to my chin. "I mean it, Ree. No one compares to you."

I search for something to say, but I'm distracted by a fever that has possessed my entire body. When he takes my hand and kisses the inside of my wrist, everything—my head, feet, arms, legs—is humming with an intoxicating vibration. His fingers trail up my arm, and staring directly into my eyes, he leans toward me, tilting his head ever so slightly to the left, and I know what he's about to do. But then we hear a chirping sound and a flash of light spews from my wristband, temporarily blinding me.

It's all gone.

I'm back in my room, lying on top of my grandmother's

quilt. My head hurts and my limbs feel heavy and numb, as if they're encased in lead. My eyelids are twitching, but that's the only part of me that's moving. I count backward in my head from one hundred, trying to relax as the Aftershock symptoms wear off. Within a minute, I can feel my legs coming back to life, each muscle spasm a bit less crippling than the last. Soon, I'm aware of a sharp, prickly sensation in my arms—it feels as though I've fallen into a small patch of thorns.

In the distance I can hear the slow drip of the broken motion-sensor bathroom sink—every drop of water a marker of a second I'm trapped inside myself.

Thankfully, the pain and paralysis fade after a few more minutes. I manage to pull off my visor and press my fingers to my temples, rubbing them in circles until my ears stop ringing. I push myself up on the bed, but fall over on my side. The dizziness makes the room pitch and revolve, so I curl my knees up to my chest and wait until I regain my equilibrium.

I distract myself by staring at the digital clock that's displayed on my InstaComm wall. I'm surprised to realize that we were in Elusion for nearly an hour. It seemed like Patrick and I were only there for a few minutes.

Oh God. Patrick.

I touch the spot on my wrist where he brushed his lips only moments earlier.

No one compares to you. . . .

My thoughts begin to topple over one another. What did he mean by that? Was he really leaning in for a kiss, or did I completely misread him? Does he want to be more than just friends?

I hug my knees even more tightly and close my eyes. I try to clear my mind, but when I do, the sound of the dripping faucet becomes louder and louder. Dad promised me yesterday that he'd fix it. Obviously, it slipped his mind, which is no surprise anymore, given how preoccupied he's been. I sit up on my bed, my legs dangling over the side, and call out to him.

"Dad! The sink is still broken!"

When there's no response, I get up and cross the room, my gait a little wobbly. I think about asking Dad about Patrick, and if he's noticed any strange behavior lately too. But I stop in my tracks when I see my reflection in the mirrored closet doors.

I'm wearing an evening gown.

I was at a party at the Simmons estate.

I was mad at Patrick for taking credit for Elusion.

My father is dead.

I cover my mouth with my hand so I can't hear my own sob. I place another hand on my stomach, because it is clenching so hard that I can't even stand up straight.

This happened to me before, and I know I shouldn't be surprised. But the shock is so intense I have to kneel down on the floor. The bottom of my dress spills out around me, creating a wavy circle of shimmering moss. My shoulders hunch forward as I rock myself back and forth in a vain attempt to dispel this devastating feeling I've been trying to avoid for months.

A long series of beeps comes from my InstaComm. I glance up with glistening eyes and see the screen morph from the digital clock to a caller ID notice.

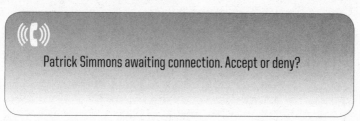

Patrick Simmons awaiting connection. Accept or deny?

My trip to Elusion must have sucked all the life out of my tab, because Patrick doesn't use my IC number very often. My body feels just as drained, my throat so raw it's hard to speak. And yet I'm surprised by how quickly I'm able to say the word.

"Deny."

FIVE

EVERYTHING ABOUT REALITY SEEMS SO
much dimmer and flatter the morning after. It's like someone
hammered a spigot into the sky and drained the last remaining
specks of tint out of it. I think I slept a total of three hours,
so I have this intense anesthetized feeling that I can't seem to
shake—not even with two *caffè macchiato*s ravaging my blood-
stream.

And being at school on a Sunday (thanks to the Department of Education's newly adopted semi-Standard 7 schedule)
is only making it worse. I forgot to do my math homework and
was late to tech ed, which allowed Mr. Herbert the opportunity to give me another twenty demerits. Now I'm only one
away from detention.

After adjusting my O2 shield, I pull up the hood of my

sweater to ward off the chill, tucking my hands into the pockets of my skirt. I walk through the long stretch of campus connecting the fifteen-story hexagon-shaped building—where my classmates and I spend most of our days toiling away for eight and a half hours straight—toward the dark, round building that houses the cafeteria.

Along the way, I'm doing all I can to compartmentalize everything that happened yesterday into the tiniest little quadrant in my brain, far away from all the receptors that process memories and pain. I try to concentrate on hopeful stuff, like how I woke up to a fresh-faced Mom making breakfast in the kitchen; how we chatted about Cathryn's party over a stack of hot pancakes covered in agave syrup; how she tossed in a load of laundry consisting of only her canary-colored scrubs, because she is going back to work at the hospital tonight.

It wasn't easy skipping the unsettling details: my odd night out with Josh and how awful I felt after coming back from Elusion with Patrick. I just didn't want to spoil the upbeat mood she was in. If she is getting her life back on track this time, I don't want anything to get in her way, especially me.

As I reach the cafeteria doors, I quickly take off my O2 shield and shove it in my bag, then swipe my passcard in front of the code reader. Once I'm inside, I'm hit with a remarkably gross stench. My eyes flick over to today's menu, which is scrolling on a digital blue screen above the chow line.

Miso meatballs with hemp hearts.

Ugh.

I cringe as I peruse the rest of the menu while an ocean of kids rushes into the cafeteria to meet up with friends, unapologetically bumping into me and bouncing me around like an anchorless raft adrift in the Florapetro-polluted waters of Lake Saint Clair. I really don't feel like dealing with the raucousness of the lunchroom today and would spend the entire period in the library if I could, but our passcards are all GPS encoded, and a monitor would hunt me down in less than five minutes.

I squint in the bright halogen lights, looking for a familiar face. The cafeteria is about half the size of a football field. In fact, it's so big that when the air quality is in the negatives, the track team uses this room for practice.

In the past, each grade used to eat together, but the school has gotten too big to do that, so there are now eight lunch periods, each lasting for exactly a half hour, the first beginning at ten thirty a.m. As a result, most of us go through the day eating really early or really late and almost all of us are always hungry. At lunchtime, we usually don't fool around with chit-chat—we just eat.

But today, something is different. Hardly anyone is paying attention to their food. Instead, everyone is frantically typing away at their tabs and talking excitedly among themselves.

"Regan!" I hear someone call out from the center of the room.

My eyes shift around, trying to locate the source of the voice, and land on Zoe Morgan, who is waving both her arms at me. Her black hair is pulled back in a tight, side-swept braid and she's wearing a snug gray cardigan and tiny blue cargo skirt with ruched knee-high black boots—actually, if those heels were any higher, she'd definitely be on the verge of a dress code violation. I look down at my choice of shoes and remember that since I was running late this morning I grabbed the first pair of shoes I could find, which just happened to be my mom's gray rubber clogs.

Great, just great.

I pull my hair into a low ponytail as I walk over to Zoe's table, which is occupied by a crew of popular seniors. I take a seat in between her and Jane Gonzales, one of the best-known student-council representatives at Hills Sector High, who manages to squeak out a hello without taking her eyes off her tablet. Zoe doesn't even bother doing either.

"Have you heard from Patrick today?" she asks.

I hesitate, wondering if he told her what happened between us in Elusion last night. I hope not. I've been avoiding all of Patrick's calls and texts for a reason. I'm still not sure what to say to him, so how can I explain anything to her?

"No, I haven't. Why?"

"It's Avery," Zoe announces, narrowing her dark eyes. "Did you see her latest vlog?"

"No." In fact, I make it a point to avoid Avery in all forms whenever I can.

"You wouldn't believe what she said about Orexis and Elusion."

I reach toward my pocket to grab my tablet, when Zoe

places a hand on my shoulder.

"Don't bother. Her whole site is shut down," she explains. "Everyone is trying to locate the video, but all record of it has been wiped out, including the sites that were streaming it."

I let out a groan. "What swill is she dishing now?"

"Avery claimed that Orexis was involved in some sort of massive consumer deception. And then she said something about how the people responsible for harming the public wouldn't 'escape' retribution or 'elude' justice, which isn't even clever if you ask me."

"As if anyone with half a brain would believe her," I say. At least, that's what I'm hoping.

"There's more," Zoe adds.

"What else?"

Zoe clears her throat. "She said that there's an object or something inside the program that's threatening users' lives."

"Oh God," I murmur.

"Patrick had her site disabled," she adds.

"Wait, did he tell *you* that?"

Zoe raises her eyebrows, as if surprised by the sharp tone of my voice. I'm not mad at her, but I am feeling like a jerk for avoiding all of Patrick's attempts to contact me. What if he was trying to alert me about this? What if he needed a friend and I wasn't there for him because I was too busy acting like an idiot?

"No. That's what people are saying, though."

"Right," I say, taking a deep breath.

"Listen, Regan," Zoe says. "Avery is in my comm class, and I know for a fact she's determined to get into the journalism program at Northwestern. She probably figures if she makes a name for herself with a high-profile, controversial story, she'll be totally unrejectable. I've been watching her numbers, and she's gained over a million followers since she started posting vlogs relating to Elusion."

Suddenly, I see Avery standing at the end of the lunch line, her tray in her hands. She's wearing her trademark horn-rimmed glasses and vintage army jacket over her uniform. Her freckled face is free of makeup, contorted into an obnoxious holier-than-thou expression as she scans the cafeteria. Our eyes meet, and she smirks as if challenging me.

If she thinks she can slander my dad, she's in for a rude awakening. "Someone has to stop her," I say.

In one swift motion, I leap off my seat and advance through the cafeteria. Ignoring Zoe's pleas to stop, I make my way toward Avery with purposeful strides. She sets her tray down at a table of drooling groupies and crosses her arms, defiant.

"Look who it is," she says smugly as I step in front of her. "One half of the Orexis dog-and-pony show."

"What's your problem?" I ask angrily. "It's not enough for you to try and ruin Patrick's news conference? This time you've gone too far."

"*I've* gone too far? Elusion is about to go live to the whole country, and your little boyfriend doesn't give two craps that he's hurting people with his lies!"

"*You* are the liar, Avery," I say, clenching my hands into fists. "I'm sick of your snide comments, and so is everyone else."

"I don't think anyone gets sick of the truth. Just ask the millions of people who tried to download that video."

"You are full of shit, you know that?"

"If that's the case, then why did Patrick shut me down?" she snaps. "Is he worried that his precious CIT approval will get revoked when they find out Elusion is addictive?"

"I went to Elusion last night to see for myself if your claims were bogus, and guess what. I'm okay. See? Not addicted to anything, or on the verge of dying!"

Avery takes a bold step forward and then another. We're about the same height, but she outweighs me by least twenty-five pounds. Yet when she looks at me with venom in her eyes, I don't even blink.

"Do you know about the firewall, Regan?" she asks smugly.

I open my mouth, praying that some solid smack talk will come out, but there's nothing but dead air. I know what a firewall is, but something in Avery's coy voice makes me think that's not what she's referring to. Even so, I can't let on that I'm confused here.

"What about it?"

"Unfortunately, I can't say." Avery makes a fake pouty face, and the kids at her table snicker in response. "You'll have to ask your boyfriend. His legal goons slapped me with a cease and desist order, so that means I can't tell anyone *what I know.* Even you. But that shouldn't matter, because he tells you everything, right? He wouldn't keep a secret from you, even if it meant telling you that your father's pet project is poisoning the minds of users. . . ."

I don't hear anything else that follows her insulting my dad. I also don't know why I can't hold back and stop myself from doing what I'm about to do. It's just impossible not to scream "Shut up!" at Avery and slam the palms of my hands into her chest as hard as I possibly can.

I catch her by surprise and send her staggering. She lands flat on her back, her glasses flying off her face as her head crashes against the floor. She turns to me and wipes her nose with the sleeve of her jacket, her eyes narrowed into tiny slits.

A group of people in the lunchroom have formed a semi-circle around us, excitedly yelling, "Fight, fight, fight, fight!"

Avery gets up slowly, but I can tell by her flushed face that she's about to lunge for me. We're interrupted by the piercing sound of an electronic panic whistle. Mrs. Allen, a tenth-grade counselor and lunch supervisor, rushes toward us, the device dangling from a chain around her neck.

"Ms. Welch!" she shouts at me. "Back off, right now!"

I'm too shocked by my own behavior to reply. I've gotten pretty angry before, but I've never put my hands on anyone.

"Avery, are you all right?" Mrs. Allen asks as she touches her hair, clearly worried the bun she's constructed on top of her head is no longer secure.

"Fine," Avery says, though the small quiver in her lip would indicate otherwise.

I smirk a little, thinking how easily shock can dissolve into satisfaction when you win a round against the Averys of this world. Too bad my victory is over the moment Mrs. Allen cuffs a cold, bony hand around my forearm and says, "Let's go."

"I'm not going to tell her I'm sorry."

Principal Caldwell lets out a heavy sigh as he leans back in his chair and folds his hands into his lap. This can mean one of two things—either he's about to give up trying to make me apologize to Avery, or he's preparing himself for another round of *Let's Rationalize with an Angry Teenager!* We've been playing this game in his office for almost twenty minutes now and I haven't given in yet, so for his sake, I hope it's option number one.

"When it comes to violence, we have a zero-tolerance policy here. I could suspend you for what happened," Caldwell says. "Now, I know you're still going through a lot at home, and I'm sensitive to that. But the only way I can let you off the hook is if you apologize to Ms. Leavenworth."

"Fine, suspend me. Anything would be better than sucking up to Avery."

It's been over an hour since my hands pressed up against her chest and sent her flying to the floor. All the rage I felt then is still here, gnawing at my heart and throbbing at the base of my skull. I wouldn't be talking to Caldwell like this if it weren't.

"Let me get this straight. You'd rather have a suspension on your permanent record than say two words to a girl you don't like?"

"Why should I tell her I'm sorry when I don't mean it? She's the one spreading lies. *She* should be apologizing."

"According to this school's code of conduct, Avery has the right to vlog about whatever she wants, as long as she doesn't compromise the school." Caldwell scratches the back of his head, his brow furrowing with frustration. "But you don't have the right to shove her, or anyone else, just because you don't like what they're saying. Can't you understand that?"

Of course I do. His argument is more than sound. But I can't back down. I won't.

"I'm not saying sorry," I say, calmly folding my hands in my lap.

"Okay." Fed up, he springs from his chair and walks over to the InstaComm wall. After he presses a couple of numbers on the glass touch screen, it comes to life, revealing a vibrant image of his olive-skinned, black-haired executive assistant. "Lillian, could you patch me in to Meredith Welch, please? I need to speak with her about her daughter, Regan."

"Yes, Mr. Caldwell," she replies, and then the screen goes black.

"Hold on," I say, bolting up from my seat. "You don't have to call my mom."

"Actually, I do."

"She's going back to work tonight; this . . . this is only going to worry her. She's been through enough."

But my attempt to reason with him is unsuccessful. "Please wait outside my office," he says. "I'll call you back after I've had a chance to speak with your mother privately."

I hear the sound of the automatic door sliding open. I see a message pop up on the InstaComm:

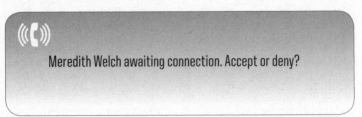

Meredith Welch awaiting connection. Accept or deny?

I reluctantly pick my bag up off the floor and slink out into the administrative office, which is filled with faculty members drinking shots of instant-brewed pod coffees and waiting for their meetings to start. My legs feel like rubber cement and I'm a little bit dizzy, so I stumble over to an acrylic bench and sit down.

I am so, *so* stupid. Fighting *the principal*? How could I not see where that would lead? I bow my head and cover my face with my hands, imagining what Caldwell is saying to my mom right now and wondering how she's going to react.

Then I see a pair of polished brown boots march toward me.

And now I'm locking eyes with Josh Heywood, who looks just as great in civilian clothes as he does in his military uniform. My lips immediately twitch up into a smile, despite the cyclone of emotions swirling inside me.

"Mind if I sit with you?" He gestures to the empty spot on the bench.

I scoot over to make room for him, pulling my bag in between my knees. I glance at my mom's ugly clogs, once again embarrassed. Why couldn't I have worn my own shoes today?

"What are you doing here?" I ask, tucking my feet under the bench.

"Admissions stuff." He leans forward, pulling his tab out of his back pocket and showing me the application form that's on the screen.

"You're transferring? To HSH?" My voice hits a squeaky pitch, a cross between excited and scared.

He smirks a little bit. Damn, he is so good at noticing my every move, no matter how slight it is. I wonder if that comes with all the military training, or if he's just paying special attention to me.

"Yeah, Caldwell told me I could reenroll here after I served my time at the academy."

Reenroll. Which means he has gone to school here before.

"Served your time? Does that mean you didn't go there voluntarily?" I ask.

He simply nods and starts keying in letters and numbers on his tab.

"So what were you in for? Anything serious?"

"Depends," he says, avoiding my eyes. "How serious is shoving someone in the cafeteria?"

Great. Josh has already heard about my run-in with Avery, which means it's already all over the school intraweb. "I don't know," I say. "Depends how much they deserved it."

He laughs, and that jittery fluttering I felt at Patrick's party is back.

Josh whispers, "I heard some of the staff talking about you while you were in with the principal. Sounds like they think Avery had it coming."

"Well, she did."

I glance at Josh's leg as it bobs up and down, and I grin. This small flash of nervousness chips away at his composed exterior, and I see a part of him that's like me—a bit frightened about letting someone new and unfamiliar get close.

"So what happened?" he asks.

"Avery made all these false allegations against Elusion on her crappy, lame vlog, and she accused Patrick of being part of some kind of cover-up. Then she started to drag my dad's name through the mud. The girl is just—"

"Speaking her mind," Josh interrupts.

"What?" I must have misheard him. Why does he keep defending her?

"Look, all I meant is . . . words are words. They don't matter as much as you think they do. What's important are the emotions behind them."

Words are words? My fingers curl around the strap of my bag, wringing it back and forth. "If that's the case, then why did Patrick force her to shut down her entire site?"

"I don't know. I didn't watch the clip. What did she say exactly?"

Just as I'm about to respond, I realize that I have no idea what Avery actually said. I never saw the video. All of my anger is based solely on what Zoe told me and what Avery admitted, which wasn't much.

"You never answered my question," I say, changing the subject. "Why did you have to go to military school?"

"I hit a guy." Josh swallows hard, and I watch his cheeks flush a dark shade of pink. "I beat him up as he was coming out of the locker room, and got expelled. That's why I was shipped off to the academy."

His chin dips down, his features strained. He seems too even-tempered to lose his cool like that, and I can't help but wonder what provoked him.

"Why?" I ask.

"This kid, he . . . he was harassing my sister. It's a long story." Josh tugs at his collar and clears his throat; then, after a short pause, he continues. "It felt good at first, taking him down like that. But later . . ."

When his voice trails off, my hand drifts over and settles on his shoulder. Josh inhales deeply and lets out a long, drawn-out breath, but then he shifts away from me so my fingers slip off his arm one by one.

"All I'm saying is, sometimes it's better to walk away than to act tough. When you cross the line and do something violent, there's no going back," he says. "It stays with you. Forever."

He stands up and puts his tab in his back pocket. "I have to go. See you in the halls."

"Okay," I say, hoping that he might look at me again and see that what he's told me hasn't made me think less of him.

But he walks straight out the door, and Caldwell calls me back into his office.

SIX

WHEN I GET BACK HOME FROM SCHOOL,
Mom has already left for work, but the glowing orange text on
the left-hand corner of the InstaComm wall shows she also left
me a video message. After tossing my bag on the floor, I plop
down on the couch and kick off her nurse clogs, extending my
legs so I can rest my feet on the padded U-shaped ottoman.
I fish out the remote from in between two seat cushions and
press a blue square button, which accesses the message from
the database.

An image slides across the screen from the right, showing
a picture of her, all prepped for a long night at Inner Sector
Medical's critical-care unit. Her hair is swept back, and she's
wearing the oatmeal T-shirt that she layers underneath the
top of her scrubs. She's even wearing a little makeup, which

brings a subtle warmth to her complexion that I haven't seen in a while. I find myself smiling at her, even though in the snapshot she's just looking straight ahead, her mouth slightly open.

I press the green oval button next and the message begins to play.

"Hi, honey. I'm sorry that we're missing each other tonight, especially after what happened today." Her gaze dips down for a second and she pauses, like she's trying to figure out the right thing to say. When she looks back up, her eyes are a little glassy, and my throat tightens.

"I don't blame you for being angry, but I had to agree with your principal about your punishment. Two weeks of detention may seem harsh to you, but it could have been a lot worse." She flashes a hint of a smile and I know the worst is over.

"I'll be back in the morning. Hopefully I'll catch you for breakfast. There are waffles in the freezer," she says, smiling. "Sleep tight."

The video ends, and I sigh in relief as I close the viewing window on the screen with the remote. The impromptu chat we had with Caldwell this afternoon was pretty brief, and I couldn't really tell how Mom was going to react once she didn't have a school administrator huffing and puffing at her. I'm so thankful that the whole thing didn't blow up in my face at home, because two weeks of detention is not going to be a walk in the park.

I'm about to shut the InstaComm off when an envelope icon

bursts to the center of the screen, spinning in a circle with the number one in the center of it. I click the Upload button on the remote, and the IP address is from a sender who's not in our list of contacts. The message has a large attachment, which instantly makes me wary, but my curiosity gets the best of me, so I open it anyway.

Hi Regan,

I was able to retrieve A's vlog. Thought you may want a look.

JH

PS: Hope you don't mind.

Zoe's in my chem class, she gave me your IC info.

I press the Launch key on the remote. As the file loads, I think about how much Josh had to go through to unearth Avery's vlog, especially since it had been completely scourged from all the Net caches.

I guess that master badge in computer science wasn't a joke.

Soon a still photo of Avery appears in front of me, her eyes already piercing through the screen. Her curly hair is hanging loose around her face and down to her shoulders, and her glasses sit on the end of her nose. I hit the Play button and then jack up the volume so I won't miss a single word.

"I have breaking news in the Elusion story. Someone with insider information got in touch with me after the big Orexis press conference announcing that Elusion received CIT approval and the program would be launched nationally," she says, her voice seemingly filled with more emotion than an aspiring journalist should really have.

I lean in, staring Avery down with a scowl.

"My source tells me that there is a hidden object inside all the Escapes—a firewall, to be exact—that lures uninhibited and vulnerable users closer to it every time they use Elusion, stimulating some kind of neurological response. We believe this firewall was specifically designed by developers at Orexis to create a biological addiction to their product so they could make *billions!*"

I throw my hands up in the air. Avery is totally fabricating things. I have *never* seen one of these firewalls of hers while in Elusion, and I was just there with Patrick.

"And it's working. Orexis stock is at an all-time high. Elusion users are finding themselves going back in more and more often, unable to control their urges. And the CIT did nothing to stop them. A new scourge is about to affect our country, turning the people we love into . . . E-fiends!"

E-fiends?

A tad dramatic, but I have to give her credit—she looks like she believes what she's saying.

"Soon my source will go on record to verify that Orexis falsified their test data to get their precious safety seal! Soon this company will be brought to its kn—"

I hit the Pause button, and given the surge of anger that's

slicing through me, I'm surprised I don't throw the remote at the screen.

But as much as I wish I could just discount Avery as a nasty, pathological liar, I can't. And that's what makes me even more frustrated.

I look deep into the freeze-framed eyes on the screen and realize I've had it all wrong. Avery isn't causing problems for Patrick out of maliciousness. She actually thinks she's saving the world. And because of her fervent belief, people are starting to take notice. People like . . . Josh.

There's only one solution: I have to prove to Avery, and to everyone else, that she's wrong. And there's only one way to do that.

I need to find the firewall.

When my eyes blink open, I have to immediately shade them with my hands. It's not Elusion's signature white light that's interfering with my vision, but an array of shocking colors. The sky is a shade of bright peach, the scattered clouds an effervescent pink so fluffy and low I'm tempted to jump up and tear off a piece like warm cotton candy. The sun is centered directly above me, a swirling, pulsating mass of purple.

I push myself up, wiggling my toes in the plum-and-bright-red-speckled sand that sparkles around me like a sheet of tie-dyed diamonds. My pale skin looks perfectly bronzed against a green halter-top bikini that magically gives me an hourglass shape.

I push myself to my feet, transfixed by the shining silver sea, its waves cresting into a foaming kaleidoscope of colors before crashing to the shore.

This is not the same tropical Thai beach that I visited the day after I found out my father was never coming home again—the one with the lush, heavy palm trees and blue-green water with dark seaweed floating in clumps underneath the surface, the one that looked like a real place. This Escape destination is a confectionary creation, rebuilt and redesigned by Patrick and his new team of programmers. The only thing that remains from before is the faint fairy-dust outline of every piece of stimulus surrounding me.

But why?

The question doesn't linger in my mind for long. The wondrous lull of trypnosis is penetrating my brain cells. A mellow breeze gently blows my hair, and I tuck it behind my ear. I turn toward the water as it begins to rise and crest, reaching into the peach sky and rushing along the shore with a thunderous roar. I stand up, my feet cushioned by the soft, cool sand, and walk toward the water, reaching it just as a frothy wave breaks. I laugh and jump back in delight as the water splashes all the way up to my stomach, causing my skin to glow. I take a step forward and then another, wading into the silver ocean. It feels as if the tide is moving not around me but *through* me, encouraging me to go farther with every wave. When I'm thigh deep in the sparkling water, a thought tugs at me and I pause.

I have a feeling that there is something I'm supposed to do.

The crash of another incoming wave distracts me, and I turn to face it head-on, welcoming the water as it spills over me. I flip on my stomach, gracefully riding the wave toward shore. When I reach shallow ground, I push back toward the sea, my legs moving in a fluid and effortless motion. I swim until I lose sight of land, then float on my back, my legs spread out in a V shape, my cheeks soaking up the rays of the sun. It's hard to explain the feeling inside me, but I trust the water to deliver me to safety.

By the time I coast back to shore and open my eyes once again, the miles of wild-colored beach have been replaced with a dense, tropical forest that's unlike anything I've ever seen before. I step out of the sea, water droplets lingering on my tanned skin as I walk toward leafy, blue-feathered palm trees with cream trunks. Tucked between them are giant flowers with brilliant red and yellow buds the size of human heads. I turn toward the palm tree and run my fingers over the fuzzy fibers of its pale trunk. It's soft, like cotton.

My gaze is diverted once again to the sparkling silver ocean, and I smile widely when I notice how all the craggy pockets of land that jut out seem like a long strand of precious multicolored jewels. The sun is beginning to set, inching closer and closer to the horizon, so I decide to skip along the shore, my feet splashing in the water. I have so much energy ripping through me that I feel strong enough to move a mountain, but for some reason, all I want to do now is collect the violet and minty green seashells that are scattered everywhere I look.

I wander and search for a while, although I have no idea for how long. But I stop when my shadow grows tall and only a small sliver of the sun remains. I breathe in the fresh air, which is tinged with a fragrance of hibiscus, determined to capture this feeling of freedom and bottle it up inside me forever.

I bend down to pick up another shell—a dark burgundy one with lots of coarse ridges—when I notice something peculiar. Off in the distance is a grayish, fuzzy wall that extends into the sky like an impenetrable fog. I feel a tingling near the base of my neck as I'm overcome with a sense of purpose.

I've left something unresolved.

What is it?

The sky is fading from peach to black as the remaining sun recedes behind a cluster of blood-red clouds.

The firewall.

I came to Elusion to find the firewall.

I drop the shells and begin to run toward the looming curtain of gray in front of me. The breeze transforms into a strong wind, blowing my strawberry-blond hair in all directions. I follow the shoreline, watching how the light colors become swallowed by darker ones. The water is changing too, the silver hue being consumed by inky darkness.

I hear a thunderous crack, followed by another and then another. And suddenly, I stop.

I'm not alone.

There's a man standing on the beach. He's not facing the water but staring directly at me, as though he's been waiting here for my arrival.

I know there's an emergency button on my wristband that would send me spiraling back to the real world, but I'm not afraid.

Even in the darkness, I recognize him.

His lips slide up in an all-too-familiar grin. "Regan," he breathes.

And then I'm racing toward him as fast as I can, my heart lodging itself in my throat. As soon as he's in range, I throw my arms around his neck. He holds me, cradling my head with his warm hands.

"My girl," he whispers.

This is real. *He* is real. I know it.

My father pulls back abruptly, staring desperately into my eyes.

"Listen to me. You're not safe," he says, shaking me by the shoulders. "No one is safe. You need to find me. . . . I'm—"

All of a sudden, I can't hear him anymore. My ears are flooded with a deafening bolt of static, and though his lips are moving, I have no clue what he's saying. The crackling sound gets so loud I almost let him go to cover my ears with my hands, but then a hurricane-force gust wallops us both, threatening to rip us apart. I grip his arms, and he holds on to me, his face straining while our bodies buckle under the intense pressure. The windstorm funnels around his legs, lifting them off the ground.

"Don't let go, Dad!" I shout. "Don't. Let. Go!"

But it's no use. Something enormous and invisible erupts from the sky and plucks him out of my grasp with one greedy snap. I watch, helpless, frozen in place as he is taken away from me, sucked behind the fuzzy gray wall.

Then I'm slapped by a quick flash of white light, and in one frightening instant . . .

I'm home.

I can't open my eyes or move my legs. The only thing I can control is my left hand, which I use to peel off my Equip visor in one sluggish movement. I try to lift my head, but it feels like I'm being weighed down by hundreds of wet stones.

I lie there, as what I just saw sinks in.

My father. He was right in front of me. I talked to him and held him in my arms.

I need to figure out what's happening. I have to call Patrick and tell him everything—even if I'm not sure what it all means.

Another minute passes by, maybe two, and I'm able to open my eyes. I'm sprawled on the couch, facing up so my gaze is trained on the ceiling. I crane my neck and push my shoulders forward, but then nausea hits my stomach, knocking me flat on my back. My head is pounding and my ears are ringing. I try to swing my arm down so I can grab my bag—my tab is in one of the interior pockets—but my arm still doesn't have full function yet.

I have to fight through this. After another thirty seconds, I regain a little more strength and slowly lower my trembling hand toward my bag. Thankfully, I left the zipper open, but when my hand dips inside for my tab, my fingertips graze the smooth, slippery touch screen and I'm unable to grasp it. I try again, focusing harder this time, pitting myself against the stiffness that's disappearing from my muscles.

Finally, I manage to wrap my fingers around the tablet, pull it out of my bag, and drag it up to my face. When I pull out my earbuds and press the Call button, I open my mouth to say Patrick's name—his number was the first one I entered into my voice-activated dialing list—but nothing comes out. It's like my throat is coated with the Florapetro grit I sometimes inhale when I forget my O2 shield.

After swallowing a few times, I'm able to say, "Call Patrick."

The tablet dials, but the call goes directly to voice mail. I let out a soft groan. Will I even be able to say more than two words right now?

"Leave a message and I'll call you back pronto," Patrick's recorded voice says in a half-business, half-playful tone.

"Patrick," I say hoarsely. "My dad. I saw him . . . in Elusion. What's—"

A long, high-pitched buzzing interrupts me, followed by an automated response:

"The recipient's inbox is now full. Good-bye."

I hang up and curse under my breath, pushing myself up on my elbows and shaking out my feet. I hope that partial message saved on Patrick's tablet, but I know I can't count on it. And I can't wait. I have to return to that beach in Thailand this very instant and figure out what's going on.

I type in my destination code, but it won't go through.

I try a second time and receive an error message, blinking on the touch screen in bold red letters like a broken traffic light.

MANDATORY LOCKOUT: YOU MAY RE-ENGAGE ELUSION IN 55:37 MINUTES.

I enter the code again, and the same message pops up. I bow my head, tears forming in the corners of my eyes. I totally forgot that my dad added this safety measure to protect people from exposing their brains to intense hypnosis without giving themselves adequate recovery time.

There has to be some kind of special administrator code that can circumvent the timer, or at least I'm praying that there is one. As luck would have it, the only person who'd know it isn't picking up his damn tablet. So I call the InstaComm at Patrick's penthouse apartment atop Erebus Tower, where I'm met with another dead end. Then I break down and call his office. I usually don't like to bother him while he's at Orexis, but obviously this is an emergency. I ask his executive assistant to patch me through to him, but after keeping me on hold for ten minutes, he tells me Patrick is at an important meeting off-site and that he'll leave word with the second executive assistant, who's in charge of his return calls.

Unbelievable.

But wait, there is another person who needs to know what happened.

Mom.

I frantically dial her private number, hoping that she'll answer right away. She can't be too far into her shift. In fact, she's probably just getting settled in at HR and going through a reorientation program or something. But soon her voice mail kicks in and I quickly press the Disconnect button on my tablet.

How can I possibly explain on a message that I saw my dad in Elusion? Mom would probably call back and ask me to come down to the hospital so the psych staff could check me out. It seems like the only thing left to do is stare at my watch for the next hour, willing each restricted minute to disappear into thin air.

When the last one finally does, my fingers fly to the touch pad of my wristband and the screen of my tablet, furiously entering every critical numeric code. Then I put on my visor and reinsert my earbuds.

When the immersion countdown begins, I feel like my chest is filling with helium. A tickling sensation ripples up and down my limbs, making all the little light-blond hairs on my skin stand on end. A large swath of incandescent light covers everything in sight, and when it dissipates, I'm transported to the same beach where I saw my father.

I look around, stunned.

There must be some mistake. This can't be the same Escape I left an hour ago. If it is, something terrible has happened here. It looks as if a bomb has exploded, leaving devastation everywhere. Fierce scarlet-colored ocean waves batter a torn charcoal shoreline. The extraordinary flowers have been scorched, so all that remain are burned fragments of stems. The forest is totally obliterated too, and the stench of decaying vegetation thickens the air so much I have to cover my nose with my hands. I'm yanked left and right by howling, storm-grade winds that spray salt water across my cold, bare skin, each and every droplet stinging me like acid rain. The wall that my father was sucked behind is nearly impossible to see, fading into the pitch-blackness that surrounds me.

The environmental conditions aren't the only things that have changed. I'm jumpy, nervous, filled with an overwhelming sense of doom. I begin hearing faint voices inside my head. As the wind strengthens and shifts, I hear them taunting me relentlessly.

You're going to lose Patrick.

Your mother doesn't care about you.

Your father is dead; don't you wish you were too?

Shaking them off, I take a deep breath and force myself toward the swirling sea, moving closer to the spot where I saw my father. Each step becomes easier, and soon I'm running, the wind blowing my hair every which way as my feet sink into the sand. As I reach the edge of the water, I trip over a piece of pale gray driftwood and fall to my knees. I push myself up as another turbocharged current of air sprays sand into my face.

"Dad!" I scream, shielding my eyes from the debris. "Where are you?"

I look toward the firewall, but I can barely make it out through the dust fragments flying around me. A clap of thunder sounds as a bolt of lightning streaks through the midnight sky, striking the beach only inches from me. I jump up and run in the other direction as hail begins to fall in heavy sheets, pelting the sand with pebble-size rocks of ice.

A roar comes from the horizon, so loud I'm certain the world is about to crumble. In the distance, far on the edge of the bubbling ocean, a cone of water rises out of the sea, twisting ferociously, like a violent tornado. I remember my father telling me a long time ago that I couldn't get hurt in Elusion, but suddenly I'm doubting him. Even so, I'm not leaving until I find him again. I crouch down in the sand, hugging my legs to my chest, bracing myself for whatever happens next.

Just as the funnel is about to suck me into its vortex, the rotating column suddenly turns away. I tilt my head up and watch as it practically flies back over the water, disappearing into the sea's horizon. But it has left something behind. A number is carved into the sand in front of me.

5020.

It's a message. A message I'm certain is from my dad.

Then, from out of nowhere, two strong arms grab me from behind and yank me up.

"I'm getting you out of here, Ree," Patrick says, holding me tight.

"No!" I say, fighting him off. "My dad is here! We have to find him!"

Patrick reaches over and presses the emergency button on my wristband.

"No!" I scream above the wind, trying with all my might to wrest myself from his grasp.

And then everything fades behind a blinding wall of light.

SEVEN

BRIGHT ORANGE-AND-BLUE FLAMES crackle and jump in front of my eyes, sending me into a mini-trance. I search my mind for a memory of the last time we used the steel-encased ethanol fireplace in the den. Thanksgiving, maybe? It was definitely on the first night the temperature bottomed out, right before it started to snow.

But I doubt everything right now.

Patrick and I have been back from Elusion for about a half hour. I can hear him in the kitchen, shouting into his tab at one of his senior programmers. The minute Aftershock wore off and Patrick could move his hands, he called Orexis, looking for an explanation as to what happened to my Escape and how I managed to see a man who has been dead since December.

My head falls forward a bit and I feel the heat of the fire on my cheeks. It reminds me of the comfort of my father's hug, and the soft timbre of his voice, but these aren't remembrances from months ago—they are images from the here and now, stolen moments that I want back more than anything in the world.

The house is suddenly silent. I feel a comforting hand on the small of my back. Patrick squats down and sits beside me, placing a steaming mug of tea on the floor near my feet and wrapping a fleece blanket around my shoulders. I raise my chin and keep my eyes focused on the flames that dance in front of us.

"You okay?" he asks.

I pull my knees up to my chest and rest my elbows on them. "What do you think?"

"Yeah, dumb question," Patrick says. "I just got off the phone with the manager of the tech crew. He can't really give me a straight answer about what might have happened until he gets a more detailed report."

"More detailed? I told you everything," I say, my voice sharper than I intend it to be. "Plus you were there. You saw for yourself."

I shouldn't act like this is Patrick's fault. He came over here as soon as he listened to my message and went searching for me in my Escape once he got my destination code off my wristband. He's always watching out for me.

"I know, but maybe you could walk me through it one more time." He sets his tab on the patch of floor between us. "Is it all right if I record this? Just so nothing gets lost in translation?"

I nod and then add a smile. Patrick has been a dot-your-i's-and-cross-your-t's kind of guy since we were kids.

He hits a button on his touch screen and says, "Go ahead."

I let out a cleansing breath. "Well, when I first got to the Thai Beach Escape, everything seemed fine, but the landscape was way different than the last time I was there." I think back to the silver water, the purple sun, and the tie-dyed sand. "The colors were all surreal and the trees were made of glass. I don't know; it was like something out of a child's dream."

Patrick loosens his necktie and slips it over his head, putting it in his jacket pocket. "Those changes were made to the World destinations a while ago, Ree. You're just noticing it now?"

When I'm quiet, I feel his hand on my shoulder and turn to face him. He doesn't say anything, but I can tell by the softness around his eyes that he realizes I have hardly been to Elusion at all since my father died.

"It's not what he would have wanted," I say.

"I know," he says quietly.

"Are all the Escapes like that?"

"Yes," he admits. "But the design changes were a business decision."

"A business decision, huh?"

"Market research suggested that making Elusion like a fantasy world would give it more commercial appeal."

"Since when do you listen to market research? You loved the way Elusion was before."

Patrick's face hardens a bit, but only for a second. He's not about to let us get off track. "So you got to the beach. What next?"

"I went for a swim in the ocean. Then I strolled through the flowers, collected some seashells."

"Sounds nice."

"It was. But then I remembered why I was there." I stretch out my legs and stare at my feet. "I got into a fight with Avery today over her vlog about the firewall. So I went there to find it and see with my own eyes, so I could walk up to her tomorrow and call her on her BS."

When he sighs in disgust and mutters, "That *stupid* video," I'm caught by surprise. From the tone of his voice, it's almost like he thinks Avery is the worst of our problems.

"As soon as I got to the firewall, the entire world started falling apart. And that's when I saw my dad. He was standing there in front of it, like he was waiting for me."

"Then he said something to you, right?"

"He warned me. He said no one was safe." Suddenly my heart sinks so fast I have trouble catching my breath. "That's when he was ripped away from me and sucked behind the firewall. Then, out of nowhere, I was zapped home."

Patrick starts cracking his knuckles. It's one of his many problem-solving techniques, and I find it terribly annoying, so I nudge him with my foot and thankfully he stops.

"The safety alert on your Equip probably detected a change in your brain chemistry and cut off the program," he says.

"But that doesn't explain why I saw my father, or what happened to me when I went back to the Escape. This tornado appeared out of the water, and it was heading straight toward me—"

"Why didn't you press the emergency button on your wristband?"

The thought hadn't even occurred to me. Maybe because I'd just seen a ghost.

"Because I wanted to . . . find my dad again," I murmur.

Patrick reaches over and puts an arm around me. "It wasn't real, Ree. I know you want to believe that somehow he might be alive, but . . ."

I slump down and lean my head against his chest. "If it wasn't real, then what was it?"

Patrick doesn't say anything in response, but I can't help noticing that his heartbeat has picked up steam.

"I'm not sure," he says. "But it doesn't have anything to do with the firewall."

Now his breathing is getting faster too.

Is there something that he's not telling me?

"How do you know?" I ask.

"Right before David died, he and I installed the firewalls ourselves to prevent hackers from infiltrating the program," he says. "All of them are application-, circuit-, and network-based, so they've kept intruders at bay, but there are assholes out there who will do anything they can to find a breach, trust me. They surround all the dumps—"

"Wait a minute," I say, my head popping back up. "What are dumps?"

"Oh, that's just programming lingo for the Escapes. Dumps are made up of basic codes with security programs in each one. Grouped together, these dumps make up the master program for Elusion, which becomes active when someone turns on the app," he explains.

"Got it. But let's skip the geek slang, okay?"

"Sorry." Patrick gives me a small smile. "Like I was saying, the firewalls surround all the Escapes. They're located about five miles from the drop point, and they connect all the Escape programs, sharing walls. They also work as a barrier, preventing users from traveling from one Escape to the other."

I look into his eyes for traces of worry or deceit, but they seem honest, like always.

I know I'm doubting everything right now. But my best friend? If I second-guess him, it'll feel like a part of my life is shattering, just like that insane scene at the beach.

"So it's like a force field then? They keep viruses out and people in."

I'm sure this is a gross understatement, but Patrick nods his head in agreement anyway.

"Exactly. They're just there to protect the user. They don't harm people inside the Escape in any way. And they sure as hell don't make them addicted."

I reach forward to get my mug of tea, but Patrick grabs it first and passes it to me. When our hands touch and his fingers linger on my skin, another reminder pops into my head.

I was dodging all of Patrick's calls and texts today. For reasons that seem kind of silly, given everything that's happened since then.

"Avery could care less about the truth; she just wants to run a smear campaign and come up with ridiculous sound bites," he adds. "Everything she said in that video was completely slanderous."

"Is that why you had her site shut down?"

"It wasn't hard to do. Our lawyers said her claims were a textbook case of defamation," he says. "Anyway, she has a lot of followers. We couldn't let her go around saying that Elusion is addictive and Orexis is falsifying data. Not when we're so close to introducing our product nationwide."

I take a sip of my tea. I don't know if the warm liquid on my tongue triggers the memory or the smell of the passionflower leaves. Regardless, I realize that I've left out an important piece of information.

"I saw a number written in the sand!" I say, my excitement nearly causing me to spill my tea all over Patrick. "It was right by the firewall, but it washed away before you showed up. Maybe it means something."

"What number?" he asks.

"Fifty-twenty," I reply.

At first his eyes have a faraway look, but after a beat he casts his gaze all around the den. "Where did you put your tab?"

"It's on the couch in the living room."

Patrick springs to his feet with a "Be right back," and in less than a minute he returns with it in his hands, typing furiously on the keypad. I stand up and glance over his shoulder.

"What are you doing?"

"I'm checking for viruses."

"But I haven't noticed anything weird on my—"

"Did you get a prompt to upgrade to a new version of the app?" he asks as he types something on the screen.

"Yeah, but I didn't have any problems with it."

"There still could have been an error in the downloading process. It could have—"

"Caused my Escape to become unstable," I say.

"And God knows what else," he says.

"Has this ever happened before?"

Instead of answering me, Patrick takes a few steps backward, a look of shock—or is it fear?—slipping over his face like a dark veil. Then he turns his back to me, as if he's trying to block my view of the tab, and begins typing on the touch screen quickly with his right hand.

"Patrick? What's wrong?" I ask.

Again, no answer. Every ounce of his attention is on the tab, where his fingertips are still skimming the touch screen at a rapid pace.

I have to admit, the way he's ignoring me is making me kind of antsy.

"Did the scan find anything?" I poke around him and reach for my tab, hoping he'll show me what he's doing. He's been pretty candid with me up until now—so his sudden need for discretion doesn't make any sense.

But Patrick pulls the tab away from me so hard that I almost trip over him. "The diagnostics haven't finished yet," he snaps.

"A simple no would've been fine," I say.

"Can you please just be quiet? I'm in the middle of something."

I've rarely seen this defensive side of Patrick, but when I have, he was trying to hide something, like his secret stash of Halloween candy or the XXX sites in his browser history.

So my hunch that he's keeping something from me—something about Elusion or my tablet—is feeling more and more like a fact.

But why? What is he afraid of?

"Give me back my tab, Pat," I say, holding out my hand. When he doesn't reply, I nudge him hard with my elbow, and he flinches. "I mean it. Give it back now."

He looks at me and clears his throat. "I really should take this into Orexis, Ree. I can have a whole team of people spend all day running protocols—"

I launch toward him and snatch the device back without Patrick putting up much of a fight. "This was a present from my dad. It was one of the last things he ever gave me, and it's not going anywhere."

I'm not proud that I played the dead-daddy card, but Patrick's odd behavior has me concerned that I can't trust him with all the personal information contained within my tab's data banks.

Like all the Net searches I did on Josh Heywood.

He puts his hands in his pockets, his brows knitting together in a fit of worry. "Just don't use your tab anymore, okay? I'll get you a new one. And don't tell anyone what happened until I figure things out—not even your mom. You have to promise me."

"Patrick, I don't understand. Tell me what's—"

"I should head out," he interjects, grabbing his tablet off the floor and stopping the recording. Then he brushes back a strand of blond hair, his eyes reddening at the corners. "Try and get some sleep, okay? We'll talk more tomorrow."

As soon as he leaves the house, the ethanol fire automatically shuts off, and I'm alone in the dark.

I lived alone, in the woods, a mile from any neighbor . . .

As another stinkball hits the wall inches away from my head and bursts open like a bubble, I run my hand over the worn, yellow page and think how lucky Thoreau was. He never had to serve detention in a crowded, stuffy lecture hall filled with about two hundred code-of-conduct offenders.

My eyes flick up once the rancid smell infects the air, and three greasy-haired boys a few rows below me burst into laughter. I had purposely taken a seat away from the fray, in one of the rows near the top of the auditorium, but my attempt at privacy has backfired. I'm up so high that Mr. Von Ziegelstein, the moderator, doesn't notice the unruliness unfolding around me. He is sitting center stage, perched on a stool with his gaze fixed solely on his tablet. Every so often he runs his fingers through his hair plugs, but other than that he's like a statue. It's almost like he's impervious to the chaos—the loud talking, music blaring, and stinkballs being launched from pellet guns by the kids in the back seats. Or perhaps he's just given up on trying to keep order in a place where nobody listens to him.

But the noise is doing much more than distracting me from reading my father's copy of *Walden*—it's pushing the anxiety I've been pinning down inside me right to the surface. I even put one of my hands on my stomach to settle the acidic feeling that hasn't left me since last night.

When I saw my father inside Elusion.

When Patrick tried to take my tablet away from me.

I shake my head, hoping to dislodge those thoughts from my mind and focus on the book again. Three girls behind me jack up the volume, the music on their tabs so loud I'm having a hard time concentrating. I wind up skimming through the small printed text and when I reach the end, I flip back through the first few chapters, my finger trailing down the side of the page. I'm just about to put the book away when my finger stops on a line that gives me a sudden case of tunnel vision. I can no longer see any other words on the page. It's like a spotlight has formed around this one sentence, so I read it over and over again.

The mass of men lead lives of quiet desperation.

That's how they seemed yesterday. Both my father and Patrick.

Desperate.

You're not safe. No one is safe. You need to find me. . . .

Just don't use the app on your tab anymore, okay? And don't tell anyone what happened . . .

Their voices are a constant loop in my head, triggering an avalanche of questions that threatens to bury me alive. Why did Patrick seem so suspicious and strange yesterday? How could those visions of my father have felt so real? What really happened at the beach in Elusion?

I'm distracted from my thoughts by a collective murmur that sweeps through the crowd, followed by a dozen or so cat-calls and whistles.

I glance down toward the front of the auditorium and see Zoe Morgan, talking to Mr. Von Ziegelstein and gesticulating like crazy. Her jet-black hair flows loose around her shoulders, and she has on a pair of patent-leather stacked heels that make her at least four inches taller than she really is. At first I wonder why she could possibly be in here. Zoe's an honors student and senior class president, and she has most of the teachers wrapped around her finger. Then I notice the length of her cargo skirt—midthigh is definitely not acceptable—and how she's cut a sexy slit up the side of it. That's at least seventy-five demerits. Pretty puny when compared to the even thousand I received for my little altercation with Avery, but still enough to earn her a brief stint in this zoo.

I shut my book and stick it back into my bag, catching a glimpse of Zoe as she makes her way into the crowded room, totally out of her element. She clutches her tab in her hands and scans the hall for an empty seat. Since there's one next to me, I stand up a little bit and wave my arms above my head, hoping that she'll see me. Our eyes lock and a smile lights up her face. As she climbs the lecture hall's steps, I can see how naturally pretty she is. Unlike at Patrick's party, there isn't a drop of makeup on her mocha-colored skin, and even so, her cheeks are a delicate shade of dark rose. When she finally reaches row GG, Zoe is huffing and puffing, like she's just finished a race.

"I am. *So* out. Of shape," she says through halting breaths.

I pat the chair beside me and laugh. "Those steps are the reason I don't take bathroom breaks."

Zoe sighs and scoots past me so she can park herself in the seat to my left. Out of the corner of my eye, I see a kid aiming a stinkball at her and shoot him a death stare that stops him in his tracks. Surprisingly, he responds with a nod of respect and slips the pellet gun back in his pocket.

"Funny, I didn't know you were a regular here," she says.

"Yeah, well, I have a pretty impressive tardy record," I reply.

"And a fight under your belt," she adds. "Can't forget that."

"It wasn't much of a fight," I say with a shrug.

"But it was a major infraction, right?" Zoe touches my arm, her lips slowly slipping into a straight line. "Did Caldwell say it was going to show up on your transcript?"

"No. He InstaCommed my mom, though. And gave me a thousand demerits."

"That's so unfair." Zoe's eyes narrow and she scowls. "Avery deserved every bit of what you gave her and more. I can't believe all that shit she said about Elusion and the Simmons family. She couldn't be more off base."

And just like that, I feel queasy. When I confronted Avery in the cafeteria, I sounded just as confident as Zoe is right now. But that was before I went to Elusion and everything I thought was certain and irrefutable was chipped away in a matter of hours.

"I bet Patrick was glad you stood up for him."

"I guess," I say, my thoughts tripping into last night, remembering Patrick's reaction when I told him about my showdown with Avery.

All he seemed to care about was her video and the possible PR damage it could do. I cared about that, too, obviously, but when visions of my father came back to haunt me, for a moment I actually contemplated the idea that the Elusion app might have some real flaws. Maybe not the one Avery is suggesting, but something that could be just as frightening.

"Do you mind if I ask you something? About Patrick?" Zoe asks.

My attention snaps back to her. "Sure."

"Does he . . . not like me or something?"

I give her a reassuring smile. "That's ridiculous. Of course he likes you."

From the way her forehead wrinkles with worry, I don't think I've convinced her.

"It's just that . . . Patrick and I were supposed to go out last night, but he canceled on me at the last minute. When he texted me, he didn't even say why."

My eyes shift away. Patrick was with me, but he didn't tell Zoe where he was and why he had to cancel their plans. He also never mentioned to me that he was supposed to see her.

Why is he being secretive about this, too?

"It gets worse. I went to his office." Zoe slouches in her seat, a shadow of embarrassment floating across her face. "I know. Totally lame stalker move, right? I just thought he was working late and I'd bring him some dinner. Cheer him up."

"That's really sweet," I say.

It was also a move straight out of Patrick's good-person playbook. I can think of a hundred things like that he has done for me, including a recent trip to the depository. Which begs the question: Why am I so hung up on the five or so minutes he wasn't acting like himself? Why can't I let it go?

"It was pathetic, Regan," she continues. "There I was, holding a bag of curried chicken, standing in the lobby of Orexis, looking like a total . . . *groupie*."

"Don't be so hard on yourself. I'm sure whatever reason he had for canceling has nothing to do with you," I say, putting a comforting hand on her shoulder. There's no sense in telling Zoe he was with me instead. Even though it was sort of an emergency situation, it would still hurt.

But it seems like she's already two steps ahead of me. "Listen, I don't want to intrude, or interfere. I really like Patrick, and I thought you guys were just friends. But if I'm wrong and you're more than that and he'd rather be with you, then . . ."

Before she can finish her thought, the recessed lights in the ceiling flicker and the sliding doors begin to open. Mr. Von Ziegelstein stands up and turns on the microphone pinned to his jacket.

"There's an early dismissal due to American Education Night," he says, his voice like sandpaper against wood. "Thank God for small miracles."

The room buzzes with shouts of joy and celebration, everyone excited to get out of detention early.

"Are you going?" Zoe asks.

"To . . . American Education Night?" The only time I ever went to that event was when Patrick, as the valedictorian of his class, was asked to speak. And even then, my parents and I found an excuse to leave shortly after he was done.

She nods.

I hesitate. "Um—I would, if I didn't already have plans . . ."

"Regan," she says, smiling. "I'm just joking. No one would be caught dead there."

I attempt a grin as we grab our bags and begin to file out of the lecture hall with our fellow delinquents. When we start to march down the steps together, she says, "You didn't answer me."

I look at her, confused.

"About Patrick," she says.

"Patrick and I are friends," I say resolutely.

At the bottom of the stairs, we're separated briefly by a massive throng of people that's clogging up the exits. I press my way through, heading toward the door, every now and then checking to make certain Zoe is okay. Once we make it into the hall, she grabs my arm, pulling me off to the side so she can talk to me privately.

"You're sure there's nothing going on between you guys?" she asks again.

On any other day, I would have said absolutely not. But if I denied it right now, that would be a lie, wouldn't it? There is *something* going on between Patrick and me—something mysterious and unfamiliar and actually kind of scary. Still, I can't avoid her follow-up question. That might give her the wrong idea entirely.

As soon as the words "We're just friends, I swear" escape my lips, I look over Zoe's shoulder and my gaze lands on my locker, which is about twenty-five feet away from us. Josh is there, waiting for me, leaning up against the wall. His hands are tucked in his pockets, and the sleeves of his gray sweater are bunched up around the elbows. He turns, staring directly at me.

I inhale sharply, my pulse accelerating. Zoe waves her hand in front of my face, breaking the spell.

She turns around to see who is vying for my attention. When she realizes that it's Josh, her lips twist up into a smirk.

"Looks like I don't have to worry about competing with you for Patrick after all."

I flinch a little bit, thinking about that moment Patrick tried to steal a kiss from me in Elusion, but when Josh smiles like he's eager to talk to me, I tell myself that Patrick's brief romantic overture was just my imagination.

"I think Buzz Cut has a thing for you," Zoe says with excitement. "He asked me for your InstaComm info in calc, and if I thought you'd go to Elusion with him. He's totally scoping for a hookup, right?"

I give her a look that's covered in pessimism, but I can't deny the fluttering in my chest. "I doubt it, Zoe."

"Well, don't keep us in suspense, then!" she says, practically pushing me in Josh's direction.

I stumble forward a little, cursing under my breath at Zoe for making me look ungraceful. But then I steady myself and take a step and then another, moving toward him as I unzip the front compartment of my bag and pull out my passcard. But the closer I get, the more I detect this nervous energy coming from him, and not the good, happy kind. In fact, his eyes are kind of bleary, and his forehead is creased with worry.

"Hey," he says, stepping to the right just enough so that I can swipe my card and open my locker.

I grab my school blazer off an inside hook and say hello, hoping he doesn't hear the happy, nervous lilt in my voice. I don't usually wear my emotions on my sleeve with just anyone, but he's beginning to turn into an exception.

Josh crosses his arms in front of his chest and leans in toward me, like he's about to conspire with me. "Do you have plans this afternoon?" he whispers.

"Not really. Why?"

"I need to take you somewhere," he says.

As I close my locker door, my heart skips a beat. Zoe was right. Josh is here to ask me out. I try to think of some witty, flirty reply as I turn back toward him. But when I see how his lips are pressed together in a tense, straight line and how his chest is rising and falling with quick, shallow breaths, all I can say is "What's wrong?"

Josh looks down at the floor, almost like he can't bear to respond, but after swallowing hard, he does.

"Everything," he says.

EIGHT

"MIND DOING SOMETHING ILLEGAL?" Josh asks.

We're outside an abandoned factory on the outskirts of the Steel Sector, our O2 shields working at maximum levels. The helmets were too heavy, so we swapped them out as soon as we arrived. There aren't air meters out here, but it doesn't matter. Everyone in Detroit knows that the toxins in this area are worse than anywhere else in the city because the wind barrels through here like a dust storm, carrying all the pollutants from the refineries.

"I don't know," I say, eyeing the eight-foot chain-link fence surrounding the old abandoned building and the looming sign warning trespassers to keep out. "How illegal is it?"

"We have to hop this so we can look around," he says, his

voice totally audible through the clear breathing shield covering his nose and mouth. "There's something inside you need to see."

I can't imagine what he means by that. My dad's HyperSoar hangar wasn't too far from here, and I'm familiar with this neighborhood, which isn't all that impressive. The large industrial fields are made up of nondescript rectangular structures that house the assembly-line workers who help piece together everything from Florapetro-fueled cars to eighteen-wheel semis. Judging by the broken windows and boarded-up entryways, the place has gone downhill in the past few months.

But before I can agree to commit the unlawful act of trespassing, Josh grabs hold of the fence with his fingers, pulling himself up. Then he climbs over, jumping down on the other side and landing firmly on his feet. The whole maneuver takes seconds, and from the smile that appears on his face, I can tell he's proud of his accomplishment.

"Did you learn that at the academy?"

"Ninja movies," he jokes. His expression turns serious, his amber eyes staring at me through the chain-link fence. "Your turn."

I shake my head.

"I'll help you," he offers.

"I'm not worried about that," I say abruptly. "I can make it over—no problem." I nod toward my skirt. "I'm just . . . not dressed for fence climbing."

He moves toward the fence, closer to me. "Oh," he says, smiling.

He takes his left hand and covers his eyes.

I scan the fence, smirking. Even though my gut is telling me that climbing a chain-link fence in a skirt and sneaking into an abandoned building with a guy I don't know that well is not the greatest decision I've ever made, I cast my reservations aside.

After adjusting the tightness on my O2 shield, I walk over to the fence and place the toe of my shoe in a hole in the wiring. My hands latch on as high as I can reach, and I pull my body up, flexing every muscle, including ones I didn't know I had.

"Good, now just lift your other leg and push up," Josh instructs.

"I thought you weren't looking!" I say, repeating my actions as I continue. It's definitely not as easy as he made it seem a moment ago. I feel my face heating up, and my fingers are already sore from gripping the cold metal wire.

"Okay, all you have to do is throw one leg over and you've got it," he says. The frosty wind prickles my legs, but I no longer care about modesty. I just want to make it to the other side.

I slip a bit, but then I manage to scale the rest of the fence, and I jump to the ground with an unsteady thud. I trip over my own feet and wobble into Josh, who catches me before I can fall. His hands grasp me firmly at the waist; the acrylic shield covering my nose and mouth is pressed against his neck. I can't help but remember how he smelled at Patrick's party—cedar with a hint of soap.

"You good?" he asks, concerned.

"Fine," I say, looking up at him.

Josh lets me go and takes a couple of steps back. "Nice job."

"Thanks."

He gestures to a door with a few slabs of wood nailed to the outside of the frame. "This way."

I follow him as he ducks underneath the planks, dodging jagged edges that threaten to rip through my jacket. Josh points to some clover-colored glass splattered across the floor and guides me around it. Then he leads me toward a stairwell marked EXIT.

"It's up a couple of floors," Josh explains.

"What is?"

Josh doesn't reply—he just starts climbing. We stop on the third landing, and I trail behind him as he pads down a long, empty hall that has strands of electric cords dangling from the ceiling. At the end, he pushes his weight against a large metal door that squeals like a trapped mouse when its hinges move, and holds it open for me.

"Proof," Josh finally answers.

The air seems clear in here, so I pull off my O2 shield and hook it to my skirt with a quick snap of a metal belt loop. Josh does the same. I look around the room, confused by the scene before me. There are tools scattered across the tops of makeshift worktables, and heaps of computer hardware fragments are practically everywhere. There are also several old, dirty mattresses, piles of MealFreeze containers, IV bags, and pill bottles littering the floor.

"Proof of what exactly?" I ask.

"That we're being lied to about Elusion."

I walk over to one of the worktables and pick up a plastic fragment that is sitting next to a broken compact drill. I hold it up to the faint light that's streaming through one of the smudged windows and study it closely. It's definitely a part of the Equip wristband—I can still see a small part of the Orexis company seal.

"Where are we?"

"An E-fiend hideout," he says, and I wince at his use of that Avery-coined term. "People come here and Escape inside Elusion for days."

"Impossible," I say, taking a step away from him. "Equips automatically shut down when your time in Elusion is up."

"What if there was a way to interfere with the communication between the Equip components and the cloud that hosts the app?"

"You mean hijack the wireless signals?"

Josh nods. "Once that happens, someone could instruct the operating system to do whatever they want."

"Like disable the safety settings," I say breathlessly. "But they'd have to know how to get past the Elusion server. Who would know how to do all that?"

"My sister," he murmurs.

It feels like all the air has been sucked out of my lungs. "But . . . aren't you the computer science master?"

"Nora fell in with this group—they're *ultra* tech geeks like

Patrick, much better than me. They spend all their time trying to break the signal down so they can stay inside their Escapes longer and stretch out the trypnosis high," he continues, his voice hard as stone. "Thought they were harmless at first, but when I came back for a visit a few weeks ago, I saw Nora and she looked like hell. Malnourished, bloodshot eyes, shaking hands. I followed her here last night. A bunch of her friends were attached to their Equips, supposedly for over twenty-four hours. Some were strung out and hooked up to IVs, desperate to Escape again as soon as they could. They were like—"

"Addicts?" *Just like Avery said.*

"Yes," Josh agrees.

"So what did you do?"

"I asked her to tell me how they were hijacking the signal, but she wouldn't," he went on. "Nora did say they had hit some kind of wall in the Escapes and they wanted to get behind it. To see what was there and how it would feel."

I know exactly what wall he's talking about, and that all it does is block hackers and act as a boundary within the Escape network. But instead of interrupting, I just listen to him closely, hoping the anxiety building inside me will stop.

"We got into this huge fight; then her friends ganged up on me and kicked me out."

"Is she okay?"

"No idea." He bows his head and rubs at the base of his neck. "I stayed outside for a couple hours, waiting for her to leave. When she didn't, I went back in and everyone was gone.

Must have slipped out the back door. Haven't seen or heard from her since. I knew I couldn't return to school . . ."

"Until you find her?" I ask.

He nods. "The only thing she left behind was this."

Josh hands me a piece of scrap paper with a strange phrase written on it at least fifty times.

HATE OUR NEW LAND

Scrawled over and over, as if done by a crazy person.

"How do you know this was Nora's?" I ask, concerned.

"It's her handwriting."

"What does it mean?" I ask him.

"I don't know." Josh takes a few steps away from me and sits down on the closest mattress. He covers his face with his hands for a second and then begins to rub his temples. "At first I thought it might be some kind of message, but maybe I'm just losing it. "

I walk over to Josh and take a seat next to him, handing him the paper. Once he takes it, he wraps his fingers gently around my wrist. I understand how he's feeling—the shock, the confusion, everything—because I've felt it too. I want to tell Josh about my insane experience with Elusion and my father and the firewall, but I keep hearing Patrick's voice, ringing in my ears, and I hesitate.

You have to promise me.

I try to focus my thoughts by glancing at the floor, and I notice that one of the IV bags is inches away from my foot. I trap it with the bottom of my shoe and drag it within reach.

I slowly let go of Josh's hand and pick it up, flipping it over to read the small type on the back.

TPN—Total Parenteral Nutrition.

The formula lists nutrients like glucose, amino acids, lipids, and dietary vitamins and minerals.

"They're using this to keep themselves hydrated and fed," I say.

You have to promise me.

What were the emotions behind my best friend's words? Fear? Guilt? Shame?

My eyes dart around the room and connect with a blue prescription bottle that's lying near the head of the mattress right next to us. I stretch backward and try to snatch it quickly, not caring that I can feel my skirt riding up my legs. When I have it in my grasp, I lean back up and read the label, but some of the information has worn off. All I can see is that the drug type begins with *Zo*, and the last name of the patient ends with an *L*.

"What do you think that's for?" Josh asks.

"I don't know," I say, squinting hard so I can make out the faint traces of lettering. Unfortunately, it doesn't work.

"Maybe it relieves pain or something."

"My mom's a nurse-practitioner; I could ask her," I offer.

Then again, that could lead to all sorts of questions—questions I'm not sure I can answer, or should.

Josh grins a little. "Thanks."

We sit there silently for a moment, both of us registering these pieces of evidence. When tallied together, they seem to point to one conclusion: Elusion has been compromised, and we have to do something about it.

Before anyone else disappears. Or worse.

"Maybe we should call Patrick," I say, half listening to an instinct that I never doubted until now.

"He knows." Josh stands abruptly and crosses his arms over his chest. "Talked to him this morning, told him everything I saw."

"What did he say?"

"He said I misinterpreted what was going on," Josh says, rolling his eyes. "Then I asked him to meet me here after school. Guess he doesn't plan on showing up."

Don't tell anyone what happened . . . You have to promise me.

"That's why I came to you. I was hoping you could help convince Patrick to take me seriously," Josh adds, his voice cracking a little.

I'm simultaneously touched and terrified by what he just said.

He wants *me* to help him. My thoughts return to Patrick, the most helpful, concerned person I've ever known. How could he completely blow Josh off like this, especially when he knows firsthand that strange things are happening with Elusion? And while he and Josh haven't really been friends over the past few years, the Patrick I know would go out of his way to be there for someone in need, even a stranger.

What has gotten into him?

"There's also your dad. He taught you everything about

Elusion, right?" Josh asks, almost willing that question into a yes. "I'm hoping you know something . . . *anything* that can give me a jump on Nora's friends."

I immediately cast my eyes away, because I can't bring myself to tell him the truth—that while I understand the general mechanics behind Elusion, Patrick was Dad's protégé.

A crashing sound suddenly echoes throughout the room, startling us both. We look to see what caused it and notice that a strong gust of wind has knocked a big shard of glass out of a nearby window frame. That's when the black spray-paint numbers on the wall beneath it nearly stop my heart.

5020.

I gasp so loudly that Josh backs away from me, uncertain of what to do. I leap up from the mattress and run over to the wall, pressing my hands over the number just to make sure that it's real. The dingy, crackling concrete under my fingernails confirms this isn't make-believe or imagined.

Whatever is happening with Josh's sister and her so-called friends is somehow connected to the vision of my father.

When Josh falls in on my right, Patrick's voice is no longer ringing in my ears. Now I hear my dad calling out.

You need to find me.

I take a deep breath, letting it out slowly before speaking again. "I saw my father in Elusion last night. He was in the Thai Beach Escape, and he talked to me."

Josh is silent for a moment, his cheeks flushing a deep shade of pink. Then he exhales and says, "Tell me everything."

As the wind outside continues to howl, I tell him over the rattling windows about my dad, the crumbling Escape, and the number 5020 carved in the sand. When I'm done, the room is as black as the oil clouds outside.

"This can't be just a coincidence," I say to Josh. "There has to be a link between what happened to me in Elusion and what's going on with Nora."

"So what do we do now?" he asks me, but when I feel him take my hand again, it's like he already knows what my answer will be.

"We find out the truth on our own."

Inside my father's study, everything is exactly as it was the morning we found out he died. His worn brown leather slippers are near the foot of his favorite nest chair. The laminate coating on his desk has a thin film of dust over it. The central air is still set at what my dad thought was the perfect temperature—sixty-eight degrees. But what stands out the most are the walls, which are covered with antique paintings and drawings in square gilded frames. Gorgeous landscape scenes filled with serene baby blue skies, rolling green hills, and picturesque lighthouses perched on towering stacks of rocks.

"When's the last time you were in here?"

I feel Josh's eyes on me, but I don't turn around when I answer him. I guess I'm a little afraid that my composure might crack if I see his face.

"Six months ago, I think." I walk over to my dad's chair

and graze my fingers along one of the armrests. "I woke up at three o'clock in the morning and wandered downstairs to the kitchen for a glass of water. On my way upstairs, I saw a light peeking out through a slit at the bottom of the study door."

I risk a glance at Josh, and I see his lips are turned up in a sweet yet concerned smile, like he regrets asking me this question.

"Dad and I didn't see each other much back then. He was always at the Orexis lab, working on Elusion, and when he was home, he was too tired for anything but small talk." I sit down in my father's chair. "I knew I shouldn't disturb him. He treated this room like a private library. But I came in anyway and"—I cover my mouth after letting out a laugh—"he was just sitting here, doing these stupid word puzzles on his tab."

Josh chuckles. "Sounds like top secret work to me."

"We wound up solving a ton of them together. We didn't even notice the sunrise through the window."

Suddenly my eyes fill up with tears, and I quickly swivel around so that my back is to Josh.

"What do you think we'll find in here?" Josh asks after a brief pause. I know he realizes I'm upset, and I appreciate him not forcing the subject.

I glance at the closet at the far left of the room. Behind its closed door, on the top shelf, there is a silver box with the Orexis logo emblazoned on the side. In it are Dad's personal items, which Patrick brought over to the house a week after my father's accident. My mother hid the box away because she couldn't bring herself to go through it.

But I have to. I don't have a choice. Something is wrong with Elusion, and this box is the only remaining unexamined piece of the life my dad left behind.

"I'm not sure," I murmur. "But hopefully there's something that will give us answers."

I get up from the chair and walk toward the closet, which opens the moment I step in front of the motion sensors. I stand up on my tiptoes and stretch, grabbing the box.

"Do you need help with that?" Josh asks, reaching up to assist me.

But when I pull it down, I'm surprised by its lightness.

"No, I'm okay. This thing is, like, less than a pound."

Josh takes the box out of my hands, holding it at different angles and inspecting it carefully. "Yeah, this looks like metal, but it's probably made of something like carbon-fiber polymer. Where do you want me to put this?"

I point to my dad's desk and Josh sets the box down. My heart in my throat, I take a laser pen out of his top desk drawer and shave through the thick strip of quick-seal across the top of the box. I breathe in deep and open it up. Inside there are only a handful of items, and one of them I've already seen before.

Tucked underneath a mug with my picture printed on it is a paperback edition of *Walden*.

At first glance, it looks like the exact same copy Patrick and I found in the lockbox, but as soon as I open it, I notice a difference. On the upper left inside corner of the cover, my father has written in neat black script:

Please return to Regan Welch.

"I love that book," I hear Josh say, and then I notice the warmth of his breath on the back of my neck. He must be reading over my shoulder.

"My dad left a copy of this book in a lockbox. My mom and I found it after he died."

I turn my attention back to the book, planning to skim through paragraph after paragraph in search of markings or notes. "There was nothing else in there. Just this." As I start to flip through the beginning, Josh says, "Wait," and puts one of his hands on mine, sending a charge of crackling energy straight to my heart.

"There's something on the copyright page," he adds.

He's right. The title of the book, *Walden*, is highlighted in a bold yellow strike, along with the last word in the author's name, *Thoreau*.

"Why'd your dad highlight the title and the author?"

I shrug. "Beats me. Let's flip through the rest of it and see if there's more."

I bend the spine of the book a bit so I can flip through the pages quickly and easily. There aren't any other highlighted portions, but when I reach chapter 3, something falls out and lands on the floor. Josh squats down to pick the object up, his sweater creeping up a bit so I catch a flash of his fair skin above his belt. When he stands up, he hands me a passcard with my father's ID number stamped on the lower right-hand corner.

"What is my dad's passcard doing in here?"

"I don't know. You think he would've had it on him when he—" Josh cuts himself off, realizing that he's about to tread on hallowed ground. "Want me to empty the box?"

I manage a nod as I think back to the day Mom and I listened to the audio files from the HyperSoar Flight Commission, which investigated my dad's accident. There was a sudden change in weather conditions. A wind sear formed in the stratosphere just as my dad was reentering from the mesosphere, causing an explosion in one of the HS-12's engines, leading to IMD—instant matter disintegration.

Nothing was left. Not one trace.

But Josh is on to something—no one in Detroit goes anywhere without their passcard. People use them to start their cars, for Christ's sake. Why would he have left it at Orexis? And how did he even get to the HyperSoar hangar without it?

"Do you think anyone from Orexis knows his passcard was in here?" I ask.

"Probably not. Someone would have had to flip through the book to find it," Josh replies.

"Do you think it's the real thing? What if it's a duplicate?"

"No way. It's illegal to have a duplicate passcard. If he misplaced it and then found it again, he'd have to turn it in."

He's right. The penalty for possessing a duplicate passcard is jail. Why would my dad risk that?

"Maybe he forgot it was in there," Josh volunteers.

"It's odd though, isn't it? That he left the passcard in a copy of *Walden*—the same book that was in the lockbox?"

Josh nods, his eyes intense as ever. Thinking.

I put the passcard in my back pocket and place the book on the table, where Josh has lined up four digital photocubes. I pick up one and shake it as hundreds of pictures of me flash before my eyes. Dressed up as an old-fashioned rag doll for Halloween, Mom's hand in mine. Smiling over a bowl of ice cream when I was five. Me and Dad watching a movie on the day he activated our first InstaComm. I hold it close to my chest and look at the other items that Josh unpacked—a small collection of ties my father kept in the office in case he was called into a meeting, a fine-toothed comb, and several multi-colored earbuds.

I look over at Josh to ask him if this is everything, and that's when I see him staring at something too.

A blue pill bottle that bears a strong resemblance to the one we found at the abandoned factory earlier.

"What is it, Josh?"

"Zolpidem," he says, pointing at the white label. "Do you think this is what Nora and her friends are taking? Starts with the same letters."

"I think Zolpidem is a sleeping pill," I say, remembering all the talks my mom gave me about abusing prescription drugs when my always-in-trouble cousin got hooked a few years ago. "Let me see it."

When I put down the photocube, he gives me the bottle,

his brows knitting together in confusion. "That can't be right. Why would they want something to make them sleep?"

"Maybe you could do a search for Zolpidem on your tab?" I suggest. "Double-check what it's used for?"

"Sure." Josh reaches into his pocket and pulls out the device. He types "Zolpidem" into the search engine on his touch screen, and a ton of links scroll in front of us. He clicks on the FDA site and reads the description of the medication. "It says here that . . . 'the principal function of Zolpidem is to aid sleep, but in very high doses the drug in powder form has been known to wake people up out of a coma-like state.'"

"Aftershock," I mumble. "If someone is inside Elusion for days, then . . ."

"The side effects are probably much stronger," Josh concludes, sighing deeply. "So the meds must counteract it somehow."

I look at the label again, but this time I read everything on it. When I do, my legs almost buckle beneath me.

Patient: David Welch
Contents: Granulated Zolpidem 30mg
Instructions: Take as directed.
Authorized by: Meredith Welch, APRN

"Are you okay?" Josh asks.

I'm not okay. Not even close.

"Why would my dad have granulated Zolpidem at his office?"

"I don't know," he says.

My eyes remain fixed on the label, even though my thoughts are going wild. "Do you think he needed it for the same reason as your sister and her friends? Do you think he might have become addicted to Elusion?"

Josh is silent for a minute. "Do you?"

Do I? I think about all the nights my dad worked late. In fact, toward the end of his life, I barely saw him. But in the moments we were together, I can't say that I saw any of the signs or symptoms that Josh said Nora had. He was still the caring father he'd always been.

Still, there's this pestering voice in the back of my head, asking me if it was possible that my dad was also one of Avery's original E-fiends?

I don't want to believe it. I *can't* believe it. But why else would he have that prescription? Who takes granulated Zolpidem? Why would my mom have prescribed him something like that?

"If my dad was addicted, do you think my mom knew? Do you think that's why she wrote him the prescription?"

He shakes his head. "I don't know your mom, but trust me, it's pretty scary seeing someone you love become addicted to anything. I can't imagine any wife enabling her husband like that."

"You're right," I say, letting out a deep breath. "If my mom had any inkling that my father might have developed some kind of weird dependency on Elusion, there was no way in hell she would've written him that prescription. And if she thought Elusion was dangerous, she never would have allowed anyone to go near it, even if it was my dad's creation."

Suddenly, a perturbed voice speaks up from behind us.

"What are you doing in here?"

I quickly shove the pill bottle into a side pocket of my skirt as I spin around. My mom is in the doorway, dressed in her scrubs and looking at us with shades of anger coloring her eyes. Since she never comes into my father's study or goes through his things, the fact that I'm doing both has got to be sacrilegious in her mind.

"I'm sorry, Mom, I thought you left for wor—"

"I forgot my dinner in the fridge, so I turned around," she snips, not even letting me get a full sentence out. "And who is he?"

I'm about to explain, when Josh pipes up and responds for me.

"Josh Heywood, ma'am." He approaches my mother with a kind, outstretched hand, and when they shake, I think I see her face soften a little. "I know Regan from school."

My mom gives him a semipolite nod and says, "Josh, could you give us a moment alone, please?"

"Sure," he replies, glancing over at me so he and I can share a sympathetic look.

Once he leaves, my mom charges over to the desk and begins putting everything back into the silver box, her lips pursed.

"Why, Regan? Why would you do this?" Her voice doesn't

have an edge to it anymore. It's just filled with disappointment.

"Do what?"

"Rifle through your father's belongings. You know how much he hates that."

A cold chill prickles at my skin when she refers to him in the present tense. She does that a lot, and I know it's because deep down she can't accept that my father's gone. She keeps his things in order at the house for the exact same reason—she desperately wants to believe that he's coming back to us. Which is why I can't seem to tell her what brought me here, or confront her about what I've found. Emotionally, she's still pretty weak.

But when I think about the passcard and the powdered Zolpidem, I wonder if there's a real chance for my mother to hold on to hope.

My dad's body was never found.

And I saw him in Elusion.

What if . . . what if my father is still alive? What if he was secretly addicted to Elusion and faked his own death because he'd rather spend his life inside the Escapes?

It hurts so much to even think he might have betrayed us like that, but I have to find a way to rule this crazy theory out—without my mother knowing.

"It won't happen again," I say, backing up toward the door.

Just as I'm about to leave, I hear her call out for me.

"Regan?"

When I turn around, she walks toward me, holding the

copy of *Walden* that Josh and I just discovered in my dad's things.

"Looks like he saved one for you, too," she says, offering it to me like a gift.

After I take it and say thanks, she pulls me into an embrace. But this time, hanging on to her doesn't make me feel stronger.

So I'm the first one to let go.

NINE

"HOME SWEET HOME," JOSH SAYS SAR-
castically, holding his helmet under his arm as he pushes open
the front door to his house.

Josh's uncle lives in a triple-wide FEMA trailer with pewter-
color siding, right in the middle of at least five hundred others
just like it. They are lined up in rows, like a huge box of mud-
covered bullets. Above them is a tangled network of satellite
dishes and power grids, a metallic weave of black electrodes
stacking into the sky. The Quartz Sector wasn't much before
but the region was practically leveled by the string of tornadoes
that struck it three years ago, and reconstruction has been slow,
probably because most of its citizens are blue-collar workers or
people on government assistance and they lacked the political
connections that were necessary to get things done.

Josh takes my helmet, setting it down alongside his on a bare laminate booth tucked into a tiny corner of the room. I run my fingers through a few knotted strands of hair and look around. It's a typical trailer layout, with a living-and-dining room suite that could practically fit inside my bedroom. A worn brown fake-leather couch is under a soot-streaked window with two mismatched nesting chairs facing it, so close they're almost touching.

I can't imagine what it must be like to live like this, displaced in what used to be a real neighborhood. Then again, I can't quite imagine going back home to the Historic Sector either, especially since my world seems to be slowly unraveling.

"Flynn won't be back for a while; he's pulling doubles at Lymestone," Josh says.

"Lymestone. That's one of the refineries, right?"

Josh nods and then hesitates, looking away. "You sure you're okay . . . hanging out here, I mean? You know, Flynn took me in because he had to, so . . . it's not exactly cozy. . . ."

"I'm fine," I assure him, trying to ease his discomfort a little. If I had to interpret the sudden halting of his speech, I'd guess there are more family secrets in Josh's past than just Nora. I find that oddly comforting.

There's an awkward beat of silence as he leans up against the front door, his hands in his pockets.

"So how long have you been staying here?" I ask.

"Just a couple weeks. My parents sold their house, and Nora and I needed a place to crash."

Josh rubs the back of his head with his hand—a gesture he performs whenever he seems a little uncomfortable. Maybe I'll see less and less of it the more we get to know each other.

"Sounds like pretty close quarters."

"You have no idea," he replies, his shoulders rolling back a little. "Nora was living by herself in our old place while it was on the market. She only moved her stuff here when it sold, but she was hardly ever around. Preferred to stay with friends and all." Josh pushes himself away from the door and turns toward the window. "When my parents split up—well, Nora took it harder than my other two sisters."

"Wow, three sisters, huh?"

A smirk catches on his lips. "Yeah, and I'm the youngest, too."

I almost tell Josh how jealous I am. The closest thing I've ever had to a brother is Patrick. Being here with Josh and listening to him talk about his family—it just gets me thinking about how important blood ties are. Even when relationships become fractured, or someone dies, the connections you have to your family are never lost.

When it came to Patrick, I always believed our friendship somehow mirrored that, but now I don't know what to think.

Out of the corner of my eye, I notice there's a photocube sitting on a side table, and just as I reach for it, I feel Josh's steady gaze on me.

I glance in his direction and hold it up. "Do you mind?"

I hope he doesn't think I'm being nosy, even though I am.

Josh answers with a noncommittal shrug, so I give it a shake. Oddly enough, there's only one digital photo flickering inside. It's a family photo, but it seems to be a couple of years old—Josh's clothes hang off his body a bit and he's a few inches shorter, his smiling face framed by a mop of copper-brown hair. He is standing outside a historic-looking brick colonial, with two of his three sisters posed next to an attractive woman with short golden hair and Josh's distinct amber eyes. Josh and another sister—more petite and wiry than the others—are positioned on the other side of a burly man with bushy russet hair and a thick handlebar mustache.

"That was two years ago, the summer before my sophomore year." Suddenly Josh is standing right next to me, his arm slightly brushing up against mine. "Nora was a senior," he says, pointing to the girl next to him. "It was the day Sally and Paige were going back to college."

I bring the photocube closer to my face so I can get a better look at Nora. Her lips are pulled into a tight smile, and her pixie cut really shows off her strong cheekbones. It's weird—I have this odd feeling like I've seen her before, but I'm not sure where. Then again, her expression is so warm; maybe I just want to believe that I know her. All my friends have pretty much fallen away since my father died—it's like they think losing a parent is contagious or something—but from the looks of Nora, I'd like to believe that she'd be the one person who'd stick by you through the hard stuff.

Then again, maybe I'm just projecting what I'm starting to feel about Josh.

"So where are Sally and Paige now?"

"Sally's in Australia. She's married and has a kid. Paige is in California, teaching."

"And your parents?"

Josh sits down on the couch, stretching his legs out. "Mom is spending time with Paige. And my dad just got a job in Alaska."

"Do any of them know about Nora?"

"No, I don't want them to worry. Not yet, anyway." He sighs. "This isn't the first time she's gone MIA. Unfortunately, they're kind of used to it."

"But you're not?"

"She's my sister," he says. "I'm always going to care what happens to her. No matter how stupid and irresponsible she acts."

That's another thing about family—I don't know what it is that compels us to give them more second chances than we give our friends, but maybe it's not something we're supposed to understand.

Just as I finish that thought in my head, I sit down next to Josh, leaving only a small space between us. Then I feel my father's passcard digging into my rear end from my back pocket.

His passcard. I lean forward and pull it out, setting it on the table in front of us. Once again, my mind is flooded with all the questions that overwhelmed me back at my house—and the crazy theory that my father might have been addicted to

Elusion and faked his death so he could disappear without a trace. While a part of me really wants to dismiss everything, the other part wants the crazy theory to be true, just to create the possibility that my dad isn't dead. Either way, Josh might be the only one who can help me make any sense of it.

"Can I get you anything to drink?" he asks, placing a warm hand on my shoulder.

Instead of answering his question, I pick up the passcard and stare it. Then all of a sudden, I glance at him and blurt out:

"What if my father is still alive?"

Josh's eyebrows creep up into two steep arches. "Are you serious?"

"I know it's a leap," I say. "But finding this passcard has made me really suspicious."

"Yeah, it's weird that we found it, but I don't see how it means your father is still alive."

"What if my dad wasn't in that plane when it disintegrated? What if it was controlled remotely? Right before he bought a HyperSoar, my dad told me that's how the CIT tested them, so I know it's possible."

Josh takes the passcard out of my hands and examines it. "So what are you trying to say? That your dad staged the crash?"

"Maybe," I say, my voice faint.

"Well, what about the FAA? If they notified your family of your dad's death, I'm guessing they had substantial proof, passcard or not," Josh says. "And even if he was addicted, do you really think your dad would do something that awful? Lie to the people he loves? And if he knew Elusion was addictive, would he allow it to be mass-produced?"

"No," I admit. The father I knew wasn't capable of that kind of recklessness. But if he really did die on that plane, how could he have left his passcard behind? Why would my dad go *anywhere* without it? Why would he keep a bottle of granulated Zolpidem at his office? And why was he protecting these copies of *Walden*?

I stand up and cross my arms in front of my chest, facing the smudged window. "I just have this strange feeling that he's still alive," I say. "That he somehow found me in my Escape to warn me."

I know how insane this sounds. Besides the passcard, the only proof I have that my dad might still be alive are these strange fragments of my father's life, and a vision of him in a make-believe world. Even so, when you put them all together, they seem like pieces of evidence—of what exactly, I'm still not sure.

"Can we use my father's passcard to find out the last place he used it?" I ask hopefully. "That could give us a strong lead."

"The only people with that kind of technology are the police," he says. "But think about how much crime there is in Detroit. How long would it take for the cops to start investigating a case they've already closed?"

"I guess," I say. "Honestly, I don't think I could bring myself to hand it over to someone else anyway. It would feel like, I don't know . . . giving up."

Josh rises and joins me near the window, handing me the passcard. "I know what it's like. When you lose someone, it's hard to let them go. You come up with a thousand excuses that will explain why they were taken from you—reasons that will make all the pain go away."

My hands begin to tremble, a crack in my seemingly calm exterior, as I admit to myself that there's some kind of rational explanation behind my dad's passcard and the drugs. But I'm not ready to accept that reality is entirely black-and-white like Josh is suggesting.

Especially since it seems Patrick wants to keep us from thinking anything is really wrong with Elusion.

"What about the number fifty-twenty?" I ask. "Don't you think it has something to do with both my vision of my dad, and your sister and her friends?"

"It could," Josh says, a wary smile forming on his lips. "I think it's pretty clear Patrick is somehow tied into all of this, too."

"Have you heard from him yet?" I ask.

I hope to God the answer is yes. Maybe Patrick messaged Josh and gave him a good reason why he didn't show up at the factory. I need to believe that I'm totally misjudging him, even if it's only for a moment. But Josh shakes his head no.

"When he was at my house, he said the problems I experienced with Elusion, and the number fifty-twenty, could be related to a downloading issue with the upgraded app, but—"

"Okay, that's a lie," Josh says, cutting me off. "If there was any kind of downloading error with the new app, you wouldn't have been able to open the program and get to Elusion in the first place."

"Are you sure?"

Josh cocks his head to the side and grimaces.

"Sorry. I forgot about the computer mastery thing."

"Listen, I know Patrick's your friend. He used to be mine, too. But if there's something wrong with Elusion, who knows how many people might get caught in the crossfire?"

"Then we need to find out what fifty-twenty means," I say. "It's the only clue we have that links our stories together."

He paces back and forth, his strides small and clipped because of how tiny the room is. "What if fifty-twenty is part of some numeric source code?"

"I don't know. Programming code is really intricate stuff. Especially the kind Patrick and my dad were doing for Elusion."

"It's still worth looking into," he says. "Did your dad leave his tab behind?"

"No, but it wouldn't matter. He kept all his files on his work computer, for security reasons. That's why he spent so much time at Orexis; everything he needed was in his lab or at his office." I clap my hands together once all my synapses start firing in unison. "*The office*. Patrick moved into my dad's office, which means—"

"He's using your father's computer." Josh finishes my sentence, his eyes brightening. "A three-panel quantum with touch recognition. Am I right?"

I recoil from him a little bit, mostly because I'm freaked out by how precise his guess was. "How'd you know that?"

"Patrick likes to brag. Told me all about it at the party," he explains. "Five feet long with a multitouch surface desk and four-foot screens. Not bad."

"Yeah, it's pretty sophisticated." I tuck my hair behind my ears and try to corral the ideas stampeding through my mind. "Do you think we could hack into it? Get the data that way?"

"No, the security on their servers is really tough to break through," he says after a pause. "And I bet they have other secure servers contracted, just to be used in an emergency, in case the main server at Orexis goes down for any reason."

Even though I'm a little discouraged by Josh's response, I press on, determined to find a way into the dark recesses of my dad's computer banks.

"Okay, what if the computer was broken into by hand?" I suggest. "The files could be sent to a remote cloud where we could access them and—"

"Hold on—all of those files are going to be encrypted and too large to send," he interjects. "And there's the touch recognition, too. The only way around that is to use a QuTap."

My heart sinks as a sigh of frustration escapes my lips. Magnetic-surge devices like QuTaps were taken off the market almost two years ago. I remember it being all over the Net. QuTaps are the only thing capable of disabling elaborate computer security systems.

"So it's impossible, then," I say, hating the defeated tone of my voice.

"I didn't say that," Josh replies.

I look at him, surprised. "Are you saying you can get one?"

"The one perk of being an academy boy is the military contacts," he says with a shy grin.

"How long would it take?" I know I sound impatient, but that's because we have no time to waste.

Josh reaches into his pocket and pulls out his tab, gazing at me as if he's standing by for an order. "I think I could track one down in a few hours."

This is our chance to get concrete facts—facts that will shine a light on this confounding mystery I've stumbled on to.

Without even thinking about the consequences, I say, "Do it."

Josh blinks a few times, apparently a little concerned about my quick decision. "Okay, but how are we going get into Orexis? Without anyone knowing what we're up to?"

"Maybe this will help." I hold up my father's passcard. "If this can get me past lobby security, I think I could talk my way into Patrick's office."

"Not a bad idea," he says.

"And if we hold on to the passcard and don't tell *anyone* what we have, who knows where else it could come in handy?"

"Okay, your secret is safe with me," Josh replies, but then

a streak of worry flashes across his face. "You sure you want to do this? If we get caught—"

"Then at least we'll get caught together," I say.

The next morning, I stand shoulder to shoulder with at least a hundred Orexis employees hurrying to get to their desks for the start of the Standard 7 shift.

It's a madhouse—exactly as I'd hoped.

Dressed in a long raincoat to hide my school uniform, I clutch my father's passcard in one hand and a bag of cinnamon buns in the other. I push my way through the crowd outside the elevator bank located in the lobby of the former Renaissance Center Hotel, where Patrick works. Although it's not as tall as the rest of the buildings in the complex, it is one of the oldest commercial structures in Detroit. It serves as the office building for only the top-level executives at Orexis and the lobby has all the ornate, old-school decorative touches of the era it was built: vaulted ceilings, marble floors, and potted palm trees. I kind of like the fact that it hasn't been modernized in any way.

I train my eyes on the closest of the three security gates, each of them manned by a Taser-wielding guard. Thankfully, none of them looks familiar to me; however, all of them appear as if they're trained to attack at the slightest provocation. Except the skinny red-haired one on the left, who is distracted and checking his tab.

Looks like I'll be entering through his lane.

When I slowly reach the entrance to the gate, I pray that the State Department hasn't deactivated my dad's passcard. Although we had a memorial service for my father, he hasn't been declared legally dead yet. There was no HyperSoar wreckage or actual physical evidence that proved he died, nor was there a mayday call or any radio correspondence with him before he was lost on radar. Josh and I did some research and found out that if there's only a presumption of death, the government can't disable someone's account until a year has passed.

So I should be safe.

My eyes rest on the yellow blinking light on the turnstile as I swipe the passcard, practically holding my breath. Suddenly, there's a shrill beeping noise and I almost lose my grip on the bag of cinnamon buns. Lucky for me, the sound is coming from the middle gate—a woman with an outstanding-ticket tag on her card. In my lane, a green light flashes and the waist-high plastic doors slide open. I exhale a sigh of relief.

Get through the crowd at the executive elevator.

The first leg of the mission accomplished. Had I gone through the regular elevators, the guards might have recognized me, and I would have had to check in. Then they would've called upstairs for visitor approval. I couldn't risk that. The staff might have made me wait downstairs until Patrick was out of his early-morning investors briefing.

I step into the elevator and swipe my card before pressing the button for the seventy-third floor. The green light flashes again.

Approved.

As the doors close, I move toward the back of the elevator, mentally repeating the master plan Josh and I cobbled together.

Get inside Patrick's office.

Text Josh on my tab and have him coach me through using the QuTap.

Find any and all codes containing 5020.

"Smells good," a woman says with a friendly wink as the elevator rockets upwards. She's dressed in a conservative black suit, with an Orexis pin attached to the lapel of her jacket. "Surprise birthday?" she asks.

"More like an olive branch."

Or a decoy, if I want to get technical.

When the elevator stops and she pushes her way to the front, she cheerfully says, "I'd forgive you, honey!"

The doors close and I step farther into the back. I'm still worried that I will recognize someone—or worse, that someone will recognize me. But as the scene in the lobby proved, faces and names are almost indistinguishable during rush hour.

Sixty-eight, sixty-nine . . .

I can do this. I *have* to do this.

Seventy-three.

The door opens on a hallway flooded with brightness. It takes me a moment to realize that it's actual sunlight. The air meter at the Inner Sector station was at negative one this morning, meaning that wind currents are minimal and air quality is good enough that O2 shields aren't required. On "nice" days like this, I guess there's no need to run Elusion ads on the glass windows, so they're crystal clear, exposing a scenic view of the thick, black water of the Detroit River and, beyond it, the towering high-rises on the shore of Windsor, Canada.

As I wander into the waiting area, I'm met with an enthusiastic squeal. It's coming from Estelle, a receptionist who has worked on this floor for as long as I can remember.

"Regan! What a surprise!" She jumps up from her swivel stool to greet me and brings me in for a big hug, her lilac-scented perfume almost overpowering me. The other receptionist, a young man with a crew cut, keeps his eyes on the InstaComm wall as he barks commands at someone in the office-services department.

"How are you, dear? And how in the world did you get up here? No one called!" Estelle says.

"Oh, I have a VIP passcard," I say with a shrug.

Not a complete lie, but still, my tongue burns a little when the half-truth slips off it.

"Courtesy of Mr. Simmons, I presume?" she says, with a knowing smile.

My dad's entire staff, most of whom now report to Patrick, have long suspected a romance between me and my best friend—which is something I must take advantage of if I want to get into his office alone.

"He's been really stressed lately, so I brought him breakfast," I say, holding up the insulated bag from the Inner Sector's best bakery. "I was hoping to surprise him."

My palms are starting to sweat, and for a second I wonder if I'm really capable of doing this. It's one thing to think about breaking into an Orexis quantum computer, and another to actually go through with it. I remind myself to act casual. Not that Estelle would ever suspect me of being a corporate spy.

"You're in luck," she says with a smile. "His briefing was canceled this morning."

My heart plummets. *Canceled?*

Estelle pauses and then sniffs the air. "Did you bring him cinnamon buns? From Mo's?"

I force a grin and nod, opening the bag, my whole plan unraveling. "Want one?"

"No, save them for Patrick. He's going to love them!" She peers at the screen on her digital data planner wristband and scrolls through the information, shaking her head in dismay when she's through. "Good Lord, he got roped into a conference call instead. But that shouldn't take too long; I could even buzz him in there and let him know you're—"

"That's okay, I can wait," I blurt with excitement. "Would it be all right if I hung out in his office?"

When Estelle's lips twitch, I fear she's going to tell me to take a seat in the lounge area. Instead she leans in a little and whispers, gesturing in the other assistant's direction. "Just don't let Andrew see you. He's so anal when it comes to rules."

I smirk as she pulls out her passcard and waves it in front of a lockpad near a set of glass doors. "I have been rooting for you two since you were kids. You are the perfect couple!"

"Thanks," I say, without looking her in the eyes.

There's less guilt that way.

Estelle glances at Andrew to see if he's paying attention, and then she turns back to me, mouthing the words "Go ahead."

I walk down a long, narrow hallway, clenching the bag in my hand, and forge ahead until I reach the corner office—the one Patrick moved into after my dad died. As soon as the motion sensors pick me up, the door opens. I haven't stepped foot in this room in months, and I'm stunned by how different it looks. The furniture is very trendy and modular. There's a glass conference table with built-in monitor capabilities, and three InstaComm walls, each of them lit up with holographic screen savers displaying natural landscape scenes.

The floor-to-ceiling window screen in the far corner of the room pictures a wooden cabin set in the middle of a dense forest of evergreens and bare trees, covered in pure, lily-white snow. I recognize it immediately—it's the cabin described in *Walden*. I can't help but think that Patrick must have kept this image as a tribute to my father.

Suddenly I feel like a cold, dead hand is squeezing my heart, and I quickly turn on my heel. It's almost as if my legs have decided to run out of here as fast as they can, regardless of what my mind has to say about it. But I plant my feet firmly on the floor, refusing to give in to these feelings of doubt. As much as I care about Patrick I simply don't think I can trust him to tell me what's going on.

I keep reminding myself of that over and over again, and

thankfully, when I pull the QuTap Josh gave me out of my pocket, I'm able to ignore everything else except for my mission. I place the cinnamon rolls on the conference table and finger the button-size piece of magnetic alloy in my hand. It's hard to believe that something this tiny can do as much as Josh claims, but as I take a seat behind my father's quantum computer, I'm about to put all my faith into it—and the person who managed to get it for me.

I set the QuTap in my lap and pull my tab out of my pocket. I wake it from sleep mode and see that Josh's avatar is blinking available on my contacts list. I tap on the touch screen, typing him a message.

Regan: I'm inside. What now?

I barely have to wait a millisecond for a reply.

Josh: Put on latex gloves, then place QuTap on panel B2.

I do exactly as he instructs, taking the gloves out of my other pocket and slowly pulling them over my hands. I need to be prepared in case the keyboard is wired for fingertip recognition and make sure I don't leave any prints.

Then I pick up the QuTap and look for the panel marked *B2*. It takes me a minute to find the labeling, but once I do, I aim the device at it, the magnetic pull practically yanking it out from between my rubbery fingers. As soon as I hear it latch on to the panel, there's a slight clicking sound. I type on my tab again.

Regan: QuTap is on. Next step?

Josh: Wait for the lights, then tell me when you see icon.

As if the computer can read Josh's texts, all the panels are alive with lines and squares of digitized white light. A virtual key-board appears at the bottom of the screen as images flash across, the fingertip analysis seemingly circumvented. I wait until the icon from the QuTap blinks on screen, a simple and neat red ball.

Regan: Icon is up.

Josh: Type in //reboot// then press //Alt+Command//

As my pulse beats triple time, I follow Josh's advice, gently tapping in the word "reboot" and hitting Alt+Command. The lighting on the panel dims a little, then flickers on and off, creating a strobe effect. I cringe, thinking I've screwed something up. Just as I'm about to tell Josh that, the lights return to normal, and at the top of the screen a message appears.

Reboot successful.

Good morning, Mr. Simmons.

Time: 7:12 a.m.

My fingers furiously dance across the screen of my tab, my left knee bouncing up and down.

Regan: It worked.

A few seconds tick by; then Josh responds.

Josh: Do generalized programming search, using this code //1r3c70rY5020//

I take a cleansing breath and stretch my fingers, biting my lower lip as I begin to type. Once I'm through, I receive a message from the computer.

I'm sorry, Mr. Simmons. We are unable to locate your information at this time.

Nothing. But then again, we didn't expect this to be easy.

Regan: No luck.

Josh: Try advanced search //4DV4NC3D 534RC|-|5020//

Again, I attempt to seek the information Josh and I desperately need, but the advanced search leads us right back to the same message.

I'm sorry, Mr. Simmons. We are unable to locate your information at this time.

I hear a noise and freeze in place, but when I realize it's the whoosh of an automatic door opening a few offices down the hall, I type on my tab at lightning speed.

I don't know how much time we have left, but it can't be a lot. Estelle said Patrick's call wouldn't run long.

Regan: That didn't work either. Abort?

Josh: No. This should do it //EyE Am ph33|1n6 |u(ky5020//

I stop to yank off my coat—it feels like a million degrees in here—and then I type in the last command Josh sent me. After I hit Enter, I say a silent prayer to the computer gods that this will turn up something. When a message rejecting my request doesn't appear right away, a surge of hope rips through me, and suddenly rows and rows of file names start piling up on the screen. There's hundreds of them, all containing the number 5020 in the programming code.

I text Josh right away.

Regan: Pay dirt.

Josh: Shit yeah!

My lips twist into a goofy, satisfied smile, but it only lasts for a brief moment.

Patrick's ever-so-charming voice is carrying through the hall. He's making his way toward his office. A shot of sheer panic jolts me out of the chair. I open both my hands, using all my fingers to copy and drag as many files as possible, dumping them into the QuTap icon. My hair falls in front of my eyes and I don't even bother to wipe it away; my heart is rattling against my ribs so loudly I'm half certain Patrick can hear.

"Wait, you're saying it's being outsourced?" he says, from behind the door. "When the hell did this happen?"

"I'm not sure. I just found out myself," says another, much deeper voice.

"Why weren't we notified?"

"Maybe it was some kind of oversight."

A bead of sweat trickles down the side of my face as I exit out of the program and give the screen a quick wipe with my elbow. Then I lunge for the magnet and pluck it off the panel. I have just enough time to stick it in my pocket and step away from the computer before Patrick enters the room.

The only thing I forget to do is take off these damn gloves.

At first Patrick doesn't even notice me, his attention directed toward the middle-aged man with glasses who is following close behind him. He's tall and handsome, wearing an expensive suit like Patrick's, with black hair and a dark ebony complexion. I recognize him immediately. Bryce Williams. He was on my dad's original Elusion design team.

With my hands behind my back, I pull the gloves off finger by finger, hoping that I'll have time to dispose of them before they realize I'm here.

"I want to know exactly when we switched over," Patrick says to him. "Find me whatever documentation you can . . ." He pauses and sniffs the air. "Wait, does it smell like cinnamon buns in here?"

Bryce spots me over Patrick's shoulder and gives him a sharp nudge in the arm—just as I snap off the last glove and curl them into a little ball.

"Regan?" Patrick's voice lilts. Obviously he's surprised to see me.

"Hey," I say, tucking the gloves in the back pocket of my cargo skirt.

"What are you doing here?"

"I brought you breakfast. Estelle let me in." I worry that this might get her in trouble, but it's either her or me, and any other excuse might raise suspicion.

Patrick squints his eyes. He looks absolutely bewildered right now. Can't say that I blame him.

"Don't you have school?" he asks.

I give him an indifferent shrug. "I'll get there eventually."

"How've you been, Regan?" Bryce pipes up, extending a hand in my direction.

"Good, thanks," I say during our polite handshake. "It's nice to see you."

"Bryce, let's catch up later, okay?" Patrick says, patting him on the shoulder.

"Yeah, sure." Bryce walks toward the door, but just before

he exits, he stops and turns around to smile at me. "We really miss your father around here, Regan."

I smile back. "Thanks."

Once the door slides closed behind him, Patrick strolls over toward the conference table, where the goodies I brought him are probably starting to get cold. Oh well. He opens the bag and breaks into a grin when he inhales. "Mo's Bakery?"

A twinge of sentimentality tugs at my heart, and all of a sudden, I feel my eyes glistening. When Patrick and I were in elementary school, my father used to spoil us with treats from Mo's every Friday. After our hands became sticky with frosting or glaze, Patrick would chase me around my house, trying to tickle me. We were so innocent then. Everything between us was easy.

"I thought you could use a pick-me-up," I say, my words sounding a bit garbled. "Besides, I owe you a thank-you for the other night."

"No thanks necessary." Patrick pulls out a black leather bucket chair from the conference table and nods at it. "Can we talk for a second?"

I nervously shift my weight from one leg to the other. If I engage in some kind of deep, emotional conversation with Patrick right now, I might lose my cool, or do something worse, like tell him what's in my back pocket. I've always had a hard time keeping secrets from him.

Which is why I need to get out of here.

"Sorry, Pat. I should probably head to school."

Patrick unbuttons his jacket and places his hands on his hips. "You weren't in such a rush a minute ago."

"I just remembered—I have a chem quiz," I lie.

But when he smirks, I know that he's on to me.

"So you're still mad at me, huh?"

"Mad? Why would I be mad?"

When he flops down into the chair, he seems more like his true eighteen-year-old self than a corporate figurehead. "Because I was kind of a jerk before I left your house."

"No you weren't," I lie again. "I mean, you were just concerned about me, right?"

"Yeah, right," he says, leaning over so his elbows rest on his knees. "That's what I wanted to discuss."

When I detect the disbelief that's coating his voice, I decide to make a bold move. "Have you gotten other complaints about Elusion?"

Given what I know about Josh's call to Patrick yesterday, if he denies that there are more flaws in the system, I'll know he has no problem with lying right to my face.

"There's a good chance the bad download is affecting your other software too. I really want you to get a new tab. You can pick it out and I'll pay for it," he says.

Wow. He's ignoring the question altogether and continuing to use this downloading error excuse, which Josh said wasn't possible. He's lying to me.

I shake my head, my blood pressure rising. "Forget it. I can get one myself."

He sighs. "I'm just trying to help, Ree. Why is that making you so angry?"

The longer I stand here talking to him, the chances of me slipping up and getting caught with the QuTap continue to skyrocket.

So I deny the obvious.

"I'm not angry," I say. "I just have to go."

As I put my hands in my coat pocket and bolt for the door, Patrick springs up from his chair and blocks my path. Now that he's only inches away from me, I can see how red and irritated his eyes are, like he's been up for days. And his cheeks are a bit sunken, too, like he hasn't been eating. My mind jumps to a conclusion—one that paints Patrick as an addict to the invention he so desperately loves. Anything to explain why he's not the trusting person I thought him to be.

"You know I'd do anything for you, right?" he says, running a jittery hand down my arm. "You're the most important person in the world to me, and I'll never let anything bad happen to you, I swear."

I nod and do my best to give him a reassuring smile as I slowly pull away.

Even though I can't help but doubt his every word, this is still something I really want to believe.

TEN

"WORK, GODDAMN IT!" JOSH SHOUTS AT
his quantum laptop, pounding on the touch screen with two
open palms.

I'm watching him as I pace inside one of the insulated glass
capsules the city built along the boardwalk of the Inner Sector
waterfront a few years ago. After school and my second stint
in detention, Josh and I decided to take a ride so we could have
a secluded spot to analyze the information on the QuTap, and
this was the first place that came to mind. Despite the "comfort" of these antitoxic fume capsules, hardly anyone comes
down here to check out the view of the Detroit River—it's so
polluted it could be mistaken for a sewage system.

As a beam of glorious sunshine filters through a lightning
bolt–shaped crack in the capsule's glass, I stop pacing and step

behind Josh, peering over his shoulder as he tries to open every file, one by one. I'm really surprised by how fast the tablet-size quantum computer works—strings of infinite number-and-letter combinations blink on the screen in a rapid-fire succession that hurts my eyes. From the way Josh is squinting, I guess it's affecting his vision too, but I don't think that's what's bothering him the most.

He leans back on the metal bench and lets out a huge groan as he runs his hands over the stubble that's sprouting on his chin.

"Just like I suspected. They're encrypted," he mutters.

"All of them?"

"I'm only halfway through the QuTap directory, but I'm pretty sure that we're screwed," he says.

I lean in and stare at the last file Josh pulled up. "It looks like a random selection of symbols, underscores, and slashes."

"I know, it sucks," Josh replies. "Every time I click on a file, I find this mess. None of my algorithms are making a dent."

I don't like the futility in his voice, so I have to convince him that giving up is not an option. "Can't we just use some decryption software to crack it?"

"Tried that already," he says, irritated. Obviously, he doesn't appreciate being second-guessed. "Orexis probably has a team of grunts policing the latest software so they can plug up any security holes. They're ten steps ahead of us."

I walk to the front of the capsule and gaze through the slight film of mildew covering the glass surface, looking out at Detroit's industrial skyline on the other side of the channel. A sun-soaked day like this only comes a few times a month, so I can actually make out all the architectural details of the high-rises—the antiquated neo-Gothic and art deco designs mixed in with more modern cylinder-style layouts; the narrow spires and old Corinthian columns and pilasters. My favorite of them all is the Florapetro Foundation Building, which has a sixty-floor spiral tower that actually rotates at a speed so slow it's hardly visible to the naked eye. And yet given how clear the conditions are right now, I feel like if I stand here, concentrating all my focus on the tower, I'll be able to see it moving.

I just have to be patient and wait for it to become real.

So I steel myself and say to Josh, "Keep trying. Please."

He doesn't answer, but I can hear him clicking away on his laptop, each stroke of his fingers hopefully bringing us closer to some kind of breakthrough. This goes on for about five to ten minutes, and my eyes never leave the tower. But with each heavy and frustrated sigh of his, my hopes begin to wither away. When thoughts of my run-in with Patrick begin to flood my head, I distract myself by tracing the concrete- and steel-infused horizon on my finger, the squeaking sound of my skin against the glass echoing inside the capsule.

And then it happens.

"I think I got something!" I hear him exclaim.

I spin around, my hair almost whipping me in the face. I stumble over to Josh and squat down next to him, my hand on his arm. "What'd you find?"

Josh redirects his eyes so they meet mine, and grins. "I only had a few files left when this one ruptured."

I tilt the laptop so I can get a better look at the screen and watch as he scrolls through pages and pages of spreadsheets filled with hundreds of diagrams that look oddly like genealogical charts. There are lots of rectangular boxes filled with sequences of letters and symbols. Connecting them together are solid and dotted lines with arrows pointing in multiple directions.

I'm not sure what to make of it.

"These are parse trees," Josh explains, pulling away from me to point at one of them. "They basically break down the source code of computer programming languages."

"It's a map?"

"Yes. The only problem is we have no idea what program it's for."

I reach over Josh and slide two of my fingers across the screen so I can zoom in on one of the trees, but enlarging the visual unfortunately doesn't give me any deeper understanding of its meaning. "This could be source code for something my dad might have been working on before Elusion."

Josh narrows his eyes, studying the figures carefully. "There are at least twelve levels of syntax being deconstructed here. What other program would have code this complex?"

"We need to know for sure, though," I counter.

"But we can't figure that out until we make sense of these trees," he says. "And this is way more complicated than what I'm used to."

"God, I wish my dad had taught me . . . then maybe I'd be able to help." I stand up, and Josh instinctively moves over on the bench, giving me room to sit down. When I do, I bring my knees up to my chest and rest the heels of my sneakers against the metal. "He spent all his time training Patrick, who was a natural at it, of course. Like everything else."

I used to admire that trait in Patrick, but the pinched sound of resentment in my voice paints a different picture altogether.

"Well, he's the last person we can go to for advice," Josh says, smirking.

I smile back.

"Listen, I might be able to get somewhere if I take the QuTap back to the person who gave it to me," he suggests, ejecting the magnetic device in question out of the laptop's side port.

I shake my head. "I don't think that's a good idea. We can't risk someone finding out what we did to get the information that's on there."

"I think I can get that point across." He pushes up his sleeves, and I take a nice, long look at his toned forearms and large hands. I see what he's getting at, but again, it's hard to picture Josh as a threat, even after what he's told me about his past.

Maybe that's because we're getting to know each other while we're most vulnerable.

"So you take the QuTap back and then what?" I ask.

old, six feet tall, and about one hundred sixty-five pounds."

The image of the reporter dims and a photo suddenly appears in her place. It's a snapshot of the boy in question. His eyes are closed and he's in a hospital gown, so the picture must have been taken after the doctors stabilized him. His cheekbones are sharp and raised, and he has a narrow chin. His coppery hair is greasy at the roots, and he has a bit of acne in a thin line across his brow.

"If you recognize this person, please contact the Florida State Bureau of—"

Josh hits the pause button, freezing the photo in front of us before the camera cuts away.

"Notice anything strange about that kid's face?" he asks me.

I search the picture with a steady gaze, and at first I don't see anything unusual, but then Josh expands the viewing window on the screen so the image is much larger. There seems to be a deep circular impression near his left temple. It doesn't appear to be a scar, because it's too perfectly shaped.

"I saw those marks on Nora's friends at the factory," he explains. "I think they're from the Equip visors."

As soon as he says that, my body reacts with a systemic tremble, like my blood sugar just dropped a thousand points.

"So you think this kid is in a coma because he's addicted to Elusion?"

"Only one way to know," he says. "We have to check out that firewall again. We aren't making enough headway with the clues we have in reality."

And in reality, time is running out.

I rise to my feet. "Okay, let's go."

Josh stands along with me, casting a tall shadow on the floor of the capsule. "Where to?"

"My house," I reply. "We should wait until my mom's an hour or two into her shift, though, so we're not interrupted like last time."

"What about when we're inside Elusion? Should we go back to the beach where your dad—"

"No, I already did that—and he wasn't there. Patrick told me that the firewalls run through all the Escapes. They're all connected. I'm not sure what Nora and her friends expect to find on the other side, but if Pat's right, that means they'd just run into another Escape."

"So where should we go?"

I smile. I have just the place in mind.

A few hours later, my head buzzes and my palms tingle with thin strips of kinetic energy. I push back the fur-trimmed hood of my white parka so that I can look up at the sky, which is a lemon yellow, lit up by an electric blue sun. Each molecule of tension that lingered in my body is being soaked up by the spongelike hold trypnosis has on my emotions, and I feel absolutely protected here.

Best of all, I have someone by my side. Someone who I really want to trust—and who looks amazing in a thick winter coat.

Josh and I are now inside the Mount Arvon Escape, perched on a narrow plateau off the mountain, towering above patches of fluffy cinnamon clouds. Everything around us is covered in glittering cherry-blossom-pink–colored snow, and the sun is giving off a magnificent spectrum of sheer rainbow-tinted light. Way, *way* down below are two rippling rivers of grape that wind their way through a valley that appears to be made out of layers of delicate eggshells. In the distance, the rivers fuse together into a glistening purple lake.

"I've never seen anything like this," I hear Josh say, his voice utterly breathless.

I inhale the cool, crisp air and exhale a turquoise-colored mist. "It's absolutely gorgeous."

Josh smiles as he unzips his black down coat to reveal a red flannel shirt. He stares at the snow-covered trees, the frustration from earlier completely gone from his eyes. "Why'd you pick this Escape again?"

I bend down, running my gloved fingers through the pink, fluffy snow. "There was a reason," I say. "I just have to think about it for a minute."

"Take your time," Josh says, throwing a backpack on the ground. "I have to figure out what this is for."

As I watch Josh dig through the bag, setting out pieces of climbing gear, I concentrate hard on the sense of purpose that's niggling at the back of my thoughts, which are still pretty gauzy at best. I try to grasp at my most recent memories, but it feels like the inside of my head is covered in the same layers of soft, delicate fur as the outside.

Josh holds up a large, sharp, J-shaped ice tool and smirks. "Cool, huh?"

Suddenly, a recollection is triggered. I've seen that object before, not more than a few months ago.

"Ah, now I get it. I was here with my dad right before he died," I say, rolling a handful of snow into a big gumdrop-looking ball.

"So are you retracing his steps?" Josh asks.

"That seems like the logical thing to do, right?"

"Logic doesn't matter here; that's why everyone loves it."

I smile at him. "Hey, you should be thanking me for figuring out why we're in these mountains."

Josh laughs, playfully throwing some snow in my direction. "Yeah, well, I wish I remembered what we're supposed to do here. Other than climb something."

Believe it or not, that particular detail has stayed with me. I don't know how, but maybe my last visit to Elusion solidified it in a dark corner of my mind.

"That's a no-brainer. Check out the firewall," I brag, lightly throwing the ball I made at Josh's chest.

When it bursts, the snowflakes cling to his coat like a glittering flush-colored badge of honor. Once I realize he isn't going to brush it away, my heart feels like it's filling with helium, and for a moment I think I'm going to float away from him.

"Okay, genius. We've got five miles to the firewall. Since we can't really go left or right, would you prefer up or down?" he asks, smiling at me.

"I'd prefer to go up, but I think down would be faster."

Josh lets out another laugh, his breath creating a cloud of turquoise, which disappears in the blink of an eye.

"What? Why are you laughing?" I say through a giddy grin.

"Nothing."

"Come on, tell me."

"It's just that . . . I don't know a lot about you, but it's obvious you're a 'go up' kind of girl."

"You really think so?"

Josh picks up a harness off the ground, tossing it to me gently. "Yeah. And I love that about you."

I jab the spiked steel plates attached to the bottom of my fire-engine-red boots into a rocky crevice. When my feet are secure, I let the rope out, rappelling a hundred feet or so before throwing my pickax against the wall of the mountain, causing a shower of pale pastel crystals to rain down on me. I pause a moment, pressing my gloved hands up against the mountain, and hold steady. I inhale and repeat the process over and over, yanking out my pickax, pushing off and rappelling downward, adrenaline flowing through my limbs. It's as if I am flying, swooping in to land.

The rush I am feeling is no longer just in my mind—I can feel it possessing every moment, every breath, every gesture. My legs are like channels of water surging toward a dam, but my arms are like ribbons tied to an old fence post, flickering in the breeze.

I land smack against the side of the mountain and pause to breathe in a fresh, jasmine-scented Nordic wind that is billowing through the atmosphere. I take off my gloves so I can feel the cold particles land upon my fingers. The snow is refreshingly cool, and it leaves a light pink stain on my hand when it melts.

"How're you doing?" Josh calls out from his perch above me.

"Great," I say, smiling up at him. "How much time do we have left?"

Josh pushes his jacket sleeve up and glances at his wristband. "Thirty minutes."

"Wow, I feel like we've been at this for hours." I look down below. When we arrived in Elusion, the ground beneath us was barely visible. And now? The trees are nothing more than tiny dark purple dots that match the lake. "Do you think we'll make it?"

"I hope so—we've gotten pretty far already."

I nod as I kick away from the mountain, bouncing back.

And just like that, everything goes haywire.

The rope slides out of my brake hand, causing me to lose my balance. It slips through my fingers as the anchor holding it lets loose. I begin to free-fall, yanking short as the rope connecting my harness to Josh pulls tight, tugging so violently against him he's thrown against the mountain, his pickax flying out of his grasp. I dangle in the air beside the mountain, held up only by my harness.

My left hand reaches for the mountain while my right continues to clutch the pickax as if my life depends on it. But it's strange—I don't feel the least bit terrified.

In fact, I feel . . . incredible.

I find a slight indentation, enough to dig my fingers in, and pull myself toward the sparkling rock, heaving my pickax so that it is wedged in place.

"I'm okay, Josh! I'm okay!" I shout.

"Regan!" he yells. "Stay still. I'm coming to get you."

Click.

I glance down. The top snap of my harness is loosening, the safety straps unbuckling as if by invisible fingers.

Click.

Another snap is undone.

"Josh!" I scream—not with terror, but delight. "My harness is giving way!"

"Don't move!" Josh quickly lowers the rope, practically diving toward me.

Click.

My free hand frantically tugs at my harness, vainly attempting to yank it closed as I dangle in midair. I kick the spiked boots into the mountain with all my might. But it's as though the ice has turned into a sheet of pink-jeweled granite.

All of a sudden, the ice shifts, causing me to lose my grip. I grab on to the pickax with both hands as my harness releases, setting Josh free.

He feels it at the same time I do.

He stops for a moment, his eyes locking on to mine. "Hang on!" he yells, releasing some slack on his rope as he plunges toward me.

But he isn't quick enough.

The ice begins to separate into long shards and tiny fragments. Suddenly my pickax has nothing left to penetrate.

I tumble backward, falling so fast the mountain is just a blur. I close my eyes as the wind rushes in my ears.

So this is how it feels to die? It doesn't seem too bad, actually.

I don't feel frightened at all.

But then I remember why I'm here—to find the firewall again—so dying today, whether it's real or not, isn't an option.

I tighten my hands around the pickax. Utilizing all my strength, I flip myself upright as my body continues to descend. I face the mountain, heaving my ax toward it as hard as I can. The ax catches the side of a large rock formation, yanking me upward. I bounce like an old string puppet, flying sideways through the air, ricocheting off the mountain and onto a huge plateau.

I hit the ground hard, rolling several times before stopping. Then I open my eyes.

In spite of the fall, I'm surprisingly unscathed. No bumps, no bruises, no scratches.

I pick up my head and look around. In front of me is an archway made out of giant blocks of ice, sparkling like a billon sea-green diamonds.

With a thump, Josh lands on the frozen surface beside me, his cheeks flushed.

"Are you okay?" he says, out of breath.

Actually, I'm better than okay.

I'm more alive than I've ever felt before.

He falls backward against the snow, as he shuts his eyes with relief. "Hey, what's your ExSet at?"

I push back the sleeve of my parka and look at my wristband. "Oh, it's . . . advanced."

Josh starts laughing. "Okay, change that right now."

"Why? Are you having trouble keeping up with me?" I joke as I type in the proper adjustments.

He kicks some ice off the blade attached to his boot and grins. "By the way, that was the coolest thing I have seen in my life. *Ever.*"

"Great, maybe we can do it again sometime."

Josh's laughing tapers off and he just lies there, staring at me. We're so close I could reach out and hold his hand. Or I could roll over a little, lean in, and tilt my head so that our brows are gently pressing together, leaving him to make the last, sweet move.

Do I dare?

"How far do you think we've gone?" he says, sitting up and brushing snow off his pants with his hands.

I crane my neck and lift my shoulders, propping my top half up with my elbows. "I don't know," I say, studying the structure looming in front of us. "It might be five miles. Maybe we should check out this ice cave. The firewall in the Thai Beach was near a cluster of rocks—kind of like a formation. Maybe this archway is another version of that."

I look over at Josh and see the rapture that's sparkling in his eyes. I can't help but hope that Elusion won't be the only place I'll ever see him this way.

The path through the ice cave looks exactly like a tunnel running through a block of iridescent mint-infused limestone. The walls are perfectly carved and rounded, the ground still covered in cherry-blossom snow. Bright rays of blue sunlight stream in through the semitransparent ceiling, and when I run my hand along the smooth tunnel walls, surface particles begin to change hues—from soft yellow to bright pink to ethereal green. It feels like I'm walking through a gigantic crystal prism.

At the end of the winding path, Josh and I stumble upon a huge cavern filled with translucent flamingo-pink stalagmites rising from the ground and glimmering harvest-gold icicles, which dangle from above like frozen caramel rain. But at the center of the cavern, about a few hundred yards away from us, is a monstrous pure-white glacier formation that stretches out like a barricade around a mythical princess's castle. I crane my neck upward to see how high it goes, but it just continues on and on, above the ceiling and into infinity.

"It's . . . *incredible*," I say. The word is such an insignificant way to describe the absolute splendor that's before us, but that's all I can muster.

Josh takes off his gloves and reaches out to touch the smooth surface of a nearby pillar-shaped stalagmite with his bare hands. "You know what? I think that frozen barrier is the firewall."

"Really? The firewall didn't look like part of the landscape in the Thai Beach Escape," I say.

"I know, but maybe the programmers are trying to make it harder to find."

"Because of what happened to me?"

"Yeah, and whatever's happening to Nora," Josh suggests.

"You're probably right," I say, unzipping my parka. The refracted blue sunlight from outside the cave is definitely causing some kind of greenhouse effect inside the cavern. There's a surge of heat that's starting to surround us, causing some of the golden icicles to drip beads of moisture on the ground.

But other than that, there isn't any strange current tearing through this Escape; no clues indicate this icy fortress is about to self-destruct.

No visions of my father, either. Lucky for me, I can't feel one shred of disappointment here. But when we leave, that will be another story altogether.

"Can you sense your dad's presence?" Josh asks, like he knows exactly what I'm thinking.

An image pops into my head—my father planting a triangular blue flag at the top of the mountain and renaming it Mount Regan. The memory of him hugging and swinging me around afterward makes me smile.

"I sort of remember being here with him last time, if that's what you mean."

"Not exactly." Josh removes his hands from the ice formation and dries them on the back of his pants. "Do you believe in . . . psychic connections?"

I press my hands against the ice like Josh did, my skin slipping and sliding along the pillar's rounded edges and rough ridges. "Like do I think it's possible for you to read my mind or something?"

Because honestly, right now, I think he can.

"No, I mean . . . do you think that it's possible to feel like someone's next to you, even though they are hundreds of miles away? Or that two people could understand each other without having to talk?"

I put my hands in my coat pockets and take a step closer to him. I know we're here to examine the firewall—to see if we can find another connection to Dad or Nora—but the only thing I can think about is how I wish Josh's arms were wrapped around me.

"Yes, I think it's possible," I reply.

Josh grins and moves toward me, his boots creating a crunching sound as he walks over the snow. His footprints blaze behind him like a row of lit candles.

"Good. I thought . . . you might think that was stupid."

I take a deep breath and then exhale, sending a foggy burst of mist into the air. "Can I ask you something?"

"Sure," he says, his lips parting to reveal another sweet smile.

"How many girls have you brought to Elusion?"

Josh's eyebrows twitch up and he gives me a funny look, but he doesn't seem offended, of course. "Why do you want to know?"

"No reason. I'm just curious."

This isn't exactly the truth, which makes me wonder—can you lie in Elusion? I doubt anyone would have a reason to. Trypnosis typically lowers your inhibitions, so what would be the motivation, really?

"Curious about what?"

I shrug. "Whether or not you've hooked up with anyone here."

Josh takes another step toward me, the icy barrier deep in the cavern looking smaller and less significant the more he closes in on me.

"That's a pretty personal question," he says.

"I'm sorry. I didn't mean to pry."

"It's okay." Josh reaches out and gently pulls my hand out of my pocket, the softness of his palm sending a tingling riptide up my arm. "One or two, I guess. I'm having trouble remembering."

My fingers entwine with his, and another crackling wave of energy travels through me at the speed of light. Josh pulls me toward him, his eyes locked with mine.

"What was it like? Kissing someone here?" I whisper.

"You mean, you've never . . ."

"No. I've only been here with my father and Patrick," I say.

Josh pushes a loose, damp strand of hair away from my

face with his thumb. "So you and Patrick . . . you're really just friends? Nothing has ever *happened* between you two?"

"Nothing has, and nothing will," I murmur. His hands travel down my back and rest on my hips, causing an electric hum to course through my body.

"Too bad for him," Josh says, his voice rather musky all of a sudden.

"Why do you say that?"

"I can tell from the way he looks at you." Josh leans in, and his lips brush against my forehead, sending my center of gravity to my neck and making my legs weak. "He wants to be more than your friend."

"So how does he look at me?" I ask.

Josh's grip on my hips becomes tighter, and in seconds almost every part of me is pressed up against him. Our world is beginning to fall away behind the veil of Elusion's white light. The stalagmites, the icicles, the snow, the frozen firewall that we came here to find are fading away, and soon we will too.

"Like this," he says, pressing his lips to mine. I clasp my hands tightly behind his back, unable to breathe, unable to think. It's as though I'm being shaken to my very core. I've never felt like this about anyone before.

But even with my eyes closed, I can tell the brightness is about to swallow us whole and take us back into the real world.

I pull him tighter, willing the light away. I'm not ready to leave.

He's kissing me harder now, his strong arms wrapped so

tightly around my waist he's practically lifting me off the ground. All I can think about is how wonderful this feels and how I want to stay here, like this, with Josh. How I don't want to go home.

But just like that, we're gone.

ELEVEN

I WANT TO KISS JOSH AGAIN.

We've been back from Elusion for a half hour, but my heart is still rattling against my rib cage. Slipping my hands under the motion-sensor faucet, I splash some lukewarm water on my face, hoping that will snap me out of this dreamy, almost lovesick state.

It doesn't help.

My brain still feels like it's wrapped in cellophane as I blindly reach for the air-dryer button on the right-hand wall. After I press it, two converging streams of hot air blow out of a nozzle and onto my hands. I lean forward and put my face right in front of the current. Once all the moisture has been sucked away from my skin, the dryer turns off automatically, and I twist back to the sink so I can check myself out in the mirror that hangs above the countertop.

My makeup is a bit smeared, so I pull some toilet paper off of the roll and blot underneath my eyes, where the damage is the worst. I adjust my scoop-neck tee so it's centered on my chest, and pull up my jeans so they're not riding so low on my hips. Now I look like I do every night, like nothing out of the ordinary has happened.

Like I haven't been climbing mountains and suffering through near-death experiences.

Like I wasn't just kissed.

But was I, *really*? As I back up against the shower door, I wonder—and worry—if Elusion is powerful enough to create feelings that don't actually exist in reality. After all, I know I don't want to be anything more than friends with Patrick, but when I was trekking around the Universe Escape with him, I have to admit, I felt . . . *something*.

Touching my fingers to my lips, I glance at the bathroom door, where Josh is waiting on the other side. My mind struggles to process what my senses keep insisting was real. And even though I have way more important things to be concerned with than a kiss, that moment is replaying itself over and over again in my thoughts.

My bare feet pad against the floor as I walk toward the door. Since we woke up, Josh and I haven't spoken much except to comment on the status of our mobility post-Aftershock.

What do I say to him now? Do I even acknowledge what happened?

I take another step forward and push the unlock button near the door, which then opens.

Josh is sitting on the edge of my bed, his head dipped down as he stares at a wrinkled piece of paper. My room suddenly feels so small. All of my attention is focused on the broadness of his shoulders; the way his waffle knit shirt hugs his muscular arms; his square jaw; and the slight beard stubble on his cheeks. But when he turns to look at me, the only thing I can see are his deep-set golden-brown eyes, which are unmistakably red in the corners.

"Hey," he says, quickly sticking the paper in his pocket and mindlessly running his hand over his short, spiked hair. "You okay?"

"I'm fine," I say. "How are you?"

Instead of answering my question, he stands up and turns away from me. That says more than words ever could.

He regrets the kiss. He wishes he could take it back.

I step away from him as I brace myself for whatever is about to come out of his mouth—a mouth that I still remember tasting like spiced apples.

"Regan," he begins, in a slightly wavering tone that only confirms my suspicions. "I'm sorry."

"Sorry about what?"

I know this is a dumb, passive-aggressive response, but a part of me wants him to admit what I fear to be true. I can't take the thought of another person not being honest with me.

There's a long silence that pretty much drives a shard of

glass into my nerves. When Josh finally turns back around, he lets out a frustrated sigh.

"It's my fault that we're back to square one," he says.

"What?"

"The firewall." Josh grits his teeth and punches an angry fist into the air. "It was right there, in that cavern. But because of me . . . we missed our chance."

I take in a breath, somewhat relieved that he's saying our kiss was a mistake for a reason that doesn't involve his feelings for me, but I realize that he's right. Our mission to scope out the firewall was temporarily derailed, and we won't be able to reenter Elusion for another half hour.

Who knows what else will go wrong by then?

All of a sudden, I hear a male voice from downstairs call out, "Regan?"

Oh God. I think I just tempted fate.

"Regan? You upstairs?"

Josh's head whips toward the bedroom door. "Is that—"

"Patrick," I whisper.

When he turns his gaze back to me, Josh looks a little panicked. "How'd he get in the house?"

"He has a courtesy code on his passcard," I reply, blood pumping through my veins like an express-line Traxx.

Josh rolls his eyes. "Great."

"What if he knows about the QuTap?"

"I think he'd sound a lot more pissed, don't you?"

I push past Josh, upset that he's not helping matters with his snarky attitude. "Just stay here. I'll get rid of him."

I rush toward the bedroom door, almost colliding with the painted glass when it doesn't slide open fast enough. I'm not really thinking now, just moving instinctively. I hurry down the hall, and when I reach the top of the steps, I call to Patrick before I even see him.

"What are you doing here?" I ask, skipping down the stairs two at a time.

"I wanted to see you," he says.

Patrick looks every inch the corporate titan, with his blond hair neatly combed and gelled, and the collar of his unbuttoned wool designer trench popped up. But his face is even more haggard than this morning. His skin is dry and pallid, and there are these light-purple circles forming underneath his eyes. His appearance is so distracting I barely notice the indigo-blue shopping bag he's holding in his left hand.

"Is everything okay?" I have to admit I'm surprised by how much I care after everything that went on today.

"Not really," he replies. "I—"

Patrick's voice catches and stops cold, his gaze traveling above me and up the stairs. I turn around to look over my shoulder and spot Josh quietly walking down the steps. My jaw slides open and I gawk at him when he finally joins me at the bottom landing.

What the hell is he doing?

"Hey," Josh says casually, staring directly at Patrick.

I can see red blotches forming on Patrick's neck—something

that only happens when he's absolutely furious.

"What's going on, Ree?" he asks, totally ignoring Josh.

"Oh, um, Josh just drove me home," I say, my stomach quivering again.

"From where? It's almost eleven," Patrick says.

Josh shifts in front of me, his eyes never leaving Patrick. "I don't think that's any of your business."

Patrick looks at the floor, backing away from both of us.

"Let me handle this, okay?" I say to Josh, nudging him in the side.

But it's like he doesn't hear me at all.

"I've been trying to get ahold of you." Josh advances on Patrick like a target, but his voice is casual and nonthreatening.

"Sorry," Patrick says. "I've been really busy. Any word from Nora?"

"No," Josh says, shaking his head. "And now it seems that she isn't the only one we should be trying to help."

Patrick sets the shopping bag on the entranceway table and shrugs. "I have no idea what you're talking about."

Josh lets out an irritated laugh. "Yeah, right."

Patrick walks around Josh and approaches me again. "What's his problem?"

I glance over at Josh, who's clasping his hands behind his head, waiting to see what I'll say. Since lying to my friend's face isn't something I've perfected yet, I just go ahead and tell him the truth.

"There's a story on the Net about this kid in Miami. The

cops found him in a coma, without any ID or passcard. They showed a photo of him and there were these indentations—"

"Christ, that's what this is about?" Patrick spins around and points at Josh. "You think the kid is sick because of Elusion?"

"I think there's something really wrong with Elusion and you know it," Josh says, pointing right back at him.

Patrick takes a step toward Josh, saying through clenched teeth, "You're paranoid, you know that? And blaming me isn't going to make that guy better any faster."

"Why didn't you meet me at the warehouse? I told you I had proof."

"IV bags? Empty pill bottles? That doesn't sound like a problem with Elusion. That sounds like you stumbled onto a bunch of druggies!" Patrick says, nearly shouting.

"Hold on a minute, Pat. Let him explain," I blurt out loudly, trying to interrupt the rising tension in the room.

Patrick quiets down but begins to pace back and forth. Then he shrugs off his coat, nearly throwing it on the floor.

"There's some kind of loophole, Patrick. People are figuring out how to break the signal between the Equip and the app so they can disable the automatic time-out. I'm telling you, you have to do something," Josh says coolly. "Recall the device, shut down the server, anything."

But when Patrick just turns away from him without answering, Josh can't contain his contempt any longer.

"You just can't admit that your precious product is

dangerous, can you? What's it going to take? Does someone need to die before—"

All of a sudden, Patrick lunges at Josh, grabbing his shirt and shoving him up against the wall.

"Patrick, stop!" I yell.

Josh doesn't move. Even though he has a few inches on Patrick and at least twenty pounds—all of it muscle—he stands still, nose to nose with him, staring him down without flinching.

With some effort, Patrick breaks eye contact and swallows, loosening his grip on Josh. Patrick lets go of him and stares at his shaking hands, as stunned as I am by his outburst. His gaze slowly turns toward me, pained and desperate. My childhood instincts kick in, and I race to his side to see if he's okay, putting my arm around him.

Then I look at Josh, who is breathing hard and, from the way he's squinting at me, wondering why I'm not comforting him.

Honestly, I'm wondering the exact same thing.

"I should go," Josh says, tightly.

"See you tomorrow" is all I can bear to say.

As Josh walks out the door, I'm filled with emptiness. This is such an utter and complete mess.

Why didn't Josh just stay in my room?

Patrick lurches away from me and drops down on the bottom step of the stairs, loosening his tie. "I'm sorry. Losing it like that. I don't know what got into me."

"What were you thinking? That's not the type of guy you are," I say.

At least not the guy I grew up with.

He puts his head in his hands, running his fingers through his hair, but when he looks back up at me, his eyes are like daggers. "And what the hell were you thinking, Ree? Inviting that guy into your house?"

And into my bedroom.

"I was being polite."

Not the best comeback in the world, but how can you argue with that?

Unfortunately, Patrick seems stumped for only a split second. "Did he tell you about his sister?"

I sit down next to him on the stairs, hugging my knees to my chest and preparing myself for a fight, because he's not going to be happy about the next bit of truth I'm about to share with him. "Yes, and I saw the warehouse."

I pause for a moment, thinking about whether or not I should tell him that I saw 5020 spray-painted on the wall there, and decide to hold on to that little piece of information until I can confer with Josh. Even though our kiss in Elusion may not have changed the shape of our relationship, we're a team now, and I don't want to jeopardize our plan by revealing too much.

"I can't believe he took you there," Patrick grunts.

"Why does that bother you so much? If there's something wrong with Elusion, don't you think I deserve to know about it?" I ask. "Josh just wants our help. His sister is missing and he's scared. Don't you get that?"

Patrick lets out a condescending laugh. "Nora is way beyond our help. She's unstable, Regan. Really troubled. She has been for years. Now Josh is acting just as insane."

"What are you trying to say?"

"I bet Nora took off, like she always does, and didn't tell Josh where she was going. And he's just freaking out. He called me yesterday, and when I said I was busy, something snapped. Now he's on some sort of vendetta."

I wonder if Patrick is aware of how crazy his ramble just sounded and how much he's sweating right now.

"Vendetta? Are you serious?"

"Yeah, like the second he feels I'm not taking him seriously, he goes and befriends you. Don't you think that's a little suspicious?"

"For your information," I say with sheer grit, "Josh and I ran into one another in the administrative office at school. He was registering and I'd just gotten my *ass* handed to me by the principal for pushing Avery, because I was standing up for *you*."

Patrick rubs his face with both hands, and then his eyes soften. "I'm just trying to—"

"Protect me? You keep saying that, but I'm not a little kid anymore."

"I know," he says. "I just want you to be careful. He's got a temper. Always has, but after his parents split, the kids kind of lost it. Nora started getting into trouble, Josh was out of control . . ."

"He hit a guy and got sent to military school. I know. He told me."

"*Hit* a guy?" Patrick says, sarcastically. "He almost *killed* someone, Ree. Beat up a kid so badly he was in the hospital for three days."

I snort at the accusation. It seems so exaggerated. "Josh doesn't seem capable of doing that. And he certainly kept calm just now when you slammed him against the wall."

"Trust me, that was for your sake. He thinks you know something, and he's willing to exploit your friendship to get to me. Isn't that obvious?"

I spring up from the stairs, stone cold angry. "Don't twist this whole thing around. This is about how *you're* not being honest with me. About Elusion, about Josh, about—"

"Wait, *I'm* not being honest?" Patrick gets up and stares me down. "What was he doing over here tonight? He was in your bedroom, wasn't he? Did I walk in on something, Regan?"

I'm shocked by how tongue-tied I become at his accusation, but I manage to squeak something out of my vocal cords.

"Now who's paranoid?"

Patrick smirks and pulls out his tab. "Josh's name was kept out of the papers because he was underage, but Trent was older, so there might be something about it in the local news archives," he says, typing and scrolling away. "Here we go. Trent Sasder. That was the name of his victim."

I glance down at the tab Patrick has shoved into my hand.

Brutal Attacker Cops Plea

The assailant of local college student Trent Sasder, 19, who was in critical care for days after suffering a brutal attack, is being set free. Insiders say the high school sophomore, who attacked Mr. Sasder outside his home, is being forced to attend Ashville Academy, a military school known for the hard-core tactics used to rehabilitate its students . . .

"How can I be sure this is even about Josh?" I say, forcing the tab back into Patrick's possession. "I bet there are plenty of other people who were sent to Ashville for the same reason."

"If you looked closely enough, you'd see the timing of the article is an exact match to when Josh left for the academy."

Maybe he's right. Maybe I don't want to look closely enough where Josh is concerned. But I'm so tired of Patrick turning the tables tonight, which is why I keep the pressure on him.

"If you were so worried about me hanging out with Josh, why didn't you say anything about this at your party?" I growl. "You knew he was driving me home. Anything could've happened, right?"

"It seemed like Ashville had straightened him out." Patrick shoves the tab back into his pocket and shrugs. "Guess I was wrong. About a lot of things."

I reach out and grab him by the shoulders, hoping to get through to him. "You know what you're wrong about? Me. You can tell me anything, Patrick, even if it's really bad. You have to trust me and let me help."

For a moment there's this look in his eyes, like he's drowning and he wants me to throw him a rope. But it vanishes in a flash. Patrick snatches his coat off the floor and walks out the front door without saying another word to me. I don't tell him to wait, but I follow him outside and stand on the stoop, watching him get into his black luxury car.

He doesn't look back. Not even once.

I realize now that my friendship with Patrick might be coming to an end, and my relationship with Josh might be over before it's had the chance to get started. But does any of this matter? When today people are missing and dying . . .

And possibly alive somewhere even though they're supposed to be dead.

When the car is out of sight, I go inside and notice the shopping bag Patrick left behind. I peek inside and see a small box with *Xr47* printed on it in large bold yellow lettering.

It's a new tablet, intended for me, I assume. Top-of-the-line, of course. The fastest one on the market, and the most expensive.

I suppose nothing's too good for Patrick Simmons's best friend.

Except for the truth.

"Regan, wait up!" I hear a high-pitched voice call out into the seven a.m. rush crowd at the Hills Sector Traxx station.

It's a dreary but wind-free day, and O2 shields aren't needed, which makes it easier to see everyone's faces. Still, there's a bitter chill and a lot of dampness in the air. I grabbed my dad's black fleece jacket as I ran out of the house early this morning, but right now it's doing little to keep me warm and dry.

I spot Zoe in the distance, waving from one of the mammoth escalators and moving her petite frame around the masses as she trots down the steps. She's wearing a bluish-violet knit cap and the hottest accessory on the market—round oversize Florapetro glasses. The tinted lenses are designed to make the world seem bright even when the sky is under siege by oil clouds.

I don't really feel like talking to anyone right now—after last night, I feel so drained. Still, I wait until Zoe catches up with me and manage a smile.

"Well?" she says, a hint of warm breath escaping her lips in a puff of white.

"Well, what?"

Zoe loops her arm through mine and pulls me closer, as if we're old friends out for a stroll. "You're not going to tell me what happened after I left you with Josh?"

I realize that the last time she saw me was the day before yesterday, right before Josh and I left school and he took me to the warehouse.

It seems like worlds ago.

"I would, but there's really nothing to tell. He and I . . . we barely know each other."

Although it's not like I haven't been trying to remedy that. After Patrick left my house last evening, I spent hours on the

Net looking for everything and anything I could find about the assault case. While my search didn't turn up anything new, the article Patrick showed me had other background details that proved the assailant was Josh. The timing was right, of course, but specifics about his family, where they lived, and the fact that the perpetrator's sister was somehow involved—all of it added up.

The scariest thing, though, is that Patrick wasn't lying about how bad this Sasder guy was hurt. He was on life support at one point.

How could Josh be so vicious?

"He's gorgeous. What more do you need to know?" Zoe grins mischievously as we walk out of the station and start off on the express pedestrian route to school.

At first, I don't really want to confide in Zoe what Patrick told me, but then it occurs to me that my best friend—the one person I could talk to about everything, the only one I could trust—might not be either of those things anymore.

"Zoe, do you know anything about Josh's . . . violent streak?"

"Violent streak?" She rolls her eyes. "That's a gross overstatement."

My eyes widen in surprise. She knows exactly what I'm referring to.

"That fight with Sasder wasn't his fault," she says defensively. "Seriously. I would know. Our parents are friends with Josh's mother, and I heard all about it."

"I read something that said Josh nearly killed that guy."

"It's a lot more complicated. After his sister Nora was assaulted—"

I practically trip over a crack in the pavement. "Nora was *assaulted*?"

"Yeah. Sasder was a total bully and ran with this group of thugs. He had been asking Nora out for weeks, and she kept turning him down. I guess he snapped one day and went after her. Gave her a concussion," Zoe says, zipping up her leather jacket as she quickens her pace. "Once Josh found out, he confronted Sasder, threatening to destroy him if he ever touched Nora again. Then Sasder and four of his goons ambushed Josh, thinking they would teach him a lesson. They didn't know Josh was Mr. Black Belt, so they had no idea he could beat the crap out of all of them."

"Wait, more than one guy attacked Josh? How come that wasn't in the article?"

"The media has spun this story at least ten different ways," she replies. "Sasder was injured the worst, and his dad's the deputy DA, so his father went after Josh with a vengeance. Couldn't get a conviction, but he used his connections to get him sent to Ashville."

I tuck my cold hands in my skirt pockets. As relieved as I am to hear that Josh isn't the monster Patrick made him out to be, I'm also just as angry. Patrick had to have known the real story about Sasder and Nora. Just how many more lies does he intend on telling me?

"What the hell is going on at school?" Zoe says, as we turn a corner.

The long stretch of campus is right in front of us. Dozens of reporters stand in the central quad, some talking into their tabs as they hold them up in front of their faces, broadcasting their reports, while other press members frantically scramble after students.

A throng of teachers is outside too, trying to escort the kids through the commotion and inside the school. I glance around to see if there are any ambulances, police cars, or other signs of trouble, but there's nothing.

"Excuse me, coming through!" a voice booms from behind us.

Before I can move, I'm shoved into Zoe by a man in a pea-coat who is flanked by three women in khaki trenches, all hurrying toward the school.

More reporters?

I grab on to Zoe, steadying her. Our tabs both start to buzz at the same time—I bet someone has sent a mass text, alerting us to what's going on. Zoe reaches into her bag to answer hers, but I ignore mine. The main building is a short distance away and I'd much rather see what's going on myself.

"Come on!" I urge Zoe.

She puts her tab away and we jog toward the central quad. Once we reach the heart of the action, we stop to watch a blond reporter interview a scrawny kid whose features are relatively generic—brown floppy hair, brown eyes, medium build—but as soon as I hear him talk into her tab, I recognize him from my tech ed class, although I can't remember his name. He's smiling at the screen, his two idiot buddies behind him doing their best to attract attention to themselves with lewd gestures and silly faces.

"Are you afraid to go to Elusion now?" the reporter asks.

Elusion? Afraid?

I step forward, getting a little closer.

"Me?" He grins as he points his thumbs toward the chest of his down-filled black vest. "No way."

"So you wouldn't hesitate to go there again, even knowing that Anthony Caldwell may have been in Elusion when he lost brain function?"

Zoe leans forward, whispering in my ear, "Anthony is Principal Caldwell's son! He and I went to preschool together, but then he moved away with his mom years ago."

I hold up my hand, motioning for Zoe to be silent.

"Nah," the boy says. "Elusion is awesome. That kid probably just screwed something up."

"Like disabling the safety settings on an Equip?" the reporter asks.

"Wait, you can do that?" he asks with interest.

The reporter turns back toward the camera, as the boys begin shoving one another, desperately trying to stay in the shot.

"Tragedy hits close to home as the students at Hills Sector High attempt to come to grips with the fact that their principal's teenage son, Anthony, was found unconscious in Miami yesterday, and an anonymous source close to the scene says that a possible connection to Elusion is suspected," she says, tucking her hair behind her left ear with a leather gloved hand. "Attempts to contact Orexis and senior product designer Patrick Simmons about whether they believe CIT rushed their approval of Elusion, or whether Equips can be tampered with, have been unsuccessful. But we will continue to bring you breaking news as the story develops."

Zoe looks at me, alarmed. "Does Patrick know about this?"

I don't answer Zoe or tell her that Josh attempted to warn Patrick about this last night. Instead I move toward a reporter in a black vinyl jacket, listening closely as she presses on her earbud, standing in front of the gray cement wall of the building.

She holds her oversize tab in front of her face, saying, "That's right, Owen. An unnamed source is confirming young Caldwell was found with distinct visor marks." I walk behind her, looking at the photo that now fills her tab. I don't get a great look, but I can see it's of Caldwell's forehead, the Equip marks clearly visible.

It's the same picture that was sent to Josh.

"Unfortunately," the reporter says ominously, "we may need to wait until Anthony Caldwell wakes up for definite confirmation on the Equip connection."

Suddenly, Zoe is bathed in a pool of light that casts shadows on her mocha skin.

"And how do you feel about all this, young lady?" says a tall, athletic man in a cashmere overcoat, pointing his tab toward her.

"What?" Zoe asks. I've never seen her exude anything but confidence; however, she wasn't expecting to be ambushed by the media. She nervously takes off her Florapetro glasses as she swallows, looking directly into the screen.

"Are you an E-fiend? Do you want to stay inside Elusion so badly that you'll do anything to make that happen?"

"No" is Zoe's simple reply.

"Ever been invited to an Elusion party in a warehouse?"

"An Elusion *party*?" Zoe asks, confused.

"Does this room look familiar?" The man shows her a picture he has blown up on his oversize tab.

"No, I've never seen this place before," Zoe says.

But the photo looks more than familiar to me.

A dark, barren room with tools scattered across the tops of makeshift worktables, dirty mattresses, and piles of computer hardware fragments. MealFreeze containers, IV bags, and pill bottles litter the floor. The only thing missing from the picture is the number 5020 spray-painted on the wall, but there's still no mistaking it.

It's the warehouse where Josh took me. The "E-fiend" hangout.

The room where he last saw Nora.

Suddenly I know who the unnamed source is, and I'm wondering how long I have before the information on the QuTap is released too.

One thing is certain—I have been played.

Without saying good-bye to Zoe, I'm off and running, and no one can stop me.

The first thing I do once I'm inside Building A is send a message to Josh.

Regan: Where r u? Need to talk ASAP.

No response.

Ignoring the warning bell, I dart toward the south side of the school, where the seniors have a huge block of lockers, my bag weighing me down but not deterring me one bit. I turn the corner and spot him waiting for the elevator less than twenty feet away.

"Josh!" I call out, but he doesn't hear me above the overwhelming chatter of our classmates, who are relentlessly gossiping about Anthony and Mr. Caldwell. He disappears inside an elevator, typing on his tab. Almost simultaneously, my phone buzzes with a message from him.

Josh: Chem lab. Tlk l8r.

He's avoiding me.

What the hell is wrong with him? I thought we were a team, and now I find out he's gone to the media without me? Is this all because of last night? I know there was tension between us right before he left my house, but in light of everything that's going on, how could he be holding that against me? Or has he found out something else that's spurred him to act sooner rather than later? Even if that's the reason, why didn't he at least give me a heads-up first?

I have to talk to Josh *now*, even if it means stalking him through the school. The information on that QuTap was taken from my dad's computer, and whether he likes it or not, it really belongs to me.

As kids begin to clear out of the hall, anxiously hurrying to get inside classrooms before the final bell, I dash to the elevator bank, pressing the up button several times in succession. I groan in frustration, watching the antiquated lights as the elevator slowly ascends, making its way to the eighth floor, where all the science labs are located.

An adjacent elevator opens and I rush inside, happy that no one else follows me in. I press the button marked with the number 8, my palms slick with perspiration and my throat dry. The last bell rings, signaling the beginning of class. I'm officially late to English. Worse yet, it means that the GPS signal on my tab will soon give my location away, and whatever administrator is nearest will happily come and collect me.

I only have a few minutes.

After what seems like an eternity, I reach the eighth floor. I quietly walk down the hall, peering in the window of each classroom to see if Josh is inside, but he isn't there. We're not allowed to have our tabs on during class, but I text him anyway, just in case.

Regan: On 8th floor. What class r u in?

Then I see something odd—the door to the B stairwell closing automatically, as if someone just entered through it.

The B stairwells are to be used only in case of emergency. In fact, I've never even been inside one. I swipe my passcard near the lockpad and the door slides open. Directly opposite me is another door that leads outside to the flat tar roof. It must be left over from before this building was remodeled, because it's heavy steel and still has a handle, which I try turning, but it won't budge.

I'm not about to retreat.

I put all of my weight against the door, pushing with my back and using my quad muscles to provide most of the force. The door nudges open, ever so slightly, allowing me to leverage all my strength to shove it the rest of the way.

That's when I see Josh on the opposite side of the roof.

Talking to Avery Leavenworth.

I can't hear a word of what they're saying, but I don't have to.

Josh is handing Avery the QuTap I used to take data off the quantum computer at Orexis.

"No!" I yell, my voice filled with pure venom.

Josh turns toward me and for a moment our eyes lock. I can't think. I can't feel. But when my gaze shifts toward Avery and she pulls her frizzy red hair back from her face and gives me a smug, self-satisfied smile, my entire body feels like it's been thrown into an inferno.

"Regan Welch!" I hear someone shout.

The deep, booming sound startles me, and I step back clumsily, crashing into a wall of bulk and flab. I turn around and see Mr. Oxbow, the tenth-grade vice principal with the highest rate of issued demerits, standing there frowning at me. I would say that he's angry, but since he always looks really aggravated, it's hard to gauge his feelings.

Even so, there's no way he could be more furious than me.

"Get to class," he says through clenched teeth. *"Now!"*

I look back toward Josh, ready to sell him and Avery out to Mr. Oxbow, but I'm too late.

They have somehow disappeared.

With everything that was important to me.

And perhaps even more.

TabTalk Message

From: Heywood, Joshua

To: Welch, Regan

5:27 p.m.

Don't be mad. I can explain. Call me when you get this.

TabTalk Message

From: Heywood, Joshua

To: Welch, Regan

6:09 p.m.

Sorry. Know I hurt u. But u have 2 hear my side of the story.

TabTalk Message

From: Welch, Meredith

To: Welch, Regan

6:33 p.m.

Are u ok? Just saw the report on Mr. Caldwell's son/
Elusion. Can't believe this is happening. InstaComm me @
work when u get home.

TabTalk Message

From: Heywood, Joshua

To: Welch, Regan

7:14 p.m.

Why aren't u answering? Pls write or call back.

TabTalk Message

From: Heywood, Joshua

To: Welch, Regan

7:29 p.m.

Going to yr place. Hope u r there.

TabTalk Message

From: Simmons, Patrick

To: Welch, Regan

7:52 p.m.

Need to c you. V urgent. Meet me @ office around 9?

TabTalk Message

From: Heywood, Joshua

To: Welch, Regan

8:47 p.m.

The Ice Cave, 10 pm. Code 9017. Pls come.

TWELVE

I'M STANDING IN FRONT OF OREXIS HEAD-quarters during an acid-rain downpour with a brand-new umbrella hovering above me. My socks are beginning to soak through, and the hems of my pants are like wet rags. As a gust of wind blows, I breathe into my O2 shield, clutching the handle of my umbrella with a death grip, my legs glued to the sidewalk.

I'm not the only one outside weathering this flash storm. I'm huddled with a pack of journalists, vloggers, and all sorts of media talking heads, who are waiting to pounce on any high-ranking Orexis official for a comment on today's big news, but they're not having much luck. There's a wall of stiff-postured security guards looming in front of all the entrances to Orexis, preventing anyone from getting too close.

Even though I've been here ten minutes, I haven't yet made my way to the door. Why?

Betrayal. Disappointment. Loneliness. Fear.

These emotions have been hitting me in rapid-fire succession ever since this morning, and I want all of them gone.

But if that's really true, why did I bother coming down here when Patrick said he needed me? I've been thinking about that question since I arrived, and I still can't answer it. Maybe I want to confront him about Anthony. Maybe I want him to comfort me about Josh. Maybe I want to confess about the QuTap before Avery can pillage it and sell me out. Those all seem like perfectly good reasons, but I haven't called to tell Patrick I'm just fifty feet away from his office building.

I can't bring myself to do it.

Another burst of torrential wind blasts me and two or three other people near the back of the horde. Soon the Inner Sector will turn into a red zone. I think back to the calm conditions from this morning. Every day, something happens to remind me how fragile our world is. It can split open over and over and over again, and nothing can prevent that.

My umbrella kicks back hard, leaving my face exposed to the elements. I wipe at my eyes, which are already burning. Once I've gotten the grit out of my lashes, I see a lone figure exiting a side door on the far left of the building—sometimes my dad would use it to beat all the foot traffic. I take a few steps away from the cluster of reporters, moving slowly so I won't arouse suspicion. As I close in, I can see the person is a woman, quite tall and wrapped in some kind of shimmering silver hooded cape, with a rebellious curl of white-blond hair poking out. My gaze shifts down and I recognize a pair of familiar jewel-toned designer shoes. Her steps become more hurried, like she's trying to escape.

"Cathryn?" I say.

Her pace grinds to a halt when she hears her name, and she looks at me with surprise. "Regan? What are you doing out here?" She quickly glances at the media camp, and when she sees they haven't detected her, she takes hold of my free hand and places it against her cheek, gasping when she feels how terribly cold my skin is. "Oh my God, you're going to freeze to death."

"I was . . . waiting f-for Patrick." Now my teeth are chattering. She's right; I just might turn into a human icicle.

"What? I sent him home an hour ago," Cathryn says, her voice sounding a bit hollowed out through the speaker on her O2. "He was being hounded. Calls, texts, everything."

I don't say anything. My mind is kind of anesthetized, and suddenly I'm having trouble reacting.

"Come with me, we'll get you warmed up." Cathryn reaches out and hails an extra-stretch luxury sedan that stealthily pulls up to the curb without its lights on. She puts her arm around me and leads me to the car. A pudgy man in a suit and cap darts out of the driver's-side door and helps us into the back.

I close my umbrella and duck inside, sliding across the

leather seat as Cathryn follows close behind me. Once the door is shut, we take off our O2 shields and she pulls her hood down, revealing a beautiful face that has not one fine line or wrinkle or any other imperfection. It's uncanny how much she and Patrick look alike. Their eyes are these serene pools of aquamarine, and they have the same chins—strong and somewhat narrow, but with this dimple that makes them both look so youthful and innocent.

She pulls off one of her gloves and presses a button on the intercom, which is located on a glass media panel built into a retractable wall adjacent to one of the windows.

"Fiske, could you please take us to the Historic Sector? And call ahead and make sure the private-access tunnels are open. It's still going to be bumper-to-bumper out on the main roads."

A voice crackles back, "Yes, ma'am."

"Are you all right?" Cathryn places her hand on my knee.

I know she's just being nice, but how can she ask me that when flocks of bloodthirsty field correspondents have surrounded Orexis, and negative reports about Elusion are running rampant on every news outlet? She doesn't seem fazed by any of it.

Not that this should catch me too off guard. I've known Patrick's mom for a long time, and she has always been a bit . . . impervious to everything. Except when her son wasn't living up to his potential.

That was the only thing that seemed to strike a nerve.

"Yes, I'm fine," I say, feeling my fingers and toes beginning to thaw.

She unhooks her cape, revealing a very expensive, high-collared silk blouse. "I'm sorry you missed Patrick. He could really use a friend right now."

I want to tell Cathryn that I could use a friend too, but mentioning that seems woefully inappropriate considering I *stole* intellectual property from her company just yesterday.

I clear my throat and ask, "How's he doing?"

"He's a nervous wreck, I'm afraid," she says, sighing. "You know how much I adore Patrick, but the slightest bit of pressure just completely overwhelms him."

It sounds as though she's criticizing him for being upset by what's happened, even though that seems like a pretty normal response, given the circumstances. I'm almost compelled to defend him. Instead, I look out the window at the lights on the curved walls of the narrow tunnel, which are creating a blurry cone of golden yellow and milky white around the sedan.

"I worry he's too much like his father," Cathryn continues, her tone now perfectly clear and pinched. "Ambitious, smart, but not cut out for the high-stakes strategizing and head games of big business."

Head games. That's exactly what Josh played with me. Last night, Patrick insinuated that Josh was acting out some kind of vendetta, and that getting close to me was part of that plan. It seemed like a wild accusation then, but now that I know Josh gave the QuTap to Avery—who literally hates me—and leaked some of the information that we were investigating together, how can I think anything else?

But what about all those messages that Josh sent me? He said he wanted to explain. His sister is still missing—maybe everything he did today was because he's desperate to get her back?

"You're being too hard on him," I say after a few seconds of silence.

Funny thing is, I don't know who I'm talking about.

"You're right," she murmurs.

When I turn back to Cathryn, her shoulders have slouched forward a little and she is wringing her hands in her lap.

Definitely not her usual body language.

"I know I've made mistakes, and he's paid the price for them," she begins.

"Like what?"

"Well, somewhere along the way, I think my pride in him became more important than what was best for him. I let him fast-track school, I let him intern at Orexis, and I let him take over the Elusion project when your father—" She stops herself. "I never said no, Regan. I haven't protected him enough."

"But you only want him to succeed," I say. "You've done whatever you could to make sure he has every opportunity to be what he wants to be."

Deep down, I've always known the truth—together she and my dad did so much more for Patrick than anyone else because he had this unlimited potential. However, I also know something Cathryn may not—that her son can keep secrets from the people he cares most about, and risk hurting people like Anthony Caldwell, Nora Heywood, and perhaps even my father.

She may be the president of Orexis, but in many ways she is merely a figurehead at the company. Cathryn doesn't run the show day-to-day. She might be totally in the dark about Elusion's apparent corruption, and someone we both know could very well want to keep it that way.

So I have to see for myself—without letting on how much I know, or the things I've found, like my dad's passcard. Josh's betrayal has made me so paranoid I can't allow myself to reveal anything.

"Cathryn, are the claims in the news about Elusion true?"

Her eyes snap back to me, the blue irises tinged with fire. Clearly, I've put her on the spot, or offended her. But soon she softens and gently runs a hand down my arm—something that Patrick used to do all the time when I was afraid.

"No, Regan," she says confidently. "Not one word of it."

The sedan takes a sharp turn in the tunnel and I lunge forward, grabbing on to the leather door handle so I don't smack up against the media screen in front of us. Cathryn is oddly unmoved, sitting straight with her legs crossed.

Once I'm tucked back into my seat, I pull the shoulder harnesses across my chest and snap them together. Then I continue on.

"But there seem to be all these pieces of—"

"Evidence?" she interjects. "A lot of the information they have is pure conjecture. And whatever proof they have of Elusion being faulty or harmful reeks of a setup. Do you know how many competitors of ours would love to see Elusion fail?" Every muscle in Cathryn's face seems to tighten as she speaks. "Do you know how many of them would be willing to pay someone off to sabotage our corporation, get our CIT approval revoked, or get us banned from the market altogether? Believe me, the number of hatemongers out there is staggering. We have sources of our own who are hunting for leads. When we find out who is responsible for this shakedown, they're going to wish they hadn't picked this fight."

My head is spinning so fast, I think I'm going to be sick. While I'm sure there are plenty of companies who would love to see Elusion fail, I know two people who share the same motives, and they are apparently working together to make it happen.

Using me to get what they want.

But does it stop there? Is there another, larger conspiracy going on, with the Josh-and-Avery connection being just the tip of the iceberg?

The sedan takes a harsh jolt when we finally come out one of the tunnels and merge onto the main road. It's enough to set me into action mode. I press the eject button on my seat harness, and as soon as it releases me, I lean over and activate the intercom.

"Pull over here, please," I say, my throat suddenly raspy.

My breathing is a little constricted too, but that eases a bit when the car slows to a stop close to a pedestrian bridge.

"Regan, wait—we're only in the Merch Sector," Cathryn says as crinkles of confusion form near her eyes.

Detroit's premier shopping district is still a far distance from home, and my mom is probably worried sick that I haven't InstaCommed her yet. But my mind is made up.

"I know. There's someone here I need to see."

It's a miracle that I'm able to make out the tiny blinking neon sign of an inconspicuous eCafé in the distance. Holding on to my umbrella, I gallop down the metal staircase of the bridge, hoping I don't slip and fall on the wet surface. The storm has lost some of its strength, but visibility is still awful, which is why traffic on the Merch Sector's central eight-lane avenue is so slow.

I block out the bellowing car horns and turn right onto the sidewalk, my sneakers sloshing through puddles filled with reflections of the national chain stores' gleaming lights. The businesses out here are open twenty-four hours because Standard 7 schedules keep many customers away until late at night, so even in this weather I have to dodge crowds of people with enormous shopping bags.

When I finally reach the eCafé's automatic glass door, I close my umbrella and go inside, where droves of motionless customers are sprawled out on couches and oversize love seats, their eyes hidden behind dark Equip visors. There are also a few surly security guards surveying the room from their prospective posts, making sure that no one can take advantage of the patrons.

I take off my O2 and put it into my bag, then pull out my tab, turning it on so I can look up the Elusion code Josh sent me a couple of hours ago. I shut the device off before I left for Orexis—I just wanted to tune out the world at that point—so when the screen lights up, there are some new texts. Two more from Josh, pleading with me to meet him at the Mount Arvon Escape; three anxious ones from Mom, wondering where I am; five from Zoe, gossiping about Anthony; and a single note from Patrick, telling me he went home to his apartment.

I let out a small sigh of relief. If Avery had somehow broken through the encrypted files on the QuTap and released that information (along with my name) to the press, I'd certainly have heard that from Patrick or Zoe by now. So all I have to do is find out why Josh gave it to her in the first place, and how he could do something that treacherous behind my back. The good thing about meeting him in Elusion is that both our defenses will be down—he'll be much more likely to be honest with me, and I won't be too angry to listen to him.

The bad thing is that I might be risking my life.

I try not to think about that as I scroll back to Josh's message and open it. Then I find an empty table and spill the contents of my bag onto it, hoping that I remembered to throw my Equip in my bag this morning, in the off chance Josh and I had to go somewhere private during the day and Escape again.

But the only piece I have is my wristband. I look at my tab—the clock reads 9:48 p.m. My heart skips as I glance around for anyone who might be Reawakening—maybe I could borrow a visor and earbuds from someone. But there's not a single soul here who isn't connected to his or her Equip, temporarily incapacitated. With the guards watching me, there is no way I can wander up to one of them and check out how much time is left on the wristband.

As soon as I sweep all my belongings back into my bag, a girl with long brown hair and a pink puffer jacket strolls out of the bathroom, the wires from her Equip earbuds dangling outside her designer messenger bag.

"Excuse me," I say, stepping in front of the girl, blocking her path.

"What?" she scowls.

I clear my throat, already embarrassed. "I know this may sound a little weird, but . . . can I borrow your Equip for a little while?"

"I'm leaving," the girl replies, attempting to step around me.

"Wait!" I move to the right, cutting her off. "It's kind of an emergency."

"Kind of an emergency?" She sneers. "I've got somewhere to be, so, you know, kind of get out of my way."

"Please!" I open my bag and pull out my passcard. "I'll give you a hundred credits for twenty minutes."

The girl raises an eyebrow, as though she's considering it. She even glances at her watch, which gives me hope.

"I'll do it for three hundred," she demands.

She's totally fleecing me here, and I would try to negotiate more if I wasn't in such a jam. I'm about to agree, when I realize that there's another problem. "I only have two hundred in my account," I blurt out. "But I'll transfer the rest to you as soon as I can."

It's pretty clear that I'm begging, and from the way the girl's lips are puckering, she actually seems disgusted by my desperation.

"You should, like, check yourself into a program or something," the girl snaps as she brushes past me and out the automatic door.

I hang my head low, humiliated.

"You're not an E-fiend, are you?" a voice says from behind me.

I spin around to see a bald middle-aged man standing behind a white Formica counter, wearing a green barista apron. Apparently he saw the whole sorry display.

"I don't think so," I say. But at the moment I'm feeling so desperate to get into Elusion and meet up with Josh, I can't help but wonder: Is this how it feels to be an addict?

"Did you hear? Someone might be in a coma because of that stupid contraption."

"I know. But I really need—"

"A nice cup of hot coffee?" the man says, grinning hopefully.

"I wish that could help." I walk toward him and sit on one of the counter stools.

"You look like you're about to jump out of your skin."

"Someone is there, waiting for me. I need to talk to him."

"Your boyfriend?"

I have no idea what Josh is to me right now, but I find myself nodding before I can make sense of my thoughts.

The man motions over my shoulder toward the back of the room.

"Listen, my coworker just took his break. He left his Equip in the staff room. You could use it for a little while if you wanted," he offers.

It's like the universe is throwing me a lifeline.

"Really?"

"Make it quick, okay?" His voice is warm and kind. "And don't die on me. That would really ruin my shift."

"Thank you so much." I reach into my bag for my passcard so I can credit him, but the man waves me off.

"Don't worry about it," he says. "Just be careful."

THIRTEEN

I DON'T KNOW HOW LONG IT TAKES ME to find the ice cave, but it definitely seems more difficult to do on my own. The rappelling moves slowly because my ExSet isn't at an advanced level like before. I also have to stop a few times and force myself to remember what exactly I'm in search of.

Thankfully, not one bit of frustration registers on my emotional spectrum. My mind and body are like balloons, rising into the frosty air, totally weightless and free. When I see the emerald-green archway that leads to the cavern, a surge of happiness wraps around my waist and chest as I remember the last time I was here.

Josh kissed me.

My head tips upward, shifting my gaze. Above me are

thousands of bright electric-purple stars, twinkling like glittering pinpricks in an ink-black sky. I follow the glow of the deep red moon, which leads me into the cave that still appears to be made of grass-colored ice. As I walk inside, the shadows from the column-shaped stalagmites and shimmering icicles dance around the soft, snow-covered floor, swirling with gorgeous pigments to form an ethereal yet distorted rainbow.

About twenty feet away, I see Josh kneeling in front of the gargantuan ice formation that stretches through the ceiling of the cave. He's wearing a navy parka and heavy, industrial boots. A backpack is securely fastened on his shoulders. His brow is furrowed as he draws something in the dazzling cherry-blossom snow.

From behind a large, gleaming green icicle, I watch him for a bit, each one of his movements deliberate yet graceful. I'm aware that I was angry with him back home, but I'm having trouble recalling why. Then I hear a little voice in my mind telling me the reason is no longer important.

Trust him.

He's your friend.

He cares about you.

So I listen and step closer, looking at what Josh is trying to create in the snow—a makeshift sketch of the firewall. But once I recognize it as the looming frozen structure in front of us, I feel a sharp, squeezing twinge near my temples. Another voice, not reassuring in the slightest, pops that amazing balloon-like feeling, and all that's left is a searing rage that almost knocks me to my knees.

The firewall.

Suddenly, I remember.

My father.

Orexis.

The QuTap.

Principle Caldwell's son.

Avery.

Everything connects in a matrix of gut-wrenching images, and I'm so furious I'm trembling. My head begins to throb with a relentless pressure behind my eyes. I close them tightly and press my fingers against my temples, but it doesn't alleviate the pain. "Regan?" I hear Josh call out, his voice questioning, like he's surprised to see me.

He walks swiftly in my direction, reaching out when I'm close enough to coax into a hug, and I quickly step to the right, dodging him and causing him to stumble. High doses of adrenaline are fueling every one of my nerve endings.

"Stay away from me!" I shout.

Josh doesn't seem as aggravated as I am, but his posture stiffens until he's as unmovable as the ice walls surrounding us. "I told you, I can explain."

"Oh, I can't wait to hear this story," I say. "I bet you and Avery came up with a great excuse for using me as a pawn in whatever scheme you two have going."

"There's no scheme," he says.

"So then why the hell did you give her the QuTap?"

"Because it belongs to her. She gave it to me. So you and I could complete our mission."

My hands ball into fists. He can't possibly be that stupid. *"What?"*

"Her father's a cybersecurity specialist. She has access to the equipment we need to decode the QuTap."

My fists are turning white with anger. I feel like pummeling him into the snow. A drop of moisture falls from the ice-covered ceiling, splattering against my pale, clenched knuckles. "So you went behind my back and asked for help from my worst enemy? Were you just playing me the whole time, so you could get information that would screw my father's old company over?"

"No! That's not what happened!" Josh yells. Apparently his feelings of aggression are now matching mine, fire for fire.

"And what about the photos of the warehouse? Did they just magically appear in the journalists' possession?"

"Look, I had to show those to Avery, too. What she did with them was kind of impulsive, but—"

"Impulsive? Do you have any idea how much trouble she can get Patrick and me in? She despises us!"

Another droplet of melted ice splatters and then another, but I'm so consumed with anger I brush them away without thinking.

"*Us?* Someone is in a hospital, hooked up to machines because of Elusion, and you're still worried about *Patrick?* That's pretty twisted." The expression on his face contorts into fury, and all of a sudden I'm reminded that Josh nearly beat a guy to within an inch of his life. I'm not scared that he will physically hurt me here, but it's another reason to lash out at him.

"Well, what about you?" I scream. "You're just like him! All you've done is lie to me!"

The drops are falling faster now. The temperature feels like it's risen at least twenty degrees since we've started arguing; the snow below our feet is quickly evaporating and creating a thick cloud of blood-colored mist.

"I have never lied to you. *Ever*."

"What about that guy you assaulted? Did you just forget to tell me that he almost died? Or what about Nora's emotional problems? You never said that she might be unstable."

We're eye to eye, nose to nose, on the verge of a real brawl.

"Go to hell!" he breathes, right into my face.

I don't think or feel. I just react. I cock my hand back and then it flies forward in an attempt to slap him. Josh ducks, avoiding the blow. As my hand hits empty air, I lose my balance and stumble toward him, my legs eventually giving way. He catches and steadies me, with one hand on my waist, the other on my shoulder. When our eyes lock, the tension in my muscles unravels almost immediately, and I can feel his body relaxing too.

Slowly, his arms bend and lead me closer to him.

My cheek is lightly pressed against Josh's chest, and I'm still breathing hard as the anger begins to dissipate. The only thing that defused the nuclear-scale fight was seeing the tenderness in Josh's eyes. He is not my enemy.

The droplets are heavier now, and falling so fast it seems to be raining.

"What's happening?" I ask, my breaths shallow and raspy. "I've never felt angry in Elusion before."

Still cradling me in his arms, Josh glances suspiciously at the giant, weeping icicles above.

"The cave is melting," he says.

We hear a loud rumbling, and the ground beneath us shifts, causing a few of the icicles to come toppling down, separating us. The ice shatters when it collides with the ground, sending a flurry of mud-brown debris in every direction. A piece strikes me in the chin, and it stings like a hornet's bite.

"Is this what happened at the beach?" Josh asks as another splinter of the frozen cavern crumbles into dark ash right beside us.

His question brings back every detail of the Thai Beach Escape, and how it seemed to self-destruct right after I saw my dad. There is no question about it. Our seething anger was no coincidence. Nor is the melting, quivering ice cave.

"We need to get out of here," Josh says, grabbing my hand and pulling me away from the firewall.

But I dig in my heels and wrestle away from Josh's grasp. "Wait!" I shout.

The earth begins to shake again, even harder this time. The giant icicles above us clatter, like a chandelier about to snap from the ceiling, as the pillars of stalagmites begin to shudder around us. Josh covers me with his body, acting like a human shield to protect me. "Press your emergency button!" he urges.

I don't want to leave. Not yet.

"Do it, Regan! Now!"

As shards of ice begin to drop from above and the towering stalagmites begin to tumble, my eyes dart around the cave in search of more solid ground. That's when I realize someone else is here, no more than a hundred feet away.

The slim build. The salt-and-pepper hair.

My father.

"Look!" I say, pointing in his direction.

Josh whips his head toward the spot I'm gesturing to. His mouth slips open in astonishment. "Is that . . . ?" he whispers.

"Dad, over here!" I wave my arms up in the air, signaling for him.

But instead of coming toward us, he turns and runs in the direction of the cave's entrance.

"Where is he going?" Josh asks.

Without answering him, I grab Josh's hand and we race after my father, navigating between the icy stalagmites that continue to fall around us. We turn a corner, and there's an earth-shattering crash as a giant icicle in the shape of a large spear breaks off from the ceiling, heading directly toward Josh. I charge at him, knocking him flat on his back and onto the ground, out of harm's way. As the piercing ice fragments continue to fall, Josh flips me around, pinning me underneath him. I attempt to push him off me, but he holds my wrists together with one hand, using his other hand to reach for the emergency button on my wristband.

He's trying to send me home.

But there's no way I'm leaving my dad this time.

"No!" I yell, but he doesn't listen or respond.

I knee him in the inner thigh and he releases me, allowing me to roll out from underneath him. I jump to my feet and Josh follows close behind; we weave around the falling icicles, miraculously making it out of the cave unscathed, and slipping out of the entranceway just as the structure begins to implode. As the earth continues to revolt and shards of ice crystals fly through the air, Josh and I hit the ground, huddling together, waiting for the madness to stop.

Then, all of a sudden, it's silent. The earth is no longer breaking apart. We appear to be safe, at least momentarily. The crystal cave is nothing more than a shredded pile of dark green ice.

"We need to go back *now*," Josh says, his lips taut. "It's too dangerous here. We have no idea what kind of damage this botched Escape is doing to us in real life."

"I'm not leaving. Not until we find where my father went."

I glance up at the night sky. The electric purple stars and the dark red moon are covered with a haze of gray, fuzzy clouds. And that's not all. The pink snow is gone, replaced by a brown sludge. Not a great sign. We may no longer be in immediate danger, but the Escape still seems like it's short-circuiting. Josh is right.

We have to hurry.

I glance up the side of the mountain and tilt my head. Over to the right, about half a mile above us, is a plateau. "If we get to that ledge up there, we'll have a view of the mountainside," I say. "Maybe we can spot him."

Before Josh can protest, I grab the backpack I left outside the ice cave and clutch his hand, yanking him along, our feet tramping through the mud and toward a narrow path. The wind begins to pick up again, barreling over the mountaintop and carrying a rank odor.

We stop directly under the plateau. The side of the mountain is craggy rock. I take off my glove and lightly run my hand over the dark stone. It's wet and slick and covered in some sort of algae-ridden slime. I look at Josh with concern as I replace my glove. "You don't have to do this. I can go alone."

He takes my backpack and opens it, then tosses me a harness. Next he drops the ice tools by our mud-covered feet. "Shut up and climb."

Before I finish closing the last snap of my harness, Josh has already dug his pickax into the side of the mountain. I swing, and when my pickax makes contact, brown grime splatters through the air. I dig my boot in, my arms above me, my hands tightly gripping the pickax.

Tier after tier, we scale what seems like miles. After a few minutes, I hear a grunt and crane my neck and see that Josh has made it to the plateau and is reaching down to help me up over the edge.

Our hands connect and he yanks me toward him, pulling

me up and onto the soggy landing. I push to my feet, hands on my knees as I take a moment to catch my breath.

"You okay?" Josh asks.

"Yeah." I nod, standing up straight as I look around. The plateau is about a hundred feet long and fifty feet wide, surrounded by a grouping of dead spruce trees with rotting branches. I spot one patch of cranberry-colored needles at the bottom of a nearby trunk. I walk over to it and crouch down to pick it up, but before I can, it fades to black and then disappears.

A sickening feeling rises from my stomach into my throat. I stand and yell through my cupped hands, "Dad!" My voice ricochets off the neighboring mountains and echoes into the cavern below us. "Dad, where are you?"

When there's no response, I head toward another group of decaying spruces, and just as I'm about to touch a decrepit limb, the entire tree turns to white and dissolves into nothingness. Then something shatters inside me, and I feel like my lungs are being clawed to shreds.

"Josh?" I whisper, my breath barely coming out of my mouth. I can't leave this Escape before I find my dad. I *won't*. "Things are disappearing!"

"I know," he replies, pointing toward the mountain range in the distance.

The dark horizon is rapidly vanishing before our eyes. It's as if someone is erasing our entire world, starting at the corners and working their way inward.

"I think our destination is being reset," Josh says, stunned.

"It's like when you clear any computer program. Unless it's been saved, everything is destroyed."

"Impossible." I'm gasping for air, my heart sputtering and stalling. I turn around and watch with horror as dying trees disintegrate one after another. With each disappearance, it feels like a hole is being carved into my bones. Even the sky is getting eaten away by this vacuum, which engulfs everything in its path, creating a blank canvas all around us.

I have no idea what all of this means. It seems like every particle in my body is being severed by this bottomless feeling of dread. But are Josh and I in any *real* physical danger? Is this exactly what happened to Anthony before he slipped into a coma?

"Dad, please! Come back!" I scream so hard I'm surprised my voice box doesn't rupture. Josh grabs my hand and squeezes.

My father isn't here. Not anymore.

Nothing is. Nothing but a pure white emptiness that's headed in our direction, threatening to wipe us out.

"Regan, we have to go," he says.

I squeeze his hand back, and he knows I understand. So we let go of each other and press the emergency buttons on our wristbands, surrendering to the all-too-familiar brightness that will carry us back home.

TabTalk Message

From: Heywood, Joshua

To: Welch, Regan

11:14 p.m.

R u okay?

TabTalk Message

From: Welch, Regan

To: Heywood, Joshua

11:20 p.m.

I'm fine. On my way 2 c Patrick.

TabTalk Message

From: Heywood, Joshua

To: Welch, Regan

11:22 p.m.

He won't listen. Not even 2 u.

TabTalk Message

From: Welch, Regan

To: Heywood, Joshua

11:25 p.m.

Yes he will. I won't give him any choice.

TabTalk Message

From: Heywood, Joshua

To: Welch, Regan

11:26 p.m.

Want me 2 come?

TabTalk Message

From: Welch, Regan

To: Heywood, Josh

11:27 p.m.

No. You've done enough damage already.

TabTalk Message

From: Heywood, Joshua

To: Welch, Regan

11:27 p.m.

Guess I deserve that.

TabTalk Message

From: Heywood, Joshua

To: Welch, Regan

11:28 p.m.

Don't u think u should hear me out b4 u cut me loose?

TabTalk Message

From: Welch, Regan

To: Heywood, Josh

11:29 p.m.

Haven't made up my mind. Until then, just let me be.

"Hey, is that David Welch's daughter?" says one of the hundred reporters who are perched outside the entrance of Erebus Tower, a steel hotel and apartment complex so tall it rises above the oil-filled clouds, practically disappearing into the sky.

"No, I don't think so," replies another reporter. "That girl is way too old to be her."

I duck my head and fight my way through the huge mob, which is at least twice the size of the one at Orexis. I pull up the hood of my jacket, thankful my O2 shield seems to be obscuring my identity. In the past few months, the media has left me alone and the sudden attention makes me feel vulnerable. I remember how Patrick was right by my side after my dad died, when the media scrutiny was at its worst, protecting me from all the interrogating questions and judgments. Making sure I was safe.

Now that Patrick himself is the target of the press's latest scandal cycle, there's nothing anyone can do to make these bloodhounds lose his scent. In fact, he can officially count me as one of the angry pack, especially after seeing my dad again and the horrifying vanishing act I just experienced in Elusion. Patrick has a lot to answer for, and tonight he's going to tell me everything.

Or else there are going to be major consequences.

As I continue to push through the throng, I glance up at the building. At almost two hundred stories, it's high enough that glass windows are allowed on the top five floors. Now that it's stopped raining, the peak of the tower appears to glow with a beautiful gauzy light. Only the wealthiest tycoons in the area actually live at Erebus, and Patrick bought one of the units just a few weeks ago.

In a million years, I never would have thought that the first time I came here would be to take my best friend down.

The media have surrounded the building, and there's a huge police presence. Stuck in the middle of the frenzy, I stand on my tiptoes and peek through the crowd enough to see that the officers are wearing protective helmets with built-in O2 shields, as if they're afraid the mob might turn violent. They are hastily trying to construct a small path so that the wealthy clientele of Erebus Tower are able to enter and leave without being mauled.

I have to make it through there somehow.

I tug the strap of my bag away from my shoulder and shimmy it down my arm, which isn't easy, since I'm pressed up against people at every turn. Then I move it to a small space in front of my knees and blindly feel through the stuff inside with my right hand. Once I locate my passcard, I wiggle enough so that I can reach my arm up and wave it around in the air, praying this hunch of mine will work.

"Let me in! I'm a resident!" I shout, hoping that one of the cops will hear me through my O2 speaker and let me through. "Please! I need to get inside!"

Luckily, someone does hear my squawking. A policeman waves a beer-bellied security guard forward, who blows a shrill whistle that makes everyone cover their ears.

"Step aside and let the young lady through!" the guard orders with a rather intimidating, deep voice.

There's a slight shift within the group, and I'm able to slip through tiny gaps here and there until I reach the path the cops are clearing out. Once I manage to make it past them, the guard takes my card and holds it up against his handheld reader. After a short beat, the words *ACCESS GRANTED, PENTHOUSE SUITE 1950AB* appear on the screen, so he nods and says, "You're good."

I breathe a sigh of relief. I was hoping Patrick had given me a courtesy code for his apartment, but I wasn't sure.

As the guard opens the electronic gate with the remote that's built into his code reader, a young, clean-shaven bellman motions for me, his arm outstretched. I grasp on to his gloved hand and he pulls me inside. The backlit onyx ceiling soars above me, casting a glow on the marble pillars that line the room. Even though it's nearly midnight, impeccably dressed hotel guests are still milling about, strolling through the area with colorful cocktails in their hands or reclining on the black and ivory French provincial–style sofas that are arranged around the fireplace.

I take off my O2 shield and wander around the lobby, looking for the right elevator. None of the chatter really registers until I find my way to the private, cordoned-off elevator bank reserved for residents and their guests. I walk into an empty one with a middle-aged couple and I press the button for the top floor.

"It's a shame," the woman says, continuing her conversation. "They found two more of those unidentified comatose kids in Miami."

Two more victims?

My fingers tighten ever so slightly around the strap of my bag.

"And a girl in Detroit, too."

I blink as a chill runs down my spine. *Three* more victims.

"Really? Where?"

"Merch Sector, I think. She had the same circular marks on her head."

I was just in the Merch Sector. Could it have been one of the people who were with me in the café? Did they experience the same thing that happened to Josh and me in Elusion? Did their Escapes erase with them in it? As my stomach free-falls, I keep my eyes glued to the doors, trying not to appear like I'm eavesdropping.

"Do you believe what they're saying? That Elusion is causing this somehow?"

"I don't know. Should we stop using our Equips? Until they figure it all out?"

"Definitely. I enjoyed myself, and the kids certainly like it, but it's not worth the risk."

The elevator doors finally whisk open, and I walk in behind the couple. Once we're inside and we've inserted our passcards into the slot, the doors slide closed and we begin to make our ascent. The couple isn't talking about Elusion anymore—now they are on to more pressing matters, like their son's lackluster grades and their daughter's class trip to Istanbul. When they step out on the 180th floor, I lean back against the elevator wall and close my eyes as I absorb what they said, hoping the solitude will help calm my nerves before I confront Patrick.

More kids in comas. Possibly all Elusion users.

A girl found here in Detroit.

My God, Patrick, what the hell is going on?

A second or two later, I'm on his floor. The walls in the hallway are a rich shade of navy blue, and hanging in a row is a collection of abstract animal paintings, creating a bizarre circus of sorts. As I walk toward Patrick's apartment, I blow out a deep breath and then another, my resolve not wavering an inch.

I take out my passcard and hold it near the lockpad, which releases the automatic interior bolt on the door. When it slides open, I storm into the apartment, calling out Patrick's name, my jaw clenched. But when I make eye contact with the person who is sitting on the couch, I'm so flustered for a minute I think I might have entered the wrong apartment.

"Zoe?" I ask.

She's pulling on one of her knee-high boots, and her cowl-neck knit top is slipping off her shoulder a little. Her long hair is tousled and loose.

Am I interrupting something?

"Regan?" Her eyes widen, not with embarrassment, just surprise. "What are you doing here?"

"I'm sorry. I don't mean to intrude," I say. "I just really need to talk to Patrick, and I couldn't get ahold of him."

"Yeah, he turned off his tab and InstaComm after I came over. There have been all these harassing messages and calls; it's such a mess."

"Where is he?"

"Bedroom," she says, pulling on her other boot and tipping her head to the hallway on her left. "He's getting dressed."

Getting *dressed*? Okay, I'm definitely interrupting something. It looks like when I didn't immediately respond to Patrick's invite, he got in touch with Zoe instead, and one thing led to another. I cross my arms in front of my chest, suddenly uncomfortable talking to her.

How . . . weird.

Zoe stands up and adjusts her shirt, then grabs her purse off the floor. She tucks her hair behind her ears, approaching me with a confident grin that I suppose would belong on any girl who'd just hooked up with one of the most eligible bachelors in the country. She also has this odd sparkle to her eyes, like she's the proud owner of something and wants me to acknowledge that it's hers and hers alone.

"You don't have to leave," I say.

"I'm just running down to the garage. Forgot my tab in my car."

Damn. I doubt Patrick is going to be very forthcoming if he knows Zoe is around. I guess I'm going to have to press him for information very hard and very fast.

"Oh. Okay. I guess I'll see you in a few minutes."

Zoe gives me a playful wink. "Great. Be right back."

When I slip aside so that she can walk past me, she takes a few steps and then I touch her shoulder. "Wait," I say.

"What's wrong?"

"Is it true? Did they find a comatose girl in Detroit?"

Zoe nods her head solemnly. "Yes, satellite radio was broadcasting the news on my drive over here. Kelly Winslow. She's a senior at some ritzy boarding school in the Heights Sector."

I find myself sighing with relief—thank God it's not Nora—but then a snap of guilt pops inside me at the thought of Kelly's family, and Principal Caldwell, having to go through this heartbreak. I think about my father, all my theories regarding his fate. How can I still not have any answers?

Zoe leaves, and for a moment I stand still. I feel like I'm in a stranger's house, somewhere I don't belong. I knew Patrick's old apartment so well, but nothing here looks familiar. The neutral gray tones. The sparse, modern furniture. The big black marble sculpture shaped like a large drop of Florapetro.

"Patrick?" I call out.

Nothing.

I inhale sharply and pull back my tense shoulders as I make my way down the hall. When I approach the sliding door, it slowly recedes. The bedroom is dim, but I can still make out Patrick's silhouette. He's lying on a king-size mattress with his legs planted on the floor, dressed in a pair of soccer shorts and a loose T-shirt. His hands are covering his face, and when I take a few cautious steps forward, his arms fall to his sides and he pushes himself up.

"Now's not a good time, Ree," he says, his eyes red and his throat completely hoarse.

"I know; I just ran into Zoe," I reply. "She went down to the garage to get her tab from her car."

There's a beat of awkward silence between us. Then he sighs, like he isn't thrilled that I knew she was here.

"Well, I'm pretty tired. It's been a long, shitty day and—"

"Listen, Patrick, we need to talk."

He laughs. "Do you have any idea how much talking I've done in the past twelve hours? My voice is almost gone."

"I don't care; this is important."

"What about when *I* wanted to talk earlier? If I remember correctly, you've been ignoring me," he counters.

"I went to Orexis to meet you, but the press had the place surrounded. Ask your mom. She saw me there. You're the one who's playing games."

He stands up and rubs the back of his neck. "I can't do this now. Let's just talk tomorrow, okay?"

"Pat, I'm not leaving here until you tell me why you keep lying to me."

"I'm not lying to you."

I roll my eyes. "Really? That's the best you can do?"

Patrick lets out a disgusted huff and tries to leave the room, but I block his path.

"When I was in Elusion tonight, my Escape practically

disintegrated. Is that what sent Anthony Caldwell and those other kids into a coma?" I say, my voice practically shaking.

"Your Escape disintegrated?" His breath catches hard on each word as he steps away from me, seemingly stunned.

"First it decomposed and then everything around me started to vanish. My emotions were raging, too. Indescribable fear mixed with uncontrollable anger. And I saw my dad again. How can you explain all that?"

"Did you go back in using your old tab?" His face contorts into a tight grimace. "You did, didn't you?"

"This isn't a downloading issue with my tab and you know it," I snap. "There are hundreds of reporters downstairs right now, here to ask you if these kids that are being found are getting hurt because of Elusion—and none of them were using my tab."

A flash of pain crosses his eyes as he drops back down on the edge of his bed.

"You owe me an explanation. If my father were here, he'd demand one, too. Or . . ."

"Or what?" he asks, twisting his head toward me.

"I'll talk to the media. I'll tell them that I've been to the warehouse. That I see visions of my dead father while I'm in Elusion. I'll tell them everything."

"So you'd betray me? Like Josh did with those photos?" Patrick narrows his eyes at me. "I thought you and I . . . After everything we've been through together, I thought we were family."

I recognize his tone of disbelief. I can't believe this is happening to us either. Last week, we meant everything in the world to each other, and now it's like we're becoming enemies.

"I don't want to. I really don't," I murmur. "But I will if I have to."

When he doesn't respond, my lower lip begins to tremble. I can't cave now, but I can't quite let go of our history together. This is so much harder than I thought it would be.

"Please, Pat. Talk to me."

He sniffles and wipes at his nose. "Okay. There are some problems. With Elusion."

The second he makes this admission, the air in the room feels a lot cooler, like someone just broke the thermostat. It's actually kind of soothing.

"Hackers are hijacking the signal between the Equip and the visors so that they can dismantle some of the safety settings and adapt the programming," he continues.

"Just like Josh said."

Patrick grips the mattress hard with his fingers. "Those morons don't comply with the product directions. They do whatever the hell they want, regardless of how dangerous it might be. And then who gets blamed? The manufacturers, the programmers, and everyone else in between! *We're* the ones who get sued and—"

I throw up a hand to put a stop to his oncoming tirade. "How were they able to do it?"

Patrick swallows hard. "I'm not sure, but there's a chance

that the new company that hosts the main server connected to the app cloud isn't carrying out the security protocols correctly, which would make it easier to hack."

I think back to the day I went to Patrick's office with the QuTap. He and Bryce were in the middle of a conversation that I was only half listening to at the time, but now it's all materializing in my head.

"I just found out that the board of directors outsourced it instead of keeping the server here, where it can be controlled and protected with the highest levels of security."

"Why would they want to do that?" I ask.

"Well, safety measures cost a lot of money. I guess when the CIT approval was just pending, they saw this as a way to trim some fat off the budget and—"

"*Are you kidding me?* Orexis is already making a killing, and Elusion hasn't even hit the national market yet!"

Patrick lets out a frustrated growl. "I just need a little more time, Ree. I can fix this!"

"How are you going to do that?"

"I can try to get the board to void the new contract some-how. I'll put together a full report of all of the incidents this month, something really convincing."

"Wait a sec, this *month*? What are you talking about? The only incidents on record have been from the past week."

"Something else happened. A week or two before I heard about Nora," he says, his shoulders hunching forward. "We got this anonymous tip on our customer service site. Someone wrote in to say that the Equip safety function, the one that cuts off the sensors in the visor and the wristband if the levels of serotonin and dopamine are too high, wasn't working. Because the signal between the app and the device had been disrupted."

"So . . . are you saying people could become addicted if they're able to reconfigure the signal?" My heart lodges itself in my chest as I wait for Patrick's response.

"It might be possible. We haven't verified that yet, though."

"Then why did you deny it when Josh confronted you?" I ask.

"Come on, Ree. There's no way I could have said anything. We didn't have a shred of data to support the claims, and all of that information is beyond confidential. I shouldn't even be telling *you* this. Do you have any idea how much trouble I could get in?"

I let out a sarcastic laugh. "Like you're not in trouble right now?"

"You know what I mean."

"No, I don't. I don't get how you can sit there and say you shouldn't be telling me what I have every right to know!" I shout.

"Well, I have responsibilities that you couldn't possibly understand," he yells back, leaping up from his bed and pointing at me. "I feel terrible about this, but I'm not the only one responsible for making the decisions. You don't understand how things work at a corporation. I have to answer to the stupid board, and investors, people who have put all of their money and time into this project. So please spare me the dramatics, okay?"

I'm completely unfazed by his attack on me. Maybe it's because I can hear Cathryn's voice telling me that Patrick is in over his head and isn't meant for the immense stress of big business. Maybe it's because of the way he's biting his lip, like he does when he's feeling guilty about something he's done or said. Or maybe it's because he really is family to me.

The thing is, none of it matters more than the safety of innocent people, and my father's legacy.

"What else is wrong with Elusion? The hijacked signals can't account for the Escapes being unstable. I haven't done anything to dismantle the settings on my Equip or the app," I say.

"This conversation is over," Patrick says, and this time he pushes right past me, practically knocking me over as he leaves the bedroom. I wobble a little but then catch myself on a nearby dresser and follow him out into the hall. There's something bigger going on here. I'm still not getting the whole story.

"And what about my dad? Why am I seeing him in Elusion?"

He doesn't even turn around. He just keeps walking away.

"Answer me, Patrick! Someone spray-painted fifty-twenty on the wall of the warehouse. I know that number means something."

"I want you to leave," he says.

"I know it's dangerous! You need to recall Elusion, and stop the national release. You need to do it before somebody gets killed."

"You don't know anything!" he shouts as I follow close

"Haven't thought that far ahead."

Just as he's about to shut his laptop down, a chirping noise comes out of the speakers. I take a peek as he pulls up his personal message system, but glance away when he catches me in the act. Thankfully, he doesn't tease me about it. Just one look at my flushed neck and he'll notice I'm embarrassed enough as it is.

"You need to see this," I hear him say.

When I shift my eyes back to Josh, his fair complexion has gone a little pale and his mouth is hanging open in shock.

"What's wrong?"

He turns his laptop toward me, and a video clip is pulled up on the screen. It's posted on the New Associated Press site, with the headline "Do You Know This Child?" Josh clicks on the Play button and the news story begins to roll. A young woman with a brunette bob and a microphone headset is standing outside a hospital's emergency-room ambulance bay. She begins:

"This afternoon, police found a comatose boy on the streets of Miami. He was rushed to the hospital, where he is being treated for severe malnourishment and possible head-related trauma."

"Turn it up," I say, dropping my legs to the ground with a thud.

Josh immediately increases the volume.

"The young man had no picture ID or passcard, so he has been admitted as a John Doe. He appears to be fifteen years behind. "None of these stories can be substantiated. Even the doctors don't have conclusive reports."

"I have proof!"

He stops so fast I almost run into him. "What's that supposed to mean?" he asks, turning around to face me.

"It means . . ." I hesitate as I meet his eyes. "I have files from your computer."

He backs away from me as if I slapped him.

"When I came to Orexis to visit you the other day, I copied them onto a QuTap."

"You're not capable of translating quantum files," Patrick says, confused.

I shift my eyes away from him.

"Of course," he says, a coldness in his voice I've never heard before. "Does this have anything to do with your new *friend* Josh?"

I don't respond.

"No one will be able to crack the files on that QuTap," he says. "Your father was the best cryptologist I've ever known, and he's the one who encased them."

"We'll see about that." I move toward the door and it whooshes open, sensing my body movement. Before I can walk out, Patrick's fingers wrap around my bicep and he squeezes, just enough for me to become momentarily frightened of him.

"Do you have any idea what you've done? You stole valuable corporate information. It's a *felony*—you could go to jail for this, Ree."

I look him in the eyes, and when I notice they are beginning to water, my legs buckle. I feel his hand slipping down my arm, his thumb tracing my skin from my elbow to my palm. After what I just told him, Patrick is still concerned about me. And if that's true, shouldn't I still be worried about him, even though he's letting me down in a way I never imagined he could?

But when I stare even deeper into his eyes, I finally see the desire-filled look that Josh told me about in Elusion. It scares me more than the forceful way he took hold of my arm only seconds ago. More than disintegrating Escapes or visions of my dead father.

"You have one day," I murmur.

Then I bolt out the door and don't look back.

FOURTEEN

IT'S NEARLY FOUR A.M., BUT I'M WIDE
awake. The light is on beside my bed, my copy of *Walden* open
on my lap. I've read it from cover to cover at least a dozen times
since I got home from Patrick's apartment a few hours ago,
trying to find something in these pages that would make up for
the fact that, thanks to Josh, Avery has the QuTap and I don't.

My focus is almost obsessive; I'm searching for hidden
meanings in each sentence, hoping that some kind of pattern
will appear. I pull out my tab and start a list of quotes that
seem to connect to each other, or sound like something my
father might say, like *Begin where you are and such as you are,
without aiming mainly to become of more worth, and with kindness aforethought go about doing good.* Or *Things do not change; we
change.*

But one line really jumps out at me every time, though I haven't yet jotted it down:

To be awake is to be alive.

I close the book and reach into my pocket, hoping to find my black stylus there so I can add it to the list, but instead I pull out a wrinkled ball of paper. I smooth it flat against my book, which is now lying in my quilt-covered lap. As my palms press firmly against the paper, ironing out the folded corners and crinkles in the middle, I look at the words that are written on the page over and over and over again in a frantic scrawl.

HATE OUR NEW LAND
HATE OUR NEW LAND
HATE OUR NEW LAND

I remember picking this note up off the floor in the foyer, where Patrick had thrown Josh up against the wall, most likely dislodging it from Josh's back pocket. Then something strange happens. Just as I'm about to fold up the paper, the words kind of blur a bit, so that some letters are sharper than others. Next my gaze shifts to the title, which is at the top of the book cover, along with the author's name.

A gasp escapes from my lips. This can't be.

I lunge over to the nesting table at the left side of my bed, where my stylus is, so I can scribble on the screen of my tab and test out my theory to see if it works, or if I'm just delirious from sleep deprivation.

I write the phrase *Hate Our New Land*, grasping the stylus hard with my fingers, and then begin to rearrange the letters, just like in the word puzzles my dad and I used to play. When I'm through, my heart is racing.

Nora's note is an anagram. The letters also spell out:

Walden Thoreau.

I erase all the letters on the tab and write everything out a second time, to make sure I didn't mess anything up, but there it is, plain as day.

HATE OUR NEW LAND

WALDEN THOREAU

I'm bursting with excitement. All this time I've been looking inside the book for answers, and the words on the cover are what have a hidden meaning. I begin scribbling on my tab—anything and everything that enters my mind.

"Why didn't you call me when you got home?"

As I catch my breath, my mother walks into my bedroom, still dressed in her scrubs, returning from her shift at the hospital.

"What are you doing back so early?" I ask.

She isn't supposed to be home until seven thirty.

"I was worried," she says, folding her hands together, and sighs, as if disappointed. "I tried reaching you on your tab for hours. If I hadn't checked the entry log at the house, I would have called the police. When I call, you answer. Got it?"

It's as if my old mom is back, the one who was in charge and not afraid to give me a little hell for screwing up. But even though it's encouraging, I doubt she's strong enough for the truth. The QuTap is with Avery now, and there's no telling what she might do with it. Everyone saw how quickly Patrick acted when Avery was just making accusations against Orexis. What she did pales in comparison to my dirty deeds. It's only a matter of time before the police are banging at my door.

"Whatever," I say as I scoot up, one hand closing around the paper and the other tucking my tab under my legs. I don't want my mom to see what I'm up to. Ever since I found the Zolpidem, I've been avoiding her. Even though I know my mom wasn't part of some grand cover-up, she did write the prescription. I'm angry that she's always been so trusting. I'm angry that she didn't ask my dad more questions. That she wasn't stronger.

"What's with the attitude?" she asks.

I lean forward and turn around, pretending to fluff my pillows as I shove the paper behind me. "You don't pick up when I call *you*," I say. "You didn't even show up at the appointment to go through Dad's lockbox."

"I see," she says, her brow furrowed with concern. "So that's what this is about? You're angry with me? Trying to teach me a lesson?"

"No," I say abruptly. What am I doing? I don't want to fight with my mom. She just returned to work. I should be encouraging her, not acting like a bratty kid. I tell myself I'm just geared up because of my recent discovery and soften the look in my eyes. "I'm sorry. I just lost track of time."

My mom tugs a clip out of her hair, which uncoils onto her shoulders. She walks over and sits on the edge of my bed. "No," she says. "*I'm* sorry. I know I've let you down lately. You've had to be strong for the both of us. I didn't realize what a burden I was placing on you."

Oh God. Even though she pretty much just summed it up, I suddenly feel a million times worse. "It's not you," I say, trying to backtrack. "This isn't a big deal. Really. I'm just . . . tired."

"Why are you still awake?"

"No reason," I say, with a shrug.

She glances behind me, where a corner of the paper is peeking out. And that's when I know she's on to me. I grab for it, but not fast enough. She whisks Nora's paper out from behind me and stands up. "Is this from your boyfriend?" she asks, waving it in front of me.

"My *boyfriend*? No!"

My mom sighs. "If you don't trust me enough to share this with me . . ."

"Oh. My. God!" Are we really having this conversation? "It's not what you think!" I shout.

Her arm drops and she looks almost hurt. "If you don't want to tell me about him . . ."

"It's not from my boyfriend," I say, exasperated. "There *is* no boyfriend."

She twirls the note in her hands, hesitating.

"Read it," I insist.

She looks at me for a second and then nods, taking her time as she opens the paper, folding out the corners and crinkles. Her eyes cloud with concern as she holds it up for me to see, as if I don't already know what it says.

HATE OUR NEW LAND
HATE OUR NEW LAND
HATE OUR NEW LAND

"Did *you* . . . write this?" she asks, horrified, like her suspicion about me being schizophrenic has been confirmed.

"It's not mine," I say quickly. "A friend's sister wrote this before she went into Elusion—and now no one knows where she is." It's time to tell the truth—at least part of it. "I think it's an anagram. Something to do with Elusion."

"An *anagram*?"

"It's like the word puzzles Dad and I used to play." I pick up my tab and, grasping the stylus hard with my fingers, I rearrange the letters, showing her how I figured it out. "I don't think this is a coincidence." I hold up my tab to demonstrate what I've done. "'Hate Our New Land' spells out 'Walden' and 'Thoreau.' And Josh found this paper at the warehouse where he last saw his sister."

"So . . . ," she says carefully, as she sits back down beside me. She puts the paper on my bedside table as she picks up the copy of *Walden*. "You think your dad left you this book so you could figure out a message from Josh's sister?"

When she says it like that, it sounds crazy. "No. I don't even know if he knew Nora. But I think he left that copy of *Walden* in his lockbox—and that other one in his office—for a reason," I say. "It's a clue. Dad knew I was the only one who could figure this out."

"And what does it have to do with Elusion?"

"I don't know." That's the one piece of the puzzle that remains out of my grasp.

"I see," she says, biting her lower lip. She looks away, embarrassed. "And you came up with this all on your own. This *Josh* didn't have anything to do with it?"

This Josh?

"Patrick told me what's going on," she admits. "He's worried about you."

A stinging burst of cold pummels me right in the back. Of course. Patrick is blaming everything on Josh.

When I left Patrick's apartment, I could've sworn I saw love in his eyes. And I knew then that any transgression I made against him would cause double the hurt and anger. I don't regret stealing the info on the QuTap, but I know too well the power of love and betrayal. The pain over Patrick's deceit has driven my desire to pursue the truth at whatever the cost. And now, apparently, Patrick's returning the favor by getting my mom involved.

"So Patrick called you?"

"No. When I couldn't get ahold of you, I called *him*. I knew that once those stories about Elusion broke, you would've wanted to make sure he was okay," she explains. "We didn't talk long. But he did tell me that you've done something out of character. That this Josh Heywood is a bad influence on you. Patrick told me all about his sister—that she ran away and he's blaming it on Elusion."

The burst of cold gnawing at my back quickly turns into a hot knife digging into my skin.

"I can't believe he . . ." I stop. "What else did he tell you?"

"He begged me to talk with you. And stop you from seeing Josh," she adds.

I roll my eyes and let out a chilling laugh. "He's warning you about me and Josh? That's hilarious."

"Listen to me, Regan. Whatever you and Patrick are fighting about, you should just let it drop for now."

"Oh really? Why?"

"Because Patrick has always been there for you, and he needs you. The company is in real trouble."

"I can't do it," I say.

"Yes, you can," she says. For a moment, I allow my eyes to meet hers, and all I see is sweetness. But then she says, "Besides, your father wants us to stick by Pat, and defend him the best we can."

Wants. Present tense.

"You're wrong," I say as I pull the copy of *Walden* out of her hands. "And this is why," I add, holding the book up as proof. "I've read *Walden* from cover to cover at least a dozen times since I got home from Patrick's apartment." Then I grab my tab and start scrolling through the notes I took. "It's all about self-reliance—going out into the wild and finding our own ways to survive. If anything, the creation of Elusion seems to have led in the opposite direction, to dependency. Patrick has changed Elusion. He's turned it into something that Dad would never have approved of. People are getting hurt. I can't sit by and let this happen."

Her eyes dim. "Patrick was right. You've done something, haven't you? What aren't you telling me?"

I hesitate briefly, wondering if she's strong enough to take what I'm about to reveal, but then I think about all I've done to look after her, like she said a moment ago, and I feel like she owes me that in return, especially now. But the actual magnitude of what I've done doesn't sink in all the way until I'm ready to confess.

So I blurt it out and get it off my chest as fast as I can.

"I broke into Dad's old quantum computer at Orexis. Then I copied a bunch of encrypted files onto a QuTap and stole them."

The stoic look on my mom's face evaporates in a heartbeat or two. In its place is a cloud of shock.

"Oh my God. Regan, that's . . . that's a—"

"Felony? I know."

She stands up and begins to pace, her hands firmly propped on her hips. "Why? Why would you do something . . . extreme like this?" I can hear the disappointment in her voice.

"It's because of this *Josh*, isn't it?" she adds. "Did he make you do this?"

"No! This was my idea." I can no longer hold in the emotions I've been bottling up for days. I blink back the tears forming in my eyes and turn my head in embarrassment as they begin to fall by the hundreds. "I wanted to find out what was wrong with Elusion."

"*Orexis* is responsible for fixing Elusion, not you," she replies, her tone softening a bit. "Your father understands that there are hidden flaws in any invention. Sometimes accidents are unpreventable."

"But they aren't being responsible, and I don't think *this* is an accident." I set *Walden* down on the mattress and spring off the bed, stepping in front of her. "Patrick has been lying to me. Lying to all of us. He denied there were problems with Elusion. That people were addicted. That people could be harmed. But when I began to investigate things, I knew he wasn't telling the truth. So I needed to force his hand. Don't you see? I *had* to do this."

My mom raises a skeptical eyebrow and sets the back of her hand upon my forehead. Then her mouth hangs opens a little bit, her lips forming a circle of worry.

"And what about me, Regan? Do you suspect me as well?"

I run my hands through my hair, like Josh does when he's trying to think straight. It doesn't help, though.

"No, of course not," I say. "It's just that weird things have been happening. When I went to Elusion last week, I saw Dad. He held me and talked to me. It was so real, Mom. He even warned me about Elusion—and then he was somehow snatched away. He disappeared into the firewall."

Mom doesn't say anything in response. She just sits down on the edge of my bed, staring at me, totally stunned.

"Patrick said it was some kind of glitch. That he wasn't really there. I mean—how could he be, unless he was still alive?"

"Regan," my mom says. "You can't think . . ." She stops, her breath catching, as if the mere thought is too incredible to even mention. I take a moment to decide what exactly to tell her. I know I shouldn't give up my one piece of leverage—the passcard—but everything else seems like fair game right now.

"I had to at least look at the possibility. I found the bottle of Zolpidem. You wrote him the prescription."

I wrap my arms around myself, and although I can feel my temperature rising and my head becoming fuzzy, I press on. "I thought, maybe he became addicted to Elusion and staged that crash. And for one awful second, maybe you knew and were helping him."

"Why? Why in the world would I do something like that?" Mom says, choking back her own tears.

"Because you didn't want to tell me the truth—he had a problem. He'd rather be in Elusion than with us."

"Oh, sweetheart," she says, taking my hands in hers and then this alarmed expression flashes across her face. "You're burning up." She places the back of her hand on my forehead again. "How long have you been sick?"

"I'm not sick!"

"You are. You don't even know what you're saying."

My tongue is thick with suspicion right now. It seems like she wants nothing more than to drop this conversation as soon as possible. Which is too bad, because I haven't even told her about the number 5020.

"You don't want to talk about this, do you?"

"You're too feverish to think straight. You need rest."

"Why were you writing him prescriptions for a drug that's strong enough to wake people out of comas? Tell me the truth!"

I didn't expect to go after her like this. And I didn't expect the pain to be so visible on her face when I did. What's happening to me? I can't be sure, but whatever it is, I'm powerless to stop it.

She looks confused for a moment and then nods, letting go of my hands and turning away from me. "That prescription for your father was for chronic insomnia. He wasn't sleeping at all when Elusion was getting ready to be sent before the CIT; he was so worried about what might happen. That his life's work might be rejected." Her voice cracks every now and then, and each time, it's like I'm cut into more pieces. I'm afraid I've pushed her too far, and when she turns around—her face pale, her eyes weary—that fear is more than realized.

"I wrote him the script because when he didn't sleep for a couple of days, he would run a high fever and get some flu-like symptoms," she continues. "Blurry vision, mood swings. Kind of like—"

"How I'm feeling." I bow my head, my shoulders caving in with humiliation. "But why do you talk about him in the present tense sometimes, and keep all his things the way they were?"

"I read somewhere that it helps with grief," she says meekly. "It makes me feel closer to him, to think that his presence is still with us in some way."

I'm so ashamed to have doubted her at all. I'm also strangely hopeful in this moment, like there's a chance she might be wrong about my dad and he's out there, somewhere, in need of my help. Still, when she walks toward me and gently eases me into a hug, I don't feel very deserving of her comfort after what I've just put her through. But then I notice how she's shuddering, and I feel a wetness collecting on the back of my shirt.

"Promise me you'll stay out of Elusion, okay? At least until they figure out what's going on. All these kids in comas . . . it's making me nervous."

I can't bring myself to outright lie and say yes, so instead I nod and squeeze her tight.

God knows how far this encounter might have set her back in her recovery, so I decide not to divulge anything else that might counteract the progress she's made. No more details about Elusion.

My mom needs to be well. I can't ruin that.

She releases me, clearing her throat. "So have you found out why you saw your father in Elusion?"

"No. I hope that information is somewhere on the QuTap," I say. "Someone else is analyzing it now."

She smiles a little bit, sort of like she might be oddly proud of me. "Why don't you lie down, okay? I'm going to make you a little something to relax. Then if you're feeling well enough later, we'll call Clarence Reynolds about all this and see what he has to say."

"Isn't that . . . Dad's lawyer?"

"Yes. I think we should tell him what you did to Patrick's computer. I'm sure he can give us some good advice about what to do next," she says as she stands. "I promise you, Regan, I'll do whatever it takes to protect you."

Just after six thirty p.m., my eyes finally open. I can't believe that I've been asleep for over twelve hours. I guess instead of waking me up for a call to the offices of Gruber, Lewis & Reynolds, my mother decided that it was best if I woke up on my own.

I'm still groggy from the small dose of Zolpidem she gave me from my father's old stash—the powder form dissolves really well in hot water, so she brewed me some spiked herbal tea. I can see why my dad used it for insomnia, because within minutes of the first sip, I was so drowsy I could barely sit upright.

I make my way down to the kitchen and see that Mom has already left for work. There are a few new dirty dishes loaded in the dishwasher, and she left me a note on the clear carbon-fiber counter backsplash:

> *Call me @ hospital if you need anything. We'll talk more tomorrow. Love you.*

My head buzzes as I defrost a peanut butter pocket sandwich. As the seconds tick down on the digital clock of the microwave, my brain begins to recharge, facts and figures blowing up like fireworks.

Patrick has less than a day to recall Elusion.

Avery still has the QuTap. If Patrick calls my bluff, what will I do?

Four lives hang in the balance, with more possibly in danger.

The microwave beeps the moment I remind myself that "Hate Our New Land" spells out "Walden Thoreau." I didn't have the chance to really examine this connection because my mother interrupted me, and now is not an ideal time to make sense of it either, because I'm stuck in an Aftershock-like limbo where my mental faculties aren't very sharp. But I do know that this is another link between Nora and my father. Leading where, though?

I pull my plate out of the microwave and walk over to the living room couch, plopping down on the center cushion and activating the InstaComm wall with the remote. Four video messages are listed—two for my mother and two for me. I highlight the icon with my school photo and then click on it, revealing two screen grabs side by side—the one on the right is of Josh, time-stamped at 4:31 p.m., and the other is of Patrick, time-stamped at 3:02 p.m. I stare at them both, comparing the different contours of their faces, which is totally irrelevant right now, I know, but my thoughts are still fuzzy and hard to control.

With his sparkling blue eyes and chiseled features, Patrick is definitely more classically handsome, someone you'd notice while walking over a pedestrian bridge during rush hour with the hope that he'd bump into you. But there's something about Josh—with his slightly asymmetrical face and the small gap in his teeth and the barely-there hair—that makes it impossible for me to get his image out of my head.

So I click on his message first, knowing in the back of my mind that the logic I just used is particularly skewed, given the dire circumstances.

Josh's image flashes to life when I hit Play and the first thing I think is that the life has been drained from his amber eyes. Suddenly I fear that there's bad news about Nora, or he's about to tell me that Avery plans to annihilate me along with Patrick.

"Hey, Regan. You weren't in school today, so I've . . . been worried about you. I know you don't want to talk, but there's so much I want to say to you."

The sincerity in his voice peels back layer after layer of distrust away from my heart. And I recognize that exhausted look on his face all too well. I want to let him back in, more than anything—for both our sakes. Going through this ordeal alone is just too much to bear. But how can I trust him again, knowing that he turned to Avery? Will there ever be a good enough reason to justify that?

"If you just give me a chance, I can make you understand everything. I know it. Please message me back."

The image freezes on Josh's profile when the message is over, and I can't move my gaze from his lips. They look so sweet and delicate, but I know from experience just how strong and seductive they are. Or at least I thought I knew. Now I'm more than aware of how Elusion is a distortion of reality, and anything felt or seen inside that virtual reality is impossible to trust. Regardless, Josh and I shared something together once, and as the resolution fades on his image, I feel like I should reach out to him, even if it's simply to tell him that I managed to break the code in Nora's note.

But instead of selecting the Contact InstaComm Caller option, I minimize Josh's window and decide to watch Patrick's message. When I click on it, Patrick's image fills the screen, his skin ashen and his brow trickling with sweat. I can tell from the background that he's at his apartment, not at work, which is highly strange for him at three in the afternoon.

"Ree, I need to see you. It's really important. No one can know we're talking and you shouldn't contact me on my tab—I think it's bugged."

I turn up the volume on the screen; his voice is but a jittery, paranoid whisper.

"Meet me in Elusion. I promise, it's safe—this Escape is under construction and not open to the public. Tonight at nine. Special invite code twenty-three hundred and one. You have to come—"

He's about to say something else, but the message is paused when a security alert flashes on the screen in bold red letters—

Visitor Request: Heywood, Josh.

I click on the View Camera One prompt and instantly I have a clear picture of the front of our house. Josh is standing on the porch wearing a black jacket and holding his motorcycle helmet. His back is to the camera, which makes it easier for me to consider clicking on Deny Access—I still haven't made up my mind about him. But then he turns to face the camera, and even with his O2 shield on I notice the tightness in his cheeks, and how the corners of his mouth are sinking. No matter how hard I try to steel myself, my anger begins to unravel and I just can't put him off anymore.

So I select the Allow Access option, and the words "Entry Granted" appear on the screen. I keep Patrick's message paused and reduce the video window so Josh won't see it when he comes through the door. I twist my hair into a low ponytail and smooth back any errant wisps with my fingers. Then I tuck my T-shirt into my capri sweatpants and turn around to greet him.

When Josh walks in the room, he looks worse than he did a few seconds ago on-screen. The veins in his neck seem to be pressing hard against his skin, and his clothes look worn and wrinkled, like he slept in them. I'm so startled by his appearance I forget that we're on the outs, and I walk over to him, reaching for his hand. His palm is damp and clammy, but then he traces his thumb over my wrist, and given my hazy, post-sedative state, that's all it takes for me to come undone.

I can't let that show, though. Not just yet.

"Are you okay?" I ask.

"Not really, but I feel a little better now that you let me in," Josh says with a tired smile.

"You look like hell. No offense," I joke, smiling back.

"Actually, this is what two days of no sleep and twenty cups of pod coffee looks like."

"I know what you mean."

Josh nods at the couch. "Mind if we sit and clear the air?"

"Sure." I let my hand slip out of his, just a fraction of an inch, but he catches it, squeezing a little so I won't let go.

Once we're comfortable on the sofa, positioned opposite each other but close enough that our knees are almost touching, he launches into a speech that sounds like he spent hours preparing.

"Regan, I know you think what I did with the QuTap was pretty shady. And you're right, giving it to Avery without checking with you first wasn't cool," he says, pausing to take a deep breath. "I should have been honest with you from the start."

"Well, you can start now instead," I say.

"I was going to use one of my Ashville contacts to get the QuTap. But when I remembered Avery's father worked for Tech Protect, I knew she could scrounge one up without much trouble."

"But how did you know that? Avery may talk about everyone else's business on her vlog, but she never reveals anything personal."

Josh glances away from me, like he's concerned how I might react to his response.

"I knew because Avery and I . . . are friends," he murmurs.

"You're *friends* with Avery?" I say, stunned. "The Avery who hates my guts Avery?"

He shrugs, embarrassed. "I met her through my sister. She and Nora are pretty close. Have been for a couple years."

I cover my face with my hands for a moment as this admission sinks in. "So I've been ragging on her all week, and you didn't think to tell me this sooner?"

"I'm sorry. I should've. I made a mistake."

"Was it a mistake?" I challenge him. "Or did you know that I wouldn't go to Orexis and steal that information off Patrick's computer if I knew Avery was somehow involved?"

Josh's eyes flick back to me. "Maybe."

I open my mouth to reply, but nothing comes out. I suppose I didn't expect him to own up to that.

"Going to Avery wasn't preplanned or anything. But she wants Nora back just as much as I do. That's why she's been so aggressive about the safety of Elusion since the beginning," he continues. "Her heart is in the right place; she just goes about things the wrong way."

"I want to believe that, Josh. I do. But honestly, Avery can't stand me because she loathes Patrick. How can you trust that she won't keep certain information to herself just to shut me out? Or that she'll leak what we've done to the public or the police? I've come too far for her to ruin everything."

"She promised that when she had a breakthrough with the QuTap, she'd set up a time to meet. She won't screw us over," he says. "Anyway, whatever crimes we've committed, she's an accessory now. Her ass is on the line too."

I hesitate. I think he believes what he's saying—I'm just not sure I can.

"I'm going to earn your trust back, I swear. Just let me show you." A faint sparkle returns to his gorgeous golden-brown eyes when he lowers his hand and gently grazes my arm. "So are we good?"

"I think so," I say, hoping that I'm not making a huge mistake by listening to my heart. "As long as you assure me that you two aren't hatching some kind of diabolical plan together."

"To do what, exactly?"

I contemplate telling Josh about what Cathryn said in her car last night—about setups and corporate spies—but it all seems so ridiculous now, especially since there's another piece of evidence that connects Nora and my father's lives. In fact, I'm kind of wondering if Cathryn maybe wasn't trying to throw me off Patrick's scent . . .

God, if we don't make more headway soon, how many more people am I going to add to this list of possible conspirators?

"Nothing, just forget it."

There's a brief moment where it seems like he's going to lean in and kiss me, but he reclines instead, slouching down so he can rest his head on the back of the sofa. I'm disappointed, but I can't really blame him for missing his cue. He's hanging on by a thread.

"So did you get anywhere with Patrick?"

"Sort of," I say.

Then I replay the whole gruesome scene at Erebus Tower, giving Josh all the details of my showdown with Patrick—what he admitted to, what I accused him of, the ultimatum I gave him, and my shocking confession about the QuTap. When I'm done giving the blow-by-blow, Josh sits there, completely dumbfounded. Actually, after listening to myself tell the story, I'm dumbfounded too.

"Wait, you bluffed Patrick Simmons, boy genius? He thinks we might crack the code."

I nod.

"Wow. Didn't think anyone but Avery could pull that off."

"And there's something else," I say. "Wait here."

I fly up the steps with a surge of adrenaline that floods through me, washing away any last residual effects from the Zolpidem. My mind is clear now, and I start writing a mental checklist of all the things I have to tell Josh about. Nora's note, first and foremost, but also what happened between my mom and me.

Once I get to my room, I grab my tab and zoom back down the stairs, where Josh is still sitting on the couch. I'm so excited to tell him about the anagram discovery that I begin prattling on about it without even noticing that he's staring at the Insta-Comm wall. I explain how I rearranged the letters in "Hate Our New Land" so they spelled out "Walden Thoreau," and bring up the diagram I drew on the tab's screen. When he doesn't react at all, that's when I realize he's not listening to me.

My eyes track his gaze and I see that Patrick's image is pulled up on the InstaComm. But the message isn't paused like before—Josh seems to have listened to the end while I was in my bedroom retrieving my tab. I'm two seconds away from chewing him out for invading my privacy when he picks up the remote and replays the last bit of Patrick's call.

"Tonight at nine. Special invite code twenty-three hundred and one. You have to come.

"I just heard from our lawyers. The news is going to break in a few hours, but I wanted to tell you myself." Patrick looks away from the camera, pausing, but when he glances back up, his eyes are heavy with a sadness I haven't seen since . . .

"Anthony Caldwell is dead," Patrick says, his voice cracking into a million pieces.

Then he leans forward and presses a button on his Insta-Comm wall, and the screen fades to black.

FIFTEEN

"SO WHY DIDN'T YOU TELL HER?" I ASK Josh. "About Anthony, or the anagram?"

He and I are strolling down the old Detroit boardwalk toward a very conspicuous-looking Avery Leavenworth. She's standing in front of the dilapidated Cullen Family Carousel, wearing the same light-enhancing sunglasses that Zoe had on the other day and a long trench coat. Her hair is pulled back into a loose, low ponytail, and her fingernails are painted black. It's almost as though she doesn't want to be recognized.

"Guess I don't want to scare the hell out of her, or give her false hope." He zips his coat up and shoves his hands in the pockets. "Besides, she's tense enough as it is already. She knows how close you are to Patrick and . . ." He shrugs.

"And what?"

"She doesn't trust you," he says, looking embarrassed.

I watch Avery as we approach, her head bobbing to the left and the right, like she's scanning the area, searching for someone or something suspicious. Like someone, namely me, has set her up. But she's wrong. I'm pretty certain there's nothing and no one around for miles, which is why Josh arranged this rendezvous at the carousel. The RiverFront Conservancy protected the landmark as long as they could, until all the small shops closed down and big businesses moved across the water to the Inner Sector.

Now this area is all but deserted and the carousel is in shambles. The rain has stopped temporarily, and though we still need our O2s, the air is clear enough to see that the paint on the wood is peeling everywhere; the mirrors at the top are all broken and shattered; some of the horses are headless or legless—probably the work of teenage vandals rather than decay. It seems very fitting, meeting Avery here. The closer we get to her, the more I feel like we're about to step onto a land mine. When she takes off her shades and her eyes settle on me, her lips break into a scowl.

Clearly, she's feeling the exact same thing.

"What about you?" I ask quietly. "Do you trust me?"

He pauses, taking his hand out of his pocket and pulling me to a stop. "Yes."

His hand slides into mine; the sensation of his palm pressed against my skin is enough to calm my worries about whatever Avery has found.

"Well, well. Aren't you two sickening," she says through her O2 speaker the moment we're in earshot.

"Don't start, Avery," Josh says, edging ahead of me a bit, a protective gesture that doesn't go unnoticed by either me or Avery.

"I'd watch out if I were you," she says snidely to Josh. "Patrick Simmons owns that ass."

"I warned you, Avery. Leave Regan alone. She's on our side." In spite of the fierce look in his eyes, he gives my hand a gentle squeeze.

She blows out a sarcastic laugh. "Yeah, right."

I let go of Josh's hand and step toward her. "I cracked Patrick's computer, didn't I? And I threatened him with the QuTap, too. If that doesn't prove that I want to help find out the truth about Elusion, I don't know what does."

"You did *what?*" Avery huffs, her forehead creased with sheer fury as she turns toward Josh. "If I get arrested for breaking that stupid cease and desist order, or anything else—"

"I didn't tell him that the QuTap was yours," I interrupt. "I just said that he had twenty-four hours to recall Elusion or I was going to the press with top secret information."

"So you bluffed?" Her green eyes cloud over with skepticism. "Without even knowing what kind of data we had?"

"Yeah, I did. And don't act like you don't do that all the time on your vlog. I bet you never even had a source at Orexis telling you anything."

"Don't you get it?" Avery says through gritted teeth. "Now

that you've tipped our hand, Patrick is probably tracking your every damn move so he can get his slimy hands on the QuTap. Do you have any clue how valuable it is?" she says, holding up the dime-size magnet.

I swallow hard and cast my gaze down on Avery's black lace-up boots, realizing that I haven't really thought about what lengths Patrick might go to in order to make sure the QuTap ends up in his possession. Sure, he said that the files could never be decoded, but maybe he was bluffing too?

I guess part of me still sees him as my friend, and that's confused a lot of the boundaries in this twisted little game we're playing. Josh must have considered that, because he didn't intentionally shame me when I told him about my showdown with Patrick.

My head bounces back up when I hear Avery chuckling like a sadistic circus clown. Her eyes flick over to Josh and she says, "What do you see in her? She's as dumb as a pile of rocks."

"Quit wasting time!" he shouts, so loudly I'm afraid his O2 might crack. "Think of those kids in a coma, Avery. They could—"

"Shut up, Josh! Just shut up!" Avery shouts.

I notice the sadness on Avery's face, and it grinds our argument to a startling halt. Suddenly dancing in the dark corners of my mind is an image of Avery at school, playfully hip-checking a girl with a purple pixie cut as they walk through the quad together, laughing and carrying on. Then another recollection follows, and I see Avery with the same girl, holding hands and smiling at each other as they talk in front of the Traxx station near campus.

Not like they're friends, but more like two girls in love.

As Avery's eyes begin to well up with tears, it all makes perfect sense. The source of Avery's anger is not much different from my own. We've both lost the people who matter most to us, people who are completely irreplaceable, and we're doing everything in our power to figure out why.

When the tears break free and streak down her cheeks, the animosity I have for her starts to soften. Josh reaches out and gently rubs her arm, like he's sorry for upsetting her. All this time, he's known Avery is his sister's girlfriend, but kept that detail from me out of respect for Avery's privacy.

After clearing her throat a couple of times, Avery says, "Okay, let me get my tab." Then she puts her sunglasses back on and rifles through her messenger bag. I lean toward Josh and place a comforting hand on his back, as if to subtly, albeit temporarily, surrender to Avery. He turns and winks at me—a sign of appreciation.

"All right, here we go." Avery brings out her tablet and slides her fingers quickly across the screen.

She spins around and lets us glance over her shoulder. Icons zip in every direction, almost making me dizzy. "First of all, you were right about the encryption. It's a beast. Like CIA-grade stuff. I hooked the QuTap up to my dad's best quantum, the one with the strongest analytic software, and it could only bust open a couple of them."

"Shit," Josh says.

"Just wait—the news gets better," Avery adds. "The parse tree you guys found wasn't programming code. That's probably why you were able to decrypt it, and why you didn't recognize it on sight, Josh."

"Then what was it for?" I ask.

"It's actually a very detailed breakdown of a *chemical* substance. Sodium pentothal. Ever heard of it?" Avery presses an icon and a diagram of a molecular structure appears, spinning in circles on an invisible axis so that it can be viewed from all angles. The lines connecting the boxes are lit up in bright indigo and the letters are a deep shade of orange.

"Yes," I reply, so quietly I'm not even sure they hear me. Then I reach over Avery and press a button on the touch screen that allows us to zoom in on the diagram. "It's a fast-acting anesthetic."

Avery raises an eyebrow. "I'm impressed."

"My mom's a nurse."

"What does it do?" Josh asks.

"Sometimes it's administered for C-sections. They used to give it to death-row prisoners, right before executions," I say. "Very powerful stuff."

"So what's the connection with Elusion?" Josh's voice is pinched with impatience.

Avery minimizes the diagram and taps on an icon that transforms itself into a brief corporate memo typed on company letterhead.

"There were a few ancillary files in the QuTap directory that I was able to bust open," she says, her gaze shifting to me. From the strained look in her eyes, I can't tell if she's furious or concerned. Given how unpredictable Avery is, maybe it's both.

"Read it," she says, passing the tab to me and stepping to the side so Josh can take a peek, too.

Confidential Memorandum
To: David Welch, Chief Product Designer
From: Bryce Williams, Senior Programmer
Subject: high responders / trypnosis

Prelim Analysis on v1 Elusion app and Equip have shown that in 8 out of 10 subject groups, adolescent users with highly responsive brain chemistry can be negatively affected by trypnosis due to their fast-growing synapses and sections of the brain that remain unconnected. (See chart 41B)

The result is oftentimes nanopsychosis, a neurological condition that can be transient or lasting, depending on the amount of exposure.

Symptoms can vary from user to user, fluctuate between mild and extreme, and can occur while inside the Escape or post-Aftershock. Inside the Escape, the most common phenomenon is false memories (visions projected from the user's subconscious, consisting of people, places, or things) blending in with the programmed stimuli and what we call an "oasis-effect" (i.e., intoxicating hallucinations associated with the firewall). Behavioral changes have been seen in users after using Elusion as well, which can include impulsivity, obsessive-compulsiveness, and other signs of addiction. (See Index for complete listing.)

Nanopsychosis can also be linked to instability within the Elusion program software, leading to Escape disruptions and emotional confabulation. This is caused when the brain, wrongly coaxed into a "fight or flight" state, essentially overloads the configurations of the system by a sharp increase of the hormone cortisol.

As far as solutions are concerned, early studies have shown that sodium pentothal can both minimize these effects as well as intensify the pleasurable reactions for those who are not high responders.

Possible administration tactics could include topical application to the skin from inside the pressure points within the wristbands, which would be undetectable to users and perhaps even CIT testers. It's inexpensive to procure as well, so it could be easily absorbed as an additional operating expense in our budget.

Please advise.

I nearly drop Avery's tab to the ground. This memo from Bryce and all the damning evidence that's in it was sent not to Patrick, but to my father. For days, I've been thinking my father might be addicted, but this document isn't conjecture—it's proof.

He knew.

My dad knew Elusion could harm people, kids like me. He knew that it could make us see things that were never there, feel things that weren't real, watch in terror as the magical world he created turned to dust, lie to the ones we love. And according to the date of the memo, he knew weeks before Elusion was submitted for CIT approval.

As my feet become anchors, threatening to bring me to my knees, I start to reject everything I just read. I can't believe my dad—the man who wanted to build a life of contributions, who wanted to give the beauty of our natural world back to us—knew that Elusion had the potential to hurt people and pushed ahead with its release. Despite all the clues and theories I've had lately, he wasn't the type of man who would authorize drugging people in order to cover up his mistakes.

"No, this has to be some kind of misunderstanding," I say, hazarding a glance across the water, because I can't look either Josh or Avery in the eyes.

"What's to misunderstand? It's all here in black and white," Avery says, snatching her tab back from me.

"Hold on, let's think about this for a minute," Josh suggests. "So everyone who has shown addiction symptoms, or had hallucinations, are young people, like us, right?"

"Yes, they're all under the age of twenty-one. It totally backs up the information in this report," says Avery.

"Nora and her friends. They've been obsessed with getting behind the firewall. That's why they started hijacking the signal in the first place. To stay in Elusion until they could find a way to do it," Josh says.

I glance back and see Avery nodding her head in agreement.

She says, "And since symptoms of nanopsychosis vary, you and Regan—"

"Experienced something totally different," I murmur, trying to ignore the pain in my chest. "Still, if my dad knew about nanopsychosis . . . he would have pulled the plug on Elusion. Or he would have at least put an age limit or something on it."

"Are you so sure about that?" Avery shoves her tab back in her bag with the force of a pile driver. "Teenagers are a *huge* part of Orexis's consumer market. If we couldn't use their product, then sales would be cut in half."

"Or kids would have just bought it on the black market," Josh adds.

"Which is why they wanted to add that chemical," Avery says. "Probably as a short-term solution to the problem."

"If they did, it looks like it backfired somehow," Josh counters. "Or it wasn't enough to fix things."

"But maybe it did fix it, for a little while at least," I reply.

"What do you mean?" Josh asks.

"Sometimes people build up immunity to medication if they're given it over long periods of time," I say, somehow channeling my mom's knowledge of all things nursing related. "Drug resistance. Maybe the sodium pentothal worked for a while, but then for some kids, the effectiveness—"

"Began to wear off," Avery concludes. "But Orexis was

willing to gamble with people's lives. That's unforgivable."

Scary thing is, she's right.

I don't know what comes over me, but I grab her arm so hard I practically dislodge it from the socket. "Were you able to find a response to this memo? *Anything* that shows what my dad told Bryce to do?"

"No." She yanks her arm away, her eyes piercing right through me. "The encryption algorithms on each of these documents were ridiculous; I was up all night running them through advanced decoding software. I nearly freaked when I extracted this one."

"What if he never read it? What if it just got lost in the data banks?" I'm grasping at anything that will help my case, but Avery is here, waiting to slap me back to reality.

"Yeah, the odds of that happening are about zero."

I take a seat on one of the benches near the carousel, resting my elbows on my thighs and covering my eyes with my hands so I won't burst into tears.

"I just . . . can't believe any of this," I say.

"The facts don't lie," Avery snaps. "Your father knew Elusion was dangerous, and there are thousands of people at risk because of him. Now I have the smoking gun I need to take everyone at Orexis down."

My hands fall to my sides, my face sizzling with frustration and anger—at her accusations, at the memo, even at myself. Just as I'm about to lash out, Josh sits down next to me, puts his arm around my shoulders, and fires away at Avery.

"If it weren't for Regan, you wouldn't have jack shit, so just shut up, okay?"

"Why are you protecting her?" she growls. "Her dad and her bastard boyfriend are responsible *for making Nora sick*. Shouldn't you be, I don't know, telling her to go to hell?"

"I know you're scared," Josh says, calmly. "And when you're scared, you like to bitch. But yelling at Regan isn't going to help us find her. You know that, right?"

"We need to make this public right away," Avery says, steamrolling right over him. "Patrick is probably already at work on a counterattack, now that he knows about the QuTap."

When I hear Patrick's name, my heart begins to pound. The voice inside my head that's been convincing me this is all some kind of grand hoax is now asking questions, like, *What if Patrick discovered the memo and has been trying to protect your dad all along? What if he's going to fix everything that's gone wrong, if you just give him a chance?*

Honestly, I don't know what to believe. I look around me and it's as though this world is breaking into fragments and disappearing, like the Mount Arvon Escape. My eyes are playing tricks on me—I'm almost certain that I see metal rungs peeling away from the base of the carousel and floating up into the night sky, as though the moon were a high-powered magnet.

"Regan?" Josh says, shaking me a little. "Are you okay?"

"Just give me a minute; I'll be fine."

I don't think that's true, but I want it to be.

Josh's arm slips away and I feel a vibration on the bench

underneath my leg. He checks his pants pocket, so it must be his tab.

"Poor baby," Avery says. "Are you worried about your father's reputation? At least he's not alive to see it go up in flames. Oops. Bad choice of words, huh?"

Before I lunge at her, Josh leaps up, waving his tab around like a madman.

"Oh, shit! It's Nora!" he says. "She just sent me a text!"

Avery gasps. "What? Let me see."

Josh hands her his tab and I stand up, craning my neck so I can get a look.

Hate Our New Land, the message says.

"Huh? What does that mean?" Avery asks, scrunching up her nose.

Josh and I share a wary glance. This time we're the ones with a secret. I have to admit, I'd much rather be on this end of it.

"Doesn't matter," he replies. "We just need to track it."

I watch as Josh drags his finger across the screen, opening his GPS. It takes only seconds for the message-sender location to be determined, but Avery and Josh look absolutely frantic, like it's taking years.

And then we have it.

49 Flat Rock Rd. QS

"Oh my God," says Avery.

"She's right outside the trailer," Josh breathes.

"Let's go, then!" Avery says, running in the direction of her car. But when she realizes no one is following her, she turns back around. "What the hell, Josh? Are you coming or not?"

Josh stares at me, the excitement unfurling like pink blossoms on his cheeks. "I have to go."

"You sure you don't have room for one more?" I manage to eke out a smile.

He's found Nora. I need to be happy for him.

"Regan, you don't have to do this. I understand. Things are . . . different now."

"Maybe. But I owe you," I say. "If my father really is responsible for all this, then I want to do everything I can to make it right. Part of that is helping you bring Nora back home."

Avery storms over to us when she sees Josh pulling me in close for a hug. I can tell that she's about to blow up again—there's a vein near her right temple that pulsates when she's reached maximum hostility levels—but Josh thankfully issues a preemptive strike.

"I'm not going anywhere without Regan," he says.

Forty-Five Flat Rock Road is nothing more than a dented mailbox.

The house behind it is simply a pile of rubble. Forty-Seven fared a little better; only half the house is missing, leaving part of its interior visible. Thanks to the rising moon and the relatively clear yet code-yellow night, Josh, Avery, and I can make out some of the upstairs rooms, but the downstairs is shrouded in darkness. Then I see it. Number Forty-Nine: a large blue house.

Although it still seems to have a solid foundation, four of the front windows are shattered and covered with swaths of plastic. There is a gigantic hole in the roof, covered by a black tarp, and from the looks of the sawed-off trees near the side of the house, I figure a heavy branch came crashing down on top of it.

We hurry toward the steps, their iron railings bent into odd spiral formations, folding out in opposite directions. I hear a crackle of thunder echoing in the distance, which is followed by the sound of wet drizzle tapping on our shoulders. As Avery starts frantically ringing the bell and banging on the door, I pull out my umbrella from my bag, open it up, and try to peer in the right-side window, but the plastic is a little too thick and smudged to see through.

"Hello?" I say, turning up the volume on my O2 so my voice can travel over a larger distance.

"Is the lock still working?" Josh asks, moving Avery aside so he can inspect the lockpad.

"Give me your passcard so I can check," Avery barks, holding her hand out at me.

I dig inside my bag, latching on to the card with my fingertips, and give it to her. Once Avery waves the card, a blinking red light appears on the lockpad.

"Yeah, it's functioning." She tosses the passcard to me, and I catch it with my free hand.

Josh nods his head to the left side of the house. "Maybe we could get in through a broken window or something."

"Good idea," I say.

He leads us down the steps and along a narrow, muddy path that winds around the house.

"Okay, here's one," Josh says, and then motions to me. "Can I use your umbrella?"

I hand it over to him and once he closes it, he uses the umbrella to knock away two pieces of jagged glass that are still attached to the window frame, which is about five feet off the ground. Then he hands it back to me and bends over, cupping his hands and weaving his fingers together. "I'll boost you up."

I nod, tossing my umbrella into the bag, and then my bag through the window. I listen to it land and I don't hear any crunching or crashing sounds, so thankfully it doesn't seem like there's anything dangerous on the other side of the wall. I put my foot into the stirrup-like hold Josh has made with his hands and grab on to the windowsill, lifting myself a little bit. Then he hoists me up, very quickly, like I don't weigh more than a puppy. When I'm level with the window, I swing my free leg over, and then the other. Soon I'm inside the house, my fingers coiled tightly around the strap of my bag, ready to use it to beat off an assailant.

"You okay in there?" Josh calls out.

"Yeah, I'm fine."

"Great, I'm sending Avery next."

Oh joy.

I pull my tab out of my bag and initiate its flashlight option, sending a small beam of brightness into the dark room. There's not much furniture or anything else in here—just a stained carpet and the middle piece of a sectional couch with rips in the upholstery. Looters must have cleared this place out not too long after the tornadoes.

I hear a thump behind me and turn to see Avery going from a crouch position to a statuesque pose. She glances around, her eyes heavy with worry, and takes a few steps until she's standing in the middle of the room.

"Nora?" she says loudly. "Are you here?"

But there's no answer.

Josh is the next one through the window, and now that we're all here, we take off our O2s and move forward, heading down a hall with uneven floorboards that leads toward the remains of the kitchen. Crumbled plaster and small pieces of glass litter the once-beautiful mosaic floor like cookie crumbs.

All of a sudden, we hear a noise. A whimper, maybe? Someone else is in this house.

"Avery, you check the front rooms," Josh whispers, reaching for his tab and, taking a cue from me, turning on the flashlight function. "Regan, you stay in the back. I'm going up."

"No, I'll go up," Avery says, pulling out a tiny bottle with a miniature spray trigger. "I've got mace."

"Of course you do," Josh says.

Avery spins around and I watch her gallop down the hall, until she turns a corner on the right. Josh follows, using his tab's light to give him better visibility, but makes a left at the end of the hallway. I listen to Avery climb the stairs, each step creaking as she places her weight on it. The creaking stops, and I know she's reached the top. My heart jackhammers inside my chest as I stand here, alone.

Then I hear another muffled cry. But it isn't coming from upstairs.

I tiptoe over to an open wooden door across from the dining room, which has nothing inside it except for a chandelier that's dangling from the ceiling by one or two electrical cords. I peer down a flight of dark steps and begin to descend, using the light from my tab as a guide.

"Nora?" I say, my voice cracking a little.

I can still hear Avery moving around on the second floor. I reach the bottom and hold up my light. The floor is granite, regulation material in what were once considered flood zones. And when this house was built, Lake Saint Clair would only have been a block away.

I hear a muffled noise.

Holding my tab in front of me, I whip around. A girl with short brown hair is cowering in the corner of the room. She's wearing only a T-shirt and underwear, curled up into the fetal position on a very thin mattress, shivering. She doesn't move. In fact, although her eyes are open, she's staring straight ahead, as if she doesn't even know I'm there.

"Regan!" I hear Josh yell from upstairs.

"Josh!" I scream. "In the basement!"

"I'm coming!" he shouts back. Then I hear him yell up to

the second floor of the house. "Avery! In the cellar!"

I kneel beside the girl, pulling off my coat and wrapping it around her fragile body. She's ice cold and barely conscious. I lean over to see if the girl is attached to an Equip, but all I can see from the light of my tab are deep visor imprint marks on her right cheek near her temple.

Josh bounds down the stairs, his strides wide and frantic.

"Is it her?" he asks with a blend of fear and excitement in his voice. He drops to his knees, as he sees her, the hopefulness in his face evaporating, which could only mean one thing.

She's not Nora.

There's a short, agonizing silence that neither one of us dares to break. Then Avery's voice suddenly shatters the quiet.

"Where is she?"

I look up and see Avery hurrying down the basement steps, so fast she nearly trips.

"Where's Nora?"

"She's not here," Josh says, standing.

"What?" Avery stumbles a bit, as if Josh's words are an actual physical blow.

He tips his head in my direction, and Avery turns to see me holding the girl who, as selfish as it sounds, we all wished was Nora. I watch helplessly as Avery dissolves into tears in front of me, covering her mouth with trembling hands.

"Oh my God" is all she can say, over and over again.

I can't help but feel sorry for her. When I lost my dad in Elusion—or hallucinated losing him, or whatever—I felt the pain of his death all over again.

The girl in my arms quivers, and as she starts to blink and moan, I run my palm across her arm a bit, hoping to wake her, but she doesn't rouse.

"We need to get her to a hospital. *Now*," I say.

Josh begins typing on his tab. "I'll call an ambulance."

"Wait!" Avery shouts at him.

"We can't wait, Avery. This girl is in trouble," he replies.

Avery storms over to me and the girl, crouching down with blazing red-rimmed eyes.

"She knows where Nora is. She needs to tell us."

"I don't think she's in any shape to answer your questions," I say.

"I don't give two craps what you think!" she snarls.

"Leave her alone, Avery," Josh warns.

But Avery doesn't listen. Instead she puts her hand on the girl's shoulder and shakes her. "Where's Nora Heywood? Answer me!"

"Stop it! You're going to hurt her!" I push Avery away with one strong, forceful hand.

"If you don't get out of my way, you're going to regret it," she threatens.

Josh stalks over to the corner and yanks Avery back by the collar of her coat. "I said leave her alone!"

When Avery falls on her butt, she looks up at Josh, her jaw clenched. "I can't believe it. Is she more important than your own sister now?"

"That's enough!" he shouts.

Before I can squeak out a word to either of them, I hear something fall to the floor beneath me. I look down and see a tablet with a neon quilted protective casing, right near the girl's limp hand. Once Avery sees it, she races over and grabs the tab greedily.

"This is Nora's," Avery said, her eyes filling with tears. "She got this from a street vendor in the Merch Sector. She had it engraved. Look!"

When Avery puts it in the palm of Josh's hand, he smiles a little as he runs his fingers over the embossed initials. "You're right—it's Nora's. Even if she was never here, this girl must have come in contact with her at some point."

"Can you turn the tab on? Maybe we can see who else she texted," I say.

Josh presses the power button several times, but no luck. "It's not working."

"That's why we have to get information out of her, before it's too late," Avery says, pointing at the girl.

I look down at her and bite my lip. Her complexion is quickly losing color. "If we don't get her to a doctor, she won't be able to tell anyone anything."

Josh starts pressing numbers on his own tab. "Regan's right; we've got to call for help."

"We'll never get clearance to see her again, especially if the doctors think this is related to Elusion. I'm sure someone at Orexis will see to that," Avery says, her eyes narrowing at me.

Josh ignores her, speaking into his tab. "Yes, we need medical assistance at Forty-Nine Flat Rock Road in the Quartz Sector."

"I'm riding with her in the ambulance," Avery says. "Just in case she comes to."

Then she stalks up the stairs of the cellar, tears soaking her cheeks. I can't blame her for being distraught.

"You . . . need . . . to find . . . me," says a weak, hoarse voice, so faint I can barely hear it over Josh's conversation with emergency dispatch.

"We found you," I reassure her. "Everything's going to be okay." At least I hope she's going to be okay. I feel the girl squirm in my arms a little, and I look down, our eyes meeting only for a brief moment because she can't keep them open for longer than a couple of seconds.

The girl reaches up and takes hold of my hand, very lightly because she's not strong enough to close her fingers.

"You're not . . . safe. No one is safe . . . behind the firewall," she murmurs before succumbing to another wave of all-consuming exhaustion, most likely brought on by nanopsychosis.

At first, I don't even recognize the words she just said to me. But then when I take her wrist, trying to check her pulse, I see something written on the palm of her hand in black ink. It's smudged and in small print, but I can tell it's a number. I hunch over a little more so I can get a closer look, and when I do, my lungs are completely drained of air.

5020.

Suddenly, the girl's voice syncs up with my father's, and they're speaking in unison in my mind.

You need to find me.

Behind the firewall.

Fifteen minutes later, Josh and I stand shoulder to shoulder under my umbrella, staring at swirling red lights as the ambulance carrying Avery and the girl drives off down Quartz Street and eventually turns a corner. The only thing illuminating the road is a blinking streetlamp that's perched a few yards away from the house we just left. Josh kicks a dented aluminum can that's lying near his feet and it bounces along the sidewalk until it collides with the stump of a dead tree.

"Nora was only a few blocks away from Flynn's trailer," he says, rubbing his eyes with the balls of his hands. "We were so close, and now we're back to square one."

"Actually, I don't think we are," I reply.

Josh bows his head and mutters, "Stop it, Regan. She's gone."

"Listen to me. That girl woke up for a minute and said practically the exact same thing my father did when I saw him in Elusion," I say, latching on to his elbow and turning him toward me. "She talked about the firewall. And I saw the number fifty-twenty written on her hand." I let go of his arm and tuck wet strands of hair behind my ears. "We can't give up, Josh. This is just too coincidental to be ignored. There's something in Elusion that we have to figure out, and we keep seeing the same clues. We have to keep pushing forward and believe that we'll find the answers. *Together.*"

"But we're at a dead end," he snaps. "The best chance we had was with the files Avery cracked; we still don't know what the significance of the anagram is, or why that number keeps showing up."

"They lead somewhere. I know they do."

"I want to believe that. I really want to, but—"

"Just trust me, please," I say, locking eyes with him. "I know that might be hard, given what you must think about my dad right now, but I'm telling you . . . these signs are *messages* from him. There's a bigger mystery here that he wants us to uncover, and if we don't keep going, we'll never know what it is. And it might be the key to everything—finding Nora, clearing his name, fixing Elusion. Everything."

Josh takes a small step away from me, gazing at me suspiciously. "So what are you trying to say? You still think your father is alive?"

"No one knows what he said to me that day. Except for you, Patrick, and my mom. How in the world did some girl I've never even met find that out?"

"You're right," he admits. "It's weird."

"It's not weird; it's a clue. Even if you don't think it's coming from my father, we have to see where it leads."

"I know you don't want to give up," he replies. "But have you considered that there's nothing left for us to do but turn that information on the QuTap over to the press and wait? I don't want to let go any more than you do. It just looks like we're out of options."

"No, we're not."

I reach into my bag and pull out my tab, checking the time on the screen.

It's 8:32. I can still make it.

"I'm going to Elusion to talk with Patrick," I say.

Instead of retreating even more, Josh gently puts his arm around my shoulders.

"I don't want you to do that." His voice isn't commanding or harsh. He's just trying to show me that he cares.

I have to admit, his touch feels wonderful.

"I'll be okay, I promise." I slip my tab back into my bag.

"What are you going to say to him?"

"I know he's running scared. Maybe if I confront him about the memo, and tell him that Avery has it, I can convince him to help us to inspect this firewall," I explain.

"Then I should come with you." I look up at him and his breath tickles my eyelashes, and I stop myself from breaking into a smile. "That way if anything happens—"

"I need to do this alone. I know I haven't been able to yet, but I think I'm the only person who can get through to him."

Josh sticks his hand out to his side, and it seems as though he's checking to see if the rain has stopped. Then he grins and takes off his O2 shield, nodding at me like he wants me to do the same. Once I close my umbrella and shove it and my O2 in my bag, he puts his hand around my wrist, turning it inward so he can kiss my palm. His eyes are still golden brown, but if I read them correctly, they're flickering with fear. He takes his other hand and places it on the small of my back, leading me so close to him. His lips press against my forehead, and then again on my right cheek, each time as delicate as a feather tracing against my skin.

And then his mouth is on mine, his hands caressing the nape of my bare neck. A rush of heat burns through my arms and legs as I reach around his strong back and hold him as tightly as I can. His tongue slips between my lips and I tremble, my mind drifting off to a distant place. As Josh pulls away, we lean our foreheads together, sighing. When he kissed me in Elusion, I wasn't sure what it meant, but I did think that nothing could ever compare to how I felt in that ice cave. I was wrong.

This is much, *much* better.

Because it's real. And I know what it means.

"Promise me something," he whispers as I press my cheek against his shoulder.

"Anything."

"Come back to me. As soon as you can."

SIXTEEN

THE FIRST THING PATRICK DOES WHEN HE
sees me in Elusion is throw his arms around me, squeezing so
tightly that I can't really move.

But I want to. More than anything, I want to be moving—
toward the firewall and whatever lies behind it. After seeing 5020 written on that girl's hand and hearing her talk like
my father, I'm convinced that there's yet another layer to this
mind-boggling mystery, and it's all hidden in the borders of the
Escapes.

Perhaps with a final answer to whether or not my father is
dead.

But now it's time for the hard part. Convincing Patrick that
he has to let go of whatever remaining secrets he's keeping,
before any more lives are lost. So far, I haven't been successful

at breaking through the suit of armor he has built for himself over the past week. Then again, from the sound of his quick breathing and the desperate way he's clutching me, maybe he's finally about to come clean.

"Thank you so much for coming," he says. "This is the only place I could think of where we couldn't be followed or monitored."

When Patrick pulls back a little and loosens his grip on me, I get a closer look at him. He's wearing a male version of my current Elusion-provided outfit—a loose, plaid flannel shirt, knee-length cargo shorts, and high-top hiking boots. His blue eyes are weary, and his skin has lost almost all of its natural pigment. Which is very odd, considering how perfect and surreal everything usually looks here.

I manage to wiggle away from Patrick's grasp and begin to glance around the rest of the Escape. We are standing in a field thick with glimmering gold stalks and geometric-shaped bushes filled with succulent berries that glow like fireflies. Above us is a pitch-black sky, with thousands of grasshopper-green numbers, letters, and symbols scattered throughout it like numerical stars.

But that's not the strangest thing about this Escape. I don't feel that euphoric hum filtering through the atmosphere and into my blood. Now that I think about it, I didn't experience that rush of energy when Patrick touched me, or the traditional brain fog either. There's just a small flurry of anticipation in my heart, like someone has injected it with a low dose of adrenaline.

"Pat? Where are we exactly?"

"This is Phase Two of the Prairie Escape," he says, his eyes not leaving my face for a moment, like he's expecting a big reaction from me. "Trypnosis isn't as intense because I'm still constructing the landscape. But it's turning out beautifully, don't you think? I tried to get all the details right."

I feel a lump form in my throat. Patrick knows all too well that I have a thing for prairies. There's a series of children's books that have been passed down through generations of my father's family, and when I was little, I was pretty obsessed with them. I loved reading about pioneer times, and I thought the characters, even the little girl at the heart of the story, were so brave. Patrick listened to me go on and on about these novels for years, and here we are, standing in a field that flawlessly resembles the hand-drawn black-and-white illustrations.

This Escape is obviously some kind of romantic, loving tribute to me, but instead of feeling flattered and appreciated, I just feel uncomfortable. He has done nothing but lie to me since the day I saw the vision of my dad in Elusion. Does he think this is enough to make up for it?

"What is it?" he asks, reaching out to me. "What's wrong?"

Instead of answering, I turn the tables on him, reminding myself that I have to stay on the offensive. "Why did you ask me to come here, Pat?"

When he steps closer to me, a lock of his blond hair falls in front of his eyes. "I wanted you to see that I'm not the monster you think I am. That I care about you more than anything."

"Pat . . . ," I begin. I don't want to discuss our relationship. Not now. Not here.

"I can feel you slipping away from me."

"I don't think you're a monster," I say, even though I'm not sure if I really mean it. But I don't argue with him about me slipping away—it's true. As scary as it is to admit, we might be at the point of no return.

"Well, then you're in the minority. The media is going wild with this story, Ree. Especially now that Anthony . . ." He trails off as his gaze casts down at the ground.

I can't blame him for not wanting to finish that sentence. Nor can I blame myself for what I'm about to say and do.

"I'm afraid it's going to get worse."

Patrick glances back up at me, his lips wrought into a tight line. "Why?"

I take a deep breath. Throwing Avery under the bus isn't something I feel good about doing, but my back is up against the wall.

"Avery has the QuTap."

His mouth hangs open a little and I notice his Adam's apple slowly bobbing up and down, like he's swallowing hard. "Avery? You've been plotting with *Avery*?"

"I didn't have a choice. You stonewalled me, and she was the only one who had the resources to crack the encrypted files," I say coolly. "And she got a few open."

Patrick just stands there, staring at me in the same tortured way I stared at Josh when I saw him handing the QuTap over to Avery. For a minute I feel a tug of sympathy at my heart, but I push it away.

"There was a memo," I continue, listening to the sound of my pulse pounding in my ears. "It was from Bryce to my father, warning about the danger of nanopsychosis. And giving him the idea to put sodium pentothal in the wristband."

Patrick brings his hands up to his face, first pressing down on his cheeks and then pushing them toward the back of his head, like he's trying to relieve the pressure. I've seen that move before. No one else might understand it, but I've known him long enough to translate—it's practically an admission of guilt.

"You know exactly what memo I'm talking about, don't you?" I say. "You've known Elusion could hurt people from the very beginning, just like my father seems to have."

"It's not like that," he says. "Do you really think he or I would have intentionally harmed anyone? Especially *you*?"

"I don't know. Maybe we should ask Principal Caldwell."

He reels back, like I've just shot him in the chest. But when he steadies himself, he levels a nasty glare at me. "You think you have everything all figured out, but you don't."

"That's why you're going tell me, Pat. *Everything*, including what's really behind the firewall," I threaten. "Because if you don't, that memo is going public and there's nothing I can do to stop it."

He shakes his head, like he's ashamed of me, which I find pretty outrageous, all things considered.

"I'm prepared to do whatever needs to be done to make this right," I say.

"You don't think I am? What's happened to us, Ree? Don't you trust me at all anymore?"

"How can I trust you?" I shout, my cheeks flushed with heat. "Your mind has been so corrupted by big business and fame that you can't even see reality!"

"Corrupted?" Patrick narrows his eyes at me. "I didn't find that memo until *after* David died. When I took over his office and started working on his quantum, it was a wreck. The files were completely disorganized, and some were even missing." He's starting to pace now, back and forth, back and forth, like a caged animal. "When I came across the memo, Elusion was already undergoing trials at the CIT. At that point, there wasn't anything I could do without sabotaging the entire project. There was way too much riding on it then, and when we got the approval, I assumed your dad and Bryce had successfully worked out all the kinks."

"So I'm supposed to believe that you never knew what they were up to? You helped my father with *every* aspect of Elusion," I say, as a slight wind blows a golden stalk against my leg.

"You're wrong, Ree," Patrick says, shaking his head. "There were parts of the Elusion creation process that even I wasn't involved in. I'm great with coding and designing the Escapes, but the trypnosis application has never been my specialty."

"Oh really? Then whose is it?"

"Bryce. Your dad chose him personally to run that division."

"So what? As soon as Josh told you about Nora, you had to have known the sodium pentothal wasn't working. You keep coming up with excuses, Pat. Problems with the app being downloaded, signals being hijacked because a new company is hosting the server—you've got an answer for everything. And you haven't done anything about it."

The breeze is turning into a full-blown wind, and I wrap my arms across my chest, trying to fend off the cold. "It's like you're in total denial. You can't bear to admit you might actually be failing."

"I'm not going to fail," Patrick says.

"It's not a crime to fail. But if you keep denying it—"

"I wouldn't lie to you, Ree!" Patrick insists.

"Then prove it," I say. "Take me behind the firewall."

Patrick lets out a sigh, and I can tell he's still holding back. "No," he says simply.

"Why not?" I ask. My heart pushes against my rib cage and I feel a little breathless. "Are you worried I'm going to suffer from nanopsychosis?"

When he spins around, I stare him down, trying to make a connection. But it's like there's barely any life left in his eyes.

"What if . . . you're already sick?" he says, his lower lip trembling a little. "This stuff about the firewall, it's nonsensical. I've told you that already. People are hallucinating things. Maybe even you."

"No, I was just with a girl who stayed too long in Elusion, and she said the exact same things my father told me when

I saw him on that beach," I say defiantly. "If anything, that proves that I'm not hallucinating."

"How?"

"Nanopsychosis can cause hallucinations based on subconscious memories. This girl would have needed to know him in real life in order to dream him in Elusion. And there's no way she could have known what he told me, unless he reached out while she was inside one of the Escapes and told her, too," I say with conviction.

But Patrick is not convinced. "You sound crazy. You know that, right?"

"I don't care what you think. I'm going to find the firewall, Pat. And if you won't go with me, I'll go alone."

"No, you won't," says a voice.

I turn around, and Josh is standing not more than ten feet away from us, wearing jeans and a blue long-sleeved knit shirt. He looks healthy and strong, like he did when I first met him at Patrick's party. "I'm going with you."

As much as I want to throw my arms around him, I know that this is the worst thing that could have possibly happened right now.

"What the hell are you doing here?" Patrick barks at Josh. Then he whips around, his face just inches from mine, his eyes blazing. "Did *you* invite him?"

"Regan didn't have anything to do with it. I stole the code off your InstaComm message and hacked my Equip so I wouldn't need an invite," Josh says to Patrick. Then he takes my hand and pulls me away. "After you left, I really started to worry. I didn't like the idea of you being in here, especially after what we saw."

"I have some bad news for you. I'm afraid Regan's little crush is affecting her mental capacity," Patrick says. "She's not thinking straight."

I feel my face get warm the way it does when I blush, but it only lasts for a second. I'm about to counter his snide remarks when I'm beaten to the punch.

"If there's something wrong with Regan or anyone else, that's on *you*," Josh says.

Patrick doesn't take criticism well, especially from someone like Josh, someone he views as competition. He shoves Josh in the shoulder to break Josh's physical contact with me.

"Ever since you met Regan, you've been trying to drive a wedge between us. You've known her for a week, Josh. *A fucking week!*"

"This has *nothing* to do with Josh. We just want this mess to be over," I say, reaching for Patrick's arm. He moves away, as if he's suddenly disgusted by the thought of me touching him. I've never seen him this upset.

"Fine, you want me to take you to the firewall?" Patrick says, grabbing hold of my wrist and twisting hard. "Then he goes home! *Now!*"

"Get your hands off her!" Josh steps in front of me, squaring off against Patrick, his fists clenched.

Without warning, I hear a crashing sound from above. I

glance up and see dark red clouds spilling across the heavens like pools of thick, clotting blood.

"Or what?" Patrick asks. He lets go of my wrist, carelessly pushing me to the side. I stumble backward a little and almost land on my rear, but I catch myself by grabbing on to an old, dying tree.

That tree wasn't there a few seconds ago.

Or was it?

"You're going to hit me?" Patrick gets right in Josh's face, spittle flying from his mouth. "Bring it on, you bastard."

Another loud crackle temporarily cuts through the tension among us as the clouds begin to herd together and partially block the green numbers that were once flickering in the sky.

"You used Regan to get to me. Admit it!" Patrick shouts, as a small white butterfly flutters in front of me, winding its way through the air in tiny circles and landing right on my collarbone.

I've never seen any live creature before in Elusion, so I'm completely stunned by its presence. I put my fingertips below its legs so it can rest on my hand, and then I bring it up for a closer look. Right away I notice a glint of gold on its wings, and I'm reminded of a line from those children's books I loved.

The butterfly with flecks of gold
Was so beautiful to behold.

Patrick must have remembered. That innocent time when he and I were simply best friends who told each other every-thing. Even now I can see that caring child within him, buried deep below the surface of this troubled young man who can't seem to tell right from wrong.

"I'm not going to fight you, Patrick," Josh says, backing away from him.

I wiggle my fingertips, and instead of flitting away, the butterfly disappears before my eyes.

"Okay, fine," I say to Patrick. "Josh goes home and you take me to the firewall."

Josh looks at me, his eyes registering his surprise. "What are you doing?"

I try to stay focused on Patrick. I can't worry about what Josh is thinking, nor can I let my personal feelings for him affect my actions.

"I have a better idea," Patrick says. "How about we go home together and get that QuTap back from Josh and his little friend Avery before they drag you down with them? If that information is released, I can't prevent Orexis from going after you. And you *will* go to jail, Regan. I don't think your mom needs to be dealing with that right now, do you?"

Bringing up my mom is blatant manipulation. He, of all people, knows how much I'd give to protect her and spare her from suffering more pain. But I can't allow my feelings for her to prevent me from doing what I know is right. And if he thought that mentioning her would make me change my mind, he's sadly mistaken.

Patrick reaches for my arm and I yank it away. "Keep your hands off me!" I shout.

"I'm taking you home, Ree!" This time he succeeds in grabbing my arm and reaches for my wristband.

He wants to send me home just like he did after I saw my dad. There's no way I'm letting him do it again.

"No!" I yell.

Josh rips Patrick's hand away from me, tossing him aside as he steps in between us. Patrick lunges at Josh, but Josh ducks, dodging the blow. Patrick lands face-first on the ground, rolling a few feet over crushed stalks before landing flat on his back.

"Give it up," Josh says to Patrick, his tone hushed and intense. It's obviously taking all of his effort to stay calm. "This needs to stop."

"*I* decide when things stop," Patrick snorts, rushing Josh again and slamming into him, knocking them both over. Josh fights back, pinning down Patrick's arms and incapacitating him.

"Have you thought about what releasing the QuTap will do to Regan?" Patrick shouts as he writhes under Josh. "You don't care what happens to her, do you? You only care about yourself."

The ground rumbles below our feet, and suddenly the prairie begins to morph into a wasteland as the golden stalks multiply, rising upward and transforming into giant black pillars of rock. A piece breaks away and hits me in the back, knocking me down.

Josh jumps up from Patrick and comes to my aide. "Are you okay?" he asks.

"The Escape is being destroyed," I say, clutching his hands as he pulls me to my feet. "It's like what happened on Mount Arvon!" Before he can respond, Patrick hits Josh with a sucker punch from behind. Patrick is about to go at Josh again, but I throw myself at him, grabbing on to him with both hands, holding him away from Josh.

"Are you insane?" I yell to Patrick. "Stop!"

My protest seems to slap him out of his rage, if only for a moment, and he wrestles away from me.

I dash back to Josh, gently cradling his face in my hands.

"So this is the way it is, Ree?" Patrick shouts. "You choose *him*?"

The golden wheat field is almost gone, rotting away before our eyes as if it's being consumed by some terrible disease.

Patrick's eyes are red and filled with such hatred I barely recognize him. "I'm not going to stand in your way, Regan. I just hope you realize what you're doing."

Then he looks away from me, pressing a button on his wristband. And just like that he's gone, vanishing into a large blast of radiant white light.

The quakes from below are becoming more frequent and intense. "We need to get to the firewall," I say, glancing at my wristband. My heart stops when I see that the dial is flashing a red warning that I've never seen before.

TIME EXPIRED

"Something's wrong. My wristband is saying that our time expired."

Josh shoves up his sleeve, looking at his wristband. His jaw drops. "Mine says the same thing," he says.

"This can't be right." I give the face of my wristband a little tap, as if that might help reset it. "We haven't been here longer than an hour—have we?"

"Press your emergency escape, Regan. *Now!*"

I press the button. Nothing happens.

Josh presses the button on his own wristband.

Once.

Twice.

Nothing.

"This Escape is under construction," I say, trying to keep calm. "Maybe the emergency button isn't connected—"

"Or maybe he disabled it," Josh interjects. His voice shakes a little, but I can't tell if he's frightened or furious. I can see sweat glistening on his forehead.

"No, he wouldn't, would he?"

"Could he have done something to your wristband when he grabbed you?"

"If you're right, then maybe the fight with you was just a ruse so he could get to your wristband too. Or maybe he did it by remote, disabling our wristbands somehow?"

But when?

The earth beneath us shifts again, sending us tumbling onto our backs. As I look up, I see that the crimson clouds have all but vanished, but the numbers in the night sky are brighter than when I first got here. They begin to flicker erratically, and then one by one grow crazy bright, each one popping like a lightbulb when it receives too much current.

"What's happening?" I can't hide how freaked out I sound.

Josh swallows, and I can see the fear on his face. "Those numbers look like source codes. I think we're reading what the programmer is logging in."

Right now.

Someone in the real world is typing in a code.

Someone who wants to hurt us.

Someone who wants to cause us pain.

The speed of the exploding numbers gets faster and faster until there are none left and the whole sky goes from ink black to angel white. When Josh and I come up to our knees, there's just a hazy afterglow as all the light fades. For a second, the world around us is cast into total blackness. It's as if I'm suddenly blind, as if Patrick has buried us alive. And then suddenly a sequence of white letters appears in the dark sky above us.

ADMINISTRATOR LOCKOUT.

The letters stay frozen in place, our only source of light.

"This was all a trap," Josh says. "I think he planned this from the start!"

I don't want to believe it, but as I stare at those words, I'm chilled to the core by the truth. I want to scream at the sky, cursing Patrick's name, but suddenly the earth shifts so violently Josh and I are torn apart from each other, flying through the air. I land on my side, my leg scraping against a sharp rock. I feel a stab of pain as deep magenta-colored blood oozes out of a nasty-looking gash.

The pain only gets worse when I remember what my dad assured me, *You can't get hurt in Elusion.*

"Regan!" Josh yells. He's been thrown hundreds of feet away, but he's already picked himself up and is running back toward me.

"You're bleeding," he says.

I push myself up, wiping away the blood that is trickling down my leg. It feels wet against my hand, dripping down onto my arm.

"Does it hurt?"

"It's just a scratch," I say. I attempt to stand, but my leg folds in pain.

Josh grabs me by the waist, steadying me as he eases us back to the ground, his eyes focused on my wounded leg. "It's more than a scratch."

He slips his shirt off over his head. His bare torso is muscular like an athlete's. He holds either side of the shoulder seam and tears, ripping off one sleeve and then the other.

He kneels beside me, wrapping the sleeves of his shirt tightly around my leg. "This should stop the bleeding." He puts what remains of his shirt back on and reaches underneath me as if he's about to carry me.

"I can walk," I insist, pushing him away.

My guilt won't allow me to accept his kindness. I'm the reason Josh is stuck here—I agreed to meet Patrick, and it looks like it was all a big setup.

I was an idiot to have ever believed in him.

There's a loud roar and the ground in front of us explodes as if a bomb has dropped. Clumps of dirt fly through the air, covering us in soot. I gag and attempt to yank the neck of my shirt up to screen my nose and mouth. But it's useless. Dust is everywhere.

A stone's throw away from us, a gigantic mound of gray rock and soil begins to rise up out of the middle of the crater, moving upward. Josh takes my hand and together we scoot backward, faster and faster, watching in awe as the earth continues to shake and reconfigure itself. In only seconds, the rock is looming over us, growing taller and taller as its base continues to spread.

Twenty feet, thirty feet, forty . . . it continues to grow as we move, the hole in the earth widening to accommodate it.

"It's a mountain," I breathe, as it sprouts above us. Unlike the rest of our surroundings, this mountain looks real, brown and gray, like some of the pictures my dad showed me when he was designing Elusion.

The earth gives a final, violent jerk, as if spitting out the painful last remnants, and stops.

At its peak, carved into the block of granite, deep and distinctive, are the same numbers that were written on the girl's hand, the same numbers that were written on the wall of the warehouse and in the sand the night I saw my dad.

5020.

"It's Mount Monadnock," I whisper as the numbers begin

to glow. "It's in New Hampshire—Emerson and Thoreau wrote about it."

Josh comes to his feet, regaining his balance but cautiously, like he's waiting for the ground to move again. When it doesn't, he straightens, staring up at the numbers. "Are you sure?"

"Positive. My dad used to have a picture of this on his tab." I forget all about my injured leg as I push myself up. The number, the mountain that he himself pointed out to me on his tab—is my father trying to send me a message?

"Dad!" I scream out, my voice echoing over the ruined prairie.

As I move toward the mountain, there's another tremor—this time accompanied by a sharp electric current that flashes like the streak of a comet's tail. I stumble forward and collide with Josh, my face against his chest.

I still don't know what those numbers mean, nor do I understand why a mountain that my father loved has suddenly burst into the Escape, but there's only one way to find out.

"We need to get to the firewall," I say.

SEVENTEEN

WE'VE BEEN WALKING FOR WHAT FEELS like miles, but every couple of minutes, I jolt to a stop.

"Did you hear something?" I ask for the trillionth time.

"This?" Josh says, stepping on one of the crumbled stone reeds. "Just me."

A prickle of disappointment crawls up the back of my neck. Ever since I saw that mountain with 5020 etched into the peak, I've been on alert for my dad's tall figure or his dark hair—convinced he might materialize in a fraction of a second. But the only sound we've heard for what feels like hours is the ground crunching underneath our feet as we shuffle through a parched world like the living dead.

No howling wind, no booming thunder—nothing. It's as if the earth has gone to sleep, leaving just the two of us, utterly and completely alone.

Yet I still hope.

I gaze up at the sky. Even though it's barely visible through the haze, we've been using the *A* in the lockout message as a sort of North Star to guide us, assuming the words in the sky are stationary. But if they're not, we're screwed. We could be walking in circles for God knows how long.

"You okay?" he asks.

"Yeah, just checking our bearings. We're still good." I begin to walk, trying to ignore the pain shooting down my leg, but then I stumble a little and Josh reaches out to put his hand on my waist, his fingers dangling there when our eyes meet.

"Maybe we should rest for a couple minutes," he suggests.

"No, I'm fine," I say. "We should keep moving."

"I know, but I can tell you're hurting. We won't be long, promise."

I reluctantly nod in agreement, exhaling like I've been holding my breath for days. "Can I ask you something?"

"Anything," he replies, with a bit of a grin.

"How do I know I don't have nanopsychosis?" I try to hide the worry in my voice but I don't think it's working. "After reading that memo, I can't help but wonder . . ."

"Is this because of what Patrick said before? About you sounding crazy?"

"I guess so." The words my father said on the beach are replaying in my mind, haunting me. "The first time I saw my dad, he told me I wasn't safe, Josh. He stared right at me when he said those words, and I swear, nothing about that felt like a hallucination."

"I believe you, Regan. And you're not sick," he says. "You know, in the mountain Escape, I saw your father too. And I've been thinking about it some more, how he ran *away* from us instead of toward us. It was kind of like he knew we would follow him. Like he wanted us to get as far away from the firewall as possible."

"So what are you saying?"

"If your dad is supposed to be some kind of false memory, or a vision or whatever, then why are his actions so logical? Why does what he said to you here, and what he's done, make so much sense?"

"You don't have to do that, Josh."

"Do what?"

"Humor me."

He pulls me into a warm hug. "Don't you get it? I'm on your side about this."

"Really?" I say, gripping his arms. "You think it could be possible that my dad is actually alive?"

"I do. And the good thing is, if he is, he's not addicted," he adds, stroking my hair gently. "The memo said nanopsychosis only affects kids our age, so the theory that he staged his own death because he was a junkie is out the window, right?"

When I glance up at him, he gives me a grin of encouragement, and it nearly melts me.

But then the words "staged his own death" form some kind of seal in my mind, rinsing over every synapse and generating a focused burst of clear thinking. My eyes snap up toward the sky, and suddenly the words "administrator lockout" have a whole new meaning for me.

"What if my father got locked inside Elusion, like we are now?"

A crease of thoughtfulness appears across his brow. "Maybe. We know Patrick is capable of it. But why?"

I hesitate, trying to piece my thoughts together.

"I don't know. What if Patrick wanted Elusion all to himself? With my dad out of the picture, he became the face of the entire project. And he was able to change the programming in whatever way he wanted, without my dad to step in and say no."

Josh nods. "Patrick has millions of dollars in his bank account. I'm sure he has the means to pay people off and make a plane accident look real."

I know my anger toward Patrick should be festering like a fast-moving infection, but instead of being mad, I almost feel giddy. We finally seem to be closing in on the right answers to all our questions.

"If your dad has been in Elusion since the accident, then how could his body survive? Look at what happened to Anthony, and he wasn't subjected to months of trypnosis," Josh says.

I know Josh is right, but I can't help but hope that my dad has found a way to stay alive. "We need to get past that firewall," I say.

He hesitates and then gives me a quick nod. "Then we better get going; there's no time to waste." He bends down to examine his makeshift bandage. "How's your leg?"

I look at my calf and notice that the bleeding has intensified. The bandage is almost soaked all the way through. When he touches it, I flinch, sensing a sharp yet throbbing pain.

His eyes slide back up toward mine. "It's getting worse, isn't it?"

"I'm okay," I say.

But that's a lie, and Josh knows it. I may not be bleeding in the real world, but apparently my brain is still registering distress.

Who knows what that could mean?

"I want you to promise me something," I whisper to him. "If my leg gets worse and—"

"I'll carry you."

"No. I want you to promise me that you'll leave me behind if you have to. That you'll get to that firewall regardless of what happens."

"Stop. You're going to be fine."

"Promise me," I insist. "Promise me that you will leave me behind if you have to."

He brushes a strand of hair away from my eyes, the corners of his mouth turning up into a smile. "I don't make promises I can't keep."

A crash of thunder sounds, and a noisy, harrowing wind thrashes around us. It only lasts a moment, but it's enough to make my lungs seize up, like they're out of air.

"Looks like Elusion doesn't like your answer," I joke, clutching Josh's hand.

"You're right," he says, the loving gaze I just witnessed gradually disappearing from his face. Now, he looks determined. Focused.

Like he's plotting something.

"You're so beautiful, Ree," he says suddenly, as he cups my chin in his hands, running his thumb over my lips.

There's an earsplitting sonic boom as a bolt of lightning cuts through the fog. Thunderclaps roar in the distance while my heart slams against my chest.

Ree? Josh has never called me that before. It's always been Patrick's nickname for me.

Another brutal gust of wind spirals all around us, covering our bodies in dust and clumps of thick mud. My hair is filthy, with bits of reed hanging from its strands. Josh grips me by my hips, holding me firmly in place so I don't topple over.

He leans into me, nuzzling my ear as he whispers, "Notice how the thunder and lightning happened the moment I called you Ree? I think Patrick's watching us somehow."

I swallow hard, trying to move whatever has suddenly lodged itself in my throat. Can Patrick actually *control* what's happening to us in this Escape? After all, he did design this one with me in mind, so perhaps this is all some kind of twisted game to him?

Josh's fingers are caressing my cheek now, his nose nestled

by my neck, and as good as this feels, I realize that he's not doing it because he's overcome by lust.

He's trying to get me out of here.

"Patrick loves you, Regan," he murmurs. "If you give him even a hint that he has a chance, he'll forgive you. He'll bring you home."

"I'm not leav—"

Josh puts a finger to my lips, quieting me. "I'm going to kiss you. I want you to break away, push me, slap me . . . make it good. Tell me you don't feel the same way. That you love Patrick."

I'm barely able to refuse before he kisses me, but even though I know this is just for effect—that this is not like before, when he really *wanted* to kiss me—I respond in spite of myself, wrapping my arms around his neck and letting my lips press against his. As if on cue, the sky explodes with light as buckets of lime green–tinted letters and numbers melt into liquid and begin to pour down on us.

Josh breaks away and gives me a gentle shake, glaring at me, his face dripping with clover-colored water.

"Regan," he whispers into my ear. "This is your chance!"

I shake my head. "I'm not going anywhere without you," I say, repeating what he told Avery when we were about to leave the carousel.

Josh exhales and his breath almost freezes in the air. The temperature is dropping by the second. Any colder and the emerald rain will turn into snow. I shiver as I look up at the lockout message, but it has totally disappeared.

"We've lost our North Star!" I shout over the next deafening clap of thunder.

"We don't need it!" Josh yells, pointing.

The rain has done something unexpected—it's lifted the fog and allowed us to see the dark, towering wall in the distance.

The stone fortress looms above us, looking like it has been standing in the same dismal patch of land for centuries. Soaked and muddy, we hold our ground in front of it, shielding our eyes from the rain as we scan upward toward the heavens, following the outline of the barrier against the sky, which is going berserk with lightning.

The wind continues to howl in protest as Josh takes a step forward, pressing his hand against the dirty, stained exterior. The wall appears to be made from roughly hewn stone bricks, each about six inches in diameter and length.

"Can we climb it?" I ask, my teeth chattering.

Josh runs his fingers around the edge of the rock, but can't get a grip. "Looks like there's some sort of ledge up there." He takes a running leap and throws his body up at an indentation in the bricks above us. He ricochets off the wall, falling backward into the mud.

He flips himself upward, his hands resting on his hips as he surveys the firewall, thinking. "Ping tunnels," he says, quickly turning toward me, his eyes blazing. "In the computer world, there's this trick hackers use. One server sends an echo signal to a proxy server, and it acts kind of like a trip wire, allowing a user to tunnel through a security network to the side of the program that's been blocked off."

"So it's kind of like locking the door and keeping the front window open?" I ask, rubbing my arms to keep warm. "The entrance to the firewall is a ping tunnel?"

Josh glances back toward the wall. "Maybe."

I scan the brick wall looming in front of me. There's no tunnel in sight. In fact, each brick looks wedged into place, as if it has been there a thousand years. "Why don't we split up and look for it?" I offer. "I'll take the left, you go right."

He wipes the rain away from his eyes with the back of his hand. "We're *not* separating."

After I nod, he runs his hand around the mortar, trailing his fingers over a brick. His torn-up shirt is soaked, clinging to his chest like a second skin. "It's probably not easy to find; otherwise more people would know about it. So look for something unusual. A hidden button. A removable brick. Anything."

Balancing my weight on my strong leg, I move slightly to the left, running my hands over the bricks. They're cold and damp, the insides rough with deep grooves, as if someone chiseled them from blocks of stone by hand. I keep going, my fingers getting covered in soot as I move from brick to brick, trailing my fingers around the edges. If we keep at our current pace, this will take forever.

I touch my fingers to another brick and notice a slight

indentation that feels different from the others. More deliberate. I lean forward, peering at it closely. A letter is etched in the middle of the brick.

"Josh!" I call out.

He rushes over, his boots kicking up wet gunk from the ground.

"Is that what I think it is?" I ask.

"It's an *A*," he says hopefully, pressing his hand against it. "It feels loose." He traces the *A* with his finger, then yanks his hand away. The letter begins to glow, bright blue rays shining out from behind.

"Did it burn you?" I ask.

He shakes his head. "No, just caught me off guard."

"What do you think it means?" I ask.

"I don't know," he says, his eyes searching the bricks around the *A*. "But maybe there are more like this."

We carefully scour the bricks, moving farther and farther away from each other, as we scramble to find another brick that has something unusual on it.

"Regan," Josh says, his voice hoarse from yelling above the rain. I limp over to him. He's standing in front of a brick with a glowing *E* in the middle, like a window into the world beyond.

"You have to trace the letter to get it to glow," he says. I nod and continue searching, working faster and faster as the downpour continues.

I look over my shoulder and see that Josh is standing in front of a glowing *T*.

A, E, T

We look at each other. Even through the rain, I can see his eyes dance with excitement. We both know we're on to something.

Swiping the soggy hair away from my eyes, I focus back on the wall as I continue my search. I'm only a few feet away from Josh when I scrape a piece of particularly stubborn moss off a brick and see some familiar etching. It's the letter *H*. I trace it with my finger and it begins to glow.

The wall groans, and loose pieces of concrete spill down from above. "Watch out!" I warn Josh as I jump back, instinctively covering my head. The wall shudders and heaves as if it's about to bury us in an avalanche of bricks. But instead of collapsing, the bricks in the wall begin to shift, sliding around and changing position until each letter is neatly stacked on top of another, resting against the muddy ground and looking like they've been there for thousands of years. I inhale sharply as I read the word the stacked letters now spell: "HATE."

I think of the piece of paper that Josh found in the warehouse: Nora's note with *Hate Our New Land* scrawled all over, the anagram that translated to *Thoreau* and *Walden*. Did she write it because she saw those words on the wall herself?

"I think this might have something to do with Nora's note," I say, purposely being cryptic in case Patrick is watching us. "It would make sense, with the anagram and all."

Josh's eyes light up, and he gives me a brief nod.

We work in silence for a few more minutes, scrambling to find other bricks with letters. And soon we find an *R* and then an *O*.

The rain pounds against us as the wind continues to howl. We work in tandem, each feeling our way. I scrape off more moss and find an *U*.

Once again, the bricks begin to quiver. There's a deep grinding sound as each brick breaks away and realigns itself like a puzzle, stopping when "OUR" is lined up horizontally, with the *O* on top of the *H* in "HATE."

It's as if we have the top and side to a door. My breath catches in my throat. Is this a way into the firewall? Did my dad make some sort of key with the anagram for Thoreau and Walden? I think so. If I'm right, and we need to spell out the words "Hate Our New Land," we're almost there.

We keep looking. Soon, we have the letters *A*, *W*, *E* and *N*.

The wall begins to shake and Josh and I step back as we witness another reconfiguration. The *A* stays in place, but the *W*, *E*, and *N* begin to move, the wall realigning until *N* is situated next to the *R* from the word "OUR." So far, we've spelled out "Hate Our New," outlining the side and top of what I think will be the door. But how is this going to work? There's only one word left to spell the last part of Nora's sentence: "land." And even if the word "land" drops vertically from the *W* and forms the other side of the door, the bricks in the middle will still be solid.

But I don't let my confusion slow me down. We keep going, more and more frantic as the storm continues to rage around us, the green rain forming deep, cold puddles that drench our feet. Soon we have two more letters: *L* and *N*.

I move farther and farther away from Josh, my arms beginning to ache from stretching and reaching and pushing against the stone bricks. The cold rain turns to sleet and lightning bolts cross the sky, every now and then slamming the ground behind us as if firing a warning shot. But I barely feel the cold or my once-throbbing leg. Adrenaline is heating my limbs and encouraging me on.

I scan the wall, searching. There has to be a *D* hidden here somewhere.

And then I see it. A brick located just below eye level, splattered with mud. I can only make out the top of a straight-edged line, but still I run toward it, scraping off the soggy dirt and the layer of fur and fuzz underneath. I drop to my knees, brushing the bricks clean, or clean enough. There's definitely a *D* under here. "I've got it!" I yell. And then I hear the roar of a train.

"Regan!" Josh yells, as the funnel cloud moves toward me at full speed. "Lay flat on the ground and get as close to the fire-wall as you can!"

Ignoring Josh's warnings, I run my fingers around the rough-hewed edges of the letter. As the *D* begins to glow, the winds hits, plucking me off the ground and throwing me into a whirlwind of debris. Around and around I spin, my body feeling like it's being ripped apart. And suddenly I'm tossed on the ground, spit out of the tornado. But I can't move. The winds are still swirling around me, holding me down. With great effort, I manage to pick my head up and look back toward the wall. I'm relieved to see Josh, on his hands and knees, seemingly unharmed, as he fights to make his way toward me, slowly battling against the wind.

Behind him I see that the word "Land" has aligned vertically, just like I thought.

The letters begin to fade away as the bricks in between them disintegrate, turning an ethereal blue.

"The wall!" I scream.

It's too small for a door. More like a tunnel, or a portal to the other side of the firewall.

I try to move again, but it's as if the tornado is purposely holding me in place. The color of the portal begins to change, its gauzy blue tint turning gray, once again becoming part of the wall.

It's closing. If we're going to go, we need to go *now*.

"Josh—leave me. Go!"

But he doesn't listen.

In an act of what looks to be extreme concentration and strength, he pushes himself to his feet, facing me.

"No!" I shout. I don't want him to come after me. I want him to get into that firewall.

But his eyes never leave mine. He charges toward me, the wind looking like it might pull the skin and muscle right off his bones. He grabs me into his arms before turning around and hurtling us both through the fading blue portal.

We land on a hard, granitelike surface and the door hardens back into a wall. I blink, my eyes adjusting to a strange fluorescent light.

"You okay?" Josh murmurs.

I nod, pushing myself up. I glance at my throbbing leg, trying not to let on how much it's hurting. The dirty bandage is torn, exposing the wound underneath. It has stopped bleeding, but it's oozing some kind of dark, goopy fluid.

As for the rest of me, my clothes are ripped and torn from the tornado and I can see fresh cuts all over my limbs, but I'm surprisingly relieved. At least we're out of the rainy cold and have made it into the tunnel. Except it's nothing like I expected.

We actually seem to be inside a small box. Tiny dazzling blue and green lights fill the walls, giving everything, even us, an ethereal turquoise glow. It's not long before the lights on the far side of the wall blink in succession, and a panel, just large enough to crawl through, opens, revealing a flight of steep steps.

Josh takes my hand and we make our way up the steps. At the top is a tunnel that is round and long and curves as if continuing forever. The same blue and green lights are embedded on the walls and ceiling, covered by a clear protective acrylic. We begin to walk, but the farther we walk, the more it feels like we're going in circles.

The same curved ceiling. The same curved floor. The same curved walls.

"Do you think Patrick can still see us in here?" I whisper. I'm following behind Josh, my hand loosely holding on to the hem of his shirt as he leads us down the narrow tube.

Josh answers my question with a question. "Do you smell something?"

He's right—an acrid scent is filling the air. A thin white cloud floats toward us, as if confirming my fear.

Smoke.

"Come on," he says, grabbing my hand, yanking me forward.

I hobble after him, the temperature and smoke increasing with each turn of the tunnel. I start to cough, my throat scratchy and raw.

"Pull up the collar of your shirt and breathe through it," Josh says.

When I yank my shirt over my nose, I trip over my feet, but luckily I catch myself on the slick sides of the plastic tunnel.

Odd.

Was I able to touch the sides before?

I continue onward, my wrists bending slightly as my arms shake with anxiety. Soon I can feel the top of the tunnel touching my head, and my stomach clenches hard. With each hurried step, the winding tunnel is narrowing and the smoky heat intensifying. I bend down, trying to wrangle my body within the confined space, and before we know it, we're crouching lower and lower until, finally, the tunnel is so small we can't stand anymore.

"On your knees," Josh says, dropping down. "It'll be easier to crawl."

But he's wrong. With my sore leg and all my cuts, it's definitely not easier. I'm wincing and trying to keep my whimpering to myself as I move forward. My eyes burn and my head pounds as the air becomes toxic, the white cloud of smoke practically strangling and blinding us. I can barely make out the lights on the tunnel walls, or even Josh's figure.

"Hold on to me, Regan," Josh pleads through a cough, urging me to move as he tugs me along by the arm. "Do you hear me? Hold on!"

For a moment, it dawns on me that we're going to die in this tunnel.

And then I see it, straight ahead. A sliver of black.

I know Josh sees it too, because he gives me an especially hard tug. "Come on!"

I follow him, blindly making my way through the smoke. The sliver of black is framing a panel at the end of the tunnel. There is no handle, no way of pushing it open. Josh slams his shoulder against it. Once, twice . . . nothing.

I hear a loud boom, and whip around. Before I have time to react, a gigantic fireball turns the corner, a sphere of flickering flames heading right toward us. I turn back toward Josh, but he's gone and so is the door, total darkness filling the empty space where it once was. I hurtle myself forward, plummeting into nothingness as the tunnel explodes behind me.

I fall no more than ten feet, landing in soft marshy ground and tumbling down a barren hill. The back of my head raps against the earth several times as I stretch out my arms, clawing with my hands for anything that might kill my momentum. When I finally roll to stop, I'm so dizzy and nauseated I have to push myself onto my knees so that I can heave. All that comes out is spit and my breath, which is raspy and thin.

I sit back, my eyes blinking rapidly, adjusting to the darkness.

I'm out of the tunnel. Beyond the firewall.

We made it.

"Josh?" I say through a sidesplitting cough.

When I stand up, each muscle in my body cries for mercy.

Where is he? Why isn't he answering me?

"Josh!" I scream.

Silence. Total and utter silence.

The world around me is beginning to come into focus. Above me is a desolate, empty sky, void of moon or stars, but thankfully with a hint of light—enough for me to make out the shadows of ravaged, scorched trees that are scattered throughout the barren landscape around me. There is very little color here: wherever *here* is. The cracked soil beneath my feet is like dried brown clay, and the hill I just fell down appears to be made of ashes and coal. I crane my neck, searching the ink-blotched horizon for Josh.

I fight the panic building in my chest. If he's not here, then where is he? Did he hurt himself trying to force our way out of the tunnel? Is it possible he didn't make it?

I can see the charred remnants of the tunnel at the top of the hill. There are still flames in the doorway, billowing outward like a five-alarm fire in a Florapetro refinery. I have to get back up there, back to the tunnel. I have to find Josh.

I start to walk, but my limp slows me down. My leg is almost numb, and I struggle to climb up the steep incline. With every wobbly step I take up the hill, the enormous planks of blue flames ahead begin to burst and spark, casting fist-size balls of blistering hot embers out into the ebony night. I put my hands over my head to protect myself from the falling, fiery debris and retreat a little from the tunnel's exit, which is completely engulfed by the incandescent blaze.

Then I push forward, again and again. I'm almost there when the tunnel shudders, collapsing on itself as it sinks down into the earth, disintegrating into a pile of black litter. I try to catch my breath. I can still feel the heat blistering my skin, even from a few hundred feet away.

I collapse to my knees, my body shaking and wracked with sobs.

"Josh, where are you?" I scream. "Josh, can you hear me? *Josh!*"

No answer. Nothing.

We made it all this way, and for what?

Josh is gone. The last person I can count on. The one person I trust.

I bend over, placing my hands on the moistureless terrain beneath me, my eyes stinging with tears. And then I hear a voice in the distance. It's not Josh, but it's still familiar. I lift my weary head, slowly pulling myself up to sit down with my legs outstretched, wiping at my eyes as I listen for Josh's voice, or any sign that he's okay.

But there's nothing but a cold, hollow silence.

I tuck my hair behind my ears, waiting, counting in my head—a measly attempt to measure the time here—but the higher the numbers climb, the worse I feel. All I can do is think about Josh and blame myself for whatever happened to him. Why didn't I help him with that door?

I can't remember. It's a blur of pain.

"Regan?" a voice whispers.

The voice is so familiar, female. Mom?

A soft, delicate laughing soon becomes amplified, like an echo deep inside a cavern.

"Where are you, sweetie?"

"Mom?" I say. "Mom, is that you?"

A faint murmur trickles down from above, slowly transforming into a booming voice that practically shakes the sky.

"I'm going to find you!" she says, with a sweet and tender laugh.

My stomach knots as I realize what I'm hearing. My mother's voice is not in the here and now, but coming from a happy memory that I have held on to for a very long time. I'm no more than four years old, and we're playing hide-and-seek. I remember the sheer delight I felt as I heard her footsteps pad across my bedroom floor. How I squealed when she whisked me up in her arms, her eyes beaming as she kissed the top of my forehead.

"I found you, Regan."

I found you.

Other voices begin to rock the darkness, pelting me back in time, like bits of hail, overlapping one another in a fever pitch.

"I'm sorry, Regan. I think you were missing the point on that essay. Maybe if you would just pay attention in class for once . . ."

Mrs. Thackeroy. My English teacher.

"Did you hear? Someone might be in a coma because of that stupid contraption."

The man at the eCafé.

"I have been rooting for you two since you were kids. You are the perfect couple!" says Estelle, Patrick's receptionist.

"I'm not going to stand in your way, Regan," Patrick growls.

The voices of the past merge into a piercing, high-pitched hum, powerful and merciless. I cover my ears and close my eyes, my thoughts turning to Josh and our trek through the tunnel.

But he's gone.

And now I'm trapped here alone, wondering if this barrage of voices is evidence that my brain is deteriorating, one neuron at a time. Or maybe my brain has already ceased to function. Maybe Josh and I never made it to the tunnel; maybe . . . maybe

I'm imagining this whole thing.

The ground rumbles and the earth begins to rupture into gigantic circles, caving in and leaving enormous black holes all around me. An aching, hungry groan rises from below, followed by another and another. I'm seized with a paralyzing panic, but I force myself up. Regardless of what Elusion is doing to my real consciousness, I intend to fight to my last breath.

I hear a hissing sound and pivot on my good leg, turning around to see something ungodly slithering out of the orifice. At least four stories long, it's a fat, slithering monster with no eyes, just a wide chomping mouth full of teeth with two tiny holes above it, like a nose. It raises its head and stops, as if smelling me. I slink back against a tree, like that will somehow provide me with protection. And then I feel something cold grab my ankle, jutting out of the wet, brown earth like a corpse rising from the dead. I try to kick it off, but it's got me in a strong grip.

I scream and then the pressure is gone from my ankle, replaced with a dirty hand over my mouth, quieting me.

"Regan," I hear a familiar voice whisper in my ear, as warm human breath touches my skin.

Josh.

EIGHTEEN

I DON'T HAVE TIME TO BE RELIEVED OR
happy or grateful that Josh is safe. As soon as he removes his
fingers from around my cheeks, a gurgling sound rises up from
inside the hideous beast that's looming in front of us.

"Hold on!" he pleads, taking my hand.

There's a split second when I notice the color of his eyes has
changed completely—from that beautiful, glassy amber that's
always mesmerized me to hollow gray. Then he yanks me by
the arm across the vast stretch of decrepit wasteland, which
spontaneously breaks apart with each of our steps, like we're
setting off hundreds of fireworks from underneath the crumbling soil.

"Where are we going?" I shout, my lungs already burning
although Josh and I just burst into a sprint.

"Anywhere but here!" he yells over another disgusting groan from the slithering worm, grabbing my wrist so that I won't fall too far behind him.

The creature bends its fleshy folds of skin, positioning itself so it can strike us, but Josh's composure isn't shaken as he expertly guides us around gaping craters in the ground and ducks sprays of rocks that are hurtling through the dank, rancid air. I ignore the pain in my leg, leaping up and to the side, keeping in sync with Josh's every sudden yet seemingly calculated move.

I make the mistake of glancing over my shoulder to see if we've gained any distance from this humongous, sickening thing. The creature has stopped and is winding its grotesque figure into a tight coil. I blink and suddenly it's plunging through the atmosphere like a sludge-covered comet.

I stumble back in surprise and my foot catches on something—probably a wide groove in the withering land—and my hand slides out of Josh's grasp, so quick the friction seems to light my palm on fire. And then I'm tumbling down, away from Josh, my body plummeting to the craggy layers of dirt and pebbles beneath me, my chin striking the ground after my knees and arms make impact. I'm lying on the ravine floor far away from Josh, who is still on top of the hill.

Another roar breaks through the night sky, practically shattering my eardrums. I can see Josh scrambling down the hill, but he's too late. The monster is already here, its mouth open wide; its jagged teeth oozing with thick, yellow drool.

There's nothing Josh can do to help me.

"Run!" I shout to him.

Just when I feel and smell the hot, stinking breath of the creature bearing down on me, Josh yells, "Behind you!"

I twist around and see a small rock formation, with a sliver of a space underneath that could protect me.

If I can get there before I'm devoured, I might have a chance.

Josh darts toward me, flailing his arms and doing whatever he can to attract the monster's attention. It works. The monster hesitates, looking away, and I crawl as fast as I can in the direction of the tiny alcove, my fingernails caked with grit and grime, my nose inhaling clouds of dust. I cough and cough but I don't stop scrambling. Just as I slip inside, the beast turns and lunges at me, as if giving one last try before I slip out of its grasp. I tuck my knees to my chest as the tongue of the beast thrashes outward from between its bloody, vein-filled gums. I close my eyes.

But just when I'm certain it's going to devour me, it seems to stop and pause. The air begins to clear and I can sense it moving away.

I open my eyes to see the remainder of a tail disappearing into a hole in the earth that has suddenly appeared no more than a few feet away from me. I let out a ragged breath and then another and another, marveling that I made it out alive. I stretch and push myself out of the alcove a little, and I see Josh coming toward me, mud particles still plastered to his cheeks, a slight smile of relief flashing across his face.

We both stop as we hear another loud, seismic rumbling. My muscles seize up as I prepare to run, expecting another monstrous worm. I look at the shaking rocky alcove right above my head and I know that I'll never make it out in time.

It all happens in an instant. One moment Josh is in my sights, and the next there's a shower of soot, ash, gravel, and rocks, my mind spinning into oblivion, and Josh's voice echoing through a sheet of blackness.

Try as I might, I can't fully open my eyes. The best I can do are these thin slits that allow only a thin stream of light. I feel limp, my arms and legs dangling at their joints, and yet somehow I'm moving. There's a sharp pressure behind my knees and around my shoulders, and my body is bouncing in a rhythmic pattern.

I think I'm being carried.

I focus all my energy on craning my neck upward, with the hopes I'll be able to make out where I am, but there's no use. I feel like a bag of bones. But I take immense comfort in knowing that Josh found a way to save me.

We aren't running anymore. We're walking.

That has to be a good sign, doesn't it?

There are whispers carrying in the air, and my brain is still so foggy I can't make any of the words out. I'm alert enough to notice that it's two low voices—two men, actually, talking to each other.

I attempt to lift my head again, and I'm able to raise it a

few inches. My eyelids peel back a little bit more too, so I can look in the direction of the person holding me in his arms. My vision is blurred, but there's no mistaking the face that's staring back at me.

My chest constricts and I struggle to breathe, even when my father's lips gently graze my forehead, like he used to kiss me before bed when I was a child.

Then a dark tunnel closes in all around me, narrowing and narrowing by the second. I can't do anything else but let myself fade away.

"Wake up, Regan."

It's my father's voice, deep and comforting.

I can feel him stroking the palm of my hand with his fingertips, each invisible line that he traces helping me to come back from wherever I just was to wherever I am. My body feels like it's encased in some kind of aluminum alloy, and I can't really move except for one thing:

I can sort of wiggle my toes.

"Good, good," he says. "Nice and easy now."

"Is this like Aftershock? Is it going to wear off?"

I feel a twitch in my lips when I hear Josh speak, and I can breathe a little, my ribs giving way so my chest rises and falls without feeling like someone just put me in a straitjacket.

"Yes and no," Dad answers. "She passed out because her delta brain waves were so strong she went into a deep dreamless state. Elusion usually only manipulates theta brain waves, which are mainly for intense meditation and light sleep."

His words crash into one another in my mind, leaving particles and pieces scattered all over the place. As my eyes begin to open, so slowly I'm not sure it's really happening, my brain tries to reassemble the fragments of my father's explanation.

Delta.

Dreamless.

"Maybe if we prop her up that might help," Josh suggests.

I feel my body weight and posture being shifted, while my eyes still seem swollen and heavy. Something soft is placed behind my head, and I can tell I'm sitting up because my lower back and legs are at a ninety-degree angle.

"Da—" That's all that will come out of my mouth.

"I'm here, Regan. Everything is going to be okay."

Even with my depreciated mental capacity, I can hear the worry in his voice.

But I don't care. My dad is with me. Finally, after all this time.

"Save your energy. Don't try to talk." Josh's voice is but a soft whisper.

"Rub her feet. Her lower extremities seem to be responding faster," my dad tells him. "We need to get her up and walking so we can get you both out of here. The firewall protects us from some of the stimuli, but it's still dangerous. And with the kind of disruption she's already suffered, she's going to have a tough enough time with Aftershock as it is."

Knuckles knead my arches and the balls of my feet, sending

a tingling sensation up through my ankles and straight to my upper thighs.

"We can't go back," I hear Josh say. The tension in his throat is unmistakable. "Patrick locked us in here."

My father's hand clenches my arm just a little bit tighter as I utilize all my strength to open my eyes. I'm sitting on the barren, marshy ground, my back resting against the trunk of a dead tree. Josh is at my feet and my dad is kneeling beside me, his familiar face lined with concern. He looks like he did when I saw him on the beach—just a little more tired and dirty.

"What are you talking about?" my father asks.

"Patrick was with us in the Escape before our wristbands stopped working. When he left, he was furious, and then there was an administrator lockout, and—"

"Dad," I whisper, trying to speak once more. He touches a hand to my cheek.

"Shhh," he says to me.

I feel my eyes starting to spasm a bit and they begin to close, even though I'm fighting to stay awake.

"Let's get her back to the compound," Dad says to Josh.

He leans closer, wrapping an arm around my shoulder. And that's when I notice his eyes. Once a deep brown, they are now the same color as Josh's: a light, vacant gray. Before I can react, I succumb to the fatigue, drifting beneath the surface once more.

The next time I come to, it's like I'm waking up in the real world. My body isn't frozen like a block of ice; my brain doesn't feel like it's sunk underwater. Even my leg, with its penetrating wound, looks almost healed. I can sit up and look around, but there isn't that much to see. I'm inside a small room that seems like it's made out of stone, kind of like a cave, only the walls here are a bright shade of ivory instead of black. I'm lying on several pieces of starchy fabric with jagged hems, so it looks like they've been torn from somewhere.

I glance down and notice that I'm still wearing the clothes I had on the Prairie Escape, but they're ripped and faded, like someone has twisted and wrung all the color out of them. My skin is surprisingly clean and I feel refreshed, like I haven't been running from monsters, breaking through walls, and rolling down hills.

When I glance back up, I notice my father, standing in the corner with his back up against the wall, his arms crossed in front of his chest. He's wearing the same clothes he wore on the beach, but like mine, they're practically devoid of color. His smile is kind as ever, and when he takes a step toward me, I leap up and meet him halfway, pulling him into a great big hug the first moment I can.

"I can't believe it's you," I say. Tears of happiness fill my eyes.

"It's me," he says softly, resting his chin on top of my head.

"I was so scared that I'd never see you again," I say.

"I know, I was too," he replies. "But we're together now. That's all that matters."

I ease myself out of his arms and glance up at him through glistening eyes. "So this is real? Wherever we are?"

"Yes, it's real."

He motions to the makeshift bed and we both sit on the edge, just like Mom and I had done only last night. Or was it longer? I've lost all track of time. I'm so confused and overwhelmed, I'm clinging to his hand like a little girl, but he doesn't seem to care.

"How's Mom doing?" he asks, as if reading my mind. "Is she okay?"

I bow my head, wondering if I should tell him the truth, but when I glance up into his eyes, the answer is right in front of me. "Uh-huh. She's doing fine."

We've all been through enough. Why make matters worse with painful truths?

"What about Josh? How is he?" I ask.

"He's fine. He's waiting outside. I wanted to talk to you. Just the two of us."

My dad is avoiding my eyes, as if he's about to tell me something I don't want to hear.

"Whatever's wrong, we can fix it," I attempt to reassure him. I thought he was dead and now I've been given a second chance. I can handle whatever he's about to tell me.

"I'm not sure that we can." The pitch of his voice deepens, taking on a somber tone that I've rarely heard from him.

"What happened, Dad? Who did this to you?" I plead.

"Josh told me you saw the memo," he says, casting his eyes away from mine. "So you know that Elusion can cause nano-psychosis in young users. And that we were trying to find a way to adapt the product so it wouldn't be dangerous."

"Yes, we do," I say. "But you need to tell me everything that went down after that. Step by step, and don't leave anything out. I can take it."

He exhales and we lock eyes again. Whatever he's about to say right now, I know in my heart he's going to be honest.

"Before we submitted Elusion to the CIT, I had Bryce Williams run a bunch of tests on subject groups, monitoring how trypnosis affected the users. Standard protocol for any type of product like ours," he explains. "I was working on programming and security networks with Patrick, and that was taking up all of my time."

I nod, vaguely remembering the countless days and nights he spent at the Orexis lab, working on Elusion. "But then Bryce discovered a problem, right?"

"Yes, he did. Something that I'd just never foreseen," he says. "I didn't anticipate how someone with a brain chemistry that was still in flux and developing would respond to trypnosis. And when he suggested sodium pentothal, it seemed like a good solution."

A gasp catches at the base of my throat and I let go of his hand. "So you went ahead anyway? Even though you knew people might be in danger of getting hurt?"

"While Patrick and I focused on the Escape design and the firewalls, Bryce did more studies, verifying that the chemical was effective," he says. "He even brought the materials to Cathryn and got her to sign off on them. He said she wanted to expedite the process and was satisfied with his results. At first, I thought this was pretty convincing evidence that we were in the clear."

"And something changed your mind?"

"Yes. After we started fitting the wristbands with the sodium pentothal, something kept eating at me. We usually approach the entire board of directors and production staff with these types of reports, at special meetings called A and Ms—Assess and Manage. The findings are presented to the group, the documents are thoroughly reviewed, and a Q and A is held. But Bryce went straight to the head of the company to receive clearance. Why would he do that?"

I bite my lip as I try to think of a reason. "Maybe he didn't want anyone to take a closer look at the reports?"

My dad nods. "That's exactly what I began to think. So one night, I logged on to my quantum and searched the shared network for the source file so I could review the documents myself. But it had been deleted. There was no trace of it anywhere."

"Was the name of the file fifty-twenty?" I ask, my heart pumping fast.

He shakes his head, placing a hand on my shoulder. "No, honey. That's a room number."

My brow knits together in confusion. "A room number? All this time, I thought . . . Really, it's a room number?"

"Yes, it's a room at Orexis," he says calmly, before taking a deep breath and finishing his thought: "Where Cathryn Simmons is holding my body hostage."

For a second I think I must have misheard him or misinterpreted what he said. "What?" I ask quietly.

"I confronted Bryce about the missing file," my dad continues, "and he just blew me off. Said it must have been some kind of downloading error."

Where have I heard that before?

"But I knew he was lying. Mostly because he was horrible at it," he says. "So I went to Cathryn and told her that we needed to halt production and hold off on submitting Elusion to CIT until we located the missing data and had it vetted the right way."

"And?" I say, encouraging him to go on.

"She seemed to agree. In fact, she thanked me for coming to her with this and told me she was going to discipline Bryce." He hesitates. "The next morning, I came to Orexis and I couldn't access my own quantum. I spent hours trying to locate the problem. Patrick even tried to help me."

"So you're sure Patrick had no idea that anything was wrong with the trypnosis?"

"I don't think so. The teams working on Elusion were very separate and didn't have the proper permission to view each other's files," he replies. "Besides, Patrick wasn't very interested in that aspect of Elusion. He loved the tech stuff, the programming and coding. The neuroscience wasn't as enticing to him, I guess. And he didn't have the right education for it either."

Patrick was telling me the truth—he didn't know anything about nanopsychosis until after my father was gone.

"Anyway, the whole quantum fiasco was a wild goose chase,"

my father goes on. "While I was caught up with that, Cathryn and Bryce submitted Elusion to CIT with falsified data behind my back," he snaps, his voice crackling with anger. "Within twenty-four hours, we had temporary approval, meaning we could release the product in three test markets."

"So what did you do?"

He gets up off the ground, his body tense and rigid. "I called them both to an after-hours meeting. Room number fifty-twenty." He pauses and clenches his hands into fists. "When they showed up, I gave them an ultimatum—either withdraw Elusion from the CIT review and stop the initial distribution of the Equips and apps, or I was going to destroy Elusion." He stops, as if remembering.

"What did Cathryn do?"

"She laughed. She didn't think I was serious. She thought that since Elusion was made up of separate entities, these Escapes, it was indestructible. And that's when I told them that each one of the Escapes was armed with a fail-safe mechanism that could destroy the entire program. No one knew about it but me."

"Oh my God," I breathe.

"Cathryn started screaming about how she would do *anything* to prevent me from sabotaging this project, and then Bryce attacked me," he says, gritting his teeth. "He got me in a pretty good choke hold, but I broke free of him, grabbed my tab, and activated the destruction mechanism."

My eyes widen with surprise. "So you did it? You took down

the network with the malware?"

"Not quite," he says. "The Elusion system is very complex, and it takes . . ." He looks at me and pauses for a minute, as if searching for the right word. "Time," he says finally. "But the moment they realized what had happened, they both subdued me, hooked me up to an Equip, and forced me into Elusion. Bryce most likely put an override on all the safety features so he could keep me here as long as they liked. And I'm sure Cathryn is paying him a lot of money to keep me alive, too."

"I don't understand. Why would they want to keep you in Elusion?"

"I know they told everyone I'm dead, and I'm sure they would kill me if they could. The only reason I'm still alive is because they can't find the destruction mechanism. I'm guessing they've found just enough proof to know that I'm telling the truth. They probably think they can scare my subconscious into telling them where it is. But it won't do them any good. I'll never tell."

I really can't believe what I'm hearing. "What about administrator access to Elusion? Does Patrick have that?"

"No way," my dad says. "He's a great programmer and can code an amazing Escape design, but he's too young for that kind of responsibility. Bryce is the only other person besides me with administrator access."

"So Patrick didn't lock Josh and me in here?"

My dad shakes his head.

"But how did Bryce even know where we were?"

"I don't know," my dad says.

That pang of guilt over Patrick is back and it's even stronger than before, and I'm still confused. There are so many more questions that I want to ask my dad—about *Walden* and the anagram—but I'm too engrossed in his story to get derailed right now.

I stand up and meet him, eye to eye. "So Elusion is going to self-destruct?"

"Yes. And the destabilization of the Escapes you experienced will be nothing compared to D-day."

My blood runs cold. If Elusion is going to destroy itself while he, Josh, and I are here, we'll most likely die. Then again, we might die anyway.

"That's why you told me it wasn't safe. That's why you asked me to find you," I say, my voice shaking with disappointment. The numbers, his message—I misinterpreted his clues, and now we're all trapped.

"It's not your fault. When I'm behind the firewall, the only messages I can get out are numbers, kind of like communicating in computer code—"

"Why didn't you just tell me all this when you saw me on the beach? Or in the ice cave?" I swallow and force myself to admit the thought that's tearing me apart. "I was at Orexis," I say. "I could've found you!"

"Even though I can get into Elusion, it's extremely dangerous for me to stay there more than a few minutes. The stimuli in Elusion are too powerful for our brains to handle—the longer a user stays inside, the more damage it causes. This place provides some protection, but it's very dangerous to be in Elusion. All of my trips there are timed, and then I'm pulled back through ping tunnels."

"But how'd you know where I was in the first place?" I ask. "And how can you control anything here?"

My dad pauses a moment, like he's unsure of the facts himself. He flashed this smirk at Patrick all the damn time.

"There's a tracking sensor on your Equip wristband," he answers. "I can access the signal in here because of the ping tunnels. The blue and green lights you saw inside the tunnel are kind of like a homing device, which only I can read."

"Wow," I say.

"As with any program, there are hundreds of ping tunnels that can be hidden by the programmer, but every time we use one to get to Elusion, it seals shut," he adds. "At this point, there are only a few tunnels left here for us to use."

"You keep saying 'here,' but I have no idea what that means," I say, rubbing my temples. "I know we're behind the firewall, but from the looks of that monster, we seem anything but safe."

"Those things can't reach us at the camp," he says, putting a hand on my shoulder. "Come on, I'll show you around. We'll sort everything out later."

I nod, giving my dad a brave grin as I stand. When we turn toward the entrance of the cave, Josh walks in. He gives me a happy smile, which I find very strange, considering what it took to get us here and what I know now about the fate of Elusion.

His broad shoulders are pulled back straight and strong, like the first night I saw him, and the darkness that usually clouds his eyes isn't there, even though they're still drained of their gorgeous amber color.

"Ready," Josh says.

"Thanks," my dad replies, giving him a nod as he walks past him. Josh takes my hand and we follow behind my dad, walking through a narrow passageway that appears to be constructed of both enamel and plaster. He seems so giddy, and it's a little unnerving.

"Ready for what?" I ask Josh.

"You'll see," he replies cryptically, bringing my hand up to his mouth and kissing it.

There's no Elusion-type buzz when his lips touch my skin, but there is a sudden warmth that gathers in the back of my head.

We exit the passageway and suddenly I'm in a vast open space, completely blank and empty, as if someone has erased every single detail of the landscape. A hearty wind begins to blow and the whiteness is pulled up from the ground like a veil. In front of me is an odd honeycomb type of structure, with loads of cave rooms just like the one I was in.

Standing in front of me are at least a dozen kids, girls and boys ranging from the ages of about thirteen to twenty, all dressed in dull, drab garments from a bunch of different Escapes. They stare at me with complete awe and wonder, as though they're seeing someone they've only heard about in folk stories and fairy tales. The crowd circles around me, a flurry of gray eyes meeting mine everywhere I look.

Positioned in the center of the group is a familiar girl with short hair and a slight frame. A girl who is looking at me, and maybe even straight through me, like we've known each other our entire lives.

A girl who looks exactly like Josh.

"Nora?"

She nods and grins as the shock registers on my face. "Hey, Regan. My brother has told me a lot about you."

Josh leans in and whispers. "All good things, of course."

This moment is beyond surreal, but when my father places his hand on the small of my back, I feel so grounded and comforted—maybe even like I'm coming home.

"Welcome to Etherworld," he says.

ACKNOWLEDGMENTS

THERE ARE SO MANY PEOPLE WHO HELPED us bring the world of this book to life, and we're so very grateful to all of them.

Big thanks goes to our families for supporting us as we worked like maniacs on this project—our husbands, Brian Klam and Ben Lindvall, for encouraging us when deadlines loomed and celebrating with us when we finally hit our stride; amazing daughters Sadie and Lily Klam, our own personal focus group; Mattie Smith Matthews, Michael and Terri Lindvall, and Barbara Robinson, for taking such good care of us during our writing "vacations"; and Yvonne Gabel, for reading the manuscript in its earliest stages and giving us great feedback. Barbara and Yvonne: as moms, you always go beyond the call of duty!

Extra special thanks to Paul C. Gabel and Ryan Guttridge, for assisting us in developing the technology for *Elusion*—there was so much we needed to learn about hypnosis, psychology, adaptive programming and the theory of complexity, and you walked us through all of it with such patience and enthusiasm. You're the best father and brother us girls could ask for!

Heartfelt appreciation also goes out to our agents, Christy Fletcher and Esther Newberg, whose tireless dedication and commitment to this project and our careers astound us; and Josie Friedman and Nick Harris, for believing in this book before it was even a book.

And of course, we have so much love for our fabulous, indefatigable editor, Sarah Shumway, whose guidance and graciousness is invaluable to us; our awesome publisher, Katherine Tegen, who continues to amaze us with her wit, wisdom, and charm—we are so proud to be on your list. We owe a great bit of debt to the rest of the Harper team: Susan Katz, Kate Jackson, Lauren Flower, Erin Fitzsimmons, Amy Ryan, Tatiana Plakhova, Karen Sherman, Kathryn Silsand, Casey McIntyre, Rhalee Hughes, and Laurel Symonds.

Lastly, we'd like to say thank you to all our dear family and friends who stood by us along the way, cheering us on whenever we needed it. You can't know how much you mean to us.

ABOUT THE AUTHORS

Claudia Gabel and Cheryl Klam met when Claudia edited Cheryl's previous novels, *Learning to Swim* and *The Pretty One*. Claudia works as an editor in New York, but she's also the author of several books for tweens and teens, including the In or Out series and the mash-up *Romeo & Juliet & Vampires*. They liked working together so much that they decided to cowrite a bunch of things, including movie proposals and TV sitcom scripts. And then one day they had the idea for *Elusion*, and the rest is the future.

You can find Claudia and Cheryl online at www.claudiagabel.com and www.cherylklam.com.